The Doors

of the

Universe

THE DOORS OF THE UNIVERSE

Sylvia Louise Engdahl

An Argo Book

Atheneum 1981 New York

LIBRARY OF CONGRESS CATALOGING IN PUBLICATION DATA

ENGDAHL, SYLVIA LOUISE.
THE DOORS OF THE UNIVERSE.

SUMMARY: AFTER DECIDING THAT GENETIC ENGINEERING PROMISES THE
ONLY SALVATION FOR THE PEOPLE ON THEIR HOSTILE PLANET, THE
SCHOLAR NOREN FINDS HE MUST BRING ABOUT THAT SALVATION
ALMOST ALONE.
[I. SCIENCE FICTION] I. TITLE.
PZ7.E6985DO   [FIC]   80–18804
ISBN 0–689–30807–8

PUBLISHED SIMULTANEOUSLY IN CANADA BY
MCCLELLAND & STEWART, LTD.
COMPOSITION BY AMERICAN–STRATFORD GRAPHIC SERVICES, INC.,
BRATTLEBORO, VERMONT
MANUFACTURED BY FAIRFIELD GRAPHICS
FAIRFIELD, PENNSYLVANIA
FIRST PRINTING JANUARY 1981
SECOND PRINTING NOVEMBER 1981

TO RICKY,

with gratitude for much inspiration.

". . . The land was barren, and brought forth neither food nor pure water, nor was there any metal; and no men lived upon it until the Founding. And on the day of the Founding men came out of the sky from the Mother Star, which is our source. But the land alone could not give us life. So the Scholars came to bless it, that it might be quickened: they built the City; and they called down from the sky Power and Machines; and they made the High Law lest we forget our origin, grow neglectful of our bounden duties, and thereby perish. Knowledge shall be kept safe within the City; it shall be held in trust until the Mother Star itself becomes visible to us. For though the Star is now beyond our seeing, it will not always be so. . . .

"There shall come a time of great exultation, when the doors of the universe shall be thrown open and every man shall rejoice. And at that time, when the Mother Star appears in the sky, the ancient knowledge shall be free to all people, and shall be spread forth over the whole earth. And Cities shall rise beyond the Tomorrow Mountains, and shall have Power, and Machines; and the Scholars will no longer be their guardians. For the Mother Star is our source and our destiny, the wellspring of our heritage; and the spirit of this Star shall abide forever in our hearts, and in those of our children, and our children's children, even unto countless generations. It is our guide and protector, without which we could not survive; it is our life's bulwark. And so long as we believe in it, no force can destroy us, though the heavens themselves be consumed! Through the time of waiting we will follow the Law; but its mysteries will be made plain when the Star appears, and the sons of men will find their own wisdom and choose their own Law."

—from the Book of the Prophecy

The Doors

of the

Universe

Prologue

THE EARLY LIFE OF THE SCHOLAR NOREN HAS BEEN TOLD IN TWO previous volumes, *This Star Shall Abide* and *Beyond the Tomorrow Mountains*. These, however, told nothing of the accomplishments that won him prominence among the shapers of his world's history. They dealt only with his adolescence: the trials through which he earned Scholar rank, the doubts that preceded his choice to assume a Scholar's full burden. The account as originally set forth ended with his discovery, in the midst of despair, of faith in what the Mother Star had come to symbolize.

That portion of his story is much like the untold stories of all other Scholars who lived during the Dark Era. All began with rebellion; all were tried and condemned by their peers for defiance of the High Law; all entered the City believing themselves doomed to death as unrepentant heretics. All proved themselves strong enough to maintain their convictions. Yet all publicly recanted for their people's sake, bearing scorn and abuse without expectation of personal gain, after learning the tragic truth behind the poetic language of the Prophecy. Voluntarily, they conceded that only under the High Law could their race survive.

These ordeals were but the prelude to more harrowing ones. Heretics were warned of the hard life to come, but not of its true nature; not until afterward were they told that their steadfastness would confer on them the Scholar rank they had supposed was hereditary. For all, acceptance of unsought Scholar status was painful; for most, as for Noren, commitment to priesthood was a step taken later, after much inner anguish. As villagers or Technicians, they had viewed Scholars—High Priests and City guardians—as a privileged caste. They had been reared to worship that caste as superhuman, and above all else they loathed the idea of being worshiped. No matter that in reality, Scholars knew less privilege than hardship. They abhorred guardianship of the world as an evil —which, of course, was the very reason they were fit to become guardians.

The caste system of the Dark Era was indeed evil. No one was more aware of this than the Scholars, whose ultimate secret was that priesthood could be earned only through the route of heresy. Scholars were Scholars not in spite of their doubt, but because of it. The essential test of incorruptibility was that they must perceive the evil and offer their lives in protest; any person in the world was eligible for Scholar status on that basis. Thus the rank was bestowed only on those who did not want what it implied. So the First Scholar planned, for he knew that otherwise his successors would not keep the Prophecy's promise. As it was, they dedicated themselves wholeheartedly to its fulfillment.

The Founders believed that until that goal was attained, survival would remain impossible without guardianship of the City's contents. They were both right and wrong. Right that the few who had escaped the Six Worlds' exploding sun could not survive on the alien world without advanced technology; right that with the planet's scant resources, their offspring could not preserve such technology in a more normally structured society—but wrong about what technological breakthrough would change the situation. Generations of Scholars kept the trust, sacrificing everything in the struggle to preserve the Six Worlds' knowledge and increase it enough to restore their people's heritage by synthesizing metal on their metal-poor planet. The breakthrough eluded them. It remained for the Scholar Noren to bring about their world's salvation.

The tale of Noren's achievement, unlike that of his early youth, sets him apart from his contemporaries. He would not wish it made public among his people any more than the First Scholar wished his own story told openly, less because it lays bare his weaknesses than because he feared it might encourage undue worship. In the case of the First Scholar, this most certainly would have happened. His martyrdom was of a bloody sort. He died at the hands of a mob he had let misunderstand him, purposely taking the blame for a tragedy in which he was blameless. The people of the Dark Era, had they known—and most especially had they known that he framed the Prophecy—would have named him more than High Priest; it would have become blasphemy to speak of him less reverently than of the Star itself. Foreseeing this, he preferred not to be named at all.

With the Scholar Noren it is somewhat different. His fate was less dramatic, though no less demanding, and not the least difficult part was his estrangement from his fellow Scholars. For those of the future it is well that the truth about him should be set down; he recorded no memories, as the First Scholar did, to be shared by the initiated through controlled dreaming. And to non-Scholars of generations past the Dark Era he abolished, he will not seem of superhuman stature, for the traditional mysteries of the priesthood will have been explained.

Yet there is a further complication. The Scholar Noren bore one

(4

secret beyond those of his priesthood, beyond those known to the men and women who, through the Dark Era, guarded the heritage of the Mother Star; and he kept it at great personal cost. The Star will blaze and fade in his world's sky—the light of its glory will reach far across the galaxy—before knowledge of that secret can come to Noren's race. Thus before this third volume of his story can be shown to his descendants, their world will have been transformed.

In the meantime, we who live under other skies will pay him the honor he deserves. Each of us, in our world's way or in our own, will say differently what his people would express in these words: May the spirit of the Star be with him.

I

THE DAY, LIKE ALL DAYS, HAD BEEN HOT; THE CLOUDS HAD DIS-
persed promptly after the morning's scheduled rain. As the hours
went by the sun had parched the villages, penetrating the thatch
roofs of their stone buildings. Now low, its light filtered by thick
air, it subdued the sharp contrast between machine processed
farmland and the surrounding wilderness of native growth, a rolling
expanse of purple-blotched grayness that stretched to the Tomorrow
Mountains. Sunlight was seldom noticed within the City, for the
domes, and most rooms of the clustered towers they ringed, were
windowless. But since long before dawn Noren had watched the
landscape from the topmost level of a tower he'd rarely entered.
Like the other converted starships that served as Inner City living
quarters, it had a view lounge at its pinnacle; and it was there that
he awaited the birth of his child.

He'd been barred from the birthing room—part of the nursery
area where infants were kept until, at the age of weaning, they
must be sent out for adoption by village families. That was off limits
to all but the mothers and attendants. By tradition, Scholars could
not see their children; even the women did not, except when no
wet nurse was available among Technician women. Talyra, as a
Technician, would nurse her own baby. Whether that would make
it easier or harder when the time came for her to give it up, he was
not sure. She'd known before she married him that Inner City life
involved sacrifices. The knowledge hadn't lessened her gladness in
pregnancy any more than it had tarnished his own elation. It would
not affect their desire for many offspring in the years to come. Yet
it did not seem fair—she'd given up so much for his sake. . . .

For the world's sake, she would say, and it was truer than she
imagined. *"In our children shall be our hope, and for them we shall
labor, generation upon generation until the Star's light comes to
us,"* she'd quoted softly the night before, when her pains began.
Talyra was devout; unlike himself, she had found the symbolic
language meaningful even during her childhood in the village. He too
now used it, not just to please her but with sincerity.

(6

"And the land shall remain fruitful, and the people shall multiply across the face of the earth," he'd replied, smiling. Then, more soberly, *"For the City shall serve the people; those within have been consecrated to that service."* He knew that Talyra indeed felt consecrated, no less than he, though in a different way; still it troubled him that she could not know the truth behind the ritual phrases. She could not know that the City and its dependent villages contained but a remnant of the race that had once inhabited six vaporized worlds of the remote Mother Star, that to bring forth babies was not only an honor and sacred duty, but a necessity if humanity was to survive. Nor could she be told the main reason why Inner City people were not free to rear families, though it was obvious enough to her that the space enclosed by the Outer City's encircling domes was limited. Only Scholars knew of the Six Worlds' fate and the new one's tragic deficiencies. They alone were aware that without the scientific research that required the City with its precious resources to remain sealed, the Prophecy might prove false.

She'd clung to his arm as they left their tiny room and walked across the intertower courtyard; at the door to the nursery area, she'd leaned against him with her dark curls damp against his shoulder. The pains were coming often; he knew they could not linger over the parting. And there was no cause to linger. Childbirth roused no apprehension in Talyra; she was a nurse-midwife by profession.

"It's nothing to worry about, Noren," she assured him happily. "Haven't I been working in the nursery ever since I entered the City? Haven't I wished for the day I could come here as a mother instead of just an attendant? Men always get nervous—that's why we keep them out. We'll send word when the child comes, you know that."

"I'll wait at the top of the tower," he told her, "where I can look at the mountains, Talyra. Ours is the only child in the world to have begun life in the mountains; maybe it means something that the wilderness gave us life instead of death."

"It gave you your faith," she murmured, kissing him. "We were blessed there from the start, darling—not simply when we were rescued. Let's always be glad our baby's beginning was so special." She drew away; reluctantly, he let her go. They'd be separated only a few days, after all. Past separations, before their marriage, had been far longer and potentially permanent; he wondered why he felt so shaken by this brief one.

"May the spirit of the Star be with you, Talyra," he said fervently, knowing these words were what she'd most wish to hear from him. The traditional farewell had become more than a formality between them, for Talyra took joy in the fact that he, once an unbeliever, had come to speak of the Star not only with reverence, but with a priest's authority.

Now the long night had passed and also the day, and still no word had come. Noren pushed aside the study viewer on which he'd tried, unsuccessfully, to concentrate. Far beyond the City, sunset was turning the yellow peaks of the Tomorrow Mountains to gold. He stared at the jagged range, the place where during the darkest crisis of his life, their child had been conceived. It was there that his outlook had changed. He did not share Talyra's belief in the Star as some sort of supernatural force; still he had felt underneath that the world's doom was not as sure as it seemed. Perhaps that was why the aircar had crashed—perhaps there'd been more involved than bad piloting on his part, for though Talyra hadn't guessed, he had fled the research outpost beyond the mountains with the intent of publicly repudiating the Prophecy. He and his friend Brek had planned to do so in front of villagers, knowing they might be stoned for the blasphemy; their discovery of the odds against success of the research had led them to consider themselves relapsed heretics. Only their own unlooked-for survival had brought Noren to his senses.

After the crash, thinking himself beyond rescue, he had felt free, for once, of his search for peace of mind; he'd shaken off the depression that had burdened his previous weeks as a Scholar. He had at last stopped doubting himself enough to accept Talyra's love. It had been a joyous union despite his assumption that they were soon to die, and afterward, he'd known she was right in maintaining that it wasn't a necessary assumption. Talyra, who knew none of the Scholars' secrets, was almost always right about the things that mattered.

On just one issue was she blind: she saw nothing bad in the fact that Scholars kept secrets. Though she'd learned that they were not superhuman, she never questioned their supremacy as High Priests and City guardians; she perceived no evil in the existence of castes that villagers thought were hereditary. And she was therefore ineligible to attain Scholar rank. Talyra simply hadn't been born to question things, Noren thought ruefully.

He could not communicate fully with Talyra. He couldn't have done so even if no obligatory secrecy had bound him. She'd come to respect the honesty that had condemned him in the village of their birth. She had protested his confinement within the walls—which was ostensibly a punishment—and had been admitted to the Inner City, given Technician rank, because she loved him enough to share it. The explanations she'd received contented her. It mattered little that she did not know, could never be allowed to know, that he'd ranked as a Scholar before committing himself to priesthood; the true nature of Scholar status was past her comprehension.

At the time of her entrance he had supposed they could not marry, for he hadn't imagined he could act as a priest without hypocrisy, and marriage to a Technician wasn't permissible while his rank was unrevealed. It would be unfair to bind a partner who was unaware of the wall that must stand between them. Though there'd have been no objection to their becoming lovers, he had held back while their future was uncertain; Talyra had been puzzled and hurt. Already she'd longed for a baby, Noren realized with chagrin, although she was as yet too young to be pitied for childlessness. In the City she wouldn't be scorned as barren women were in the villages. He had assumed that since she could not rear a family, a delay in childbearing wouldn't disturb her—or that if it did, she would break off her betrothal to him. At least that was what he liked to tell himself, though he knew he'd been too absorbed by his own problems to give enough thought to hers. There had been a time when he'd not cared to live, much less to love.

Then, in the mountains, everything had changed. He'd thrown problems to the wind and followed his instincts, and instinct led him not only to love, but to strive beyond reason for their survival and their child's. They'd had no sure knowledge, of course, that there was a child; yet what couple would believe their first union unfruitful?

He couldn't remind Talyra that she would not live long enough to give birth; certainly he couldn't remind her that perhaps she had failed to conceive. More significantly, he found he could not tell her that it made no difference to the world one way or the other. Science had proven the Prophecy vain; according to all logic, the human race was doomed by the alien world's lack of resources. But he could not destroy Talyra's faith. This too had been instinct, and through this, he'd discovered buried faith of his own that had reconciled him to priesthood.

The role of a Scholar was to work toward a scientific breakthrough that could fulfill the Prophecy's promises; the role of a priest was to affirm the Prophecy without evidence. He no longer felt the two were inconsistent.

He owed much to the child he would never be permitted to see, Noren thought: the child who would grow up as a villager—where, and under what name, he would not be told—and who, knowing nothing of his or her parentage, might someday in turn fight the apparent injustice of the High Law. . . .

"Noren—"

He looked up, expecting news from the nursery, but it was Brek who stood in the doorway. "I guess you're wondering why I didn't

9)

come to the refectory," Noren said. It was their habit to take their noon meal together in the Hall of Scholars, the central tower where as advanced students, they normally worked, though Noren ate his other meals with Talyra in the commons open to Technicians. "I wasn't hungry, I'm as nervous as all fathers—just wait till it's your turn!" Brek, quite recently, had married a fellow-Scholar; their delight in their own coming child had been plain.

Brek hesitated. "By the Star, Brek," Noren went on, "it's taking a long time, isn't it? Should it take this long?"

"Noren, Beris asked me to tell you. They've sent for a doctor." Brek's tone was even, too even.

A *doctor?* Noren went white; rarely had he heard of a doctor being called to attend a birth. The villages had no resident doctors; babies were delivered by nurse-midwives, trained, as Talyra had been trained in adolescence, for a vocation accorded semi-religious status. In the City there was no cause to usurp their prerogatives. Besides, it was improper to intervene in the process of bringing forth life. Only if the child were in danger. . . .

Vaguely, from his boyhood, he recalled that babies sometimes died. So too, in the village, had mothers who were frail. It was not a thing discussed often, unless perhaps among women—though he had never known a woman whose eagerness for another child wouldn't have overshadowed such thoughts.

"I think you'd better come," Brek was saying.

As they descended in the lift, other boyhood memories pushed into Noren's mind. The child might be past saving . . . against many ills doctors were powerless. They'd failed to save his mother, who'd been poisoned by accidental contact with native briars that encroached on the edge of a grainfield. He now knew she couldn't have been helped; the poison had no antidote. But at the time he'd been bitter. It was not right, he'd thought, that Technicians, emissaries of the all-knowing Scholars, should control medical equipment as they did all objects containing metal. He'd been unaware then of how pitifully little equipment there was to control, or of how long it must last before metal could be synthesized and Six Worlds' technology restored to everyone.

Had the Six Worlds had ways of ensuring safe births? The computers could answer that, of course; he wondered, suddenly, if any past Scholar had been moved to ask. He himself was prone to ask futile questions as well as practical ones, a tendency not widely shared when it could lead only to frustration.

Brek was silent. That in itself was eloquent—Brek, Noren reflected, knew him much too well to offer false reassurances.

It had never occurred to Noren that the baby might die. He could face that himself, he supposed; he was inured to grim circumstances. The seasons since his marriage had been the happiest of his life, too good, he'd sometimes felt, to last. But Talyra's sorrow he might find past bearing. It was so unjust that she should suffer . . . after all the grief and hardship he'd brought her in the past, he'd wanted to make her content. He'd vowed not to let her see that a priest could have doubts, or that even when closest to her he knew loneliness.

Was it only because of her pregnancy that he'd succeeded? If the child died, if she was desolate over what she'd surely perceive as a failure as well as a sorrow, would her intuition again lead her to sense that his own desolation went deeper? "You are what you are," she had told him long ago, "and our loving each other wouldn't make any difference." It hadn't; for a time this had seemed unimportant, yet throughout that time, the child had bridged the gulf between them. . . .

Talyra would blame herself if it wasn't healthy; village women always did, and she'd been reared as a villager. It wouldn't matter that no one in the City would consider her blameworthy. Noren cursed inwardly. Village society, backward in all ways because of its technological stagnation, was both sexist and intolerant; Talyra might be openminded enough to be talked out of most prejudices, but she wouldn't listen to him on a subject viewed as the province of women. Among Technicians there was less stigma attached to the loss of a child. Brek's wife Beris had been born a Technician, in the Outer City, as had Brek himself; maybe later on Beris would be able to help.

Yet Brek had said Beris sent the message—that was odd, since she was neither midwife nor nursery attendant. As a Scholar, Beris had work of her own in water purification control, vital life-support work she could not leave except in an emergency. As they reached the nursery level, Noren faced Brek, asking abruptly, "What's Beris doing here?"

"She—she was called as a priest, Noren. I don't know the details."

The door where he and Talyra had parted was in front of them; Noren pushed and found it locked. He felt disoriented, as if he were in one of the controlled dreams that were a part of a Scholar's training. Beris called as a priest? To be sure, no male priest would be summoned to the birthing room, so she was a logical choice; there were not many Scholar women, since village rearing didn't encourage heresy among girls, and comparatively few of the young ones that Talyra knew well had assumed the blue robe of priesthood. But why should a priest be needed at all? At the service for the dead, yes, if the baby didn't survive; but that would be held later, and elsewhere. He would be expected to preside himself, at least Talyra would expect it, and for her sake he would find the courage, disturbing though that particular service had always been to him. What other solace could a priest offer? Had they felt only a robed Scholar could break the news of her baby's danger? That didn't make sense—Talyra would know! She was a midwife; if the delivery didn't go well, she would know what was happening.

She'd rarely spoken to him of her work. He knew only that she liked it, liked helping to bring new life into the world. Yet there had been times when she'd come to their room troubled, her usual vitality dimmed by sadness she would not explain; it struck him now that she might have seen babies die before. Perhaps she had seen more than one kind of pain. That women suffered physically during childbirth was something everyone knew and no one mentioned. It was taken for granted that the lasting joy outweighed the temporary discomfort. Midwives were taught to employ a modified form of hypnosis that lessened pain without affecting consciousness, or so he'd been told, though Talyra wasn't aware that the ritual procedures she followed served such a purpose. Doctors—and often priests—could induce full hypnotic anesthesia. Had Beris been summoned for that reason? Had Talyra's pain been abnormally severe, could that be why they'd sought a doctor's aid? Anguish rose in Noren; her confidence had been so great, he had not guessed she might be undergoing a real ordeal.

"I've got to go in there," he told Brek. Having never been one to let custom stand in his way, he felt no hesitancy.

"You can't do any good now. When you can, they'll call you—"

"For the Star's sake, she may need me! The doctor may not be here yet, she may be suffering—she's not been trained to accept hypnosis as we have, and she's not awed enough by a blue robe to let just any priest put her under."

"Beris said something about drugs."

"Drugs for childbirth?" Drugs were scarce and precious, not to be used where hypnosis would serve and surely not on anyone who wasn't ill; Talyra would not accept them during the biggest moment of her life. Unless her baby had already died . . . but no, not even then; Talyra was no coward.

"I don't understand," he protested.

"Neither do I," Brek said. "We don't know enough about these things; sometimes I think women keep too much to themselves. I'd never have thought it could be risky for Talyra. She's young and strong—"

Stunned, Noren burst out, "You mean there's danger to *Talyra*? Not just to the child?" In sudden panic he threw his weight against the door, but it would not yield.

Brek grasped his arm, pulling him aside. "The child was stillborn, I think," he admitted.

The door slid back and Beris emerged, still wearing the ceremonial blue robe over her work clothes. She blocked Noren's way.

"Let's go down," she said quietly. "I know a room that's empty where we can go."

"I've got to see Talyra."

"You can't, not here."

"Where, then?" He wondered if they would move her to the infirmary; he knew nothing of what illness might strike during a delivery.

"Noren." Beris kept her voice steady. "It was over faster than anyone expected. Talyra is dead."

Later, he wondered how Brek and Beris had gotten him to the lift. They took him to a room on the next level that was temporarily unused; once there, he collapsed on the narrow couch and gave way to tears. For a long time they said nothing, but simply let him weep.

When he was able to talk, there was little Beris could tell him. "It happens," she said. "Usually with older women, or those who've never been strong; but occasionally it happens with a girl who seems healthy. Talyra knew that. She knew better than most of us; all midwives do."

"She never said—"

"Of course not. You would be the last person to whom she'd have said such a thing."

"Did it happen on the Six Worlds, too?" Noren asked bitterly. "Or could she have been saved-there?"

"I don't know. At least I don't know if she could have been saved at this stage. It's possible—they had equipment we haven't the metal to produce, and they could tell beforehand if there were complications, so that their doctors could be prepared. Sometimes they delivered babies surgically before labor even began."

Beris paused, glancing uncomfortably at Brek; her own pregnancy, though not yet apparent, could scarcely be far from their thoughts. "Talyra wasn't a Scholar—she didn't know how it was on the Six Worlds. But I do. I suppose men don't absorb all that I did from the dreams the Founders recorded . . . but you do know it wasn't the same as here. I mean, people didn't have the same feelings—"

Noren nodded. The Six Worlds had been overpopulated; women hadn't been allowed more than two children, and they'd had drugs to prevent unplanned pregnancies. Hard though it was to imagine, people hadn't minded; at any rate, that was what all the records said. Sterility hadn't been considered a curse. Some couples had purposely chosen to have no offspring at all; they had made love without wishing for their love to outlast their lifetime.

"Well," Beris went on, "it was the custom there for women to be seen by doctors, not just during delivery, but all through pregnancy.

13)

They knew a long time ahead if things weren't going right. And so pregnancies that were judged dangerous were—terminated."

Noren was speechless. Brek, aghast, murmured, "You mean deliberately? They killed unborn children?"

"Their society didn't look on it as killing. And it wasn't done often once they had sure contraceptives—only when the child would die anyway, or when the mother's health was at stake."

"Talyra would not have done it at all," declared Noren.

"No. That's what I'm trying to say, Noren. She wouldn't have, even if the option had been open, because in our culture we just can't feel the way our ancestors did. Our situation is different. So unless the Six Worlds' medical equipment could have saved her without hurting the baby, our having that equipment wouldn't have changed anything."

But the baby died too, Noren thought. She'd given her life for nothing. Perhaps these things happened, but why—why to Talyra? It was the sort of useless question that had always plagued him, yet he could not let it rest.

"She was so strong, she loved life so much . . . there's got to be a *reason*," he said slowly. He recalled how in the aftermath of the crash, Talyra's indomitable spirit had kindled his own will to live. She had refused to let him give in; all the hardships—the terror of the attack by subhuman mutants, the heat, the exhaustion, the hunger and above all the thirst—had left Talyra untouched. How could she have come through all that, only to die as a result of the love that had led to their near-miraculous rescue?

"She believed the Star would protect her," he persisted, "even in the mountains where we *knew* we were dying, she kept believing! You were there, Brek—you saw. I couldn't disillusion her. That was what pulled us through. It's so ironic for her faith to let her down in the end."

"Talyra was a realist," Brek declared. "I remember she said, 'If we die expecting to live, we'll be none the worse for it; but if we stop living because we expect to die, we'll have thrown away our own lives.' "

"She didn't feel faith had let her down," Beris added. "It comforted her! She knew she'd lost too much blood, she'd seen such cases before—and she wanted the ritual blessing. That's why I was sent for."

"You gave it to her, Beris? You said those words to a dying person as if they were true?" Noren frowned. *May the spirit of the Mother Star abide with you, and with your children, and your children's children; may you gain strength from its presence, trusting in the surety of its power.* He had conceded the words were valid when said to the living, who were concerned for the welfare of future generations; but in the context of death—death not only of

(14

oneself but of one's only child—they took on a whole new meaning.

"I've never used ritual phrases lightly, not as a priest, anyway," Beris answered. "The words do express truth, just as much as the ones you say every time you preside at Vespers. Of course I said them, and part of the service for the child, too, because she wanted to hear it."

He turned away, realizing that though he himself could not have denied Talyra's wish, he'd have been choking back more than tears. "A priest gives hope," he said softly, "that's what Stefred told me when I agreed to assume the robe. It's a—a mockery to use the symbols where there's nothing left to hope for."

"But Noren—" Beris broke off, seeing Brek's face; she did not know Noren's mind as Brek did. "Talyra hoped for *you,*" she continued quietly. "The last thing she said to me was, 'Tell Noren I love him.' "

Noren sat motionless, already feeling the return of the emptiness that had paralyzed him during his weeks at the research outpost. Brek and Beris seemed far away, their voices echoes of a world he no longer inhabited.

"This isn't the time to tell you this," Beris was saying, "but Talyra made me promise. She said you must have more children, that it's important, because otherwise the world will lose twice as much—"

"She knew I wouldn't want anyone's children but hers."

"That's why she said it—she did know. She knew you don't hold with custom and might not choose someone else just for duty's sake. And there was something about what happened in the mountains that I didn't understand, she said it would become pointless, what you suffered there."

"I suppose she meant your drinking so little water," Brek said. To Beris he added, "I never told you the whole story. Noren nearly died of dehydration; he couldn't drink as much impure water as Talyra and I could because he'd already drunk some as a boy in the village."

"You'd drunk impure water without need?" Beris was shocked.

"Just for a few days before I was arrested," Noren assured her. "I didn't believe in the High Law then, not any of it; it wasn't only the injustice that made me a heretic. And I'd decided I'd outgrown nursery tales about stream water turning people into idiots."

"But then how could you dare to—"

"I was tested for genetic damage, just as Brek was after we got back from the mountains. He must have explained about that, or else you wouldn't have married him. Anyway, I'd been told how much more I could safely drink, and in the wilderness I kept within that limit for Talyra's sake. We'd *seen* the mutants, you know. Talyra hadn't heard of genetics, but she knew they were subhuman because their ancestors drank the water . . . and, well, even though I thought we'd die there, I couldn't let her fear, while we were sleeping together—" He broke off and concluded miserably, "She was right; it's turned out to have been pointless. I'm not likely to want another child."

"If you say that, it's like telling Talyra your love for her made you stop caring about the future. That it was hurtful to you."

"To *me?*" Wretchedly he mumbled, "If it weren't for me, Talyra might have lived a long, happy life in the village."

"How could she have? She'd surely have tried to have children, so the same thing would have happened."

"Would it?" Noren burst out, "Beris, my child may have killed Talyra! You've learned all these things about pregnancy, things they knew on the Six Worlds—hasn't it occurred to you it may not always be the woman's fault when things go wrong? How much do you know about genetics?"

"Not much," she admitted. "I don't think anyone does, beyond the fact that technology's needed for survival here because something in the water and soil damages genes if it's not removed."

"There must be more detail than that in the computers—they preserve all the Six Worlds' science, and more must have been known in the Founders' time." The idea came slowly; as it formed, Noren wondered why no one had ever spoken of it. "In the dreams, the Founders knew the genetic damage was unavoidable without soil and water processing. Yet there weren't any subhuman mutants then. The mutants came later, as the offspring of rebels who fled to the mountains rather than accept the First Scholar's rule. That means the First Scholar *predicted* the mutation, and he couldn't have done that without understanding what genes are! What's more, there must have been cases of genetic damage on the Six Worlds themselves, because the concept wasn't a new one. Perhaps there were mutations that didn't destroy the mind."

"Genetic diseases, yes," Beris agreed. "I did get that much from one dream. But not necessarily mutations. A lot of people had defective genes to begin with, only not all the genes a person has affect that person, or all her offspring."

"Why aren't some of our offspring still affected, then?"

"The Founders—women and men both—passed genetic tests," Brek reflected. "Don't you remember, Noren? When they knew their sun was going to nova, how they chose the people eligible to draw lots for the starships?"

"And there was something about genetics in the First Scholar's plan, too," Noren recalled. "It was one of the reasons he wouldn't let Scholars' children be reared in the City, even the Outer City. Their being sent to the villages had something to do with what he called the gene pool."

"You're right, there's got to be a lot of stored information," said Brek. "I suppose no one's ever taken time to study it because it's so irrelevant to our work now. Till we find a way to synthesize metal, so that soil and water processing can continue indefinitely, it doesn't make any difference whether we understand genes or not. Understanding can't prevent the damage, only technology can."

True, thought Noren grimly. Still, he'd always wanted to understand things—and to him, this was no longer irrelevant.

It was near midnight when he returned to his own quarters. At Brek's insistence he had accepted bread and a hot drink, knowing that one should not go more than a full day without nourishment. "Or without sleep," Brek said worriedly. Tactfully, he avoided any direct suggestion about hypnotic sedation.

"I'll sleep," Noren said quickly. He did not see how he could do so in the bed he'd shared with Talyra, but the Inner City was crowded; barring the infirmary, there was nowhere else to sleep. And after all, rooms were nearly identical, having once been cabins aboard the Founders' starships. There were no personal furnishings, for such materials as could be manufactured were allocated to the Outer City, while the Inner City practiced an austerity that even to villagers, who had wicker and colored cloth, would have seemed strange. Talyra had kept her few belongings neatly stored in a compartment beneath the bed; none would be in evidence to torment him.

"Noren," Brek continued hesitantly, "the service tomorrow—"

"I'll be all right."

"Will you preside?"

"I—I can't, Brek."

"I understand, of course. So will everyone. But it's your right, so I had to ask."

"You don't understand at all," Noren told him. "I wouldn't crack up emotionally. I'd like to be the one to speak about Talyra, what she was, what her life meant to us. It's the ritual part I can't do."

He thought back to the first such service he had ever attended, the one for his mother, and how awful he'd felt hearing the Technicians, who in the villages performed priestly functions by proxy, read the false, hollow phrases over her body. His mother had *believed* those things; she'd believed both her life and death served some mystical power, the power of a star not yet even visible in the sky.

He had since learned it was not all a lie. But the service for the dead was not part of the Prophecy that science might fulfill. Nor did it deal only with the Mother Star. It was one thing to accept the Star as a symbol of the unknowable—as he'd done when he assumed priesthood—as well as of the heritage from the Six Worlds. Symbols no longer bothered him. But in this ceremony alone, the Founders had gone further. "I'm not like you and Beris," he told Brek. "I can't feel the words about death symbolize truth."

The night dragged on. Noren could not cry any more, even when alone; he did not believe any emotion would return to him. He'd been right, perhaps, when despair had first gripped him, the year before at the outpost. His marriage had been only a brief reprieve.

Toward dawn he drifted into sleep and was immediately caught up in nightmare, the old nightmare induced by the controlled dreams through which Scholar candidates learned of the Founding. He was the First Scholar, yet at the same time, himself; the woman dying in his arms had Talyra's face, Talyra's voice. . . . He surfaced, telling himself as always that it was just a dream, Talyra still lived, in experiencing the First Scholar's emotions he had drawn images from his own memory. But when fully conscious, he knew that never again would it be a dream from which he could wake up.

The First Scholar too had lost his wife. She had killed herself because she could not bear the knowledge that the Six Worlds were destroyed. That had been what convinced the First Scholar that the secret of the nova must be kept; it was a key episode, so despite its pain it was one new Scholars had to go through. What kind of woman would prefer death to serving the future? Noren wondered. Talyra wouldn't have! Why then had Talyra died? There was no sense in any of it . . . the First Scholar's wife had served the future after all, for her husband's decision had hinged on hers, the symbolic interpretation of the Mother Star itself had hinged on it. How could the future be served by senseless tragedy?

In the morning he viewed the bodies privately, dry-eyed, before they were shrouded and moved to the open courtyard. Because Talyra had been a Technician, the service was not held within the Hall of Scholars. Except for the absence of kinfolk, with whom all Inner City people sacrificed contact, it was more like a village ceremony; and for this Noren was thankful. Ritual of one sort or another could be more easily dismissed as routine in mixed groups than when only Scholars were present.

Alone, for Brek had quietly assumed the presiding priest's place, Noren joined the gathered mourners as they began the traditional hymn. He was too much a loner to want others' sympathy, though there were many present who would offer it. The ceremony was a thing to live through. So, perhaps, would be all his days to come. Reason told him his work in nuclear physics was futile, and without Talyra to bolster his faith. . . .

How proud she'd been when he first put on the blue robe, and how needless his fear that it would turn her love to a deference he would abhor. Not till he was much older would he be required to assume the burden of appearing at public ceremonies outside the Gates, where villagers and Technicians would kneel to him. In the Inner City such customs were not observed; the robes, in fact, were rarely worn except for formal officiation. But like the other acknowledged Scholars in attendance, he wore his now, as befitted the solemnity of the occasion.

He had steeled himself to the words of committal; the shock of understanding them had worn off since he'd first heard them as a Scholar. Recycling of bodies with the ancient converters from the starships was necessary to future generations in an alien world that did not provide enough of the trace elements on which biological existence depended. In any case, he had never shared the villagers' reverent awe at the thought that when one's body was taken into the City, one somehow became part of the life cycle only Scholars could comprehend. He'd long since resigned himself to the fact that the physical side of this holy mystery was all too earthly.

It was the other part that still disturbed him. *"For as this spirit abides with us, so shall it with her; it will be made manifest in ways beyond our vision. . . ."* Sunlight beat down between the glistening towers onto Noren's uplifted face; he closed his eyes, marveling at the sincerity in Brek's voice.

Villagers and Technicians believed that Scholars were omniscient, that they *knew* what happened after death. Did not the Scholars know the answers to all other mysteries: why crops would not grow in unquickened soil, how impure water could turn sane men into idiots, and even how Machines had come into the world? Having been enlightened as to these latter things, Noren himself had not, at first, doubted that the former was equally explicable. He grew hot at the memory of his naiveté when he'd queried the computer complex about death, and of his stunned disillusionment at its inability to provide any information. He'd been a mere adolescent then, of course. The past year had taught him much. His emotions had become less involved, at least as far as his own fate was concerned. But now, Talyra. . . .

"Her place is assured among those who lived before her and those who will come after, those by whom the Star is seen and their children's children's children, even unto infinite and unending time. And not in memory alone does she survive, for the universe is vast. Were the doors now closed to us reopened, as in time they shall be, still there would remain that wall through which there is no door save that through which she has passed. . . ."

Somehow, said of Talyra, it seemed less incredible than it always had to him. Surely Talyra wasn't just . . . extinguished. He could not imagine a universe in which Talyra had ceased to exist.

He had studied the computers' records of the Six Worlds' religions; he'd learned that belief in continuance after death had been common though not, by the time of the Founders, widely accepted among scientists. He had wondered why the Founders—all trained as scientists—had put it into the liturgy; for in establishing themselves as priests, they had been scrupulous about proclaiming only those ideas in which they sincerely believed. To the First Scholar, who had planned this, the test of a false religion was not whether someone had made up its symbols on purpose, but whether that person had been aiming to defraud. The Founders had been required to cloak certain facts in symbolism, but they had not practiced deception. They had meant everything they said. How, Noren had asked himself, could they have meant what they seemed to be saying in the service for the dead, especially after they'd seen thirty billion people die in the vaporization of the Six Worlds?

Now, suddenly, he understood. It had been the First Scholar's influence, the dreams' influence! They'd all experienced the death of the First Scholar's wife: experienced it in personal terms—just as he, Noren, had—as a result of the dual identity one assumed in controlled dreaming. The dream material, even in its most complete version, was edited. The Founders had recorded memories for posterity, knowing that only so could they convey the reality of the Six Worlds' tragic end to those in whose hands survival of their race must rest, but they'd had a right to some privacy; even the First Scholar had edited his thoughts to remove such personal ones as would contribute nothing to comprehension of future problems. Thus his image of his wife's personality had not been preserved. But he had loved her. No doubt he'd indeed felt that somewhere in the universe she must, in some way, live—such a feeling might even remain in the recordings. Each dreamer drew different things from them according to his or her own background. The Founders, having lost loved ones to the nova, might well have clung to emotion as if it were the First Scholar's actual conviction. After his martyrdom they had revered him, as all Scholars still did, striving to emulate him in everything.

It was ironic. To the First Scholar himself, faith not based on evidence hadn't come easily. "Did you suppose he was born with it?" the Scholar Stefred had said when Noren, on his return from the mountains, had begun to perceive the real nature of commitment to the Prophecy. Stefred had always maintained that Noren's mind was very like the First Scholar's.

From his place in the inner circle Noren glanced around, expecting to see Stefred among the blue-robed figures closest to him. Astonishingly, he was absent. It was unthinkable that he wouldn't attend this service, out of friendship not only for him but for Talyra, whose entry to the City he had arranged; unthinkable too that Brek would have neglected to tell him of her death.

(20

Noren himself had not sought out Stefred, nor did he intend to do so. There was no help for this sort of pain. As head of recruitment and a skilled psychiatrist, Stefred knew all young Scholars' deepest feelings; he had guided them through the ordeals of inquisition, enlightenment and recantation. He had aided their adjustment to the status they'd neither sought nor welcomed. He'd been their first friend in the Inner City and remained, to all, a warm one. But though he'd want to help, he was uncompromisingly honest—he would not try to argue away grief.

Yet neither would he ignore it. Could he be tied up with urgent Council business? Noren had not entered the Hall of Scholars for two days; he had heard none of the current rumors about the City's affairs. Abruptly, it occurred to him that these affairs had not halted, that little as they now mattered to him, they would go right on. The effort to fulfill the Prophecy would go on, hopeless though it was. He had committed himself to participation. For a time he'd had faith that it was worthwhile. Had that been only for the child's sake?

He'd thought such faith, once discovered, would be permanent. But perhaps it had never been valid at all; perhaps it had been a mere feeling, no better founded than this unexpected feeling that Talyra's true self still lived on.

". . . *so may the spirit of the Star be with her, and with us all.*" Brek stopped speaking; there was a long silence. Gradually Noren became aware that men stood ready to lift the shroud, that they were waiting for his signal.

Stepping forward, he dropped his eyes. There was nothing to be seen, of course, but dazzling white cloth; wherever Talyra was, she could not be there. Nor could the child—the boy, he'd been told—in whom they'd taken such joy. *Oh, Talyra,* he thought, *it wasn't the way we imagined. The wilderness gave us death after all.*

When it was over, Brek took him to the refectory, persuaded him to eat. "Stefred sent a message," he said. "He'd like you to stop by his study—"

"I don't need to do that."

"You and your starcursed pride," murmured Brek. "I should have known better than to say it that way. I know you don't need therapy from Stefred. So does he. But after all, his own wife died—and he still mourns her; he's never looked at anyone else. It's no wonder if he's sorry he couldn't be at the service and wants to tell you so personally. You owe him the chance, when he's so troubled right now himself."

"Troubled? Why?"

"You haven't heard? Everyone's mystified. We don't know what the problem is, except that he's working with a heretic who's been reacting badly to the dreams. Apparently he doesn't dare leave her."

"Not at all?" The testing and enlightenment of a Scholar candidate took several weeks of intensive therapy, climaxed by the grueling ceremony of public recantation; but not all phases demanded Stefred's presence. There were rest periods, and some of the machine-induced dreams could be controlled by assistants.

"Well, he won't leave his suite at all; he's having his meals brought to him. And he's monitoring the entire dream sequence personally. As far as that goes, he handled the inquisition personally after the first hour or so—the observers were sent out. I don't suppose we'll ever hear what happened."

"No," agreed Noren, "but it must have been rough for them both." Any candidate experiencing the dreams had been judged trustworthy. That meant she had stood up to Stefred despite real terror, which in Technicians—and most female heretics had been born to that caste—could sometimes be hard to induce. Technicians weren't overwhelmed by City surroundings, as villagers were; stress had to be artificially applied. Stefred was expert; he knew how to do it harmlessly, and when necessary he could be ruthless. It was for the candidate's own benefit: no one unsure of his or her inner strength could endure the outwardly-degrading recantation ceremony, or accept the "rewards" that came after. One must be certain in one's own mind that one hadn't sold out. If that certainty could be engendered only through extreme measures, Stefred would use them; but he would not enjoy the process.

"The odd thing," Brek went on, "is that she's a village woman. Yet at first, I'm told, she was fearless. Everyone who saw her noticed—she was as self-composed as an experienced initiate. It was almost unnatural."

Slowly, Noren nodded. It was indeed odd that a villager, brought straight from a Stone Age environment into the awesome City—believing she'd be put to death there for her convictions—could be so cool under questioning that Stefred would have to employ unusual tactics. But they would learn nothing of her background. Not only were closed-door sessions with Stefred treated as confidential, but no questions were asked in the Inner City about newcomers' past lives. This convention had been established because the true significance of heresy must be concealed from the uninitiated, but it was also a matter of courtesy. Former heretics, who were by nature nonconformists, had not always behaved admirably in youth; it was considered tactless to risk embarrassing anyone. And it was cruel to stir memories of loved ones with whom no reunion would ever be possible.

"What's strangest," Noren reflected, "is that someone strong-willed enough to need special handling would be endangered by the dreams. They're hard for everybody at first. A person who wasn't bothered by what the Founders did wouldn't be a fit successor. But close monitoring—that's used only for the most terrifying ones, the ones that could induce physical shock. I never heard of monitoring the whole series."

"Could he have put her under too much stress beforehand, maybe?"

"Stefred? He's never miscalculated; you know that!"

"I do know," Brek replied. "Yet now he's worried. No one's seen him since Orison the night before last, and then he looked— well, as if he needed that kind of reassurance. Since he's willing to talk to you—"

"I'll find out what I can." It was true enough, Noren realized, that only pride had made him resolve not to go to Stefred, the one person in the City to whom he could speak freely of sorrow. He did not want false comfort; but that was exactly what Stefred never gave.

But there was another encounter that had priority. On the verge of taking the lift up to the tower suite in which he'd met so many past crises, Noren moved his hand instead to the button for "down."

At the foundation of the Hall of Scholars was the computer complex, most sacred of all places in the City because there alone the accumulated knowledge of the Six Worlds was preserved. To Noren, knowledge had seemed sacred from his earliest boyhood; to all Scholars, its guardianship was a holy responsibility. The information stored in the computers was irreplaceable. If lost, it could not be regained, and without that information, human survival would become impossible. Unrestricted access to it was the right of every Scholar; priesthood wasn't a condition—but it was in contact with the computer complex that Noren felt most nearly as he supposed a priest ought to feel. The computers held such truth as was knowable. He knew better, now, than to think that they held *all* truth, but they held all his human race had uncovered, all he was likely to find in his own world.

In this only, there was happiness he had not shared with Talyra. It was the single aspect of his life her loss would not diminish. But he could not accept the joys of learning without also accepting the demands. *I care more for truth than for comfort,* he'd declared at his trial. He'd been a mere boy, fresh from the village school; it sounded naively melodramatic now. He had known even then that most people would think it foolish. The village councilmen had been appalled by his blasphemous presumption and had sent him to the City as a condemned prisoner. During the subsequent inquisition, however, Stefred had not thought it foolish; he'd called it the

23)

key point in his defense. Stefred, who knew more than any village council about uncomfortable truths, had challenged him to choose. He could not now revoke the choice he had made.

Noren sat at a console, not yet touching the keys, glad that in the dim blue light of the computer room no one would notice his hesitancy. He had never been afraid of knowledge. He'd learned early that it could be painful to possess as well as to acquire; he had shut it out at times; still he could not consciously deny that knowing was better than not knowing. Somewhere in the computers was information that could tell him: had actions of his killed Talyra?

Quite possibly they had. If so, it was fitting retribution for the mistakes on his part that had led to the crash in the mountains . . . yet how could things work like that? *She* had been guiltless!

He himself was not. He had by his rashness destroyed one of the world's few aircars; its loss might affect the well-being of generations yet unborn. He'd thought himself willing to destroy people's hope at the cost of his own life. These events were behind him now. Stefred had said he must look forward, not back. Yet considering the death of the child. . . .

Could the child have been harmed by the mountain water after all? Though Noren's genes hadn't been affected by it, Talyra had not been tested; they'd said it was more complicated with a woman, that it would demand surgery for which they had no proper equipment and which would in any case be risky during her pregnancy. But Talyra had drunk no more of the water than Brek, whose test result showed no harm—not nearly as much as the officially established limit. Still, if genetics hadn't been studied since the Founders' time, did anyone really know how exact the limit was?

All the science of the Six Worlds was in computer memory. He had access to all of it if he could frame the right questions. Since becoming a Scholar, he'd acquired skill in questioning, a process that demanded deep thought. It would not be possible simply to ask why Talyra had died, or even why the baby had; the program couldn't respond to a query of that kind. His questions must be specific. He must analyze the issues, however hard they were to face.

Suppose there had been damage to Talyra's genes, suppose the limit was not the same for everyone—even so, the mutation caused by impure water wasn't lethal. The mutants in the mountains, despite subhuman brains, were all too healthy. Besides, the baby most likely had been conceived the first night. Impure water was harmful only to reproductive cells, not to embryos . . . wasn't it? He frowned, struggling with concepts unfamiliar to him, as a new thought came into his mind.

He knew little about pregnancy. Such things were not studied—

babies came and were welcomed; one did not ponder how they grew. Beris had said that on the Six Worlds doctors had known more. Had they known what could harm an embryo during the first days of its existence?

A child newly conceived was alive; like all living things it needed water; it must get this through its mother's blood. But it was surely very small. So could a small amount of some damaging substance hurt it, even if the mother herself was not damaged?

This, he knew, was the kind of question that was answerable. Whether or not anyone had asked it before in the City, the program would reply as promptly as if the query concerned recent experiments. His hands trembling, Noren keyed, CAN AN UNBORN CHILD BE HARMED BY WHAT ITS MOTHER CONSUMES EARLY IN PREGNANCY?

Instantly the screen before him displayed, YES.

EVEN IF SHE HERSELF IS NOT MADE ILL?

YES. SUCH DAMAGE IS CALLED TERATOGENIC.

IS THAT THE SAME AS MUTATION?

NO, IT IS A DIFFERENT TYPE OF GENETIC ERROR. TERATOGENIC DAMAGE IS NOT INHERITED BY THE CHILD'S OFFSPRING.

SUCH A CHILD SOMETIMES LIVES, THEN?

USUALLY IT LIVES, BUT IS DISEASED OR DEFORMED.

CAN TERATOGENIC DAMAGE CAUSE IT TO BE STILLBORN?

OCCASIONALLY. MORE OFTEN, LETHAL DAMAGE WOULD RESULT IN EARLY MISCARRIAGE.

Noren gripped the edge of the console keyboard, fighting sick despair. If it could happen, it was reasonable to assume that it *had* happened, given the fact that the impurities of the water had been in Talyra's bloodstream throughout her first week of pregnancy. He drew deep breaths; then, with effort, continued, IF SUCH A CHILD IS STILLBORN, CAN THIS CAUSE THE DEATH OF THE MOTHER?

NOT DIRECTLY. IN RARE CASES TERATOGENIC DAMAGE MIGHT LEAD TO COMPLICATIONS IN DELIVERY. CAN YOU SUPPLY SPECIFIC DATA?

WHAT SORT OF DATA?

GENETIC DATA THAT WOULD PERMIT THE PROBABILITY TO BE CALCULATED.

No, thought Noren in dismay. He could not supply that. But the Founders could have—otherwise the computer wouldn't be programmed to ask for it.

He knew nothing about biology, but he was well-trained in higher mathematics; the calculation of probabilities was something he understood. HOW MANY INPUT VARIABLES ARE INVOLVED? he ventured.

THE ENTIRE GENOTYPE OF BOTH PARENTS MAY BE RELEVANT. THE PROGRAM CAN DETERMINE SIGNIFICANT VARIABLES FROM THAT,

25)

PLUS CHEMICAL ANALYSIS OF THE SUBSTANCE IN QUESTION AND ITS TIME OF CONSUMPTION. THERE MAY BE OTHER ENVIRONMENTAL VARIABLES ALSO.

Genotype? He did not know the word; fortunately computer programs were patient with stupid questions. DEFINE GENOTYPE, he commanded.

GENOTYPE IS THE GENETIC MAKEUP OF AN INDIVIDUAL ORGANISM, THE SPECIFIC SET OF GENES IN ITS CELLS.

HOW LARGE IS THE SET IN HUMANS? Noren inquired, thinking that perhaps some doctor would help him list his own genes in a form suitable for input. Incredibly, he found himself staring at a six-digit figure.

THAT IS THE NUMBER OF GENES THAT MAY VARY? he asked in disbelief.

IT IS THE NUMBER WITH WHICH THE PROGRAM DEALS. THE SET IS LARGER, BUT SOME GENES ARE REDUNDANT OR OF UNKNOWN FUNCTION.

No wonder the Scholars hadn't devoted time to studying the field, thought Noren. Genetics must be as complicated as nuclear physics. And surely even a knowledgeable person couldn't key in that many separate bits of data; it would tie up a console for weeks. WHAT IS THE INPUT FORMAT FOR GENOTYPE? he queried.

THE ANALYSIS CAN BE MADE DIRECTLY FROM A BLOOD SAMPLE THROUGH THE USE OF AUXILIARY INPUT EQUIPMENT.

Did such equipment still exist? It must; the Founders had been careful to write the program in a way compatible with the facilities preserved for their descendants. So his own genotype could evidently be analyzed. For Talyra's, it was too late. If he had known before her body was sent to the converters. . . . Perhaps it was best that he had not, that he could obtain no real estimate of the odds, for they would not be zero, and they might prove conclusively that having a child under other circumstances wouldn't have been fatal. Yet he could not just drop the matter. *It happens,* Beris had said. *Occasionally it happens with a girl who seems healthy.* Generations of women had accepted that, when all along the computers had been able to calculate probabilities in specific cases! Why had the Founders made no mention of this in the High Law?

Because, he saw, it would not fit the High Law's purpose. The original population of the colony had been dangerously small, so small that maximum increase had been deemed desirable even though it would hasten the depletion of resources. Thus for survival's sake the High Law encouraged childbearing; it forbade all contraception, not only the drugs that couldn't be manufactured with available resources. There was no longer need for such a prohibition—any decent couple would be outraged at the mere thought of the things Scholars knew about from the old records. He himself

(26

had been more shocked by them than by the literal meaning behind the phrases referring to disposition of bodies. But this hadn't been true in the Founders' time. The Founders had grown up in a society where overpopulation was a serious problem; they had considered it natural and even admirable to limit births. They'd assumed that if people went on computing the odds of trouble when medical facilities were inadequate, no one would take any risk at all.

Yet . . . there were nevertheless perplexities. Why, for instance, had he come upon this knowledge only through purposeful inquiry? Basic information about human reproduction was not obscure, and the sexual customs of the Six Worlds were known to any Scholar familiar with material about the vanished culture; there were allusions to them even in dreams. Scientific details, on the other hand —and especially those related to genetics—received practically no mention. It was almost as if references to the topic had been deliberately omitted from the reading matter of the Scholars themselves. And that was strange; not only was access to knowledge supposed to be unrestricted, but genetics was the very thing most pertinent to understanding of the alien world's limitations. Guardianship of the City was justifiable only because it was the sole alternative to genetic damage: so the Founders had believed, so all Scholars since had agreed. There was no question about this fact; but why was it thought sufficient to know that it was true if the computers had detailed information about why it was true, about the biological mechanism that produced the damage?

And why hadn't the First Scholar's recorded thoughts dealt with the subject more fully?

Having raised these issues, Noren could not fail to pursue them; it was not in him to let such things ride. CAN THE PROBABLE CAUSE OF THE MOTHER'S DEATH BE ESTIMATED WITHOUT HER GENOTYPE? he asked.

NOT ACCURATELY. A ROUGH APPROXIMATION CAN BE MADE.

That was better than nothing. SHE CONSUMED UNPURIFIED WATER, he keyed. FOR CHEMICAL ANALYSIS REFER TO MEMORY. The computers had more information about what was in it than he did, after all.

AMOUNT AND TIME OF CONSUMPTION?

MINIMUM DAILY RATION; FIRST SIX DAYS OF PREGNANCY OR LESS.

FOOD DURING THIS PERIOD?

NONE AT ALL. They had agreed to starve—there'd been no safe food, so he, Brek and Talyra had calmly discussed it and decided that starvation would be preferable to an adaptation that would lead to production of subhuman offspring. Had she even then been carrying a defective baby?

QUALITY OF PRENATAL MEDICAL CARE?

Again, NONE.

27)

ANY EXPOSURE TO RADIATION?

No, Talyra hadn't entered the power plant; and though he himself had worked both there and in nuclear research labs, any failure of the shielding would have been detected. No case of radiation exposure had occurred since the accident that had killed Stefred's wife. But wait . . . *radiation?*

There had been the mystifying radiation given off by the alien sphere.

It had brought about their rescue. They'd found the little sphere in the mountains, an artifact from some other solar system, long ago abandoned by the mysterious Visitors who'd mined and depleted this planet's scant metal resources before humans from the Six Worlds had arrived. He had manipulated it, made it radiate—an alarm had been triggered in the monitoring section of the computer complex. Thus an aircar had been sent out from the City and had located them. But he'd been unable to walk after retrieving the sphere from the rock niche where it had lain; it had been Talyra who, at his instructions, had carried it to the open plateau and turned it on.

Since then, the sphere had been studied at the research outpost. It had been pronounced harmless; the radiation it emitted was of a previously unknown sort and no one could tell what it was for, but it didn't seem to hurt anybody. It caused no mutations in fowl, the only creatures available to test it on. There were no facilities for taking it apart or attempting its duplication, but as the only artifact of the Visitors ever discovered, it had been observed with great fascination by the few Scholars fortunate enough to draw duty at the newly built outpost: duty welcomed as respite from lifelong Inner City confinement. Were any of those Scholars pregnant? One thing was sure—no woman who'd touched the sphere as early in pregnancy as Talyra could yet have given birth, for Talyra had been the first.

CAN TERATOGENIC DAMAGE BE CAUSED BY RADIATION HARMLESS TO ADULTS? Noren asked.

YES.

BY THE UNKNOWN RADIATION THAT LAST YEAR TRIGGERED AN ALARM?

INSUFFICIENT DATA, replied the screen tersely. That was what it always said when one asked a question for which the programmers hadn't had an answer.

Noren dropped his head, burying his face in his folded arms. He was indeed responsible, he thought despairingly—for the child's death and no doubt Talyra's also, for would it not be too great a coincidence if she'd died of some other cause? As a scientist, he could see that there was no conclusive proof. But how could he ever, in the face of so many suspicious factors, believe otherwise?

And for how many more deaths might he become responsible, if women at the outpost now carried unborn children damaged by the sphere?

It would have been better not to have found it. It would have been better if they had died in the mountains, as they'd expected they would. Yet Talyra had viewed its discovery as a confirmation of her faith. She'd believed the spirit of the Mother Star would guard them, and in her eyes it *had*—they had been led to an utterly unpredictable deliverance, as the Prophecy proclaimed would some-day happen for all mankind. *Though our peril be great even unto the last generation of our endurance, in the end man shall prevail; and the doors of the universe shall once again be thrown open to him.* . . . On the basis of the analogy, he had accepted priesthood. So great an irony as that was past bearing. . . .

No. The whole chain of events had begun with his unwillingness to live with his own failings; he would not make the same mistake twice. Wearily, Noren sat upright once more and went on questioning.

II

AS DUSK CAME ON, NOREN WAITED ALONE IN STEFRED'S SECLUDED study high in the Hall of Scholars. Beyond the window three waning moons hung between the lighted pinnacles of adjacent towers. There had been moonlight on the plateau in the mountains, too, he found himself thinking, the harsh, desolate wasteland that to him and Talyra had been a place of beauty. And long before, the same three crescents had shone on the village square where they'd made their first pledge of love. Life had been simple then, despite his dissatisfaction with its injustice and his inner knowledge that he might someday face punishment for heresy. He hadn't imagined how much things could change.

What was left for him now? he thought numbly. It would be better if he had some constructive job to turn to. He didn't expect happiness—without Talyra, how could he know happiness again? Nor did he still look for peace of mind. But tomorrow morning would come, and the next, and the next . . . he would have to do something, since no one was idle in the City, and how could he go back to work—futile work—when all hope for its success was dead in him?

This was not a question to ask Stefred, or for that matter, anyone else. Even from Brek, he knew, he would receive an all-too-ready answer. It would be said that if his actions had caused deaths, that was all the more reason why he was obligated to work toward the ultimate preservation of lives. By many of his fellow-priests, in fact, he would be told that if he'd survived last year's events at high cost, it was because he might be destined to preserve humanity; that was the basis on which they'd justified the loss of the aircar. He must therefore avoid letting the issue be raised in the light of what he'd learned about the baby, for he could not endure the thought of its life, and Talyra's, being figured into the balance. The proffered answers would no doubt be the same.

No price would be thought too high for his salvation. He, Noren, was regarded by most as a genius who, in his later years, would bring about the advance in physics needed to realize the Founders'

(30

hope of synthesizing metal through nuclear fusion. All efforts of past generations to achieve this had been proven vain by last year's experiments; a flaw had appeared at the level of basic scientific theory. The computers now said the task was impossible. The priests, however, maintained that it could not be impossible—that since nothing else could enable their species to survive, an unforeseen breakthrough would occur if they kept working. Noren was viewed as the most likely person to make it.

He did not share this confidence; he himself had never been deluded about the chances of his talent producing such an outcome. His very gift for the work showed him, with a clarity not apparent to others, that the limits imposed by available facilities were absolute. More and more, since his return from the outpost where future experimentation was to be tried, he had seen that the research would be fruitless. Study, like priesthood, was for him a gesture—a gesture that sustained people's hope, unlike the destructive one through which he'd sought to deny life by declaring all hope fraudulent. He had acknowledged the value of faith and had even felt its power, but he'd found it couldn't alter his scientific pessimism.

At times, with Talyra, he had forgotten all this. The end would not come in his lifetime, and he'd lived as if long-term survival of his people were indeed assured. He'd been on his way to becoming like everyone else. But he couldn't have gone on with that forever, he thought, suddenly overcome by a sadness that was more than grief. He was not like everyone else; he never had been. . . .

The door slid aside, and Stefred stood for a moment in the lighted opening; Noren rose to greet him, and they gripped hands. "Noren," he said quietly. "I-I've no words."

"They aren't needed," Noren replied. With Stefred this was true; he had an uncanny ability to convey the warmth of his feelings even when forced to speak words not easy to hear.

"I can't tell you it will stop hurting. I've been through it, and I know better. But in time—"

"You've never remarried."

"That's different."

"How?" demanded Noren. Stefred wasn't an old man—more than old enough to be his father, no doubt, but in a world where most married in adolescence, that did not make him old in years. Furthermore, everyone who knew Stefred liked and admired him; he'd scarcely have had trouble finding another wife.

"My position's awkward," he replied painfully. "There is a—a bond that develops between me and each candidate I examine; you know that. With the men it means lasting friendship. With the women it could mean more; ethics require me to suppress all such thoughts while acting in my professional role. Later . . . there've been several women I might have approached later, but by then they'd chosen others."

"You could marry a Technician, though."

"Could I? Noren, every Technician who enters the Inner City kneels to me in a formal audience during application for admission, seeks my blessing, thinks me of supernatural stature! I can't hide my rank while getting acquainted with the newcomers, as the rest of you can." His voice dropped as he added with bitterness, "No Technician woman would refuse me; she would feel awed by the thought of bearing my child. It goes without saying that I don't want love on that basis."

Of course not, Noren realized. Because in the villages most heretics were men, the balance between sexes would not be equal in the Inner City if Technician girls weren't brought in; but the religious devotion of these girls, who considered it a high honor to be accepted for lifelong confinement within the walls, was not exploited. They assumed they were to be courted by their peers. Stefred, who must appear robed at the admission interview and accept the near-worship accorded High Priests, was doomed to a unique sort of loneliness.

And loneliness wasn't his heaviest burden. Meeting his eyes, Noren noticed the shadows beneath them, the lines of fatigue and worry in his face. Only a real emergency would have kept Stefred from the service for Talyra; he'd just now returned from a dream-monitoring session with a candidate whom he must consider in peril of cracking up. "This is a bad time for me to have come," Noren apologized. "I know you can't tell me the details, but people have heard rumors."

Stefred crossed to his desk and slumped wearily into its chair, not bothering to turn on the lamp. "I'll tell you this," he said after a short pause. "I'm—afraid, Noren. For the first time, I'm dealing with someone I'm afraid I can't bring through."

"She's not strong enough?" Noren sat down again, sensing that Stefred really wanted to talk about it. Detached though he felt, the situation puzzled him. If the girl lacked courage, that judgment would have been made earlier, before it was too late to pursue the heresy charge less rigorously and give her Technician rank. Once secrets had been revealed to her, she must be isolated from Technicians for the rest of her life if she proved unable to withstand the full sequence of ordeals that led to Scholar status. Since this would mean not mere confinement to the Inner City but true imprisonment, it was indeed a dismaying prospect—but surely a remote one. Stefred knew how to bring out the best in people.

"Oh, she's strong," he was saying, "she's more than strong enough; she's the most promising candidate I've seen in a long

(32

time. If I fail, the tragedy won't be just hers and mine; it will affect all of us."

"But then if it's just some personal reaction to the dreams, can't you help her deal with it?" Stefred, Noren knew, would never violate anyone's confidence, let alone reveal a confession made under the drugs, which, in a private inquisition, he must have used. However, it was no secret that things in a candidate's background could make particular aspects of the dreams unduly trying, and in such cases, hypnotic aid was normally given.

"She's concealing too much from me," Stefred said. "There's a wall in her mind I can't get past, and I wouldn't be justified in breaching it even if I could. I'm already sure she meets the qualifications; she hates the caste system as much as we all do and will gladly work toward its abolishment if she finds herself on top. I've no warrant to invade her privacy except to determine that. You know I can't probe her subconscious merely to spare her suffering."

"Not unless she consents," Noren agreed. "Still, if you'll risk killing her otherwise. . . ." It was possible, in theory, for someone who'd identified closely with the First Scholar to literally share his death in the last dream, the crucial one that dealt with the Prophecy's origin—without which no person fit for Scholar status would be willing to affirm its validity.

"The last dream's not the problem. If it were, I could handle it; she'd need temporary isolation, perhaps, but given time, I could prepare her. What seems to be happening is that she's too intuitive —the recruiting scheme wasn't designed to deal with someone who grasps things outside any conceivable past experience." He leaned forward, frowning. "Noren, what if you'd guessed the extent of the editing in the candidates' version of the dreams? Could you have gone through with voluntary recantation?"

"No," Noren said. "No, I based my decision on first-hand knowledge of the First Scholar's motives. When you told me afterward about the editing I was furious—I thought for a moment you'd manipulated things to deceive me."

"Lianne," Stefred reflected, "underwent more anguish than any person I have ever monitored in the first dream. It's not enjoyable for anyone—it can't be; watching a sun nova and consume its planets isn't an easy experience. But most candidates are detached at that stage; it's nightmare, not reality. Not till later does the reality sink in. Lianne got it all; from what she said after she regained consciousness, I know she got everything the First Scholar felt—but of course, without his foreknowledge."

"Everything? But she couldn't have known what populated worlds are like," protested Noren, remembering his own slow absorption of the idea that not just one City but thousands had been wiped out in that single surge of intolerable fire.

"I wasn't sure she could take another session," Stefred went on, "but she was willing, and I went ahead with close monitoring. Her physiological responses showed she was coping; I thought we'd passed the crisis. And then, when she woke, the first thing she said to me was, " 'Why have you edited it so much?' "

"Oh, Stefred."

"You see what's going to happen. She'll stick to her refusal to recant even after finishing the sequence; precisely because she *is* strong, is perceptive, she'll hold out on the grounds that I've kept part of the truth from her. Her very fitness to become one of us will force her into a position that deprives her of the chance."

"That's awful. It's one thing to make that choice out of real disagreement with the First Scholar's decision, but to have to live with its consequences because of a false suspicion that you're cheating—"

"I know," Stefred sighed, "especially since I have cause to believe she doesn't disagree. The dreams wouldn't affect her so deeply if she didn't share his convictions. For that matter, she wouldn't be unsatisfied by the explanation I've given her about the editing."

"Stefred," Noren mused, "why wasn't I unsatisfied? You told me thoughts beyond my comprehension had been removed from the recording, and I took your word."

"It was true in your case," replied Stefred grimly. "With Lianne I've come close to lying."

Noren stared at him in bafflement. Stefred never lied to anyone; that was why even candidates under stress learned to trust him. "I don't see," he admitted, "how the partial truth can be less valid in her case than in mine."

"Neither do I, really. Even mature candidates don't notice what's absent from the First Scholar's thoughts at first; his world is too strange and distracting. As for you, though, you were very young, Noren. You didn't miss the deleted emotions because you'd never imagined such feelings, and they'd have been truly beyond you. That's one reason we see to it that known heretics are brought to trial in adolescence."

"Is she an older woman?" Noren asked, surprised. The majority of people with heretical tendencies did reveal them early, though since opportunity to earn Scholar status was every citizen's birthright, older candidates occasionally appeared.

"Well, not adolescent, certainly. Oddly enough, her age is one of the things she won't tell me. She was a stranger in the village where she was arrested, so we don't know her real identity, and all she'll say is that she has no children—which, barring some medical cause, means she's unconventional in more than her opinions. She can't have lacked suitors; she's quite pretty, in an unusual sort of way." He shook his head, obviously perplexed. "Her face looks young, but her mind seems as old as any I've encountered. The full version of the dreams would not be incomprehensible to her, and she's well aware of that."

"The full version . . . wait a minute! Are you saying she's concerned about things in the *full* version, the one I haven't been through myself yet, not just the second version that contains the plan for the succession scheme?" Shaken from his stupor, Noren realized that he'd nearly forgotten such a version existed. He had been told about it when in deciding to accept priesthood, he'd inquired about the First Scholar's personal religious beliefs; but it covered much more than religion. Though its ultimate effect on most dreamers was heartening, the First Scholar's trust in the future had been hard-won; his recorded memories were said to involve agonizing periods of doubt and near-suicidal depression. Ordinarily only experienced Scholars chose to grapple with these feelings; Noren, who'd tasted them in his own life, had nevertheless been advised to wait awhile.

That advice had been given just after the return from the wilderness, he reflected. Stefred had known then that Talyra might have conceived a child there; had he also known there was risk of a disastrous outcome? Was there something related to such an outcome in the full version of the First Scholar's memories, something there'd have been no use in worrying about while awaiting the birth? It was all too likely. The First Scholar had been absolutely positive that genetic damage was unavoidable without technology to compensate for the alien environment; the edited recordings emphasized this certainty, for nothing else could justify guardianship of the City. But, Noren thought suddenly, it was not a fact he'd have accepted without strong proof. . . .

"Yes," Stefred was saying, "she sees the questions you did recognize last year as things he must have thought about. Life, death, why novas wipe out worlds—you know what I mean. And the despair, Noren. She perceives he'd have experienced despair, not just horror and regret."

"Does she also sense that he rose out of it?" inquired Noren. In the end the First Scholar had met death fearlessly, with genuine conviction that the world was to be saved—but could a person who knew about despair guess that? Perhaps he'd not guessed it himself during the bad times. And perhaps it wouldn't have happened that way at all if he'd known what had since been discovered about the impossibility of synthesizing metal.

"I think she does," Stefred replied, "though I admit I don't know just why. I haven't even hinted; my only recourse has been

to hope she'll assume I'm withholding the worst parts out of mis-
guided kindness. Actually, of course, to use the full recording
would be a mercy in her case. She—she has begged for it, Noren;
it is very hard to subject her to as much torment as I must." Incredibly, his voice faltered as if he were struggling to hold back
emotion he could not share even with a fellow-Scholar.

"Torment? But why is it any worse than what came before,
when she knew Scholars weren't telling her all she wanted to know?"
Noren asked. Obviously the full recording could not be used; it
included references to the secret of the succession. But if the feelings it contained were so painful, to keep it from candidates not
yet informed about the hopeful ending seemed indeed kind as well
as essential.

Stefred, once more in full command of himself, explained, "Right
now she's suffering in a way that should never be necessary: she
reaches for thoughts that won't come, knowing full well what sort
should come. You know how hard it is to reach out that way in the
dreams; you had courage enough to reach further than most—but
you were too inexperienced in life to absorb all the data you received. The real gaps you accepted as mystery. If I put you through
the candidates' version now, you'd find it intolerable to be held
within its limits."

Limits . . . yes, the City, too, had once seemed limitless,
thought Noren, looking out from the dim room to the closely
grouped towers that blocked most of the night sky. He had thought
he could never exhaust the well of knowledge preserved here in the
City. He'd thought there could be no need to seek beyond. Even
when he'd found that limits did exist, he had told himself he could
live within them. He had resolved to play the game because there
was no other; he had stopped reaching for what he knew would
never come.

Was this strange village girl, who by her reaching took on
torment even Stefred felt was excessive, less of a realist than he?
That was hardly the way she'd been described—yet she was evidently unwilling to stop.

He'd changed so much since his own initiation . . . but in what
direction? How many directions? He knew more, and yet perhaps
he'd lost something, too, something besides Talyra. He did not
feel like the same person; perhaps he'd lost part of himself. Confused, cold with apprehension he did not understand, he heard his
own voice ask, "What if you put me through the full version now?
I—I think the time's come when I need to know what's in it."

"Not when you're burdened by grief, you don't," Stefred said
gently. "Maybe in a year or two."

"No," declared Noren, suddenly very sure of what he was looking for. "Not in a year or two—now."

He had thought Stefred would be unwilling even to discuss it at a time when he was preoccupied, a time when the Dream Machine was obviously not available in any case—candidates always had priority for controlled dreaming, and there was always a waiting list of Scholars who'd signed up to experience library dreams through which they could learn more about the Six Worlds. Surprisingly, Stefred seemed eager to dissuade him from a decision that could simply have been delayed.

"The part about his wife," he said. "That would hurt, now, more than you expect; you'd experience it in a very personal way."

"But he did come to terms with it."

"Are you thinking you might be helped to do the same?"

"Well, yes, that too," Noren said, realizing this was true. "But I have something else in mind." No doubt Stefred assumed that he hadn't guessed, that he still needed protection from knowledge of his own blameworthiness in what had happened; maybe that was why he'd suddenly averted his eyes, as if stricken by remembrance of something better left unspoken. But if so—if Stefred knew portions of the First Scholar's memories did deal with the problem of genetic damage—that was all the more reason for proceeding as soon as the equipment was free.

It was unlike Stefred to avoid anyone's gaze; normally he was brutally straightforward about harsh reality, thereby inspiring people to rise to the challenge. To be sure, he was expert in masking his feelings for good purpose; but Noren knew all those games and had always found them exhilarating. Now his tone was oddly uncertain. "Noren, it's not like the first times through," he said. "You don't just relive nightmare and wake up with new knowledge. What you gain from the full version is more subtle: emotions, value judgments, that take a lifetime to interpret even after you've shared the First Scholar's view of them. In fact it contains some feelings none of his successors have ever managed to interpret. It's a harrowing experience. Ideally it should be spread out over many weeks, one step at a time."

"But you say this village woman, this Lianne, wouldn't be harmed by getting the whole thing fast, under stress of heresy proceedings."

"I'm balancing perils. To her, we are liars if we make it seem too simple; and since that may lead her to choose permanent imprisonment through misunderstanding of our aims, she has nothing to lose."

"Neither have I," Noren muttered. Then, because Stefred had heard and reacted, he added quickly, "I mean, would I suffer more than I'm already suffering? I'm not going to feel *good,* whatever I do now."

37)

"No—and I wouldn't have you believe I'd try to distract you from sorrow that's natural and unavoidable."

"I don't want distraction," said Noren, thinking that no such aim on Stefred's part had been implied by any of his comments. "It's just that I—I have to move on, Stefred. I can't slip back into the mold, or I'll end up paralyzed, the way I was at the outpost."

"There's risk of something worse than that," Stefred said with artificial, measured coldness. "You might be thrown into a depression more serious than last year's, and the recovery could be a good deal slower."

Perhaps, but last year too Stefred had cautioned him and had assumed responsibility before the Council when things seemed to be turning out wrong. Yet he had not felt it was wrong for either of them to take risks. Looking at him now, Noren could see plainly that he was deeply troubled. He would consider it his fault if Lianne got hurt, however unavoidable his actions had been in the case. He was not judging objectively in this separate matter—he simply didn't want another crackup on his conscience.

"You know me better than to warn me away from the truth," Noren said levelly.

Stefred nodded without answering, and Noren saw, suddenly, that it was unfair to let him bear any part of the accountability for his own future undertakings. "The decision's mine," he went on. "As a committed priest I have the right of access to the entire heritage left us by the First Scholar; that's the rule."

"It is," Stefred replied reluctantly, "though I never expected to hear you claim the prerogatives of the priesthood in opposition to me." He lowered his head, so that his face was hidden, but the pain in his voice was unmistakable.

In confusion and remorse, Noren went to him and touched his shoulder. "Stefred, I'm sorry. We're both under strain; I shouldn't even be here tonight. Certainly I shouldn't be talking about my problems when you've got a big one of your own to deal with. But —but I can't play it both ways; I can't go on acting a priest's role without taking full responsibility for what I do. You're my friend, you always will be. I'm grateful for the way you've helped me—and I know what you gambled for my sake when I was too proud to seek help—but I'm not a candidate any more, not even a trainee. You can decide what's best for Lianne, but not for me. Not any longer."

For a time Stefred was silent. Then he said, barely audibly. "Do you mean that, Noren? You're willing to go counter to my advice in this?"

"Yes. I'm sorry if I've hurt you—I never wanted to. It—it just didn't come out the way I meant it to." Like so much else, he thought in misery. Stefred's friendship had been the one firm thing left to count on.

(38

With evident effort, Stefred smiled. "You haven't hurt me," he said. "Did you imagine I'd think less of you for having a mind of your own? It's what we demand of heretics in the first place, after all."

"Oh, of course you wanted me to stand out against you while you seemed to be supporting injustice. But—"

"But it's harder to do when you're aware my job's to support *you.*"

"This isn't just a matter of pride, this time."

"No. It's more a matter of growth."

Startled, Noren felt his face redden. "What a fool I've been," he murmured. "You've known that it is, all along."

"Well, I've known you're a promising innovator."

"For the Star's sake, are we back to that?" exclaimed Noren impatiently. "That's part of the trouble; I'm sick of hearing about my so-called promise! I'm sick of having everyone expect something of me that I'll never be able to deliver. I know you think I'll achieve great things someday, but I just can't take your word for it."

"I realize you can't," Stefred admitted sadly. "That's part of the pattern; one sign of your promise is your inability to take anyone's word for something you've reached the point of doubting."

"That's the same thing you see in Lianne," Noren observed.

"One of the things, yes."

"Then you're manipulating me again, and I'm letting you! It's why you've told me as much about her reaction to the dreams as you have; you knew I'd see the comparison—"

"No!" Stefred burst out, wrenching his chair around to face Noren directly. "By the Star, Noren, I never anticipated this. It didn't occur to me it could help till you proposed it yourself. Eventually, yes; we both knew you'd choose it eventually—you're too much like him not to want awareness of all he went through. But no wish of mine led you to suggest it now, not—not unless you can read my mind."

"You do think it may help me, then."

"I don't presume to judge; you've taken the decision into your own hands." At Noren's look he added, "I guess that sounded sarcastic. Forgive me; I'm slow tonight. As you said, we're both under strain. I honestly don't know if it will help you. My thought was—elsewhere."

On Lianne, yes, as it should be. "I'd better go," Noren said.

As he reached the door, Stefred stood up. "Noren . . . wait," he said softly.

"I've already said more than enough I'm sorry for."

"You've changed your mind?"

"About the full version of the dreams? No, of course not; but I shouldn't have bothered you with it. I'll sign up for the first open time slot on the regular schedule sheet."

"They're not like library recordings. They have to be monitored."

"Oh, come on, Stefred—they won't send me into physical shock or anything. Not at this stage."

"I trust not. Nevertheless monitoring's standard procedure. Does that alter your enthusiasm?" Restlessly, Stefred paced back and forth between the desk and the window, his indecision more evident than ever.

"What it alters," said Noren sharply, "is my optimism about how soon my theoretical right of access is going to take effect. You can always give me a medical disqualification, and since you're the only one in the City qualified to monitor controlled dreaming—"

"Don't reproach me for a circumstance I've spent the past two nights regretting," said Stefred wearily. "Just sit down again and listen."

Noren sat. "Since I can't read your mind," he said, "I think it's time you told me what's going on in it."

With resignation, as if conceding defeat in some inner battle, Stefred said, "There's one way I could help Lianne, a way I've not let myself consider. If I could use the full recording—"

"You'd waive the requirement that she can't know in advance what recantation will lead to?" exclaimed Noren, astonished. Stefred wasn't one to go by the rule book, but to violate that particular policy would be unthinkable. The key to the succession was that Scholar rank could be attained only by those who did not want it, who most certainly would not accept it as payment for submission to necessary evils. "It would be self-defeating, if you want my opinion," he went on. "She'll never recant if she knows what she stands to gain; none of the rest of us would have."

"The recording could be re-edited, the secret parts taken out."

"If that's feasible, why haven't you done it?" asked Noren in bewilderment.

"Because as you say, I'm the only person in the City qualified to monitor controlled dreaming at all, let alone the form of monitoring used in the editing process." He met Noren's eyes for the first time since the dreams had been mentioned. "Did you think I could sit down at a computer console and push keys, as if I were editing a study tape? The computers can't read thought recordings, you know—they've got to be processed by sleeping human minds."

Abruptly, Noren understood. "You need a volunteer to work with."

"Unfortunately, yes. I'd prefer to take the dreamer's role myself."

"That would be a waste of machine time," said Noren, keeping his voice light, "considering that I'm going through those dreams as soon as possible anyway."

"I suppose you are," Stefred said, his voice low, "and I can't deny that I'm tempted to take advantage of that. I—I did manipulate you, perhaps—not purposely, and not by plan, yet I won't pretend I didn't know underneath that you'd force my hand if I argued."

"You also knew all that argument wasn't necessary. If you'd explained what was at stake in the first place—"

"If I'd done that, I wouldn't have been sure you wanted this experience for its own sake. And I couldn't weigh her welfare against yours."

"Then you're slipping," Noren said. "I'm a priest—and she is a prisoner in our hands. There's no question about whose welfare comes first; any one of us would offer, wouldn't we?"

"But I couldn't use just anyone, and the very things that make you a suitable subject will make it more grueling for you than for others."

"What things?" asked Noren, beginning to realize that he was not quite sure what he'd volunteered for.

"Your likeness to the First Scholar—and your willingness to reach for his entire thought. I couldn't rely on someone whose mind would retreat from the rough parts; there'd be danger of missing something significant."

"I don't understand the technique," Noren admitted. "I thought the monitors showed only physiological responses. Is there a way they can indicate content, too?"

"Not directly. It has to be done with hypnotic suggestion—in this case, commands to respond physiologically in some unmistakable way whenever a thought we must delete comes into your mind. You'll be unconscious, of course; you won't feel anything."

"You—you stop each time?"

"The master recording? Not with this kind of material; to keep stopping and starting would drive you insane. No, it's possible to synchronize the timing so that I can make the actual edited copy later, by feeding small sections into my own mind while I'm awake, as if I were working with a recording of my own thoughts, or with something briefer and less emotional." He smiled, seeming more like himself, like the Stefred in whom it was impossible to lack confidence. "It's a safe procedure; that much I can promise."

"I'm not worried."

"That's because you know little of what's involved. Under some conditions such hypnosis can be extremely dangerous; I wouldn't dare to try it on a person whose mind I hadn't previously explored —which rules out older Scholars originally examined by my predecessor. You, however, I know. Your peril lies not in what I'm going to do to you, but in your reaction to the dreams themselves."

"That's a chance I have to take," Noren said firmly.

"You realize this must be begun now, tonight, and the whole series must be completed in quick succession without proper rest breaks?"

Noren nodded. They could afford no delay; having once started the dreams, a candidate could not be permitted long conscious intervals in which to notice discrepancies caused by the necessary omission of the secrets, nor could she be kept under sedation indefinitely.

"You aren't in fit shape for it," Stefred said unhappily. "Only this morning you held rites for your wife—"

I killed my wife, Noren thought, *and if I can do anything toward salvaging some other woman's future, that may help even the score.* Aloud he said, "If I back out now, how will I feel if Lianne is lost to us? If I must see her isolated, knowing I might have prevented it? Will that heal me, Stefred?"

"It's too late for either of us to back out," Stefred conceded. Silhouetted against the window, his face in shadow, he went on, "You're right, I'm slipping—but I'm human; I saw you suffer last year in a way I don't want to see again. I staked my conscience and my career on my conviction that you'd take no harm from it; and my belief in you was justified. You took not harm, but strength. I know perfectly well that if you run into problems with this, the same thing will happen. You've always been strong. You'll withstand it."

"I should hope I'll withstand it as well as an uninitiated village girl," replied Noren, indignant. But he was aware that sorrow and exhaustion had made him reckless, that if he were not already half-dreaming, he would be afraid.

He came to his senses in the Dream Machine's small cubicle; when he opened his eyes, he could see at first only the pattern of dials, switches and colored lights that covered its walls. He was still reclining, and became aware that electrodes were taped not only to his head but to other parts of his body; dimly, he recalled Stefred's telling him to remove his tunic before beginning the ritual of hypnotic sedation that, during his time in the City, had become familiar to him. Stefred bent over him now, the concern in his manner all too plain.

"Is it over?" Noren asked. "I—I don't remember anything!"

"It hasn't started yet." Stefred sat on a stool close to the reclining chair, his eyes on Noren's. "I had to wake you; there's something troubling you that you haven't told me about."

"What makes you think so?"

"I did some routine checking in preparation for giving you hypnotic commands and found evidence of psychological trauma that's never been there before. It's too risky for me to proceed without understanding it, yet I'm not willing to probe your mind without your permission."

"What sort of evidence?" Noren asked slowly.

"Basically, Noren, you respect yourself," Stefred said. "You've never felt guilty about being *you,* or about not seeing things just as other people do. That's one of the things we go into quite deeply with heretics; the self-confidence that results in defiance of conventions has to be genuine. Yours was extraordinarily so. Now it is—shaken."

"Well, after what happened last year—"

"I know you doubted yourself then. But it was never a deep-seated doubt; though it caused you pain, what lay underneath was more powerful than your conscious feelings. That was how I knew you'd come through. What I find now is a bit more serious." Sighing, he declared, "You have the right of privacy, but not the right to force me to work in unknown territory. I must have your consent to probe, or we call this off."

Noren turned his face aside. "It's nothing so complicated," he said. "I'd rather not talk about it, but if you really need to know, I'll tell you outright. I guess it's true I don't respect myself much now; I guess I never will, because I—I killed Talyra."

Stefred shook his head. "To feel guilt after the death of a loved one is a normal thing. Especially when a man's wife dies in childbirth, he can't help thinking he's partly to blame. I would be much surprised if I found no such feelings in you. What I do find is more than that. It's as if you are torn by a belief that you've done some real and avoidable wrong."

"Oh, it's real enough. I did kill her, Stefred. Not just by getting her pregnant—by getting her into a situation that caused genetic damage to the child."

"You know better than that," said Stefred, surprised. "You've been tested; your reproductive cells are undamaged. She drank far less unpurified water than you've drunk, and anyway, the mutation doesn't kill."

"I've been through all this with the computers! There's a lot of information no one ever talks about. Isn't it in the dreams?"

"These dreams? I'm not sure what you mean."

Briefly, Noren summarized what he had learned. "The Founders knew, they must have," he concluded. "I thought you did too, that it was why you were afraid I could get hurt by knowing all the First Scholar's thoughts."

For a long time Stefred was silent. "No," he said finally, "no, the First Scholar didn't record any thoughts about mutation beyond the basic facts in the edited recordings. That does seem strange, now that you raise the issue—you're right that he must have known much more. As to this teratogenic damage, the danger's never occurred to anyone. There's nothing edible here that could cause it, after all."

No, thought Noren, nothing to eat but products of caged fowl and grain grown in machine-treated fields; nothing to drink but tea and ale, both of which were, of course, made with purified water. And the few drugs kept for emergencies had rarely been used on anyone who happened to be pregnant.

"Even if the child did suffer such damage," Stefred went on, "you've no cause to assume that was the reason Talyra herself died."

"But it might have been. Could my knowing this account for what you found in my mind?"

"Yes, it could. Guilt based on rational grounds, as if, for instance, she'd died in the crash of the aircar—there are people who wouldn't feel to blame, but you're not one of them." He sighed and continued soberly, "I won't try to tell you that because you meant no harm, had no way of predicting any harm, it shouldn't bother you; that's unrealistic. It does bother you. I—I haven't an answer for you, Noren."

"Well, I didn't expect you would have," Noren said, relieved that Stefred hadn't attempted to offer empty consolation. "That's why I wasn't going to mention it. Can we go on, now?"

"I'm not sure. With a trauma I can't remove, a relevant one—"

"Relevant? The First Scholar had no part in his wife's death."

"No," Stefred agreed. "Not in that—but there are some perplexing feelings in these dreams, guilt feelings that are quite strong; and you see, Noren, I can't give you hypnotic suggestions to remain detached from them. That would set up a conflict your subconscious mind couldn't resolve."

"Guilt—in the First Scholar's thoughts? Besides the guilt he acknowledged about sealing the City and establishing the caste system?" Noren was incredulous. "Surely he never did anything else bad enough to suffer over."

"Hard as it is to believe, he seems to have—we don't know what. You realize that what we call the full version isn't actually unedited; he did some editing himself to remove private things. The cause of his submerged suffering is one of the things he deleted."

"But he wouldn't—I mean, he wasn't self-righteous; if he'd done anything he was sorry for, he wouldn't hide it," Noren protested. "And if he did want to hide it, why didn't he remove all record of his emotions about it at the same time?"

"Those are questions no one has ever been able to answer. After he died, the Founders wondered, too. Even his contemporaries couldn't believe he'd had grounds for the feelings in these recordings." Stefred frowned. "Nevertheless, they are there. Which means, Noren, that when you experience them, you'll transfer them to your

(44

own situation—not getting a cause from his mind, you'll draw it from your own, just as you'll still see Talyra's face instead of his wife's."

"If that's true," Noren said, "then there's no way around it. I can't live my whole life without going through these dreams—you said a while ago we both know I've got to do it eventually."

"Yes. But if you've chosen to undertake it now because of a hope that you'll gain more understanding of genetic damage, I can't let you proceed on that basis. Though people do draw different things from the recordings, that's too big an area for all of us to have missed."

"Which in itself is a mystery I can't back away from. Besides . . . this guilt you say he felt . . . there are two ways to look at it. He came to terms with that, too, evidently."

"You're wise beyond your years," Stefred murmured. "I can't contradict you—just so you realize that the real thing won't be as easy to deal with as the theory."

"Is it ever? Look, Stefred, I hope you don't think I'm so stupid as not to feel any fear of this, especially if we're going straight through to—to the end." Lying back against the padding of the chair, relaxing his body only by effort of will, Noren could not suppress the chill spreading through him; the end—the facing of the mob, the pain of the wounds, the dying—was very hard.

"Actually, the danger in the last dream is negligible for you now," Stefred told him, "far less than during your first subjection to it, when you were less mature and when you had no foreknowledge of the outcome. We'll go right on through, though of course I'll monitor for your safety as well as for the editing." He turned to check a panel of dials; as he did so, Noren caught sight of motion in the doorway to the corridor.

A woman stood there, dressed in the beige tunic and trousers all Inner City people wore, yet looking somehow strange in them. She was too tall, for one thing; her skin was too pale; and her hair. . . .

"I woke," she said simply. "So I thought it must be time to go on. Probably I should not have come here—but then, my door wasn't locked, and I suppose you're not surprised if a heretic doesn't stick to the rules of proper behavior."

Noren stared. Cool, self-composed, strong—yes, she was all that, and more. He had never seen a woman with so much poise. Nor had he seen one with piercing blue eyes and hair near-white in youth. . . .

Her hair! That was what was wrong—her hair had already been cut short. Stefred had not mentioned that; but of course he wouldn't have, for the indignities she'd suffered before entering the City need never be generally known. The cropping of one's hair was among the humiliations to which one submitted voluntarily on the day of

45)

one's public recantation; short hair was therefore common, and in no way mortifying, among young Scholars. No one who'd not seen her during her candidacy would suspect that Lianne had borne such a badge of shame beforehand.

How had it happened? The High Law stated specifically that convicted heretics must be turned over to the Scholars unharmed; no village official would have dared to cut this woman's hair after her trial. Only earlier, during the night in jail, perhaps, as the best friend of his childhood had been murdered by an enraged mob, as he himself, while in bonds, had been beaten senseless by drunken bullies—but even they had not gone so far as to crop his hair. If that had been done to Lianne, what more had she undergone? Had she hidden the rest from Stefred, unable to speak of it, not yet guessing, of course, the depth of understanding and compassion he would ultimately offer her? How painful it must have been for him to put her through an inquisition harsh enough to buoy her self-esteem.

Whatever he'd done, it had been successful. Despite the shorn curls, she held her head high, as if she were already on the platform outside the Gates, already grasping the symbolic significance of that ritual exposure to an abusive crowd. Small wonder he considered her promising.

Only a moment had passed since she'd spoken; Stefred, his back to the doorway, had not seen her enter. As he swung around, startled, Noren glimpsed his eyes, and for an instant there was more in them than professional concern. *Of course,* Noren thought. *She's a match for him, certainly!* And then, *No wonder he feared his decision to let me do this wasn't objective enough.*

He hoped fervently that Lianne wouldn't choose a suitor before Stefred was free to seek her love.

She stepped forward into the cubicle. "It was stupid of me not to realize that I must wait my turn," she said. Then, to Noren, "Are you a heretic, too?"

He could not give her any clue, of course; he said shortly, "I'm a Scholar."

"But you're as afraid as I am!" Her blue eyes penetrated him, then suddenly she lowered them, regretting, apparently, that she'd revealed such intuition of his thought.

"It's frightening for everyone, sometimes," Noren told her. "Still we choose to dream."

"To learn, as I'm learning?"

"Yes—or to reach beyond what can be learned." He had not expressed this even to Stefred; he was not quite sure that it made sense.

Lianne's eyes met his again. "You're afraid of something past

(46

what will happen in the dreams," she declared, as if her mind and his could somehow touch.

"Of what will happen in the world, perhaps."

She said softly, with soberness that was not fear, "I think you and I have much in common."

"We both have ordeals ahead," he agreed.

"May the spirit of the Star be with you in yours." The conventional words, as she spoke them, sounded rehearsed and yet deeply sincere; it was odd, he thought, that a heretic not yet fully enlightened could impart so much meaning to them. Noren was still wondering at it when Stefred took his hand, and at his silent nod of assent, put him into deep trance. Afterwards, Lianne's voice was the last he remembered hearing.

III

THE NIGHTMARE WAS UNLIKE ANYTHING ONE MIGHT IMAGINE; HE knew of no words that could convey its content. There were no thoughts: not his, not the First Scholar's, not anyone's. There was only horror and revulsion. This horror . . . nameless, shapeless . . . was part of him, or he of it; the scope of it had no boundaries. He knew it not from sight or sound but as pure emotion. It was as if he'd fallen into another dimension . . . no, as if he'd created such a dimension and had been trapped there. Its evil was of his own making, yet he'd meant no evil; he had tried to achieve something good. He must not stop trying, though he knew he would be punished for it by this unbearable deprivation of all rational connection to the universe he knew, to the form of life he knew. . . .

There were no concrete images in the nightmare itself, but just before waking he saw the mutant—not an adult mutant such as he'd killed in the mountains, but a hideous mutant child. Its body was like that of a human child just able to walk, but it was not human. It was mindless. There was only emptiness behind its eyes. Noren came to himself with long gasps, not sure if he'd been sobbing or retching. *By the Star,* he thought, *not again! I can't take it again—*

Gradually his head cleared. He sat up, finding himself as always in his own quarters, his own bed, knowing that many weeks had passed since his first waking from this agony. Knowing, too, that more weeks—perhaps years—might go by before he'd be free of it, if indeed he ever would be. He wondered how long his courage would last.

It was not a recollection of anything in the controlled dreams. Those had been all right: terrible at times, of course, but also uplifting. Though he'd shared depths of the First Scholar's feelings that surpassed anything in the edited versions, the heights, too, had been correspondingly more intense. He had begun to grasp what it meant to come to terms with depression and fear that couldn't be banished, evil that was part of a world from which no escape existed. He'd felt the rising of a faith that was more than escape, and

(48

pondering it, he knew why the full version of the recording was considered worth going through. It had not solved his problems, yet he'd gained lasting food for thought; it would be a long time, he realized, before he could consciously understand all he had learned from the First Scholar.

About the controlled dreams he had no regrets, except for disappointment at the fact that they'd indeed contained no additional ideas on the subject of genetic damage. But the ensuing nightmare was another matter.

Even Stefred was puzzled. It wasn't the kind of problem he'd anticipated; and at first, during the long, deep follow-up discussions they'd had after the completion of the machine-induced dream sequence, he had said Noren had reacted remarkably well to the ordeal. There had been no signs of trouble then. Even the inexplicable guilt feelings of the First Scholar's later years—which Noren perceived less as remorse than as a grief too dark and too personal for any dreamer's comprehension—had not been unduly disturbing.

He had gone back to his own quarters, resigned to a return to study. In the days that followed, his grief for Talyra, though still painful, had gradually receded; he found himself not thinking about her till some small, sharp reminder—the sight of a Technician girl's red bead necklace, for instance—brought back a temporary wave of engulfing sorrow. He'd quelled his rage at the way of things, recalling acceptance he'd drawn from the First Scholar's mind; and once he had even presided at Vespers. He'd said the ritual phrases of hope with renewed confidence that they might, in the end, prove true.

Then the nightmare had begun.

The first time he'd discounted it as fatigue mixed with too much ale. The second night he was more shaken, yet during the day he'd carried on and had relaxed with Brek and Beris in the evening. He'd been only a little apprehensive when he left them at bedtime; but that night, the third, had been the worst of all. After that, he'd been unable to eat, and as darkness came he'd gone in helpless, shamefaced panic to Stefred for formal consultation.

"It's nothing to worry about," Stefred had said calmly, though his eyes were troubled. "First we'll check to see if it's my fault."

"Stefred, that's nonsense—"

"Possibly not. There shouldn't have been risk in what I did to you, but I was so tired that week I may have botched it, left you with some posthypnotic suggestion that's creating a problem. If so, I can remove it; you must let me explore, Noren."

Seeing the logic, Noren had agreed to further hypnosis, but it had solved nothing. "If a person were to have recurrent nightmares of this sort without cause, we would call him ill," Stefred said, "but in

49)

your case we know the cause. It hit you harder than I believed it could, despite all my misgivings; you're handling it better than you realize."

"But other people who go through the full version of the dreams don't react this way. Even Lianne——"

"Lianne owes a great deal to you, Noren. She has said so."

"You told her about me?" That surprised him; he did not want her assuming he'd done it for her sake when that hadn't been his main motive.

"Not specifically. After her recantation, though, when I had to explain the edited secrets, she guessed a good deal more than I'd have expected she could about why I'd finally yielded to her request for less editing of other things. Lianne's adapted to the Inner City fast, and she's remarkably good at putting two and two together."

Although she was now a Scholar, Noren had not seen Lianne often, for her work shift was at night. Surprisingly, despite obvious scientific aptitude, she had not chosen to study nuclear physics; instead, she was working as a technical assistant in the controlled dreaming lab. Ordinary dream material, not the First Scholar's thoughts but memories other Founders had recorded of the Six Worlds, required no monitoring; those who wished to experience such dreams did so during normal sleep hours. Someone must be on duty to operate the equipment, but this was not skilled work, and the job was often given to young, new Scholars who had not yet chosen permanent vocations—those most eager to dream of the Six Worlds themselves when the Dream Machine wasn't being used for anything of higher priority.

"Why did Lianne withstand the full version better than I did, when she has so much less experience?" Noren persisted.

Stefred's look was grave, yet a little perplexed. "Perhaps because you haven't forgiven yourself for what happened to Talyra."

Noren frowned. "You said I might transfer the First Scholar's guilt to my own situation—but that's not how it is in the nightmare; Talyra isn't in it. None of the personal things are involved. I do still feel guilty about them, but I've . . . accepted that."

"I know," Stefred agreed. "You acknowledge it consciously, which in theory should keep it from causing you subconscious trouble. Yet there's the image of the mutant." He continued thoughtfully, "That might have appeared anyway in your natural dreams; you and Brek are the only people living who've actually seen mutants, and now that you fear your stillborn child might have been like that—well, we may be dealing with a separate problem. It's not the sort of thing the First Scholar's memories could have triggered in you."

"I'm sure it's not," Noren declared. Certainly there'd been no thoughts about mutants in the recording; he had been alert for

(50

them. "Besides, the focus of the nightmare is something else, something I can't put a name to, not an image at all—something I can't face because I can't even define what it is."

Stefred appraised him searchingly. "Noren, posthypnotic suggestion could free you of this nightmare, let you sleep peacefully. Do you want that kind of help?"

"No!" Noren burst out.

"Why not?"

"Because—because it wouldn't solve anything; I'd still not know *why.*"

"Given a choice, you prefer to go on suffering?"

"I—I deserve it, I guess. Or it wouldn't be happening."

Soberly, Stefred reflected, "That could be true."

"That it's punishment? Oh, Stefred, you don't really believe the spirit of the Mother Star can reach down and strike me, the way villagers would think!" No such preposterous idea was implied by official liturgy; only the villagers' corrupted notions of blasphemy endowed the Star with power to punish.

"Of course I don't," Stefred assured him. "But you are quite capable of punishing yourself; your subconscious mind can do more than you realize, and you are strong enough to take a good deal of voluntary punishment."

"You mean that's really what's happening?"

"It's one of the things that can happen. But it's not a healthy response, and with you I think the situation's more complex. You don't despise yourself enough now to abandon all constructive aims for destructive ones, any more than you did last year."

"By the Star, Stefred, I *want* to do something constructive! Only I—I feel so helpless, because there's nothing to do." He remembered just in time not to mention the uselessness of his work specifically.

"You're still searching for something."

"Yes, I suppose so. It was why I insisted on the dreams . . . but I seem to have hit a dead end."

"I'm not so sure," Stefred said slowly. He was silent for a while, then went on. "You want to get to the bottom of this. You don't want me to stop it for you artificially—which, incidentally, I was counting on when I offered to, because suppression of such a dream might do you real harm. So we're going to have to wait and see what happens."

"You mean I've got to just—live with it?" Noren faltered. Talyra's sad voice echoed in his memory: *You simply have to live with the consequences of what you are.* She had not blamed him for being different, but she'd always felt it would doom him to suffering, and for that, she had wept.

"For the time being. I'm not callous; I know how bad it is, and

51)

I'm too much of a realist to tell you not to let it frighten you; in fact the best advice I can give you is not to fight that—fighting will only make it worse." Pressing Noren's hand, he added, "Come back to me in a week or two if the nightmare doesn't stop; there are some other things I can do if necessary."

It had not stopped. It hadn't come every night, but Noren had learned to fear sleep. At first he'd thrown himself into his work in the daytime; that was a strategy that had brought him through bad times before. It was no longer one that worked. He found it wholly impossible to fix his mind on the mathematical problems he had once found engrossing. The image of the mutant child haunted him, looming between the study viewer and his eyes.

One day in desperation, unable to work, unable to face Brek's well-meant solicitude or to confess that he had not eaten, he'd hidden in the computer room. Idly, without conscious plan, he had asked, IS THERE A TRAINING PROGRAM IN GENETICS? The computers were programmed to give systematic training in sciences relevant to the Scholars' work, training designed to enable young people with no schooling beyond that offered in the villages—the mere rudiments of reading, writing and arithmetic—to rapidly master material that on the Six Worlds would have required years to absorb. It was done through individually generated study tapes, intensive quizzing, and memorization of details under hypnosis: a fast-paced, demanding process, yet enjoyable if one wished to learn. Noren had been through such programs in math, physics and chemistry; he knew there were certain others. But he did not expect genetics to be among them. Surprisingly, it was.

Feeling uncomfortable about so blatant a departure from the job to which he was committed, he told himself that a short break could do no harm; he was only going through the motions with regard to nuclear physics anyhow. He embarked on the genetics program—and soon found why the Founders had provided it for the benefit of posterity. No one could possibly be expected to assemble such a program from scratch after fulfillment of the Prophecy; no non-specialist would be able to ask the right questions. The basic vocabulary and concepts alone took him days to acquire even with hypnotic aid. He had not known what genetics involved; he'd assumed it just had something to do with reproduction and biological inheritance. He hadn't imagined every cell in every organism's body was continuously controlled by the interactions of countless genes. In fact he'd had no real idea of what a gene was—that it consisted of a chemical code so complex as to demand computer analysis amazed and fascinated him. No wonder the First Scholar's memories contained no details about genetics; they contained no details about the mathematics of nuclear reactions, either.

(52

The short break from physics stretched on, week after week. Noren's days became bearable; often they extended from one to the next—it was a good excuse for not sleeping. It was customary for Scholars pursuing specific training programs to work far into the night; among the young initiates, this was viewed as a game, a challenge. To force one's mind to the point of exhaustion was a gesture of protest against living a life one had looked upon as privileged. Noren was past that stage; he'd long since learned that the so-called "privilege" of Scholar rank entailed hardship and deprivation beyond the imagination of the relatively prosperous villagers. But his long hours in the computer room were not thought strange; even Brek accepted a new study program as a legitimate retreat from grief. That it was also a retreat from terror, Noren confided to no one.

Now, however, waking again from the nightmare, he knew that he could retreat no more. He'd completed the formal training sequence and had reached the point where in other sciences one could progress further only with the aid of a tutor. No one was qualified to tutor him in genetics—he himself already knew more about it than anyone had learned for generations. In any case, what a tutor did was to introduce trainees to applications of the knowledge they'd acquired. Genetics had no applications, not in this world, anyway. On the Six Worlds, which had had a tremendous variety of plant and animal life, it had been used for agriculture—it had been, during the last centuries of the civilization's existence, a major weapon in the battle against hunger. The Six Worlds had been overpopulated and short of food. Genetic alteration of crops and livestock had increased the supply. But there was no food shortage on this alien planet, and no edible lifeforms either, other than the few imported ones already fully utilized. No genetic alteration of native lifeforms could overcome the fact that they were based on alien, damaging chemistry, incompatible with human life; that was the reason human life wasn't going to be possible after the irreplaceable soil and water purification equipment gave out. . . .

Everything led back to that one inescapable fact.

Noren, sitting on the side of his bed, found himself literally, physically sick—sick from fatigue, from frustration, from terror and despair. He had honestly tried to act constructively. He'd put fear out of his mind while learning, and what he'd learned was *important*—all preserved knowledge was important, it all reflected the Six Worlds' rise. The Six Worlds' people, his people, had penetrated so far into the mysteries of the universe . . . how much further might they have gone? It was too late, now. He had learned something worth learning, but he could not pass it on. Someday he would die. Eventually his whole species would die—not in some dim, unforeseeable future but by a known date, not many generations ahead. All the effort would prove useless. Grief and guilt had driven him to a personal effort that was even more abortive than the work he'd abandoned; he'd learned a whole new complex of ideas, ideas that should be exciting, and they could be of no use whatsoever. This despair was worse than the despair he'd begun with.

The First Scholar had felt despair too; by sharing it in the dreams, one was supposed to learn the way out. One suffered, but one got past that. In real life, Noren realized suddenly, he wasn't going to get past it. The way out was through action; the First Scholar's life had been full of action: hard action, action sometimes justifiable only as the lesser of evils, yet action he believed would save his people. He had not faced a situation where the more knowledge he gained, the more clearly he saw that no such action was open to him. *It's no wonder,* Noren thought, *that I feel trapped in the nightmare. . . .*

He reached for the washbasin, a white plastic basin since, without metal for pump parts, adequate plumbing was a luxury the City's towers did without. His sickness was no mere feeling. He hadn't thought he had eaten enough to be so sick; perhaps the cup of tea he'd forced down had been a mistake.

At length, when he was able to stand, he mustered his courage and returned to Stefred, knowing that no alternative remained.

He consented to deep probing not only under hypnosis, but under drugs. A time came when he found himself conscious; Stefred was saying to him, "I'd like to monitor the nightmare itself, Noren."

"I'm not sure I can go to sleep; I'm not even tired any more." Saying this, Noren realized he'd undergone prolonged sedation.

"I can induce it, if you'll let me. It can't be done against your will."

Thinking that it had happened against his will all too many times, but ashamed to admit he did not feel he could endure it one time more, Noren agreed. The session was grueling despite Stefred's calm support, and he came to himself shivering, soaked with sweat.

"What's wrong with me?" he murmured, for the first time dreading the relentless honesty on which his trust in Stefred was founded. "I could always cope before; even during my first days at the outpost, when I'd panicked in space and thought I was losing my sanity, I *didn't* lose it—"

"That thought's what scares you most," Stefred observed, "much more than the nightmare does."

"Yes," Noren confessed in a low voice. He had never seen insanity, but he'd learned enough from the computers to know it existed. "They told us when we were little, in the village, that we'd turn into idiots if we drank impure water," he reflected. "I laughed then because I didn't believe it. And now, of course, I know better, I know it can't happen that way to me. I even know it wasn't just like that with my child—" This was true; he had learned from his study of genetics that Talyra's baby could not have been like the mutants after all; it had perhaps suffered teratogenic damage, but not the same sort of damage that had produced the subhuman creatures in the mountains.

"Is the child in the nightmare some kind of symbol not only of what did happen, but of what I'm afraid is happening to my mind?" he continued. "Things are so . . . so mixed up—all tied together somehow. The First Scholar's feelings, too! When I'm awake, I remember his good feelings; why do only bad ones, indescribable ones, come in my sleep?"

"This is hard to say to you," Stefred admitted, "but I don't know. And I've no means of finding out."

"You can't cure me?" whispered Noren, appalled. He had not wanted to seek help, but he'd never doubted Stefred's ability to provide it.

"There's nothing to cure, Noren. You are not sick; you've in no way lost touch with reality. Difficult though it is for you to accept my estimation of you, I am professionally qualified to diagnose mental illness." He smiled, though it was obviously an effort for him. "If you can't take my word, you're accusing me either of incompetence or of dishonesty."

Noren raised his head. Put that way, the judgment was indisputable. "You're telling me the nightmare may not stop," he said shakily.

"I wish I could tell you otherwise," replied Stefred gently. "But you want the truth, and the truth is that we're faced with something beyond my skill to analyze. Your sanity is not in question, and the monitoring has shown that the nightmare's harmless to you. That's as far as I'm able to see; you will have to find your own way."

"I'm willing to try," Noren said, "but I—I don't think I'm equal to it."

"With that, I'm on firmer ground," said Stefred, his smile genuine now. "There are ways of proving to you that you are. At least there would be if you were a candidate and still afraid of me so that I could demonstrate how much you can endure of your own free will."

"But this isn't like what you do to candidates; no one could bear it voluntarily—"

"No? Suppose when you'd come to me as a heretic, convinced that my aim was to pressure you into submission, I had induced such terror in you—I could, you know—and demanded your recantation as the price of freeing you of it. Would you have knelt to me and begged my mercy?"

55)

"Well, of course not," declared Noren. "What a silly question, Stefred."

"To you, it is. To someone to whom it wasn't, I would never pose it."

"I see your point," Noren conceded. "Why doesn't it make me feel any better?"

"Because you don't yet see that you're in a comparable situation." Seriously, Stefred went on, "Noren, the mind is strange, and there's much about it we can't comprehend. Of this much I'm sure, though: what is happening to you is happening by your own inner choice. Strength, not weakness, has brought the ordeal upon you."

"I don't understand."

"I've told you in the past," Stefred reminded him, "that a strong person can open his mind to things a weaker one wouldn't be willing to confront. The subconscious mind gives you whatever protection you need—there are psychoses and drugs that can circumvent that, but in you I find no trace of interference with normal functioning. Therefore you are experiencing something you're able to handle and that is in some way purposeful."

"But what constructive purpose could it serve?"

"That, I can't answer."

"I suppose the fact that it's unpleasant doesn't rule out inner choice," Noren said slowly. "After all, we do suffer voluntarily when we reach out in the controlled dreams. You know, what you said about Lianne, when she was being subjected to the candidates' version of the recordings . . . it—it's a little like that, I think. As if I'm trapped by intolerable limits, reaching for something that isn't there. In the nightmare it's always just beyond the edge, where I can't touch it. Is that a reasonable analogy?"

Stefred leaned forward. "It could be more than analogy," he said, his voice edged with excitement. "Think: did you feel this at all in the controlled dreams?"

"Well, I was definitely reaching for something I didn't find. Only the rest was so overwhelming that I didn't mind much, any more than I minded the limits of the candidates' version when I was younger."

"We don't understand just how controlled dreaming works," Stefred mused. "We're sure only that the dreamer has a certain degree of freedom. The more courage you have to reach out, the more you gain—"

"You told me that the very first time I was subjected to it," Noren recalled.

"Yes. You've always had that kind of courage—from your earliest childhood you've sought knowledge, and even from the first dream you took more than was forced on you. And your identification with the First Scholar is exceptionally strong. I can't guess what you

(56

drew from the full version of his thoughts—but conceivably, it was more than the rest of us have gotten. We've always known the editing he did for privacy left gaps we can't fill."

"Could that cause nightmares, the way the gaps in the partial recording were agony for Lianne?"

"Yes," said Stefred thoughtfully. "Yes, it could. The unanswerable questions he pondered aren't disturbing you, not in the sense of giving you nightmares, anyway. But something he *knew,* yet deleted . . . if it was an emotional thing, a significant one—"

"But why would he delete anything significant? His goal was to pass on all his knowledge; surely he took out only personal details that were no one's business but his own."

"That's the puzzle," Stefred agreed. "He wouldn't have removed anything his successors would care about. And he was skilled in the editing process; he wouldn't have left gaps that could cause a dreamer to suffer."

"I wonder. He wouldn't have left any that would cause harm— but you say that what's happening to me is not harmful. You say I've chosen to experience more than was forced on me. He made a lot of plans that depend on people being willing to do that."

"For fulfilling the Prophecy, yes—but we know those plans."

True, thought Noren, and yet—"What if I were to stop shrinking from the nightmare, enter it as I would a controlled dream?" he asked.

"That would be a very wise approach," Stefred answered soberly, "but I can't tell you where it would lead. Noren, if you have taken something unprecedented from the First Scholar's memories, you are already past the point where I can counsel you." He smiled and added, "But then, I've always believed you'll move beyond me one way or another in time."

Of course, as the world's most promising nuclear physicist, Noren thought bitterly—but on the verge of an exasperated reply, he became aware that Stefred was no longer trying to reassure him. On the contrary, he had just presented him with the most frightening challenge of all.

Lying sleepless, Noren courted nightmare, wishing with full sincerity that it would overtake him. Seldom had it come, lately, and when it had, he'd been able to draw nothing more from it. Though it was still acutely painful, he no longer found it terrifying, for he was increasingly convinced that its emotions had originated not with him but with the First Scholar—and it was something he wanted desperately to understand.

Stefred had been speculating about direct transfer from a recorder's subconscious mind to a dreamer's; he had reread all the information in the computers about the thought recording process and had even reexperienced the First Scholar's recordings himself in the hope that he'd get from them whatever Noren had gotten. That hadn't happened. Noren, embarrassed, realized that now more than ever, Stefred regarded him as having some special rapport with the First Scholar that set him apart from everyone else. He was torn; he did not want such a position—yet could Stefred conceivably be right? Was there something buried in his mind, perhaps, that could explain why he felt unlike other people, even the people who shared his concern for knowledge, the Scholars with whom he'd once thought he wouldn't be a misfit?

He had always been a misfit as a boy in the village. He'd never gotten on well with his father and brothers; they had not cared about any of the things that mattered to him, and the reverse had also been true. Once he had despised them, as he'd despised the village life they had found satisfying. He was no longer so callous; for all their rough ways, they had been honest men who'd worked hard and who would leave many descendants. He wondered sometimes what had happened to them. Did they still feel shame at his having been convicted of heresy? The severance of family ties demanded of Inner City residents had been no sacrifice for him, though for most others he knew, it was; it bothered him a little to realize that he'd had nothing to lose.

Except, of course, Talyra. And he had not lost her because of his heretical ideas after all. Ironically, he had lost her for no purpose whatsoever; and worse, she'd lost her own life. . . .

The First Scholar had come to terms with grief. But his wife had chosen to die—chosen tragically and mistakenly, to be sure, but nevertheless she had made her own decision. Talyra hadn't. He could never reconcile himself to that! If some end had been served by it, something she would have chosen had she known . . . but there was nothing. He could endure his own guilt. He knew, from the dreams, that the First Scholar had lived with some terrible and mysterious horror for which he'd felt to blame, and he had endured it, he could never have been at peace in the end if he had not. The end, the deathbed recording, contained no traces of any horror; there was sadness in it, and physical pain, but otherwise only hope: the exultant hope that had engendered the Prophecy. For himself, Noren thought, there would never be hope again. Talyra had died uselessly, and the things she'd believed in, the things the Prophecy said, were never going to come true in any case.

It always came back to that.

Turning over in the dark, the total darkness of a windowless room in which for lack of metal wire, there could be no illumination when no battery-powered lamp was in use, he found himself thinking again about genetics. It was strange he could not put that out of his mind. He'd long since learned all he could about it, lacking practical applications to focus on; he had satisfied his curiosity as to the specific way in which unprocessed soil and water of this world damaged human reproductive cells. It was an incredibly complex process requiring understanding of both chemistry and biology at the molecular level; he'd spent weeks wholly immersed in it, and even so, only the mental discipline acquired from his past study of nuclear physics had enabled him to master the concepts. He was by now, he supposed, the greatest authority on useless information who'd ever lived in the City. The greatest shirker of responsibility, too, people would say, had he not gone back to an outward pretense of devotion to the unattainable goal of metal synthesization.

Yet he could not let his new knowledge drop. He did not know why. It wasn't escape from terror any longer, nor was it still escape from the futility of his official work—for was not genetics equally futile?

How frustrating that he couldn't justify devoting more time to it. He would like to experiment. He might genetically modify some native plant to grow in treated soil, and that would give people relief from the monotony of a diet based on a single crop; but the cost would be too high, not only in his time, but in the time the land-treatment machines would last. A second crop would be welcomed by village farmers; they would want extra fields to grow it in. The Founders had been wise to provide only one kind of food. They had also been wise, perhaps, not to encourage even the Scholars to learn that if it were not for the limitation imposed by the machines' durability span—which had been calculated on the basis of necessary population increase—more variety would be possible.

The Founders had made just one practical use of genetic knowledge: they had developed the work-beasts. Everyone knew that, of course; even the villagers said that the work-beasts had been created by the Scholars at the time of the Founding. It was one of the notions he had scorned during his boyhood, but from the dreams of his enlightenment as a Scholar candidate, he had learned to his astonishment that it was true. Animal embryos had been brought from the Six Worlds and had been genetically altered so that they could eat native vegetation and drink from streams. They were essential to the villagers as beasts of burden as well as for hides, tallow and bone; what a pity that there wasn't a way to make the meat usable, too. But genetic alteration couldn't accomplish that. Work-beast flesh, like any creature's, contained chemical traces of the food and water that had nourished it; the High Law decreed that it must be burned. You couldn't deal with the damaging substance in the soil and water by biological modification of what people consumed. The problem—the biological problem—was not in the food sources, but in people themselves. . . .

Noren sat upright, his heart pounding. Why wasn't it possible to make biological modifications to *people?*

It was all too possible in nature. That was the trouble. The mutants were biologically changed. They ate native vegetation and drank from streams as work-beasts did; what had been accomplished with the work-beasts was called controlled mutation. It had been detrimental to their intelligence, not as seriously as in the case of the mutants descended from humans, since the beasts hadn't been very intelligent to begin with, but a similar type of brain damage had been involved. *Only it needn't have been.* He had studied the research done by the Founders, and he knew; with hindsight it had been recognized that the brain damage could have been avoided. The world had needed strong work-beasts, fast, more than it had needed smart ones; the researchers had been working against time, and they had not tried to deal with the complexities of the genes that regulated brain development. Later on, they could not retrace their steps, for the inherited brain damage was irreversible.

But if that damage had been needless, if it could be averted if controlled mutation were done in the right way, why couldn't mutation in people also be controlled? Biologically, genetically, people were animals. . . .

He fumbled for the lamp, suddenly unable to bear the darkness. He knew he would not sleep until he had discovered the answer.

There must be an answer, of course. The Founders were not stupid; they could scarcely have failed to perceive what he had just perceived. They would hardly have established a system they loathed, a caste system they knew to be evil, if there had been any alternate means of human survival—they had maintained over and over again that they would not. They'd experienced heartbreak during their decision and its implementation. The factors in the decision had been considered in full and painful detail by the First Scholar, who had suffered most agonizingly over it. Noren knew, beyond any possible question, that the First Scholar would not have done the things he did if there had been any choice. Nor would he have overlooked any conceivable future way of saving humanity from extinction.

But it was surely very strange that his recorded memories hadn't included any regret about whatever it was that precluded controlled genetic alteration of humans.

Noren pulled on his clothes, his hands shaking, and took a small lantern; it was so late that the corridor lamps had been turned off. Outside, only the lights at the tower pinnacles still burned. He strode across the courtyard to the Hall of Scholars. The computers could tell him what he needed to know. They preserved all knowledge, and the answers he now sought had once been known. They must have been.

(60

He looked up at the dazzling tower lights and the faint stars that showed between them. Off to his left was the red-gold glow of Little Moon, now rising. *As bright as Little Moon,* said the Prophecy; the Mother Star, when it appeared in the sky, would outshine any other. He would not live to see that, but his people must . . . his descendants must. Talyra had been right, he knew; he must eventually have other children. He did not feel he would want love again, not for itself, but he did want to believe that his offspring would live after him. She'd understood that, and her last thought for him had been to send word that she understood.

The towers . . . the City . . . to him they had always been a symbol. Of the future. Of the knowledge he craved. Outside, as a heretic, he'd gazed at them with more longing than he could bear. Had he offered his life for conviction's sake alone, or only because without access to knowledge it had meant little to him? To be sure, he'd refused such access when to test him, it had been offered in the form of a bribe; he had not been willing to take something unjustifiably withheld from others. But City confinement had been no more a hardship for him than separation from his family had. In his very arrest he'd had nothing to lose, though he'd believed himself soon to die. Had it been right to accept priesthood when he'd made no real sacrifice?

Approaching the computer room, he knew again that it had been. The essence of priesthood, for him at least, was guardianship of knowledge and extension of it—only by that means could knowledge ultimately be made free to all people. Only through its use could metal become available. Yes, that aim might fail, probably would fail; in the end everything would be lost . . . but the human race must die striving for life.

Suppose, just suppose, it had been possible to alter humans genetically so that the species need not die. Noren realized, with his hand poised above a console keyboard, that he did not want to crush this fantasy yet. The replies to his questions were going to crush it. But suppose that option *had* been open to the Founders— the Prophecy's promises would already have been fulfilled! He would be living in the era all Scholars wished to see; the City would long since have been thrown open, knowledge and machines would be available to everyone. . . .

Or would they?

No! There would be no more metal than there already was. Its synthesization wouldn't have been achieved, and in fact it wouldn't need to be achieved—people wouldn't even have kept working toward it. If people could drink unpurified water and eat plants grown in untreated soil, they could survive *without* metal, *without* machines!

But the knowledge in the computers could not.

Computers depended on metal parts and on a continuous supply of nuclear power. The knowledge in them was in the form of electrical impulses. If the power failed, that knowledge would be lost. The Founders had known this; it had been one of their main reasons for sealing the City, for if the knowledge were to be lost, the machines essential to survival would be lost too, along with any chance of ever obtaining the metal for more machines. . . .

It was a circle. If it was broken, humanity would die; yet if it had been broken in another way, a way that had enabled humans to live without the City . . . then the City would no longer exist. He would be living the Stone Age life of the villagers, and without metal resources, without people trained to preserve even the remnants of a metal-based technology, there would be no possibility of regaining such a technology in the future.

The universe would be closed to his race. Forever.

The accumulated knowledge of the Six Worlds would be lost forever.

And the First Scholar must have foreseen that outcome.

Numb, paralyzed, Noren closed his eyes; the room had begun to swim dizzily around him. The nightmare that had eluded him earlier was assailing him now; though he was still conscious, he began to feel the familiar horror. He no longer wanted to understand its basis. He knew he could not face such understanding. He knew what significant facts the First Scholar had edited from his memories; he wished he could edit them from his own.

He should go now, walk away from the computers, forget genetics and return to his study of physics. Life would go on, as it had gone on throughout the generations since the Founding. As it would go on for a few more after him. No one else would learn what he had learned. People would be content. The villagers and Technicians would be content because they believed the Prophecy, and the Scholars would be content because they had faith in their power to bring about the Prophecy's fulfillment. *There shall come a time of great exultation . . . and at that time, when the Mother Star appears in the sky, the ancient knowledge shall be free to all people, and shall be spread forth over the whole earth. And Cities shall rise beyond the Tomorrow Mountains, and shall have Power, and Machines; and the Scholars will no longer be their guardians.* Everyone believed that. Would they be happier knowing that it was false? Had he not faced exactly the same decision last year, when he'd first lost confidence in the nuclear research, and had Talyra not died because of his mistaken attempt to offer truth in place of illusion?

But it was not the same. Then, truth as he'd seen it had been a destructive truth. He could not have saved anyone by exposing the Prophecy's emptiness. He could not, by sacrificing all he personally valued, have enabled future generations to live.

(62

Could he now?

Could the Founders have done so? The First Scholar?

They had not, certainly, been insincere in what they did; their suffering had been real. They had made a choice, a hard one, too hard to impose on their successors, and they had made it for humanity's benefit. They had chosen a relatively short era of social evil to attain a long era of future advance, evidently. He did not have to judge whether they'd been right or wrong; the option was no longer open. For him, knowing that synthesization of metal had been proven scientifically impossible on this planet, the choice was simply between preservation of knowledge and a chance for permanent preservation of life . . . if in fact there was now any choice at all.

He had better start finding out, Noren told himself grimly. If he left the computers without knowing, he might lack the courage to come again.

Afterward, he did not remember his whole line of questioning; he was dazed and couldn't be sure which of his words triggered a long-hidden branch in the control program. For a time, quite a long time, he was conversing normally; then all of a sudden he found himself waiting, the light at the top of his console glowing orange, as auxiliary memory was searched.

A wait in itself was not unusual; information about subjects not of immediate concern to the world was kept in auxiliary storage to be called up only on request. The computer complex, he'd been told, was not really well designed for its role as a central library. It had been put together from the separate smaller computer systems of the dismantled ships of the starfleet: a task the Founders had accomplished under the extreme handicaps of having no materials or equipment for the manufacture of extra parts and, even worse, of being unable to risk loss of any memory content during the integration process—which meant the whole job had to be done without shutting down the power even momentarily. The resulting system therefore consisted of numerous interlinked units rather than one large random-access one. It was no great problem; rarely did anyone need data such as he'd just requested. Yet he had already waited once upon his initial request for the genetics file, which he'd supposed was a single entity . . . evidently, that wasn't the case.

There had been a contingency plan, then. The Founders had not burned their bridges; they had known metal synthesization might fail. He was, he supposed, going to be given specific instruction in the process of modifying human genes. How excited he'd have been if this had happened earlier tonight, before he'd perceived the implications! He wondered if the program would spell them out. Probably not, he thought bitterly; no doubt the Founders hoped the implementer of the contingency plan would work as an unwitting tool. So much for the sacred principle of access to knowledge for the priesthood, and the even more sacred one of equal share in the burdens. . . .

That was what hurt worst, Noren saw. He had never wanted to be a priest, but he had come to feel it was wrong to refuse the responsibility. He had become convinced that the priests' world-view was genuine, that the role involved no sham or delusion. Now it seemed that the whole edifice had been built on sham after all. When in recantation, one went through symbolic reenactment of the First Scholar's death, one believed one had shared the full burden of the Founders' moral dilemma; but if they had made the hardest choice of all and then hidden the fact that such choice existed, their successors had been duped! The Scholars were all tools. Right from the beginning it had been that way. How could the First Scholar have been a party to that—how could he have founded a religion on such a basis, a religion he'd believed valid? In the dreams he *had* believed; those feelings couldn't have been faked. . . .

Words appeared on the console screen. YOU HAVE ASKED QUESTIONS THAT PROVE YOU ARE NOT OF THE FIRST GENERATION. HOW MANY PLANET YEARS HAVE PASSED SINCE THE ARRIVAL OF THE FINAL EXPEDITION?

But the computer knew that! thought Noren in amazement. It was the computer that had kept track of the time since the Founding; the Scholars relied on its internal clock. *It* told *them,* not the other way around. Odd, too, that the word "Founding" had not been used in the question. "The final expedition" was an obsolete phrase, one he knew only because the First Scholar had used it in the dreams.

He was not a trained programmer, but he'd learned enough since becoming a Scholar to realize that the normal executive program was no longer operating; the information he was to receive had been so well protected that it was not to be processed by the integrated system at all. Some vestige of a first-generation master routine had assumed control. Slowly he keyed in the requested number of years.

HAS METAL YET BEEN SYNTHESIZED? the program asked.

NO. THAT IS NOW KNOWN TO BE IMPOSSIBLE. He might not be given the full truth unless he made clear from the outset that there was no remaining hope in the original plan.

YOUR INQUIRIES CONCERN GENETICS. HAVE YOU COMPLETED THE TRAINING PROGRAM IN THAT SCIENCE?

YES.

YOU MUST BE EXAMINED WITH REGARD TO YOUR READINESS TO RECEIVE FURTHER INFORMATION. THE TEST IS EXTREMELY DIFFI-

(64

CULT AND WILL REQUIRE SEVERAL HOURS. ARE YOU WILLING TO UNDERTAKE IT NOW?

YES, replied Noren. He was a fool, probably; the night was far gone and he was giddy with fatigue and emotion. Common sense told him that he would do better on such a test if he took it when fresh. But having come this far, he could not back away.

He had been tested many times before by the computer system, though never as a prerequisite to obtaining answers to his questions. Usually information was simply presented; if one couldn't understand it, one had to study up on background material and then ask again. Testing was reserved for the formal training programs, and it was made very arduous. One was pushed to the limits of one's individual capacity and a little beyond; computer programs excelled at that. Noren had learned not to mind it. Once he'd discovered that tolerance of one's failures was a carefully calculated factor in the scoring, he had even learned to enjoy the challenge. But no previous test had come close to the one to which he was now subjected.

At first it was simply a matter of understanding basic concepts of genetics, not too different from the tests in the training program he'd recently completed. Then, when he thought he was nearing the end, a new phase began. It turned into a fast-response exercise. This was similar to the "game" in which, as a new Scholar, he'd been trained in the mental discipline needed for advanced study; he knew how to deal with it. He was aware that he was not expected to respond within the allotted time to every question; the aim was to see how well he could cope with confusion. But in this case, the confusion was compounded. Not only did the questions demand thought, being full of technical details often over his head, but irrelevant inquiries were interspersed, presumably to throw him off the track. He was asked about his personal life. He was asked his opinion of various Inner City policies. Noren tried ignoring these superfluous matters, but that did not suit the testers' strategy; he found that if he neglected to respond to *any* demand, however foolish, he would be forced to restart the current series of technical problems from the beginning. And to make things even rougher, he was given no feedback whatsoever concerning his scores.

This went on literally for hours.

Eventually, when he was trembling with exhaustion, the screen cleared, and a nine-digit figure appeared upon it. MEMORIZE THIS ACCESS CODE, he was told. OTHERWISE, IF YOU SEEK INFORMATION FROM THIS FILE IN THE FUTURE, YOU WILL BE REQUIRED TO REPEAT THE TEST.

Too overcome to protest, Noren committed the digits to memory. What, for the Star's sake, was wrong with his name? The computer system kept track of everyone's test scores, but name was the only identification needed to refer to them.

UNDER NO CIRCUMSTANCES PUT THE CODE IN WRITING, the instructions continued. IT HAS BEEN RANDOMLY GENERATED AND IS RECORDED ONLY WITH YOUR TEST RESULTS. EVERY PRECAUTION MUST BE TAKEN TO ENSURE THAT WHAT I AM ABOUT TO TELL YOU IS NOT COMMUNICATED TO ANYONE I'VE HAD NO OPPORTUNITY TO JUDGE.

Noren stared incredulously. The reason for using an access code had become clear enough, but the word "I" created a greater mystery.

FORGIVE ME FOR TESTING YOU SO RIGOROUSLY, the displayed wording went on. IT WAS NECESSARY. SURVIVAL ON THIS PLANET MAY DEPEND ON MY SECRET BEING PASSED TO A PERSON WHO WILL USE IT WISELY. I DO NOT KNOW HOW THE WORLD'S CULTURE WILL CHANGE AFTER I AM GONE. I KNOW ONLY THAT I CANNOT LET THIS KNOWLEDGE PERISH, AS MY FRIENDS WOULD WISH.

Who had programmed this? The computer never referred to itself by personal pronouns; he was reading the words of some past Scholar who'd chosen to speak to posterity as an individual—who had, moreover, carefully chosen to whom he would speak. The Founders had not done things that way. Everything, even the separate control routine, indicated that the file had been added to the system not as an official contingency plan, but secretly.

DO YOUR CONTEMPORARIES STILL HAVE HOPE OF SYNTHESIZING METAL?

YES, Noren replied. I MYSELF HAVE NONE.

IS YOUR INTEREST IN GENETICS SHARED BY OTHERS?

I HAVE TOLD THEM NOTHING OF SIGNIFICANCE. THEY THINK IT A MERE PASTIME.

YOU ARE IN A DIFFICULT POSITION, THEN, MUCH MORE DIFFICULT THAN YOU KNOW. I HAD HOPED IT WOULD BE OTHERWISE.

It gave him an uncanny feeling to see such phrasing; it was as if he were conversing with a conscious being, though he knew his responses would merely determine which of various preprogrammed statements would be presented to him. In the same way as in a programmed text, the writer had provided comments to fit differing circumstances. I HAVE GUESSED A GREAT DEAL ABOUT THE DIFFICULTIES, Noren confessed. I HAVE GUESSED WHY INFORMATION ABOUT HUMAN GENETICS WAS CONCEALED RY THE FOUNDERS.

YOUR GUESS IS UNLIKELY TO BE CORRECT, FOR IF YOU KNEW THE REASON, YOU WOULD NOT HAVE HAD TO GUESS—IT WOULD HAVE SEEMED OBVIOUS. POSSIBLY YOU THINK WE WERE UNWILLING TO LOSE THE CHANCE OF PRESERVING THE SIX WORLDS' KNOWLEDGE. DO YOU APPROVE OF CONCEALMENT FOR THAT PURPOSE?

(66

Noren hesitated. Finally he responded, I HAVE NEVER APPROVED OF DECEIT.

THAT IS TO YOUR CREDIT. BUT YOU ARE EMBARKING ON A COURSE INVOLVING FAR MORE COMPLEX ISSUES THAN THE ONE YOU HAVE IMAGINED.

This was like what Stefred had said to him long ago, Noren recalled, during his candidacy, when he'd objected to the withholding of the truth about the nova from non-Scholars. Was it really so much worse for the Scholars themselves to have been kept in partial ignorance? No . . . but the Founders had *lied!* The First Scholar had lied! They had said specifically to their successors that there was *no means of human survival* apart from guardianship of the City. To be sure, the First Scholar had lied to the villagers of his own time by pretending to be an insane tyrant; he had told open falsehoods about his motives. Yet that was different. He had not led them to make moral choices on false grounds.

The programmer of this file had been very clever. By using the personal pronouns he had created an illusion that encouraged trust. Perhaps he'd been one of the Founders after all; he had said "we" at one point. There might, of course, have been a rebel among the Founders; but what basis was there for judging such a person's credibility? He, Noren, had been judged, and he saw now he had been judged on more than his knowledge of genetics; the seemingly irrelevant personal questions had been the most significant of all. He had undergone a thorough psychological examination. How was he to evaluate whoever had devised that? How much of the programmed sympathy could he believe?

WHOSE WORDS ARE THESE? he inquired, not really hoping for a meaningful answer. Few of the Founders were remembered by name, since when they'd assumed priesthood they had chosen anonymity in fear of worship.

Promptly, as if the statement had no greater import than any other computerized response, an answer was displayed. YOU KNOW ME. I WAS LEADER OF THE FINAL EXPEDITION FROM THE SIX WORLDS, AND SO FAR, I HAVE LED THE CITY. SOON, WITHIN A FEW WEEKS AT MOST, I MUST DIE; IF IT DOES NOT SO HAPPEN I SHALL DESTROY THIS FILE, FOR I CANNOT RISK ITS DISCOVERY DURING MY LIFETIME.

The First Scholar himself? Utterly bewildered, Noren sat motionless, trying to quiet the racing of his heart.

ARE MY RECORDED MEMORIES FAMILIAR TO YOU?

YES, Noren keyed, glad that no fuller reply was needed; his hands were unsteady.

IN THEIR FULLEST FORM?

YES. BUT EVEN THAT WAS EDITED BY . . . YOURSELF.

67)

THAT IS TRUE. AND IF YOU NOW KNOW ENOUGH TO ASK THE QUESTIONS YOU'VE ASKED AND TO RESPOND AS YOU'VE RESPONDED, YOU HAVE GROUNDS TO DISTRUST ME.

Noren paused; how could one possibly tell the First Scholar that one distrusted him? Perhaps this whole night's experience was unreal, not a thing truly happening. Perhaps he was still in his own bed. . . .

He was aware, suddenly, that it was *not* happening—not distrust. Though logic did give him grounds for it, logic wasn't what mattered. He had shared this man's inner thoughts and emotions, had done so repeatedly; he could not help trusting him! He would always trust him, just as after experiencing the candidates' version of the dreams, he had trusted enough to recant on that basis. Logic had told him then that the Scholars might deceive him; but in controlled dreaming there could be no deceit. Editing, yes. Since the First Scholar could not possibly have done what the evidence indicated he'd done, perhaps someone had tampered with the recordings later, reedited them as Stefred had prepared the version for Lianne—that, in fact, might explain the incomplete cuts that had caused his nightmare. Things could indeed be cut from thought recordings—but the thoughts that weren't cut could not be altered. Having shared the First Scholar's mind, Noren knew positively that he was trustworthy.

I STILL TRUST YOU, he declared. BUT THERE IS MUCH I WISH TO KNOW. He hoped this secret file had been designed as a crosscheck; since tampering was technically feasible, the First Scholar might have foreseen that it could occur.

YOUR QUESTIONS WILL BE ANSWERED. BUT BEFORE I CAN TELL YOU ANYTHING CRUCIAL I MUST ASK YOU FOR A COMMITMENT. WILL YOU PROMISE TO PURSUE FULL ENLIGHTENMENT WITH REGARD TO THE ISSUES THAT HAVE BEEN CONCEALED, NO MATTER HOW MUCH YOU MAY SUFFER FROM IT?

YES! The First Scholar too had been forced to trust, Noren perceived; no promise keyed into a computer could be binding except in the mind of the person who made it—yet he would feel bound. Had the psychological examination predicted that he would?

I MUST SUBJECT YOU TO A GRIM ORDEAL. I AM DEEPLY SORRY, BUT IT IS UNAVOIDABLE. I CAN GIVE YOU NO ASSURANCE THAT IT WILL BE HARMLESS TO YOU; IT MAY PROVE SERIOUSLY DISTURBING —YET OUR PEOPLE'S FUTURE WELFARE IS AT STAKE. AND YOU HAVE THE RIGHT TO KNOW THE FACTS IT WILL REVEAL.

I AM NOT AFRAID TO KNOW, Noren replied, aware that although this was not wholly true, any other response would be unthinkable.

OF THAT, I HAVE MADE SURE: YOU HAVE BEEN TESTED IN MORE WAYS THAN YOU REALIZE. THE STATEMENT NEXT IN SEQUENCE IN THIS PROGRAM WOULD NOT BE PRESENTED TO YOU IF YOU WERE NOT BOTH QUALIFIED AND COMMITTED TO ACT UPON IT. ITS MERE

EXISTENCE IN COMPUTER MEMORY IS DANGEROUS.

The screen went blank for an instant, and Noren drew breath. Then more words appeared. THE KNOWLEDGE YOU SEEK CANNOT BE EXPLAINED VERBALLY. YOU MUST ACQUIRE IT THROUGH A DREAM. THERE IS A HIDDEN RECORDING; I HAVE PUT IT WHERE IT CANNOT BE FOUND BY ACCIDENT. I AM RELYING ON YOU TO EXPERIENCE THAT RECORDING, AND TO LET NO ONE ELSE KNOW OF IT UNTIL YOU HAVE DONE SO.

A dream, an *unknown* dream, hidden for generations? The shock of the idea wasn't unwelcome; Noren's mood began to rise. There was some tremendous secret here, something far more complex than he'd imagined, and perhaps even . . . hope! Valid hope for the world! He felt ashamed to have doubted the First Scholar even briefly.

ARE YOU WILLING TO FOLLOW THESE INSTRUCTIONS?

YES. The hardest part would be keeping it from Stefred. . . .

I WARN YOU THAT THE DREAM WILL NOT BE PLEASANT.

NONE OF THEM ARE, Noren acknowledged. Not the First Scholar's, anyway.

THIS CONTAINS ELEMENTS NOT PRESENT IN THE OTHERS, BOTH IN RECORDING TECHNIQUE AND IN CONTENT. YOU WILL UNDERGO CONSIDERABLE STRESS.

More than in the deathbed recording? But of course, when the First Scholar had programmed these words, he hadn't expected to make that one; it had been the result of the last-minute inspiration he'd had about the Prophecy. He had planned his martyrdom—to prevent widespread violence, he'd purposely incited the villagers to kill him—but he had not known when he made those plans that all future Scholar candidates would experience his death, or be required to ceremonially reenact it. He had not yet conceived of viewing the Mother Star as a symbol, even.

So one could hardly swear by the Star to do as he asked. Feeling foolish at the thought that he'd been about to do just that, Noren keyed simply, WHERE WILL I FIND THE RECORDING?

IN THE OLDEST DOME, BEHIND THE MAIN RADIOPHONE CONTROL BOARD. THERE IS A SMALL LOCKED PANEL. The lock's combination followed; Noren memorized it.

Putting the recording in a dome rather than a tower had been a brilliant tactic, he saw. If it had been concealed anywhere in the Inner City, Scholars might easily have come across it; but the Technicians of the Outer City, bound by the High Law to avoid touching machines they hadn't been personally trained to handle, would never disturb its hiding place. A combination lock would be a "machine" in their eyes, and to tamper with it would be sacrilege.

ONCE YOU HAVE EXPERIENCED THE DREAM, YOU MUST BE THE

SOLE JUDGE OF WHETHER IT SHOULD BE SHARED WITH YOUR CON-
TEMPORARIES. YOU MUST ALSO MAKE CERTAIN OTHER JUDGMENTS.
THEY WILL NOT BE EASY.

WILL I RECEIVE FURTHER INSTRUCTION?

THIS FILE CONTAINS DATA YOU MAY CHOOSE TO RETRIEVE. I
HAVE LEFT YOU NO MORE WORDS. I CAN OFFER YOU NO COUNSEL,
FOR CIRCUMSTANCES IN YOUR TIME WILL NOT BE THE SAME AS IN
MINE. MAY THE INFINITE SPIRIT GUIDE AND PROTECT YOU; AS I
DIE, YOU WILL BE IN MY THOUGHTS.

Stunned, Noren absorbed the significance of this final message,
written mere weeks before the First Scholar's death, the death he
himself, dreaming, had come near to sharing. The full version of
that particular recording was, of course, wholly unedited. And there
was a mystery about it. "There's a sense of deliberate effort to channel his mind away from something that haunted him," Stefred had
said. "The self-control needed for that would have been staggering,
especially for someone in as much pain as he was. And it seems so
unnecessary. No one would have thought less of him for failing to
hide his private worries."

He had not intended to make such a recording. Faced with an
impelling reason to make it, he'd been obliged to guard this secret.

At that time, had he indeed thought of the successor to whom
the secret would be passed? In the deathbed dream one's thoughts
were framed in the symbolic language of the Prophecy, since one
had known those words all one's life. But they had not been written
till after the First Scholar's time; the recording itself contained only
the concepts, later translated into poetic phrasing. There was controversy over the interpretation of some passages. *We are strong in
the faith that as those of the past were sustained, so shall we be
also: what must be sought shall be found, what was lost shall be
regained, what is needful to life will not be denied us.* . . . That
was usually taken to mean that the First Scholar had been absolutely
positive that somehow or other, the synthesization of metal would
be achieved. But could the underlying idea have been a less specific
one?

Had the First Scholar, dying, believed that some future priest
might find a different solution?

IV

THE OUTER CITY, EXCEPT FOR THE DOME CONTAINING THE POWER plant, was normally off limits to Scholars, certainly to Scholars young enough to be recognized by Technicians as former heretics. For those who'd grown up there and were known, like Brek and Beris, there could be no exceptions; it was lucky, Noren thought, that the task of finding the secret recording hadn't fallen to one of them. He himself took little risk; in the oldest dome, which was partitioned into areas for what few pieces of manufacturing equipment existed in the world, he would not even attract much attention. To go there was a violation of policy, but priests were expected to evaluate policy in the light of circumstances. He did not need to ask anyone's permission.

But he would have to go robed. That fundamental rule couldn't be set aside. Only Inner City Technicians knew that Scholars were ordinary mortals; the Outer City ones viewed them as villagers did. As a small boy, Noren had assumed they wore *only* robes, with no clothes underneath! Thinking them ageless and sexless, it had not occurred to him to wonder if they ever took them off. He'd devoted some thought to this later, to be sure, but it was one of his more heretical speculations—his mother would have labeled it blasphemy.

He carried the blue robe, folded, from his room to the gates of the exit dome; then, passing through them into the corridor that led to the City's main Gates, he slipped it on and secured the fastenings. Never before had he appeared robed to anyone but Inner City people, and it was not a milestone he looked forward to. Ceremonial appearances, on the platform outside the Gates or in audience chambers, were demanded only of older Scholars. He'd rather hoped, as did many young initiates, that a research breakthrough would make it possible to eliminate the caste system before he got that old. Was this now conceivable, perhaps, if research in genetics could bring about long-term survival?

Though he hadn't explored the Outer City, he had studied a map; a corridor intersecting the one to the Gates connected the domes in the ring, which had no openings to the Inner City courtyard they enclosed. The oldest dome, the one built before the Founding, was adjacent to the one he'd first entered. It was silent there; work did not begin this soon after dawn. But men were on duty in the radiophone room. All the villages had radiophone links to the City, not only for the transaction of routine business, but for requesting emergency medical aid. He himself, after his escape from jail, had been forced to handle a village radiophone; masquerading as a Technician in the uniform Brek had risked giving him, he'd been viewed with awe by the villager in charge of it simply for managing, to his own surprise, to replace a dead power cell. How long ago that seemed!

He stepped into the compartment and resolutely approached the main control board. The two Technicians sitting there rose from their chairs and, turning to him in deference, they knelt.

Noren froze. He had known, of course, that it would happen, but he'd not let himself remember. It was so *wrong*. . . .

Wrong, but necessary—as his abhorrence of it, too, was necessary. He was not supposed to enjoy it. Anybody who might enjoy it would have been screened out during the inquisition Scholar candidates underwent. The blue robe helped, at least. The robes were identical; they, not their wearers, inspired reverence. To these Technicians he was not a man, but a symbol. He was not receiving personal homage. *A High Priest does not receive,* Stefred had assured him. *He gives.* . . .

"May the spirit of the Star be with you," he said quietly. "Please return to your duties; I only wish to inspect the equipment."

He walked around the control board, which was set out from the wall; behind it were cabinets, and one did indeed have a combination lock. Rapidly he opened it, feeling awe at the thought that the last fingers to touch it had been those of the First Scholar, generations ago. There was no dust in the domes, for prolonged exposure to the planet's atmosphere was corrosive to most Six Worlds alloys and the air was therefore filtered. No Technician would have questioned the strange device, any more than the two now present questioned his need to inspect it. The panel swung open. Noren removed a sealed plastic container and relocked the cache.

As he returned to the corridor, he found he was shaking less from possession of a sacred relic than from the turmoil that the kneeling of the Technicians had stirred in him. Necessary, yes . . . but it should not have to be! The First Scholar would *not* have designed it, given choice! If by genetic change people could be enabled to live without the City, he would not have perpetuated the caste system any longer than was necessary to effect such change—even if it meant the City's ultimate destruction. Even if it meant loss of the computers' knowledge. And he, Noren, could not do so either, he thought in agony. Would the recording he now

(72

carried give him power to abolish the castes, power that for some reason hadn't been available to the First Scholar?

He had been psychologically tested. He had been warned of difficulties past imagining. And it had been made clear that for the recording to fall into the wrong hands would be disastrous. Abruptly, Noren saw what might lie beneath these measures.

All Scholars were trustworthy; the selection process ensured that. All were honest. But they did not all agree on matters of policy . . . and to eliminate need for the City would not only cause knowledge to be lost, but would leave the Prophecy unfulfilled. Priesthood meant affirmation of the Prophecy. If its promises came into conflict with the more basic issue of human survival. . . .

He held the recording under the folds of his robe, wishing there were a duplicate copy back in the cache.

For the present, the big problem was how to experience the dream secretly. Thought recordings weren't private property, and they were not carried around; he couldn't simply walk into the dream room and hand it to the person on duty. Nor did he know how to operate the Dream Machine himself, even if it should be unattended long enough. And it wouldn't be. He might have to wait weeks for a time slot without priority authorization from Stefred—yet he could not tell Stefred, excited though Stefred would be by an ancient recording's discovery.

It was still early; the past night's scheduled dreamer might just be waking. Right now would be best! The prospect of prolonged delay was more than Noren could stand. Stefred wouldn't be around at this hour when he wasn't working with a candidate. Who would be?

Lianne, probably. All at once he recalled Stefred's words: *Lianne owes a great deal to you, Noren. She has said so.* And Lianne was so new at the job that she might not know that such a request was unprecedented. Even if she did realize, somehow he knew she wouldn't feel bound by the rule book . . . not Lianne. She was too mysterious a person to refuse involvement in further mystery.

His pace quickened as he crossed the Inner City courtyard, his priest's robe once again folded over his arm. The upper level of the Hall of Scholars was deserted; most people were at breakfast. Noren had no appetite, nor did he feel lethargic from lack of sleep—which was fortunate, he thought with detachment, since the coming sleep of controlled dreaming would be anything but restful.

Lianne was in the dreamer's chair, the headband nearly covering her cropped curls. At first, thinking her unconscious, he turned away in disappointment. Then to his astonishment she sat upright, smiling not only with recognition but with welcome. She reached out for the switch on the panel beside her; a blue light turned to yellow.

Noren stared at her. "You were getting input while you were awake?" Stefred could do that; it was a step in the editing process and must also have been done by his professional predecessors. Not by other people, however.

"Just sampling the library. There are so many dreams I want to experience, and not nearly enough time—I was trying to choose one."

"For your next scheduled session, you mean?"

"It's this morning. There's no one else due until noon."

Then he must take a quick plunge. "Lianne," he asked bluntly, "can you keep a secret?"

Her smile became unreadable. "I'm rather good at that, actually."

"Even from Stefred?" Too late, he recalled that Stefred was attracted to this woman and that weeks had passed since his professional relationship to her had ended; conceivably they were already lovers.

No hint of that showed in her expression. "Especially from Stefred," she told him. "Because I've had practice." She raised the reclining chair and removed the wired band from her head. "It's hard, isn't it, with Stefred—once you know him well, you want to tell him everything. But when you've an earlier commitment to keep quiet—"

"A commitment to other heretics?" It was the only thing he could imagine a candidate being obliged to conceal, and he had been told she'd concealed a great deal during her inquisition. "Stefred doesn't probe for that. He wouldn't want you to betray anyone's confidence. At the beginning, though, when he's testing you, he lets you worry about it."

"I know." It sounded, oddly, as if she knew more from her brief experience than he himself had learned in the past two years. "Stefred and I understand each other. He knows I've kept something from him, yet he's never tried to pry it out of me. I'm told past lives aren't mentioned in the City. I suppose everyone must be curious about mine."

"Well, we're human. And there were rumors about your reaction to the dreams, so that when you chose to work here, despite how bad it had been for you at first—"

"But you've all experienced them; you know . . . oh, maybe you don't. *You*, though, Noren—" She broke off, embarrassed. "I guess I've heard rumors, too."

"What rumors?"

"That you're a lot like the First Scholar."

"You mean because I'm supposed to turn into some sort of scientific genius? That isn't going to happen, Lianne. Oh, I'll work toward it, but I'm not going to come up with any radical new nuclear theory; it's not possible." This was the sort of thing he'd resolved not to say to people, but with the situation now about to change. . . .

Surprisingly, Lianne didn't argue. "I'm not talking about what you'll accomplish. I meant outlook, strength—knowing life's not as simple as most people try to make it. That sort of likeness."

"I didn't realize there were any rumors about that. Stefred knows, but he wouldn't talk about me that way."

She didn't meet his eyes. "He wouldn't—he hasn't! I suppose it . . . it must be what he calls my gift of empathy."

"Empathy?"

"Sensing people's feelings. That's why he's training me in psychiatry." She caught his wordless surprise and went on, "You didn't know? Of course not, most of the women who take shifts in the dream room aren't his personal students, they're just temporary assistants. I'm to study medicine and psychology, help with interviewing and so forth."

"I didn't know Stefred wanted any help."

"Noren—I'm a lot younger than he is. Someday he'll have to choose a successor. He's waited—"

"For someone with the right talents. I see." *I see more than she's saying,* he thought.

Though he had not spoken this aloud, she blushed. "Maybe you've heard—other things. They're not true. It's not that I don't like Stefred, I do! He's one of the most admirable men I've ever known. I'm truly sorry I can't feel as he wishes I did. When he asked me to marry him, though, I had to say no. I don't plan ever to marry."

How sad, Noren thought, for both of them. She must have loved someone in the village, someone she'd never see again. Or was he the heretic she was protecting? Perhaps, now that she'd been enlightened, she was hoping that someday he too would earn Scholar status.

"You're being trained as Stefred's heir," Noren said slowly, "and you know he wants to marry you—yet still you keep secrets from him?"

"I told you, he's aware of that."

"All the same, I shouldn't have come to you with mine."

"Is it against Stefred's best interests?"

"No. No, it's more like what you said—a prior commitment. A—a higher loyalty, if you like. But he'd give almost anything, personally, to know it."

"He'd feel that way about some of my secrets, too. That's why it hurts to keep them." Beyond doubt she was sincere; Noren perceived that it hurt her with an intensity he couldn't account for.

"I can't tell you everything," he began, wondering why he dared tell her anything at all. "I never planned to; I thought you'd be too inexperienced to realize how much I was holding back. I see you aren't. But if you're willing to be stuck with something else that'll be hard to hide—"

"For you, I'm willing," she said softly, again averting her eyes.

He pulled the recording from his tunic. "I'm not free to say where I got this," he declared, "and I can't pretend it's normal for me to be carrying it around. But it's a dream I have to go through. Soon."

She took the container and broke the seal to examine the cylinder within. "How long is it?"

"I've no idea."

"You haven't experienced it before, then."

"I'm not even sure what's in it, except that it's—significant."

She studied him, once more seeming to grasp thoughts he hadn't expressed. "You've got mixed feelings. Is there any chance it needs monitoring?" At his hesitation she added firmly, "I have to know."

"I suppose you do. It's not fair not to warn you that we could run into trouble. It—it's probably pretty nightmarish, Lianne. Theoretically I guess it should be monitored. That's one reason I can't let Stefred find out; he knows me so well that if he was monitoring, he'd see it's too important a thing for me to keep to myself. In fact under hypnosis I might talk freely to him—it's something I've no deep determination to hide."

"So you were going to just give it to one of the untrained assistants, have her put you under and close the door on you as if it were a sightseeing tour of the Six Worlds?"

"I hadn't any choice."

Lianne frowned. "Are you sure this was prepared by someone qualified, that it's not raw thoughts of a person who might have been emotionally disturbed?"

"Absolutely. Whatever strong emotions are in it are there for a purpose." In desperation he added, "Look, I wish I could explain more, but I'm bound, and I—I *have* to do this."

"I believe you. But you don't have to do it without monitoring." As he drew breath to protest, she rose from the chair and inserted the cylinder into the machine. Her back to him, she said, "Noren, you're trusting me awfully far. I could do more than tell Stefred, you know; I could copy this while it's running and experience it later myself."

Appalled, he could do no more than stand silent; he had not known the equipment well enough to foresee that possibility.

Lianne turned to face him. "I won't, of course—which you realize, or you'd be calling this session off. So get into the chair."

He obeyed, discovering that now that the moment was upon him, he was terrified. The First Scholar had warned that this dream might not be harmless.

"We're going to have to trust each other," Lianne said quietly. "I won't tell Stefred—and you mustn't tell him that I know more skills than he's taught me." She tilted the chair all the way back and then with quick, deft fingers she unfastened Noren's tunic and began taping monitor electrodes to his chest.

"Lianne, how can you possibly—"

"Know how to monitor, when I've never even had a chance to observe such a session? That's like asking you how you got hold of a recording with a seal that's been intact since before your grandparents were born."

He remained silent as she adjusted the band to his head. "I didn't have to be so honest with you," she pointed out. "I could have attached the monitors after you were asleep. But you're too tired to be plunged into this without deep sedation; I'll bet you haven't closed your eyes since the night before last. I'm going to put you into trance, and for that, you've got to trust me completely. You've got to know I'm hiding no more than I'm required to hide—and that I'm competent."

"Stefred hasn't taught you deep trance techniques yet, either."

"Hardly." Her voice was even, yet somehow reassuring. "Nevertheless, this isn't the first time I've used them. And there's something else we need to consider. If you fear you might speak openly to Stefred under hypnosis, you might to me. I won't probe, but if you talk freely—"

"You wouldn't understand enough of it to matter." He looked up into her face and then murmured, "Or would you?"

"It depends on what you mean by 'matter.' You say you've no underlying determination to hide the dream content, yet you were ready to risk physical shock rather than confide in Stefred."

"Well . . . Lianne, it's not just a—a personal thing. Stefred couldn't treat it as a medical confidence; it may be relevant to fulfilling the Prophecy, so he'd be obligated to tell the whole Council."

"I'm not bound to that yet. I haven't assumed priesthood." She appraised him thoughtfully. "But *you* have."

"Yes." He saw that he would have to say more. "If a person's been given cause to suspect a conflict could arise between fulfilling the Prophecy and following the First Scholar's plans, what should he do?"

"In your place," she declared, "I'd be sure I knew all the facts before getting the Council involved. And Stefred is one of its senior members."

Noren didn't answer her. Lying still for the first time since last night's inspiration, he found his mind beginning to drift. It touched questions he'd overlooked before. Genetic alteration of humans . . . but *how?* The analysis and modification of genetic material itself was something he'd studied; it would surely work with human cells as well as animal ones. But how would that help? The work-beast modification had been done on embryos. There'd been no room aboard the starships for animals; the embryos had been transported in test tubes. They had in fact been conceived in test tubes on the Six Worlds: an agricultural technique he had read about. Such a thing could hardly be arranged with humans, even if people would tolerate the idea of it, which of course they would not. There was only one way of conceiving babies, after all; the mere suggestion of interference would be indecent . . . and besides, there just wasn't any means by which. . . .

He felt his face grow hot. Lianne was bending over him; he caught sight of a monitor light flashing red. It was a good thing her "gift of empathy" didn't extend to the actual reading of minds.

"I'll put you in trance, now," Lianne said. "I won't use quite the routine you're used to, but it'll work the same if you want it to." As her hand closed on his she added seriously, "Being scared of the dream is all right. But you mustn't be nervous about *me*. I understand all kinds of feelings. I suppose you don't expect that from women, even Scholar women."

"Old ones, maybe, who've been priests for a long time."

"But the young ones, scientists or not, are still influenced by village customs. Noren, I've never thought the way the villagers do."

"Of course not. You became a heretic."

"I don't mean just that."

An idea came to him. "Were you accused of witchcraft?" That could explain a lot. Most alleged witches, village women reputed to have strange powers, were innocent of real heresy and were given Technician status if condemned and delivered to the City; but there were occasional exceptions. And according to Stefred, some witches did use hypnosis.

Lianne laughed. "Witchcraft? No, but I probably would have been if people had known more about me. I'm—different. I can't pretend not to be."

"I used to feel that way myself, sometimes. As if I belonged in some other world."

Very quietly she said, "That's a good way to describe it."

"I think if I'd heard then about the Visitors, the aliens who left the sphere we found in the mountains. . . . Do you know about that, yet?"

"Yes," Lianne said. "I do. I'd like you to tell me more, though, Noren . . . only first you need to sleep. . . ."

She was skillful; he didn't have time for apprehension.

As in the other dreams, he was the First Scholar, but retained consciousness of his own identity. He was standing in a wide space within the inner courtyard of the City—it was a time when not all the towers had been erected, so he knew it was some years before the end of the First Scholar's life. The images of the dream, having been recorded as a long-ago memory, were less clear than in most. But the emotions were strong. Though he could not yet comprehend them, Noren was immediately aware that these were the undefined emotions of his nightmare.

Reaching out as he'd learned to do, he found he could gain no quick understanding of his situation. It was like his first experience in controlled dreaming, when he'd lacked the background to interpret what came into his mind, when he had sensed only that the First Scholar's underlying thoughts were acutely painful. He would not grasp what was happening till he heard words spoken by himself and people around him; he must confront it one step at a time.

And the feelings were worse than those in the earlier controlled dreams. There was horror of a different sort from the horror he'd felt while watching the nova, or during the Founders' reluctant seizure of power. Then, he had been horrified by things outside himself. Even while letting the village people think him a dictator, he'd known that he was not what he was forced to seem and that he was not going to hurt anybody. Now he knew the course he planned might bring someone harm. Indeed, it might bring harm to one intimately close to him. . . .

"It is unthinkable," said the man who stood beside him.

"So was our sealing of the City," Noren replied. "That went against all our ethical principles, too."

"Yes, but we had no choice; there was no other chance for human survival," the man replied. The personalities of the First Scholar's companions were dim in the dreams, for he'd focused not on them, but on issues, in recording his memories for posterity. Noren was aware, however, that this man was one of his best friends; they were discussing something that to the Founders as a group would be unmentionable. "We supported you," the friend continued, "because you convinced us that without preservation of the City, our grandchildren's generation would be subhuman. It's presumptuous to tell you that my conscience bears a heavy load. I know yours bears more than mine, and that you suffer from it. I will simply say I cannot bear a heavier load than I now carry—nor can any of us. We could not violate ourselves as you ask even if we saw justification."

"Do you not see it? Death of our human race will be just as bad generations from now as it would be for our grandchildren."

"*Will* be? Generations from now, a way to synthesize metal will have been found! The technology can be maintained indefinitely then; the City will be thrown open, and more cities will be built. That's your own plan; you've made us believe in it—"

"It is my hope," said Noren in a low voice. "And I have planned for its fulfillment. But it is not sure." With dismay he realized, as himself, that the First Scholar had never been sure! In the full version of the officially-preserved dreams, he had experienced these doubts and the despair to which they led; but there had been editing, the First Scholar's own editing, still. What he was feeling now had been removed. This was not just discouragement, not just lack of proof that synthesization of metal could be achieved. It was rationally based pessimism akin to what he, Noren, had developed later, when there'd been many years of unsuccessful experiments. From the beginning the true odds against success had been concealed.

"Think," he found himself saying as the First Scholar. "There are avenues our descendants can try; nuclear fusion may indeed prove the key to artificial production of metallic elements. But what if it's inherently impossible to do it that way? No doubt metal can be synthesized, but a likelier route to that goal would be a unified field theory—a way to transform energy directly into matter. You know that as well as I do."

"If nuclear fusion won't work, the unified field thory will be developed. Past physicists have failed, yes, but they never gave it top priority, as our successors will."

"There won't be the facilities to develop a unified field theory, let alone test it," stated Noren bluntly. "If that weren't so, I'd have taken that route to begin with. But it would demand an accelerator larger than the City's circumference, containing more metal than we've got tied up in the life-support equipment. You'd know that, too, if you weren't afraid to think it through."

"You're treading on dangerous ground," replied his companion, after a short pause. "You're coming close to telling me that we have sacrificed peace of conscience in a futile cause, that those who died aboard the starships—your wife, for instance—were perhaps wiser than we were."

"No! There is a chance for survival in what we're doing; otherwise there'd be no chance at all."

"That's not good enough. Most of us couldn't live under this much stress without full belief in the goal."

"I know," agreed Noren. "That's why I'm approaching people individually with the alternate one."

"Oh? I assumed it was because you have the decency not to discuss obscenities in front of the women."

"I have approached some women," he replied quietly. "This thing is not obscene; you are too blinded by tradition to be objective. The Six Worlds are gone, now. A taboo on human genetic research should never have existed even there—but here, it is as meaningless and fatal as our taboo against drinking unpurified water would have been on our native planet."

"That may be true. Yet I tell you I'd risk extinction rather than experiment with the genes of my unborn children, and I don't think you'll get any different reaction from the others."

"I know that, too," Noren confessed. "You are the last person on my list, and it's true that the rest reacted as you did. All except . . . one." He, the First Scholar, let the memory flood into his mind; and as Noren he accepted it, letting the despair engulf him. Only one supporter, just one whose intelligence, whose natural faith in the future, overrode the conditioning of her rearing—and perhaps it was for his sake that she'd opened her mind. Why should she bear the whole burden, she for whom he cared more than anyone else in the whole City?

Dimly, in the part of himself that was Noren, he felt surprise. The First Scholar had not remarried in all the years he'd lived after the death of his wife, and there were no thoughts of love in any of the other dreams; it was a thing many Scholars had found strange. No grief for his wife remained in the later recordings, and his own plans for the new culture encouraged the production of offspring. It was odd that he had not set an example, for in all other ways he had lived by the precepts of the High Law he'd designed. Now, the thoughts coming into his mind made plain that far more editing had been done in the official record than anyone had guessed.

But though they were thoughts of love, they were not happy thoughts. The recording, of course, had been made many years after the events with which it dealt; the mental discipline required to make such a recording, keeping later emotions below the surface, must have been tremendous. Noren perceived that the First Scholar had not wholly succeeded—the horror of his feelings was not all apprehension, there was recollection involved also. In the dream it was like precognition. Terror began to rise in him; he was doomed to proceed step by step toward disaster.

"You acknowledge, then, that we must continue as we've started?" asked his friend.

"Yes," he agreed shortly. He had approached only the people he felt might be receptive to an even more drastic plan than the one he'd originally set in motion, and they had rejected it. He'd foreseen that they would, but he had been obliged to try. There was no further step he could take to win open support. He must pursue the alternate course in secret, since he was unwilling to let future survival rest on the nuclear fusion work alone.

Yet there was risk. If anyone found out what he was doing, he would lose his place of leadership. His companions had accepted much from him, but for this, they would despise him and would vote him down. Even the original plan would then be doomed; there were steps in it he had not confided to the others. There was the matter of his calculated martyrdom, which would ultimately be necessary in order to win the enduring allegiance both of the villagers and of the City's future stewards. Without it, there would eventually be fighting. Those who told him no such system as he'd established could last without bloodshed were right; they did not guess that he knew this, and that he expected the blood to be his own. But it would not work unless he retained leadership until the time for it was ripe.

Was he to die for nothing in the end? He was willing to die, but not without the belief that future generations would live. Synthesization of metal would save them, but it was by no means the most promising way to do so; he'd realized that from the start, though he'd edited this realization from the thought recordings. The recordings weren't for posterity alone; they were experienced as dreams by his fellow Founders, and there was too much peril in confronting his contemporaries either with doubt about metal synthesization or with its alternative.

Genetic engineering . . . the mere mention of it was branded as obscenity! The taboo was so strong that the way out of the survival problem had not even occurred to the biologists who'd worked on the animal embryos brought for beasts of burden. They'd genetically modified them to accept a diet of native vegetation, yet had never reasoned that the same principle might work on human beings.

As things stood, the human race could never adapt biologically to the native environment. The damaging substance in the water and soil would result in offspring of subhuman mentality; within a generation there would be no human beings left. But it was so needless! A simple genetic alteration to permit the alien substance to be metabolized, and the damage would no longer occur. It would not have to be done in any generation but the present one; the alteration, once made, would be inherited. Water and soil purification would never again be necessary.

There would be a price, oh, yes—a terrible price. The City's technology would be permanently lost. The technology couldn't be maintained without the caste system, and the caste system was justifiable only because there was no way of surviving without it. Once people could drink unpurified water and eat native plants, the City must be thrown open. Its resources would be used up quickly, for they must be equally shared among members of present generations instead of being preserved for future ones. Some metal must be diverted to farming and craft tools. The research could not continue long; it would be doomed to fail even if metal synthesization was theoretically possible. Once the machines wore out, no more could ever be built.

This prospect, to him, was a grief beyond measure—yet as the price of ultimate human survival, of a free and open society that could survive, it would be endurable. Perhaps some might disagree. But so far, they were not even considering that issue. They could not look far enough ahead to confront it, so great was the taboo on human genetic engineering itself.

The Six Worlds, long before the invention of the stardrive, had banned all research into human genetic engineering. The very idea of developing the ability to modify the genes of future generations had been rejected; all interference with procreation, in fact, had become anathema once sure contraceptive drugs had been perfected. As for medically assisted conception, that had been abandoned as contrary to the public interest. It had been declared that human reproduction was not the business of science.

To be sure, there had been legitimate worries about abuse. There had been all too strong a chance that governments would try, by any scientific means that existed, to control people. Genetic engineering techniques had been discovered while the mother world's governments were still primitive and corrupt. Use of such techniques on humans was indeed a potential that might have been misused.

Ironically, however, people's justified fears of its abuse had been magnified into distorted ones. Genetic engineering would have been no more dangerous than other scientific capabilities that had been used wrongly, but there had been many political reasons for opposition to it. It was known, for instance, that it might lead not only to misuse, but to elimination of genetic disease and to longer lifespan. Yet such benefits had been less well publicized than the dangers. The Six Worlds' governments had not wanted to spend money on the research that could lead to starships, and they had not liked the thought of people traveling to other solar systems beyond their control; so they'd encouraged the notion that it was wise to ban anything that might ultimately result in a population increase.

By the time interstellar travel became a reality—just in time, as it turned out, to save one small colony from the nova—human genetic engineering was a forgotten concept. People had been conditioned to believe that application of science to alteration of human genes, unlike all other medical science, was somehow "unnatural." Perhaps, eventually, this might have changed. The new unified government of the Six Worlds was neither corrupt nor restrictive; sooner or later scientists would have become interested in genetic research again, and though they'd have met public opposition, they would not have been held back by a legal ban. He, the First Scholar, would have seen to that, for he'd been in a position to form policy. But then had come discovery of the impending nova . . . and it was too late.

If it had not been for the ban, specific techniques for genetically adapting to the alien world would have been already available, even routine; he had known this when he received the mandate to lead the final expedition. He had known when he made his plans that if his ancestors had not restricted freedom of research, those plans would not have been necessary. *There would have been no need to establish the caste system in the new world at all.*

Noren, absorbing this thought, grew cold with the dismay of it. The Founders and all generations since had upheld a system they knew was evil, supposing that the necessity for it was an unavoidable quirk of fate. No one could have prevented the destruction of the Six Worlds. No one could have made the new world different. But if the Six Worlds had not taken a wrong turning, if people there had been allowed to pursue knowledge freely as he himself had always believed it should be pursued, the evil could have been avoided! And the First Scholar *knew*. No wonder he'd kept this particular recording hidden.

But there were worse things in it than the pain of knowing what might have been. The First Scholar wouldn't have used a dream instead of a computerized text if all he'd had to present was Six Worlds' history; what had happened so far was only background. . . .

The scene shifted, as happens in dreams, but he soon realized that there was a shift of time as well as scene. It came to him that several recordings had been spliced; episodes that would normally be separate dreams were to be experienced in unbroken sequence, without intervening rest periods. He had been warned that he would be placed under great stress, yet he had not expected that after all he'd gone through in the past, he could be as afraid as this. For the first time in controlled dreaming, Noren found himself fighting to be free of an experience he did not wish to share. Resolutely he willed to surrender. His own identity was primary now; and with a corner of his mind he remembered, thankfully, that Lianne was monitoring the safety of his sleeping body. Unaccountably, he saw an image of her face: a pale oval framed with white curls, eyes searching him. Then he was caught up again in the mind and body of the First Scholar.

He was with Talyra. He was happy—he could not think beyond that; the future did not matter while he was with her. . . .

It was not Talyra, of course, but the woman the First Scholar had loved. Sitting on the edge of the bed, he became aware that he had not seen her at all in the dream; he had experienced only feelings. He, Noren, could not associate such feelings with anyone but Talyra, but as the First Scholar they'd been aroused in him by the woman now at his side. Since the recording contained no pictures, her form was dim; but from his thoughts he knew that she was beautiful and good and that she was the most important person in his life.

"We are committed now," she said, her voice trembling a little.

"Are you afraid?"

"Not for myself. Not even for you, though you've risked the most; you chose to take the chance. But the child—"

"I know," he replied grimly. "The child didn't choose. Yet there's no other way."

"It has to be tried," she agreed. "We owe it to the generations who'll come after us."

"To those that might not come after us if we fail to try."

"Yes. Still, I don't feel good about it. I never will."

"We've done the best thing," he said reassuringly, although he did not feel good about it either. Gradually, Noren perceived that "we" referred not to the Founders as a group, as it usually did in the dreams, but to himself and this woman alone. And he knew what they had done.

She was a geneticist, one of those who'd worked on the modification of the work-beast embryos. Secretly, with the aid of the computers, she had determined what alteration of human genes would be needed to enable people to drink unpurified water. But of course, she could not modify human embryos in the same way she'd done the animal ones; that would indeed be unthinkable, and it would not be practical in any case. In humans, the genetic modification must be made in adults, made in such a way that it would be inherited by their children. The concept wasn't new; on the Six Worlds, some genetic work with animals had been done in that way. Genes of adults could indeed be changed.

But it had never been tried on humans before.

So again they must accept an evil that, except for the ban on human genetic research, could have been prevented. On the Six Worlds, far more animal tests would have been done before such a technique was considered ready for human testing, but in the new world no biologically similar animals existed. All medical tests must be done on human volunteers. She had wanted to try it on herself, to alter her own genes. He, the First Scholar, hadn't let her do that. His unwillingness to expose her to such a risk had not been what had convinced her; in the end, he'd argued that she was young enough to have other babies and that the colony needed children. If the test should fail, the person on whom it was done could have no more offspring. It was better for that person to be a man. He had persuaded her to try the genetic alteration on him.

That did not mean she took no personal risk, however, for it was she who would bear the child. And the child might not be normal. They knew that; they knew they were experimenting with

85)

a human being who'd been given no choice. They hated themselves for it. The child might be mutant . . . the horror of that engulfed Noren; he saw again the image of the mutant child that had appeared in his nightmare. This must come from his own mind, for reaching into the First Scholar's memory, he was aware that unlike himself, the First Scholar hadn't actually seen any mutants of the sort that later inhabited the mountains. He knew the result of drinking unpurified water only from the record of what had happened to the planet's first explorers. He, too, felt horror, but it did not come from personal experience, at least his recorded memory included no experience; there was a—a foreboding, somehow. . . .

Perhaps it was only fear. He had drunk the water *on purpose*. He'd had to; there was no other way to test the genetic alteration. That alteration had been made in his body—it had been done with a vaccine—and then he had deliberately drunk more unpurified water than was considered safe. Theoretically, the genetic alteration made it safe; his body should now be able to metabolize the damaging substance in the water. His genes should not have been damaged by drinking. But how had he found the courage to put such a thing to the test?

He wondered, even as the First Scholar he wondered. Now that it was too late to turn back, he did not feel courageous at all.

"What will we do if . . . ?" the woman questioned, not for the first time.

"We will face that if we must," he told her. "Don't worry now; there's no point in worrying before the child is born." There was no way of knowing beforehand if the water had damaged his genes; the computer system was not yet programmed for the sperm tests routine in Noren's own time. The two of them must simply wait. For her, he felt, that would be even harder than for him—to know the child she'd conceived might be a mutant seemed past any woman's bearing. Yet she had been willing. She believed, as he did, that it was a lesser evil than to passively accept the odds against survival without genetic change.

He embraced her, trying not to think of the future. It was not only peace of conscience they were prepared to sacrifice, and not only the anguish they might feel about the child that they were risking. Nor was the risk of his position as leader what troubled his emotions. They would lose everything if their child wasn't normal; they would even lose each other. That was why they hadn't married. He wanted to marry her, he planned to do so once they knew the experiment's outcome—surely, he told himself, it would succeed! But if it did not, then she must be free to marry someone else; only on the grounds that the world needed her future children had he persuaded her to try the genetic change on him instead of on herself. He

(86

could have no more children if this test failed. He had drunk the water, and if damage had been done it was irreversible.

They had been lovers before he had drunk it; they'd been careful, since they had not wanted a child until they were ready to make the test, but the worst an unexpected pregnancy could have caused would have been delay. Later, should there prove to be genetic damage, they could take no chance at all. There would be no question of sterilization, for the colony's gene pool was considered a resource and he could not tell any doctor what he had done. He could not marry her, and he could not remain her lover, either, even if she chose to reject all other suitors.

As the dream became hazy and began to shift, Noren understood with dismay why it was that all thoughts of love had been edited from the First Scholar's later memories.

She whom he loved was no longer in his arms; she receded from him, and feeling her go, he knew it was forever. He knew the test had not succeeded. As Noren, he'd known this all along, underneath—if it had been successful, the course of history would have been different—and the First Scholar had known also, for the recording had been made not before the child's birth, but long afterward. This was the submerged horror that had been in the dream from the beginning.

The horror not only of this controlled dream, but of his nightmare. The mutant child had been real. . . .

He knew what he would be required to face, both in the dream and after waking.

The mist cleared; once more he found that time and place had altered. In terror, he perceived that he would be given not knowledge alone, but direct experience. He must not retreat from it. He, Noren, had been chosen—but he had also been permitted to choose. As the First Scholar, he knew that the incomplete editing in the officially preserved recordings had been deliberate, that it was designed as a test and as an invitation. This horror would not be forced on anyone. Only a person willing to confront it consciously would reach the point where he must look into the eyes of his mutant son.

Perhaps the dream had not been intended to be so vivid. Perhaps if he'd not met mutants in the mountains, an event the First Scholar couldn't anticipate, he would see the child no more clearly than the mother. In her he sensed pain and felt it as his own; but her face was still shadowy. The child stood out in sharp contrast, mindless, but with the body of a human. It had light skin and reddish curls and it was old enough to walk.

He clutched the woman's hand. He still loved her, deeply and hopelessly. They no longer lived as lovers, of course, but they let it be assumed that they did; it was the only way they could explain their refusal to take other partners. All the Founders had originally been married, since only married couples had been selected for the starships, but with the passage of years open love affairs occurred among those widowed or separated. That their leader should have such an affair did not bother anyone. That he should neither remarry nor love would, in view of the need for children, be less acceptable.

"There is no more time," she said to him with sorrow. "The child is old enough to be weaned, and I can keep it in my room no longer. You know I can't; by your own rule all others must give up their babies. People will not like it if you make an exception of yours."

"No," he agreed, "but perhaps they will tolerate it. They will not tolerate the truth." So far, no one had gotten a close look at the child's face; she had told them it was sickly and had allowed no one but herself to tend it. Now it should be sent to the dome where the rest of the Founders' offspring were being reared to become the new and essential Technician caste. But that was impossible. This child was not merely retarded, it was of subhuman mentality—and a doctor could determine why. Everyone knew what damage unpurified water caused; without that knowledge they would not have gone along with the sealing of the City. They all knew such water wouldn't be drunk accidentally. She was a geneticist, and to some he'd argued for genetic engineering. If they saw the child, they would guess the truth, and his chance to establish a lasting society would be lost.

Somehow it had not occurred to him beforehand that such a child would live.

He'd assumed that if the test failed, the child would die in infancy. The mutant children of the exploratory team had died; their brains had been sent to the Six Worlds for autopsy. That was how the nature of the genetic damage had become known. Yet, he now realized, the mutation itself was not lethal; the colonists' descendants, if not saved by future science, would not die but would become subhuman. He really did not know how the other mutant babies had died. He perceived that he hadn't wanted to know.

But he could imagine. *Her* courage had not faltered; for more than a year she had nursed this mutant—one couldn't think of it as one would think of a human baby—and had borne the sight of its empty stare. There was no love in it. She had treated it gently, but it was not a docile creature, and he knew, sickened, that when it was older its mindless rages would turn to animal ferocity. Loose in the wilderness, it would survive for that very reason. *The mutants in the mountains were cannibals,* Noren thought, remembering all too well . . . but as the First Scholar he did not have foreknowledge; he simply doubted that another woman, one who'd not taken a calculated risk with the resolve to bear the consequences, would have nourished such an infant at her breast.

"We can no longer hide it," she told him, "yet the truth must not be known. There is only one thing I can do."

Stunned, appalled, he waited, not daring to answer her. For the first time he feared that perhaps he should not be leader after all; he'd handled countless bad situations and had often been called wise and brave, yet now he felt utterly helpless. He did not see anything they could do, though he knew the welfare of future generations might hinge no less on this decision than on his others.

Calmly, holding back tears, she continued, "I must leave the City. Though it's forbidden, there are no guards, and when I'm gone, no one will guess the reason."

"No! Dearest, you can't!"

"It's the only way. And there's nothing more I can do here in any case. I have analyzed the genotypes; I know where I may have gone wrong—but nothing can be proven without more testing. I'd be willing to try again, I would even take another lover if there were anyone we could trust. But there's no hope of that. I can help you only by going. I've enough medical knowledge to be useful in the village, and you know I won't betray the City's secrets to the people there."

"You don't understand," he protested. "There've been rebels in the village, those unwilling to acknowledge dependence on water piped from the City. They are outcasts. They drink from streams, and most flee to the mountains before they give birth. If you take the child to the village, you may be forced to follow them."

It was more than he could endure. The present inhabitants of the village, colonists who'd been shut out of the City, had been born on the Six Worlds; they knew the danger of the water as well as the Founders did. Their leaders would not permit violation of the already-sacred rule: those who incurred genetic damage, or who bore damaged children, could not live among them. His most painful visions were of the rebels he'd failed to save, those he could not contrive to take into the City as he took other dissidents. They faced worse than peril and hardship in the mountains, worse than the production of subhuman offspring; observing his own child, he knew that when such offspring grew to maturity their parents would be endangered by them.

He could not let her take so great a risk as that. Yet neither could he prevent it. She had nursed the child; it was animal, not human, yet if he killed it to save her, she would not forgive him . . . nor would he ever forgive himself.

"My darling, I know what may happen," she said steadily. "But what choice have I?"

89)

"You have none," he heard himself whisper. "We made our choice long ago, both of us."

"Do you regret it?"

"No. We did wrong, and we must pay for it—yet what we did was best. Not to try to prevent extinction would have been a greater wrong. For all children to be like this would be the worst form of extinction."

"I've left the genetic data in the computers. Will people of the future try again, perhaps?"

They *must,* he thought. Not only to ensure survival if metal synthesization failed, but so that her suffering would not be vain. "They will," he promised. "I'll see that the knowledge is passed to them. That won't be easy to manage, but neither will the—the rest of my plans. I can arrange it so that things work out."

He had not told her that in the end he himself must die at the hands of the villagers; it was the only secret he had kept from her. Were it not for that, he thought despairingly, he might go with her, as he longed to do—he would rather share her lot than stay behind as leader. He no longer wanted to lead. The burden was too heavy; without her, he might not be able to bear up under it; others might do a better job of leading than he. But there was no other who would carry through the ultimate phase of his plan.

Resolutely, he lifted the child, held it in his arms, his face for the moment averted.

"Don't torture yourself," she murmured. "That serves no purpose."

"It serves our successors," he said. "This is necessary for the same reason I observed the nova from the starship; there are certain lessons they can learn only from thought recordings. They'll know the evils we established, the closed City and the castes. They must be shown the larger evils with which we had to deal."

"The nova, yes. But how can you record personal contact with a mutant? How can you explain it?"

"To most future dreamers I can't. In time, though, there will be a person who won't shrink from the truth. That person may succeed where we've failed."

He turned the child toward him and, for the first time since its early infancy, fixed his own eyes on its vacant ones.

And now, there could be no question from whose mind the image came. Like the nova, it was burned indelibly into the memory of the First Scholar, and the recollection was sustained during the recording process in such a way as to overwhelm whoever experienced the dream. It would make no difference, Noren knew, if he had never seen other subhuman mutants, never been attacked by them and killed them as in fact he had; he would draw from this moment the full shock of all he'd previously undergone. The mindless creature cloaked in human flesh would be no less revolting to him if he'd never been tormented by fears about Talyra's baby, for as the First Scholar he knew that this was *his* child. He knew also that in the end, its mother had been driven with it into the mountains.

But that was not the worst. The First Scholar, in subjecting him to this, had meant him to know the agony of personal involvement, yes; but the true evil was not in involvement but in the illustration of what might happen to the whole human race. This was a warning not of the consequences of action, but of those that might follow inaction. The First Scholar had taken the fathering of this child upon himself, as he'd later taken the villagers' wrath at their exclusion from the City, to spare future generations. Better that his genes should be damaged than that everyone's should. . . .

And it was not to justify himself that the First Scholar had made the recording. He had made it for a chosen heir. *That person may succeed where we've failed,* his words echoed. He, Noren, had said them, yet as the dream faded and his own identity emerged from it, he was not sure that he wanted to wake.

V

NOREN KNEW, OF COURSE, WHAT HE MUST DO. THE SECRET FILE
gave him the results of the work done in the Founders' time; the
mother of the First Scholar's child had left specific, detailed data
and an analysis of what she believed had gone wrong. Though
theoretically, it would have been possible to proceed without further
preliminaries, the stakes were so high that he must move slowly.
He must develop his skills by personally repeating such work as was
possible to do with animals; it was necessary to design and carry
through experiments like those done on the Six Worlds, using a vaccine to produce genetic changes in adult creatures and verifying
that these changes were passed on to the next generation. None of
this was original research—the computers contained complete information about it, and in fact were equipped to handle the actual
physical analysis of the genetic material in living cells. But to him,
biology was a new field, and he had no one to tutor him. He had
to become absolutely sure of his own competence.

He expected the work to be hard, and it was. But it was not
nearly as hard as the things he'd thought would be easy.

His first impulse, after waking from the dream, was to tell everyone about it. Surely all Scholars would be elated to hear that a
means had been found whereby survival could be assured and the
caste system abolished! That they must face personal risks, suffer
new conflicts of conscience, would not deter anyone; they'd earned
Scholar rank in the first place on the basis of their willingness to
make such sacrifices. Noren shrank from the thought of the chance
he himself must take—but he didn't intend to let that stop him.
Was he to be less courageous than the First Scholar? Besides, it
would be easier under the circumstances of his own time; at least
he could be tested for genetic damage and need not fear the actual
birth of a subhuman mutant. And he'd have plenty of support.

Or would he? On reflection, he remembered that even before the
dream he had perceived that there would be controversy.

Perhaps the Scholars of his era weren't bound by the taboo that
had shaped the Founders' views. But they were dedicated to the

Prophecy. If this new work succeeded, the Prophecy would not come true. To be sure, it wasn't going to come true in any case; metal synthesization wasn't going to become possible. But his fellow priests didn't believe that. They believed he, Noren, could *make* it possible! If he were to stand up after Orison some night and suggest abandoning the effort. . . .

No, like the First Scholar, he would have to approach people one at a time.

A few days after the dream, once he'd outlined in his own mind the course he must follow, he sought out Brek. Brek was the only close friend he had, aside from Stefred; though he was on good terms with everyone in the Inner City, he didn't form friendships easily. He was a loner by nature; he always had been. Because Brek, as a Technician, had helped him escape the village jail, and because Noren had later been involved in Brek's own initiation into Scholar status, a bond had developed between them. But he had spent most of his free time with Talyra, not Brek. Since her death he'd avoided social contacts. He'd wanted to be alone, and he had not wanted to intrude—at meals, for instance—when Brek and Beris were together. Or was it simply that it hurt too much to see them as a couple, to see Beris glowing with happiness about their coming child?

Talyra . . . waiting for Brek in the refectory where they'd agreed to meet, Noren's thoughts returned to Talyra. If only things had been different. If only. . . .

No, he thought suddenly. No, if Talyra had lived, things would not have worked out well at all. He could not, of course, have asked Talyra to take the risk.

There would be no risk of producing a mutant like those in the mountains; he could be tested for the genetic damage that would cause that, so if his experiment failed as far as such damage was concerned, he would lose only his ability to father normal children. He could be sterilized and continue a normal married life. Sterility was, to be sure, grounds for divorce; but Talyra would not have divorced him. She'd have borne the disgrace of childlessness rather than do that, and he could have told her in the symbolic language that what had happened was the result of his work as a Scholar.

But the other risk, the risk that would follow success in his trial use of the vaccine, would be one to which he could not have exposed her. He could not have done so even if he'd been willing; it would have been against fundamental policy, for medical experimentation was done on Scholars, and Scholars alone. Technicians could not participate. They could not give informed consent, since they could not be informed. If he successfully altered his own genes so that unpurified water caused no detectable damage to his reproductive cells, that would not prove his children would be normal

—it would only mean they wouldn't be subhuman. They might suffer genetic damage of some other sort. A genetic change to a parent could, in theory, cause any number of unpredictable side effects in the offspring. He would have no way of knowing beforehand; and having a child would be the second, and most crucial, part of the test he must carry out. And that test could not have involved Talyra. To ask a woman to experiment with her baby would be even worse than to ask her to permit medical research on her own body; such a request could be made only of a Scholar woman. Oh, Talyra—like any Inner City Technician—would have gladly volunteered if told it served the spirit of the Star; but that would not be "informed consent." It would be unthinkable for a priest to exploit religious devotion in that way.

So if Talyra had lived . . . well, to wonder what he'd have done was pointless. Yet, now what? A loveless marriage, he supposed, to some Scholar who like himself cared more about human survival than personal happiness. He could no doubt find a bride easily, for though in the village, where girls chose steady men who'd be good providers, he'd been considered a poor match, in the City different qualities were admired.

It was past noon when Brek joined him, and Noren was in no mood to waste words. He filled his meal tray automatically, and they were barely seated at their table before he burst out, "What would you do, Brek, if you had a chance to help make sure of human survival on this planet—and it meant changing your ideas about the Prophecy, supporting steps you'd hate?"

Startled, Brek replied, "You know what I'd do. We all made that decision when we recanted. What's the point of going through it again?"

"That's what I want to talk about. We may have to." As quickly as possible he explained, omitting only what had been revealed in the dream. For some reason he'd begun to feel that the First Scholar's role was a secret to be held in reserve.

Brek heard him out. Then, slowly, he said, "Noren, I know you're discouraged about nuclear research. Everybody's discouraged. But it's not hopeless—you decided when you accepted priesthood that it's not. We've been through all this before, too—"

"No, it's different now, Brek! When I assumed the robe, I did it because I'd discovered that I believe a way will be found for us to survive. I didn't know what way. Nobody knew—that was the whole point of faith! Well, this is the way; we don't have to rely on faith any longer."

"I've still got faith."

"That's fine, but it's not enough, not when there's a means of action. Just sitting back and having faith was constructive when we

(94

had no other choice, but now that there's an alternative, we've got to *act*."

"I'm studying physics," Brek insisted. "That's action. But you, Noren, you aren't really trying any more, are you?" He hesitated; it was obvious he wished the discussion hadn't gotten started. "I haven't said anything till now," he continued unhappily. "Nobody's wanted to—we all know how hard things have been for you since Talyra died. Only . . . only people are beginning to wonder how long your mourning's going to interfere with the work that needs doing."

"You don't think I'm serious about what I just told you?"

Brek dropped his eyes. "I—I don't see how you could be. Oh, I know you're honest about it. You're the most honest person I've ever known; you always were. But—but it's not quite the same, you know, to get all this abstract information out of the computer as it would be to do what you're talking about doing. Stop and think what it would mean for a man—" He broke off, embarrassed not by the subject itself but by the sudden realization that it might be tactless to speak of it to a friend whose wife had recently died.

"I've thought," Noren assured him. Grimly, he recalled the dream, which he was now sure he must not mention. Brek had not yet experienced the full version of the First Scholar's official recordings; he wouldn't be qualified for exposure to the secret one until he had done so. Perhaps he wouldn't be qualified even then—the First Scholar had taken care not to impose it on anyone who was unready. He had foreseen that not all his successors would be ruled by reason, any more than his contemporaries had been. With dismay, Noren began to grasp the magnitude of the task he himself had been chosen to take on.

He was not good with people. He had no inborn gift for sensing their emotions, persuading them to see things as he saw them. For a while, when they'd both been younger, he had influenced Brek strongly by his confident expression of heretical opinions; but Brek, who had admired his courage more than his realism, had long ago learned to use his own mind.

"I have thought, Brek," Noren repeated. "Don't try to spare me."

"All right, then—have you pictured how you'd feel if it were you, your wife instead of Beris—"

"Do you suppose I'd ask this of you and Beris without trying it on myself first?" Noren demanded.

"No," said Brek in a low voice. "No, you wouldn't. I'm sorry; it was unfair to assume you haven't considered remarriage. Only . . . that doesn't really change things. One test wouldn't be enough. And you just aren't going to find anybody else with your kind of tough-mindedness."

"What kind?"

"The willingness to sacrifice everything to logic . . . to—to set aside all human decency, all normal feelings . . . for an ideal. For a future none of us will live to see. I'd give my life, Noren, but I wouldn't—well, I hate to be so blunt, but I wouldn't sleep with Beris knowing I could beget a genetic freak. You know how I feel! In the mountains you suffered agony rather than drink that water—"

"For Talyra's sake. Talyra couldn't have consented; Beris can. She's not only a Scholar, she's even accepted priesthood—doesn't she have the right to decide for herself?"

"For herself, but not for me—and not, I think, for the child, who wouldn't be a Scholar, wouldn't even be consulted. I don't believe any of us have that right. If you want the truth, which I know you always do, I'm giving it to you."

That was the beginning. Noren knew, then, that he was indeed going to face more difficulties than he'd imagined.

He spoke, without receiving any encouragement, to several other men, ones he felt he could trust to keep quiet about it—young ones either unmarried or married to Scholars. The older men he avoided in fear they might let some rumor reach the Council; more and more, he saw it was too soon to get the Council involved. For that reason, dishonest though it made him feel, he hid all hint of his new goal from Stefred; ostensibly out of pride, he let Stefred assume he was still learning to live with the nightmare. It was hard not to enlist his aid, especially since Stefred would surely support the plan. If anyone was tough-minded, he was. But Noren knew that Stefred hadn't enough power to sway the Council alone.

He needed a woman's viewpoint. He'd expected to receive this from Beris, but after what Brek had said, discussing it with Beris was out of the question. So was discussing it with anyone else's wife, and to ask one of the unattached Scholar women might look like—well, like a proposal. He was not ready for that yet. He went, therefore, to Lianne, who he knew wouldn't take it that way, and who had specifically claimed to understand all kinds of upsetting feelings. It occurred to him that her gift of empathy might be very useful under the circumstances.

Lianne listened, and she wasn't shocked. Noren realized, after they'd talked a while, that her remarks had been very neutral, very noncommital. "What about it, Lianne?" he demanded finally. "Would you support this if it came up in a general meeting?" Not yet having committed herself to the priesthood, Lianne wouldn't be entitled to vote at a meeting even if there should be one; but he valued her opinion.

"Noren," she said soberly, "I—I don't think you should rely on what I think. I'm different. I told you that. I'm not like other women

(96

here; I don't plan to marry—I've never even wanted a baby. So how can I give you an answer that's valid?"

"You've never *wanted* a baby?" He had never heard of a woman being quite that different.

"Well, the rest of my feelings are normal," she said, turning red. "Noren, how can you be so brilliant and yet so blind to what is custom and what isn't? You've dreamed plenty of library dreams. You know lots of women on the Six Worlds didn't want babies. That doesn't mean they didn't want—" She broke off. "Look, I wouldn't be embarrassed if you weren't, but you are, and I—I'm making things worse with every word I say! Go get some other woman's opinion."

"Wait," he said. "You can answer the other question. Do you believe we should do what we have to do to survive, even though it means not fulfilling the whole Prophecy, the part about cities and machines for everyone?" He'd received surprisingly little opposition on those grounds, from the people he'd talked to; the discussion had always turned to more emotional channels and then broken off too soon.

"Yes," Lianne declared. "I believe we should. But that's not what the argument will be about. It will be, among other things, about whether we can survive and fulfill the Prophecy, too." Her composure restored, she gave him a strangely compassionate look. "You're in a more difficult position than you know," she said, her voice so low that she seemed to be speaking mainly to herself.

That was exactly what the First Scholar had said to him.

Having exhausted the supply of potential allies in whom it seemed safe to confide, Noren turned to the work itself, feeling that once he proved the method practical, people would be easier to convince. But that too involved serious problems. He hadn't anticipated having to keep the animal experimentation secret; he'd thought that before he reached the stage where it was necessary, the project would be officially approved. It was one thing to spend a lot of time in the computer room studying genetics—for all people knew, he might be developing some wonderful new mathematical basis for the synthesization of metal. Nuclear experimentation was at a standstill in any case, since for the past year the existing theory had been recognized as inadequate. It was not hard to explain why he stayed away from the nuclear research lab. Explaining a desire to work in the biology lab was another matter.

Scholars were, to be sure, free to choose their own work; Council approval was not required except for things involving allocation of irreplaceable resources. Major decisions, matters of basic policy or of the use of metal, demanded approval not only by the Council but by vote of all committed priests in a general meeting. The use of one's time, however, was one's own business, in theory, anyway. In practice, use of it for any nonessential purpose was not a way to win friends.

There was no essential work for a Scholar in biology; such equipment as existed was used almost exclusively for the training of doctors, most of whom were Technicians—and this meant it was located in the Outer City. The only lab Noren was free to visit easily was for medical research, which was done in the Inner City because of the requirement that all volunteer subjects must be Scholars. There was little such research, for facilities were too limited. Metal instruments, drugs—they just couldn't be manufactured, not the complex ones common on the Six Worlds; many disorders that had been conquered there were incurable here, and would remain so. The lethal diseases of the new world, against which no one had natural immunity, were controlled by vaccines developed in the first generation; these were now manufactured in the Outer City and routinely administered to each generation of children by Technicians. A search did continue for antidotes to the poisons given off by native plants, and better treatments were being developed for illnesses caused by them; this was the only real area of progress, and the one in which volunteer subjects were used.

Noren had participated once, shortly after his entry to the Inner City. Then, he'd known nothing about what was going on; he'd been miserably sick and had not paid attention to the equipment, which, for lack of adequate space, was crowded into a compartment adjacent to the room where he lay. Thinking back, it occurred to him that he'd have had easy access to it—and a good excuse for running experiments merely for his amusement. Bacteria, viruses . . . he would have to learn to work with them before he could try experiments with animals in any case; he would have to prepare the vaccines. A vaccine to be used for genetic alteration did not work in the same way as one to produce immunity against disease, and it wasn't made in the same way either. But to an observer who'd never heard of genetic engineering, one culture dish would look like another. . . .

Yet there was just no legitimate reason he could offer for spending weeks in that laboratory. Even Stefred might start wondering if he did, for Stefred knew he wouldn't abandon all useful endeavors for what could only seem an obsession with a fascinating hobby. Realizing this, Noren evolved a quite desperate plan.

After absorbing everything he could from the First Scholar's records, he thought through every detail of the lab work carefully, transferring essential data to computer-generated study tapes. Unobtrusively, he gathered the necessary supplies, even making one trip to an Outer City lab not visited by a Scholar within memory; a whole roomful of Technicians knelt in silence while he took what he needed, none of them questioning, and none ever likely to encounter another Scholar to whom they'd venture to mention the incident. At night, he stored everything in the cabinets of the medical research lab, which like all Inner City facilities was unlocked. Since Scholars had complete trust in each others' integrity, by custom they made no checks either on people or on equipment. One bore full responsibility for one's own acts.

When ready he went to see the doctor in charge of medical research. "I'm not getting anywhere studying physics," he stated honestly, "and—and right now I can't face any more of it. I've got to have some kind of break, yet I can't just sit around without doing anything useful."

"Have you talked to Stefred?"

"Yes, weeks ago. He says I'm not ill. Yet I haven't been able to get back into my work routine."

The doctor sighed. "What you need is a vacation."

"A what?" Noren had never encountered the word.

"On the Six Worlds, people took time off from work, a few weeks out of every year, usually. Took trips just for a change of scene. Sometimes I think we'd be more productive in the long run if we could do that, though it wouldn't be acceptable in our society. The outpost helps; what a pity you've already been there."

"Yes." It was indeed a pity, for he could accomplish a great deal more at the outpost; he could even experiment on work-beasts. The thought of bringing one of the gigantic, clumsy work-beasts into the Inner City was, of course, ludicrous, so his "animal experiments" here would have to be confined to fowl. But the outpost was new, and all Scholars were eager for terms of duty outside the walls that had traditionally imprisoned them. It would be years before he got a second chance. "I need a change of scene, all right," Noren continued. "That's why I thought if I could be of use to you—"

"I'm sorry," replied the doctor, shaking his head. "I won't tell you what you already know, that we all feel you're most useful in physics and would be wasting your talent if you were to switch fields. You're brilliant; I'm sure you'd make a fine medical researcher. But Noren, it takes long study. I can't use an untrained lab assistant."

"Of course you can't. That's not what I mean. I had in mind volunteering for something more—restful." He tried to put a brave face on it.

"There's a long list of volunteers. Besides, a week or so of bed rest wouldn't—"

"Wouldn't solve anything for either of us," Noren agreed. "Look, your project data's in the computers like everyone else's; I have the right of access to it—which I've made use of. I know what you haven't any volunteers for, haven't requested any for because it would take too much time away from their own work. You've developed a new treatment for purple fever."

Frowning, the doctor observed, "You're serious! I think maybe you should check back with Stefred."

"What for? So that he can tell me I'm too honest with myself to resolve my subconscious conflicts by coming down with some psychosomatic illness, one that might confine me to the infirmary for weeks without being of practical benefit to anyone?"

"You've got a point, I'll admit. And there's no denying that purple fever's a real problem in the villages." He appraised Noren thoughtfully. "If you've read that report, you know we can't cure it; it has to run its course. The treatment, if it works, will make it somewhat less painful and less apt to produce permanent crippling —that's all."

"There's no significant danger of crippling, is there?"

"Not if you don't overexert yourself. Villagers often do."

"I won't set foot out of this lab," Noren declared fervently.

The next few days were worse than he'd anticipated. He had been warned that he'd be given no hypnotic anesthesia, which after all would defeat the purpose of the experiment; villagers couldn't be kept under hypnosis during long-term illnesses since doctors couldn't be in constant attendance away from the City. There was a hospital to which injured patients could be taken by aircar, but purple fever victims couldn't be moved. Painkilling drugs were un-available, but now a specific drug had been developed that might partially alleviate the symptoms. To test it, however, the subject must be in a position to describe his symptoms. Noren found them indescribable.

At the onset he had merely a fierce headache and shooting pains throughout his body, which he decided he could tolerate. Not till he tried to sit up on waking did it occur to him to be frightened— he felt sure his spine had fractured. The next thing he knew, he was lying flat, immobile, and the room seemed darker; he realized that he must have passed out.

"How's the headache?" the doctor asked.

"Worse." The point was to provide data, not to display stoicism. With effort, Noren managed to whisper, "I don't think your drug works very well."

"It hasn't had a chance; it's designed to treat the disease, not ward it off. I'll give you the first injection now. By tomorrow night you should start feeling some improvement." Encouragingly, he added, "If you're wondering whether this experiment's worth doing, remember that an untreated villager feels no improvement for at least a week."

He could not move his head without pain so intense he feared he'd cry out with it. He couldn't move his limbs or torso either, and in fact was cautioned that to do so would be "overexertion" at this stage. He lay motionless, dreading every muscular twitch, for three full days; after that, he was asked to try lifting his head slightly, or an arm or leg, to judge whether it was getting easier. "Easier" wasn't exactly the word, but it became possible. "The real benefits are in the convalescent phase," the doctor told him. "Without treatment a victim of purple fever is bedridden for six weeks or more and may never regain full use of the muscles if they're taxed too soon. But you're recovering nicely. Before long you'll be moving around the lab." Noren wasn't in shape to believe this confirmation of what he'd counted on.

The fifth morning, Lianne appeared instead of the doctor. "I'm glad to see you haven't turned purple, anyway," she said. From her smile he could not quite tell if she was joking.

"Didn't you ever hear about purple fever in your village?" he asked her. "It's the *plant* that's purple, the plant with the spores that cause it."

"My mother must have forgotten to warn me."

"I guess she didn't warn you that it's contagious, either. I thought they weren't going to let anyone in here."

"I'm a medical student, remember? Stefred won't require me to be a full-fledged physician as Six Worlds psychiatrists were; he isn't one himself, because his work's with healthy people instead of sick ones. But we do have to know the basics." She stood calmly at the edge of the cot, looking down at him with emotion he couldn't define. "You can sit up now, but don't make any rapid movements. I'll help."

"Seriously, Lianne, you could catch this—"

"If I do, there's a proven treatment—but I'm not going to. Lift yourself slowly and don't turn your head. The motion's going to hurt, but you need to begin getting used to it."

He started to speak, but as he raised his back the pain knocked the breath out of him. Lianne laid her hand lightly on his shoulder. Gradually his fear ebbed, leaving a purely physical agony that didn't seem to bother him as much as its severity warranted. Noren's spirits rose. Maybe the plan was going to work after all. For a while, he'd wondered whether he might have overestimated his own stamina.

"In a couple of days you'll be ready to sit at the lab bench," Lianne said. "I'll be around a good deal if you need anything."

"You mean you've been assigned to work in here?" he burst out, dismayed. No other experiments were in progress, and he'd assumed the chance of contagion would ensure his privacy.

"Let's just say I've chosen this week to start my student lab projects," she said evenly. "That way, no one will touch what's on the bench; you don't want somebody else to barge in here and mess up your test tubes, do you? It would be an awful waste of heroic fortitude."

And so, for the next six weeks, the work proceeded more smoothly than he'd imagined it would; he did not even have to invent a story about needing a pastime to keep his mind off the continuous ache of his muscles. The doctor assumed all the paraphernalia was Lianne's. Actually, she did very little on her own. When present she watched him gravely, quietly; sometimes he got the feeling that she knew more about what he was doing than her comments revealed. She had guessed his purpose through uncanny intuition combined with her knowledge of his ultimate aim—but how could she possibly know that he'd progressed to the point of splicing genes?

His physical weakness, the pain of motion and the persistent headache, failed to handicap him greatly; he was not sure just why. Though to concentrate on his task took effort and to steady his hands throughout the hours of intricate lab work was a bigger challenge than he'd foreseen, he found that he was enjoying it. He was truly accomplishing something, after so many seasons of futile study—that must be the reason. Yet he felt something more was involved. Confidence, perhaps, confidence not only in his mind but in his control over his body? As a village boy he'd considered himself too awkward even to make a good craftsman. Now, though, things seemed to be happening to him that extended beyond the ability to cope with the effects of the disease. Lianne taught him to allocate his strength, to relax totally except when his movements demanded tension; then later, when the doctor pronounced it safe, she taught him exercises to recondition his muscles. Evidently her medical training was including physical therapy techniques. Or, he reflected, perhaps she'd been a village witch after all. People did go to witch-women with ailments such as purple fever, for which the Technicians could provide no help; and the fact that she hadn't been charged with witchcraft didn't mean she'd never practiced any of the healing methods associated with it.

He found himself wishing that he could confide more fully in Lianne, perhaps even let her experience the dream—but that would be too unfair to Stefred. It would be, even if it weren't for Stefred's personal interest in her; and in view of that factor, the mere prospect of a close friendship made him uncomfortable. There were times when he saw something in her face that made him turn away. Only the recency of Talyra's death allowed him to accept Lianne's companionship, Noren realized; he was doing enough behind Stefred's back without creating a false impression that he was a rival for the one woman whose love Stefred wanted.

After some weeks in the lab, Lianne brought him fertilized eggs, and he proceeded from gene splicing in bacteria to the manipulation of genes of higher organisms. Some of the eggs hatched, and he went further. Finally she managed to smuggle in a grown hen, which he successfully injected with a gene-altering vaccine. She took a sample of the hen's blood to the computers and returned with a tape proving that its genotype had indeed been modified. Thereafter, the hen laid eggs, the analysis of which proved that the modification had affected reproductive cells. Lianne took the hen away and returned, in due time, with chicks. Analysis of their blood was unnecessary; they had blue tailfeathers. "Did you know what you were doing," she inquired, "or did it just happen?"

"I knew." He frowned and added, "But I didn't know they were going to hatch early."

"I hope not. I have enough trouble hiding a poultry coop on the aircar deck without having to explain blue-tailed fowl—I was going to bring them in here before they hatched. And I'm going to have to get rid of the rooster pretty soon; you have no idea what a noise it makes."

What an odd thing to say, Noren thought. He'd grown up on a farm and so, presumably, had she—or at least she'd lived near one; no village dwelling was beyond the noise of cockcrow. "It's not only the idea of someone seeing them that worries me," he said. "I was working with a regulatory gene, one that affects timing of development. They wouldn't normally have tailfeathers at all so soon after hatching; I used the blue coloring just for a marker. Well, I speeded up the appearance of tailfeathers all right, but evidently I speeded up hatching, too. Either the computer's gene mapping for fowl isn't accurate or else I fumbled."

"No complex experiment works perfectly the first time it's tried," Lianne said, sounding as if she'd been a Scholar for decades.

"Lianne," Noren declared grimly, "the big one has *got* to."

"From your standpoint, yes. But if it should fail, if you can have no more children, you'll still have a chance to—"

"I'll have no chance, and you know it! People won't accept the idea even now; what chance would they give me after a failure?"

"I can't answer that," she admitted in a low voice. "One step at a time, I guess. What comes next?"

"I find out what went wrong here and try a few other alterations. Till that's done, I'm afraid you'll have to hang onto the rooster." He wondered where he'd be now under his original plan, which hadn't included steps demanding outside aid. As she turned to go he went on, "Lianne? What are they saying about me? In the refectory, I mean, not officially."

"They're upset," she told him frankly. "Oh, they admire courage, Noren—but any Scholar would have been willing to undergo purple fever if there'd been a request for volunteers; I talked to one young man whose father was crippled by it, and he thinks you usurped his rightful role. The rest see the dark half of your motive. They interpret your being here as a retreat from working toward metal synthesization, and they know that you wouldn't retreat if you didn't feel hopeless, so they're depressed."

"Then maybe they'll be readier to consider an alternative, knowing they can't rely on me the way they've been doing."

"Don't count on it. The goal was set by the First Scholar, not by you; and if they decide they can't rely on you, they'll blame you rather than the goal itself." Gently she added, "Retreat from hope isn't appropriate conduct for a priest."

"You say that as if you were quoting it."

"Not the words. But it's what all the older people are thinking."

Slowly, he observed, "You also say it as if you agree with it, even now that you know human survival and the other hopes aren't necessarily tied together. Yet you've not accepted priesthood yourself—and you've helped me get away with neglecting 'appropriate conduct.' Could it be that you're slipping back into heresy, Lianne?"

"If you mean am I questioning the validity of the official religion," she told him, "then no, I'm not. My reasons for not becoming a priest are . . . personal. I support the aims of the priesthood and share the underlying faith. So do you, Noren."

"For a while I was convinced I did. But it's tangled up with so many things that aren't true, won't be true if humanity does survive."

Faith was a way of dealing with unanswerable questions. Yet now, Noren thought miserably, some of those questions could be answered—and the answer was *no*. Cities and machines for everyone. Knowledge free to everyone, all human knowledge, past and future, being expanded "even unto infinite and unending time," as the poet had expressed it. *Knowledge shall be kept safe within the City; it shall be held in trust until the Mother Star itself becomes visible to us.* The Mother Star, symbol of the unknowable . . . until the unknowable becomes clear, then? He had believed that. He'd been sure there would still be priests, as searchers for truth though not as a social caste, after the Prophecy was fulfilled; he'd believed they would explore the universe. *There shall come a time of great exultation, when the doors of the universe shall be thrown open and every man shall rejoice.* . . . What was priesthood without that goal? What was faith without it? Faith in survival wasn't enough. . . .

"Of course it's tangled," Lianne declared. "Religions usually are. *Were,* I mean, on the Six Worlds," she corrected hastily, as if the past tense wasn't obvious in her use of the plural. "But Noren, you aren't going to get very far with people just by proving chicks can be given blue tailfeathers. So maybe you'll have to try to untangle it."

* * *

By the time he was fully recovered and discharged from the medical lab, Noren had taken the experimentation as far as he could with fowl and had even started work with human blood serum. His results with the latter had been confirmed by computer analysis but were not, of course, ready for actual testing. He'd spliced human genes in test tubes, but to prepare a live-virus vaccine for human use would have been far too dangerous without the Outer City's facilities, even if he'd had the time. And he had no more time. He considered faking a relapse, but that would have negated the success of the purple fever treatment, which had been declared ready for village use. Or else, if the doctor had caught on, his malingering would have put an end to what little sympathy his fellow Scholars still had for him.

They were cool enough as it was. They didn't show it openly—they went out of their way not to, in fact—but he could tell how they felt. During his past bad times, they'd been sympathetic; yet he'd refused all sympathy, rebuffed every offer of help, not because he disliked people but because he had never known how to respond to them. Perhaps he'd indeed been guilty of what Brek had termed "starcursed pride." In any case, Noren reflected ruefully, he'd provided more than enough excuse for them to stop trying and let their real feelings surface.

There was nothing personal in these feelings; Lianne told him that, and he believed her. He could see the logic: he had become a symbol. He was the ordained heir, the youth destined to achieve the long-sought breakthrough and, by synthesizing metal, fulfill the Prophecy! He had been viewed as heir even by his first tutor Grenald, an aged man whose own lifework had failed, and who, last Founding Day, had died whispering Noren's name. That had seemed significant to people, for the failure of Grenald's research had frightened them. Fear, not moralism, prompted their current disapproval; for if Noren could not advance the work, could anyone? And he was refusing the role in which he'd been cast.

How very ironic, he thought, when he'd indeed been chosen heir to a different task—and by the First Scholar himself.

Would people support the new goal if they knew the full truth about the First Scholar? Logically, they should; the reverence felt for him should guarantee its acceptance. Though he hadn't been able to get it accepted in his own time, present circumstances weren't the same—and the Founders hadn't venerated him as Scholars now did. He probably hadn't foreseen such veneration when he wrote the programmed cautions . . . still, he'd already planned his martyrdom, already taken steps to ensure that it wouldn't lead to his worship outside the City. And he'd nevertheless hidden the

105)

secret not only from his contemporaries but from most successors; something about that made Noren uneasy.

Yet he himself couldn't delay indefinitely. Free to come and go within the City, he felt weak and helpless not so much from the lingering effects of illness as from the fact that he was blocked from any action. He could not return to physics, yet he couldn't study genetics, either. He could do no more with human genes without better lab facilities, and he could get them only with Council approval. There was other necessary work, many years of it, which during the hours he'd been bedridden he had analyzed: grain must be enabled to grow in untreated soil and to recover trace elements from organic fertilizers, which could in the future include workbeast manure, more efficiently than at present; irradiation of seed must be made unnecessary; the need for weather control must be eliminated; immunity against disease must be made heritable. There were feasible genetic solutions to these problems; the secret file dealt with some of them. But they all depended on the basic alteration of human metabolism being implemented. That alteration had to be tried first, and soon—for it couldn't be made in the whole species until it was proven in a third generation. Only if his grandchildren were normal could implementation of the change safely proceed in the villages!

He could afford no more lost time. Even without support among the younger Scholars, he must risk telling Stefred.

"I'm glad you've finally come," Stefred said when Noren appeared at his study door three nights after leaving the medical lab.

"You don't know why I'm here yet." Noren was sure of this; Lianne had sworn she'd revealed nothing.

Stefred, his smile warm and unsuspecting, pulled another chair close to his. "I thought I did," he said, "but now—" He broke off, sensing that this wasn't to be like their previous talks. "You're—older, Noren."

"You thought I went into retreat, I suppose, and that I've come out to find myself still in need of help." Noren hoped his own smile was warm; he wanted desperately to preserve this friendship despite the strains he'd been forced to put on it. "I do need help, Stefred, but not the kind you think."

"Right now I'm not sure what to think," Stefred admitted. "Your face gives the lie to all the rumors I've been hearing. Obviously you're not here to consult me in my professional capactiy."

"More in your executive capacity. I couldn't come to you sooner; I've learned something I wasn't ready to bring to the Council. Now I've got to. But it's going to shake people up—even you, Stefred." Painfully he added, "Especially you, because you're going to hate me for having concealed it from you."

Stefred waited silently. Noren continued, finding it hard to frame the words, "You remember what we suspected about my nightmare? We were right."

"That you got something the rest of us missed from the First Scholar's memories?" Obviously Stefred was wounded, though he tried to keep his tone even.

"Something he purposely concealed. He arranged things so that I'd uncover it, or that somebody would, anyway. There were—tests, not just what's buried in the official dreams, but some in the computer system that he programmed personally."

"Secretly?" Stefred burst out incredulously.

"Yes. With elaborate precautions. I couldn't get at the file again easily if I ever forgot my access code."

The delaying action didn't work; Stefred had caught the key word. "What," he asked in distress, "do you mean by the *official* dreams?"

"You've just guessed, I think." Unhappily, Noren held out the recording, which till now had been hidden in his own room, wrapped in the blue robe no other Scholar would touch during his lifetime; belatedly it occurred to him that this would have been a poor place for it if by some unforeseen chance he'd died of purple fever. "By the Star, Stefred," he went on, "I wish I didn't have to hurt you so much, but you're going to figure out the answer to the next logical question too, and I can't help matters by trying to avoid it. I've been through this dream, and you know I couldn't have done that without Lianne's help."

"Has she been through it, too?" Stefred's voice was very low.

"No. She doesn't know who made it or what it contains, though she and a few others have heard some related facts. The First Scholar told me in plain words that I've got to be sole judge of whether to share it."

"That gives you a great deal of power," Stefred said slowly.

"I never asked for it. But I've come to see I may need it—so though I can't expect you not to inform the Council, I need a promise that you'll go through this yourself first and that you won't copy it when you do."

"You have my word." Holding the container carefully between cupped hands, Stefred asked, "Am I to assume it's on the same level as the full version of the others?"

"Not exactly," Noren said. "It's got the things he edited out of the others. It's . . . rough. Very rough. You won't enjoy it."

"I suppose I should count myself fortunate that you're not telling me it should be monitored, which would make me ineligible till Lianne's trained."

"Don't laugh. For anyone but you, it does demand monitoring —and for some people we'll need an edited version." How unreal it seemed, Noren thought, for him to be offering Stefred advice on such a matter. He rose to go, knowing that before he reached the turn of the corridor, tonight's scheduled user of the Dream Machine would be bumped by a priority requisition. He hoped Lianne was on duty; perhaps he should have checked and waited for a night when she was sure to be. It was hard to imagine Stefred needing monitoring, yet with no advance preparation . . . well, it wouldn't hurt, and she could start it after he was unconscious.

"Stefred," he warned, realizing that perhaps he hadn't been explicit enough, "this isn't just a private memory, though parts of it are—well, personal. It's the most important thing any of us have learned since his era. Till now we haven't been given the whole plan, you see."

Startled, Stefred demanded, "It affects the future? The Prophecy?"

"I told you it's Council business."

"I thought you meant simply because of the right-of-access rule. If it's relevant to his plan, then why—"

"I'll explain if you want. But it might be better to see what someone without preconceptions draws from the recording."

"You're right. Come back, say, around midnight."

"No. You can do without monitoring, but not without sedation before and after. Surely there's somebody qualified in hypnosis you can call on." He didn't know whether Lianne had yet disclosed her talent in that area. "I was psychologically tested before receiving this. I assume your training means you can cope with it. All the same, it'll be stress."

When Noren returned the next morning, Stefred looked even more shaken than he'd expected him to be. His face was ashen. "What were you doing these past weeks in the medical lab?" he began without preamble.

"You know, or else you wouldn't be asking."

"And Lianne?"

"She watched, mostly, and helped me get supplies. It was her own idea," he added hastily. "You know how intuitive she is; she guessed why I'd gone in, just from my having gotten her opinion of the basic concept."

"Is she committed?"

"To what?" Noren hesitated; at first he'd assumed "committed" was a reference to priesthood, as it normally was.

"To this—experiment." For the first time in the years they'd known each other, Stefred lashed out in anger. "The Star curse you, Noren—you know what I mean."

Noren turned white. "Lianne—with *me*? What do you think I am?"

There was a long silence. Finally, in control of himself, Stefred said levelly, "I think you're the most dangerous man in the City, because you believe you've inherited a sacred charge, and you're strong enough to let nothing stand in your way. If I was wrong about the extent of Lianne's involvement, I apologize. But she visited you daily while you lived in that lab; she made excuses to go there—I could see she looked forward to it. And she is the only unmarried woman you know well who might wholeheartedly support what you're trying to do."

Bowing his head, Noren mumbled, "She's the only supporter I've found, all right. We were working with fowl; she kept a coop for me on the aircar deck. I got as far as modified chicks."

Stefred didn't respond at first. When he did, he sounded no happier. "Please forgive the emotional outburst," he said, "but you know better than I do what going through that dream is like. Last night I thought you must be exaggerating; I was wrong. Only there's so much you don't yet see." He got up and came to Noren, who was still standing. "Noren, about Lianne—she has refused me. She's made plain that she won't change her mind. If you and she were to love each other, I wouldn't begrudge your happiness. Did you think I was accusing you of taking her from me?"

"Weren't you? I wouldn't blame you; I can see how it must have looked."

"You misunderstand. She's refused me; whoever she chooses will have my blessing. What I feared was that she might have accepted a sacrificial role in this genetic scheme, as apparently she has." At Noren's protest he went on, "Oh, I realize it hasn't gone that far yet. But if she encourages preliminary lab work, she will go further, if not with you then with someone else."

"And you can't endure the thought of her babies being genetically modified?" Noren burst out, astonished. "Stefred, you're a psychiatrist! You're training her to be a psychiatrist! Surely you don't feel the way the Founders did, with their taboo; I mean—you couldn't call it obscene just because it might involve Lianne."

"No," Stefred agreed, "though you'll find people today who will feel it's an obscenity; traditions like that don't disappear in a static society. But as to Lianne, I am human, Noren, and I love her too much to see her hurt in a futile cause."

The implication of the last phrase didn't strike Noren immediately; he was absorbed with the sudden realization that for Stefred, the woman in the dream would have been Lianne—it was just as well if she hadn't been present to monitor after all. "I'd hoped," he said frankly, "that in time, if it works with me, you and she—"

"You thought I'd support this goal?"

"Why yes, in the Council for now, but later personally, too." The evident reluctance bewildered him; it had never occurred to him that Stefred would be anything but a strong ally.

"I'd better make clear from the start," Stefred said, "that it won't get my support in the Council or in any other way, and in general meeting I will vote against it. I will fight you by every means at my disposal, Noren. When I said you are now dangerous, I meant that."

Noren, stunned, was unable to reply. Not evading his eyes, Stefred continued, "If I'd had the courage of my convictions, I would have destroyed that recording this morning. I didn't. I couldn't take it upon myself to do that; it's part of the heritage to which all priests have a right—or perhaps the right is only yours. A man's memories are his own, to bequeath as he sees fit; I'd need to see what he told you in words to know for whom he recorded them. I know only this: the situation has changed since he did so, and if you use them as he intended, may the Star help us all. We will lose everything that's been achieved on this world, and in the end our descendants will die."

"Oh, no, Stefred. The genetic change is feasible—do you think I won't test enough to be sure? I know I can do it, do it safely."

Grimly, Stefred conceded, "No doubt you can. That's precisely what worries me."

"Then when you say we'll lose everything—"

"We don't live in the world the First Scholar knew. We have a culture built on the Prophecy."

"Do you suppose I haven't thought about that? I know there'll be a fight in the Council over it; to some of the older priests, the Prophecy is more than it was ever designed to be—more important than survival, even, because they're not realists. Well, you know how I feel about the City, about the preservation of knowledge! About fulfilling the promise to give machines and knowledge to everyone. About . . . reopening the universe. You can't possibly believe I'd find it easy to give up those things, or that I haven't been through every aspect of what we'll be sacrificing, over and over—" Noren's eyes stung; it was incredible that Stefred, of all people, would fail to understand.

Stefred sighed. "Sit down, Noren. I've been harsh, I'm afraid—you have lived for many weeks with the conviction that you can save future generations by working toward the end of all that you most value; it's cruel to crush your hopes. Yet I must. The whole issue's vastly more complicated than it seems on the surface."

"The *surface?*" Noren protested, declining to sit.

"Of course you have gone deeper in many ways: into all the emotions the First Scholar felt, and worse, because you've seen what came after—the mutants, the—the descendants, perhaps, of his own child."

"I may have killed one of those in the direct line," Noren mumbled.

"And so for you, the horror is even greater than what he intended you to bear—yet you are bearing it. He chose his successor well. The tragedy is that you were born too late."

"A priest," said Noren dryly, "is not supposed to say it's too late for hope."

"Or to tolerate unnecessary evils?" Stefred took his arm, drew him toward the window; they looked down between the towers to the outer circle of domes. Though they could not see the Gates or the broad platform beyond, that place was vivid in every Scholar's memory. "You have been there only once, outside of the dream in which you faced death there as the First Scholar," Stefred said. "You took abuse at your recantation feeling very much a hero. But I have appeared on that platform countless times as presiding priest—at Benison; at the blessing of seed after harvest; at more recantations than I like to recall; even, one year, as chief celebrant on the Day of the Prophecy. On all those occasions I have stood impassive while crowds knelt to me and paid me homage, which is something neither you nor he ever had to endure. The evil of the caste system, to me and to the others old enough for ceremonial responsibility, is hardly an abstract one. Do you think for one minute that in a choice between life without this system and the City's preservation, I'd hesitate to sacrifice the City?"

"I didn't," Noren said. "Yet now you're hesitating."

"No, there is nothing hesitant about what I'm doing. I am telling you there is no such choice. For the First Scholar, there was, and I imagine you've made yours as he did—but he could not foresee what changes would occur after his time. If he had envisioned a society like ours, he'd have warned you. I think, Noren, he must have hoped for the secret to be found within a generation or two. And in any case, remember, he hadn't gotten the idea for the Prophecy when he made the hidden recording; that inspiration came to him only as he lay dying."

"What would he have warned me about?" Noren questioned, inwardly aware that the First Scholar had indeed said he could not know how the world's culture would change, and had mentioned that difficult judgments would be necessary.

"That the physical ability to survive might not be enough to keep humanity from perishing."

"I see why that was true when he made the decision to keep the destruction of the Six Worlds secret—people would have been so hopeless that they wouldn't have defied their instincts enough to avoid unpurified water. You're going to say, I suppose, that they'll be hopeless again without the Prophecy, that they rely on it as their ancestors relied on being part of the Six Worlds' civilization. It will be different now, though. They won't have to defy instinct; they can live off the land."

"Noren," Stefred said sadly, "after all these generations there's no such instinct left. The land is alien. Life, now, comes from the

City, and the City alone. The instinct to live is embodied in the High Law. Can you imagine people breaking it willingly?"

"But if we tell them—"

"Tell them what? If the next time I speak from the platform outside the Gates, I were to tell people they can now drink impure water and eat food not grown in quickened fields, would they go home and do it?"

"It wouldn't be that simple," Noren acknowledged. He hadn't thought about it before, but of course villagers would not do that. "We'd have to be ruthless, I guess," he said slowly, "as the Founders were when they established the City in the first place. We might have to cut off the piped water supply, and certainly we'd have to stop treating land. But we could do it without harming anyone."

"Could we?" Stefred turned to him. "If the day comes when you figure out how to do it without harming anyone—or even without setting off enough violence to seriously threaten the long-term survival of our species—then perhaps I'll back you after all. Until then, consider me an opponent. And I am not just challenging you; I mean it. I will fight this idea all the way."

Dismayed, Noren saw that he did mean it; he would not merely withhold support, but would lead active opposition against which the goal of changing people genetically could not possibly win approval. And yet, he thought, Stefred had called him dangerous, considered the recording itself dangerous . . . and therefore must feel he could succeed.

That there was no chance of getting the Council to sanction genetic research became more and more apparent as, one after another, its members experienced the dream. Noren knew he couldn't prevent their doing so. He had been free to return it to the cache from which he'd obtained it, but having revealed it to Stefred, he could not keep it from other priests, all of whom had equal right to the truth. Realizing this, he felt at first there should be a general announcement of what had been learned, but to his own surprise he held back, some inner sense in conflict with his normal desire for full openness. Stefred and his fellow Council members concurred. "We've got a delicately balanced society in the Inner City," he said, "and our reverence for the First Scholar is its focal point. If you stand up in a meeting and declare that the mutants in the mountains are descended from him, you'll deal a blow not only to your own aims, but to the rest of his plans—which he himself knew."

It was true enough, Noren saw, that even to enlightened priests such a statement would be akin to blasphemy; only by experiencing the dream itself could they understand. It was therefore made available to those who chose to go through what was described as a difficult and unnecessary ordeal. Since the experiencing of the full version of the other dreams was made a condition for exposure to the new one, few younger Scholars sought it. How, and by whom, a previously unknown recording had been discovered was told only to the Council; and the Council said that it contained private memories irrelevant to life in the present era.

Noren did not contest this judgment. He knew that if he joined battle too soon, he would lose. He allowed even Stefred to believe that for the time being at least, he was willing to let the matter drop.

He could see that Stefred's arguments were valid; after discussing them for hours, he was forced to agree that people couldn't survive the sudden loss of all they believed in. Even for the Prophecy's fulfillment, the making of cities and machines available to all, there was an elaborate plan for a transition period; though most non-Scholars assumed everything would happen on the day of the Star's first appearance, of course that wasn't how it would be. The Founders' plan for the transition was gradual, and it did ensure that no one would get hurt by the changes. The trouble was that it assumed survival would demand continued observance of most provisions of the High Law; it made no allowance for abolishing the whole Law along with the castes. And of course, the transition plan was also based on people being given what the Prophecy promised them.

"If genetic change had been initiated in the First Scholar's time or soon after," Stefred said, "there'd have been a chance for a culture based on the conditions in this world to develop. But now, if people's established values should fail them, they wouldn't be able to develop anything new. Innovation has been repressed too long. Without adequate natural resources, it can't start again, not with a population as small as ours would be."

"But we've grown since the Founders' time—"

"Those gains would be lost. There would be fighting, Noren. Bad as our world is, we've at least kept it free of mass violence; but if its culture disintegrated, the survivors would kill each other off. They'd fight over the pure water in the rain-catchment cisterns, over the last remaining land-treatment machines. . . . ."

Yes, thought Noren—they would. He knew only too well that they would. But the First Scholar's companions aboard the starship had told him his plan for the Founding would lead to violence, too. . . .

Besides, there was no alternative. Without synthesization of metal everyone was going to die anyway when the machines wore out—and metal synthesization was a lost cause. That was the thing no one but himself seemed willing to face. Eventually, no doubt, others would reach the point of facing it; but by then it might indeed be too late. The genetic change couldn't be considered proven until it had been inherited by its developers' grandchildren.

Without quite knowing why, Noren began going to Orison, a religious observance open only to Scholars. He had previously avoided this; he'd gone instead to Vespers with Talyra, and after her death he'd rarely attended either service. Orison had always disturbed him; there'd been a period when it had even frightened him. So many unanswerables, so many fine words that might not come true. . . . *There is no surety save in the light that sustained our forefathers; no hope but in that which lies beyond our sphere; and our future is vain except as we have faith. Yet though our peril be great even unto the last generation of our endurance, in the end man shall prevail; and the doors of the universe shall once again be thrown open to him. Not on this world only, but on myriad worlds of innumerable suns shall the spirit of the Star abide. . . .* To him, at the time of his earliest awareness of the Prophecy's futility, this sort of liturgy had been more a terror than a comfort. Now it became piercing anguish. And yet he was drawn, somehow.

One evening, as he stood silently with eyes raised to the prismatic glass sunburst, symbolic of the Mother Star, that emblazoned the ceiling of the Hall of Scholars assembly room, comprehension came to him; it struck him so forcibly that he grew dizzy. How blind he'd been! He had thought he'd learned something of faith. He'd known its emotional impact before; on the day of his commitment to the priesthood he'd been deeply moved by these very symbols. It had not lasted, not the emotion . . . but that had been faith in which he'd had *no choice.* No choice but to die, anyway, as they'd all have died in the mountains if his subconscious faith had not sustained them. That was one kind, a necessary kind: simply to go on because there was nothing else to do. But it demanded no real action. Faith and action weren't opposites; all at once Noren perceived what an act of faith involved. There had to be choice in it, a decision that might go either way; one must *choose* a road that might lead nowhere.

"*. . . so, therefore, we consecrate ourselves to stewardship, to the ensuring of human survival; and may the spirit of the Star be our guide.*" Into the familiar words Noren put for the first time a commitment to risk of failure; and he knew he would never be quite the same person as before.

Late that night, robed, he went to the lab in the Outer City lab where vaccines were manufactured. Because equipment was limited, the work there was done in shifts; there were always workers present. They were trained microbiologists, far older and more experienced than he; still they knelt to him, addressing him as "Reverend Sir"— Noren thought ruefully that he'd have preferred another siege of purple fever. One did what one must, however. He gave orders, and since the High Law commanded obedience, he was asked for no explanations. It was unheard of for a Scholar to visit Technicians instead of sending for them, still more so for him to require a virulent virus strain and use of one of the few existing biological safety cabinets so that he could work with it personally; but people didn't question the ways of Scholars. If it occurred to them that it was ludicrous and downright hazardous for him to put a lab coat over a flowing blue robe, they refrained from saying so.

Noren returned to the lab many nights, carrying sealed test tubes to the computers for analysis in the hour before dawn. At length, after a passage of weeks, he carefully but matter-of-factly injected himself with his new vaccine.

As he prepared to leave, he told the lab chief he wouldn't return in the near future, receiving the usual courteous acknowledgment. He started toward the door, feeling lightheaded with a mixture of relief and fear; but the Technician's voice stopped him. "Reverend Sir—we would be honored by your blessing."

Noren turned; he owed them that. It had been a breach of etiquette to necessitate their working in a "superior being's" presence night after night, one for which he'd have been severely criticized by fellow priests; furthermore he had delayed their own work by preempting scarce equipment. These people were entitled to all he could give them. Holding out his hands in the formal gesture of benediction, he nodded, and the lab workers clustered around him. He'd used the words often enough at Vespers, but never in personal audience, never to people kneeling, awaiting his touch. *"May the spirit of the Mother Star abide with you, and with your children, and your children's children. . . ."*

Your children's children. He hoped so; he hoped it would be a more tangible blessing than he could offer in mere words.

For three weeks after that he waited, his dread growing. He did not expect the injection to harm him—although in any experimental work there was that possibility—for he'd modified the virus to remove its toxic effects as well as to give it genes for the capabilities he wanted it to have. Nor did he worry about whether it would spread throughout the cells of his body; that could be, and was, confirmed by computer analysis of blood and tissue samples. Whether the added genes would work as expected was another matter entirely; and to test that, he'd have only one chance. Once he'd drunk unpurified water, there would be no turning back.

And the next step? A marriage of convenience, he had thought. Well, he'd be willing; what he'd had with Talyra could never be duplicated, and it was respectable, even customary, for a man to marry without being in love. But who was there to marry? There were very few unmarried Scholar women, and all of those young enough to bear children had plenty of suitors. Though he might successfully court someone, he didn't want to do that. It wasn't just that most girls wouldn't support the genetic research—he could probably find one who would share his belief in its necessity. She would ultimately get hurt, however. Even if his child was normal, she'd get hurt, for she would want him to love her in a way he could not; and what if later, she met someone who did?

No, it would not be right for him to bind anyone. It would be fairer if there was no expectation of permanence on either side.

For couples to be lovers was not unusual; in the Inner City, where families couldn't be reared, it was not frowned upon. But a girl could still be hurt that way; she could fall in love and be heartbroken over a breakup even if there had been no promises. Asking someone to bear a genetically altered child was bad enough without that. Now that the time was at hand, Noren knew he was unwilling to let it happen.

To be sure, there were women among the Scholars who loved casually. In the case of most such women, he feared, birth of a normal child would not prove much about any particular man's genes. However, there were exceptions. There was Veldry, for example. Veldry had been faithful to her lovers; she was a decent enough person. It was just that she couldn't seem to be happy with anyone for more than a year or two. To swear by the Star to be faithful forever wasn't her sort of commitment.

Veldry was always doing unexpected things, Noren reflected. She was, for instance, one of the few younger women who'd chosen to experience the newly discovered dream. Admittedly, she liked newness. But there was more to it than that; she'd been through the full version of the First Scholar's memories earlier, and one didn't undergo that ordeal merely for love of novelty. Perhaps he was unfair to her in considering her shallow because of her short-term personal relationships. She might be just the person to commit herself to an experiment in genetics; she'd already had several babies, and she was, after all, a Scholar who had passed all the tests of dedication to the welfare of future generations. Yet he could not help the way he felt. He wanted a child, a child to live after him—and he did not want Veldry to be that child's mother.

So if he could not marry, and could not bring himself to start a casual love affair either, what was left? He knew underneath that just one course was left; he'd known even before Stefred had spoken of it. Looking back on those days of recovery from purple fever, he saw that Stefred had been right. Lianne would wholeheartedly support the goal. But there had been more in her friendship than desire to work toward ensuring human survival. She had refused Stefred, as she would no doubt refuse any man for whom she had no deep feelings, and had declared she did not want marriage. Yet Noren knew, from the way she'd looked at him, that Lianne would not refuse his love.

He did not love her as he'd loved Talyra. He wouldn't pretend to, wouldn't want to pretend even if he could. But if it must be someone

—and Talyra herself had said he must have children—he could not honestly tell himself that he didn't want it to be Lianne.

More than a half a year had passed since his discovery of the First Scholar's secret when Noren, knowing the vaccine had had more than enough time to act on him, took the irrevocable step. Under cover of darkness he unflinchingly violated the High Law's most sacred precept.

On the east side of the Inner City courtyard was a sort of garden. It was just outside the dome containing the water purification plant; in the triangular area between that dome's wall and the adjacent one were rocks, some native shrubs, and a waterfall. The water poured out of a spout in the wall, draining back into the dome after splashing into a stone basin. This water was, of course, unpurified; and it had practical functions as well as aesthetic ones. Its main use came when the purification plant underwent one of its periodic partial breakdowns; on those occasions people too old to have children drank there, since most of the pipes to the Inner City, which always bore the brunt of resource shortages, were cut off. Also, if one wore long plastic gloves, the impure water could be used for washing articles that weren't absorbent. Perhaps the chief reason for the waterfall, however, was psychological. Villagers lived within sight and sound of cool water they were forbidden to touch, despite year-round blistering heat; for Scholars to do the same was a poignant reminder of the alien planet's restrictions.

Staring at the moonlit glimmer of the plunging water, Noren thought back to the day he'd first quenched his thirst in a forbidden stream. How triumphant he'd felt, how sure that by defying the High Law he was asserting his trust in his own mind, his independence from foolish taboos! He'd turned out to be wrong, that time. . . .

Then there was the other time, the time in the mountains, the days when in agony of thirst and fever, he'd barely moistened his lips. Had that restraint indeed been meaningless? No, for if he'd suffered genetic damage then, he could not be doing this work now; and if no one else was willing to do it, the future of the world might be different. But there was still no sense in what had happened to Talyra. If he were now married to her, there'd be problems, yet her death and the child's had been too high a price for avoiding them.

No! All of a sudden, he saw . . . *even her death wasn't meaningless!* If she and the child hadn't died, he would never have begun to study genetics. The secret might never have been found. The means of human survival might never have been imagined by anyone.

Holding to this thought, inspired by it, Noren thrust his cupped hands into the waterfall and, over and over again, he drank.

VI

THE WEEKS OF WAITING WERE HARD, AS NOREN HAD KNOWN THEY would be. And he also knew that this was just the beginning. If the water he'd drunk had damaged his genes, the obstacles to continuing the work might prove insurmountable; that prospect he refused to think about. But if it hadn't, he would nevertheless face a long period during which his self-discipline would be severely tested. For that, he began to prepare himself.

He could do nothing active toward the goal till enough time had elapsed for the water's effect on him to become detectable. To spend that time in pointless reanalysis of the genetic work was a temptation; yet that would only be putting off his return to physics. He realized that he had to return. Once a child was conceived, seasons must pass before the experiment's outcome was known, and during those seasons, when no progress could be made in genetic research, he must pretend to have abandoned his interest in it. He must earn the other Scholars' respect again, so that later, armed with proof that the genetic change worked, he would have hope of winning support. Furthermore, he must provide evidence that metal synthesization was a lost cause. He owed people that, he felt.

And he owed it to his child-to-be.

At night, alone in the dark, he worried about the child. What he'd resolved to do was wrong; he could not deny that. Though the mother would consent, the child could not. And it was wrong to experiment on *any* unconsenting human being!

Yet the choice was between risk to a few babies and the sure extinction of the entire human race. He *was* sure—as sure as it was humanly possible to be—that metal could not be synthesized in any way short of a Unified Field Theory, which, as the First Scholar had known, could not be developed and tested without large-scale equipment unobtainable here. Wrong as it was to experiment with his child, to let humanity die when the life-support machines wore out would be a greater wrong.

If he could find a mathematical basis for a Unified Field Theory, Noren thought—show how metal had to be synthesized in principle

—people might admit that their faith was misplaced. This, then, would be his task. It was an impossible one; the greatest physicists of the Six Worlds had sought a Unified Field Theory for centuries, and the chances of his coming up with it within his lifetime, let alone within the next year, were therefore effectively zero. Yet he had to do something with the year! And if he was going to do this, he'd do it honestly. It would demand mental discipline surpassing any he'd previously attempted, but that wasn't an entirely unpleasant prospect, even knowing himself foredoomed to failure. It would help keep fear of a worse failure from his mind.

The day after reaching this decision, he mentioned it to Lianne. He'd been seeking her company casually, in the refectory and in other gathering places, since injecting himself with the vaccine. She did not know about that; he had not yet told her how far he'd gone in genetics, or how far he planned to go. That must wait till he had checked the impure water's effect on him. But considering what he planned to ask of her, he must strengthen their friendship; though he would not court her as if he loved her, he could scarcely ignore her until it was time to broach the subject. And he discovered, with some surprise, that he did not want to ignore her. That troubled him; it seemed disloyal to Talyra. Having pledged himself to Talyra in midadolescence, he'd never paid attention to any other girl. Now he found himself enjoying Lianne's companionship—even, on occasion, looking forward to the time when they would share more than companionship. How could he? he wondered.

Lianne knew how he still felt about Talyra; he was sure she did, for though she quite evidently welcomed his company, she was as careful as he to shy away from anything suggesting courtship. She was on guard, he felt, against displaying her feelings, and sometimes joy in her eyes turned to pain. Yet it was not his lack of ardor that was hurting her. Lianne's pain went deeper; whatever her secrets, they seemed to weigh heavily upon her, and Noren sensed that he could not have helped even if his heart had been free to give.

Nor did Lianne need help. She was . . . self-sufficient; he could not doubt her ability to handle problems. For some reason, however, her self-sufficiency was unlike his own—she was not a loner, as he was, and nobody thought her cold or unapproachable. Lianne radiated warmth. He felt comfortable in her presence, despite the fact that her mind was inscrutable. Her wisdom was baffling at times, but never irritating. The Unified Field Theory, for instance. . . .

"It's not a thing I can explain," Noren told her, "not to someone who hasn't studied physics. But matter and energy are—well, two aspects of the same thing. The power plant converts matter to energy. If we really understood the relationship, completely understood it, we might reverse the process, convert energy to matter, to metal, perhaps—"

"But you don't have the facilities you'd need to learn how all the forces are related, let alone the subnuclear particles," Lianne replied promptly. "They hadn't established the identity of forces on the Six Worlds, even studying particles with far higher energies than we can produce here."

Noren gaped, incredulous. To be sure, Lianne had experienced the secret dream by now, and the First Scholar had spoken of the Unified Field Theory in that dream; but had he thought specifically about forces and particles? Even if he had, how could a village woman—one now studying psychiatry, not physics—have drawn their significance from the recording?

"The mathematical foundation could be laid," she went on, "only I think it's beyond you, Noren." She sounded almost as if she felt duty-bound to inform him.

"Of course it's beyond me," he agreed. "That's the point! It's beyond all of us; that's what I've got to prove before I can make people accept the alternative."

"Can you really work with math at that level, or are you going to fake it?"

Noren's instinctive angry retort never reached his lips; the implications of Lianne's question were too astonishing. Even the ability to fake the math would mean he'd progressed beyond other physicists who would check—thus Lianne realized there were various levels beyond. That fact could be learned from the computers . . . but not without a very thorough grounding in mathematics. It was something he himself had perceived comparatively recently.

"Fakery," he replied quietly, "is something I've never been willing to stand for."

"So I thought," she murmured, troubled. She seemed about to say more, yet held back. "It's so hot," she burst out, "let's find someplace cooler! I don't see how people bear this endless heat."

The heat was, to be sure, scorching, as it always was outside and had been every day within Noren's memory; the cool interiors of the towers and domes had been startling to him on his initial entry to the City. Lianne had been in the City less than a year. "We'll go indoors if you like," he said, wondering if her white hair and extraordinarily pale skin made her sensitive to sunlight.

"I guess that's our only choice. Don't you wish, though, that we could walk somewhere in the shade, under trees?"

"You've been spending too much time with library dreams," he told her, smiling. He knew what trees were; five of the Six Worlds had had them.

"Dreams?" Lianne, who made incredibly complex connections between abstract things, was often dense about simple ones.

"Yes—hasn't Stefred explained about them? The pleasant ones

aren't just recreation; they're designed to show us what this world hasn't got, to make us feel the lacks in a way non-Scholars don't. So that we'll never be satisfied, always keep struggling. And maybe someday, once we have metal, we can find a better planet—" He broke off, aware with renewed anguish that this goal was among those that must be renounced.

"I didn't mean to stir that up," Lianne said hastily. "I'm not quite sure how I managed to."

"What you said about trees, of course. Why not ask for an ocean?"

She turned even paler than her normal coloring, as if the casual remark had been an unpardonable slip of some kind. Noren took her arm. "Lianne—don't be sorry! I have to learn to bear this; we all do. It's just that when we've believed in the Prophecy so long, believed not only in survival but in a better future—"

"Yes," she agreed; but she was still trembling. "Yet a—a simple thing like *trees*—"

"We could have them, maybe!" Noren cried excitedly. "That might be done with genetic engineering, after the essential jobs are finished. There are plants with thick stems, they just aren't strong enough to stand upright. I never thought before, but in principle I could alter them. There's a lot I could do! Oh, I know we're going to lose the City—the power and the computers—in time, but as long as I'm alive I can keep them going; I can keep the genetic technology long enough to make this world better for our descendants. And though we don't have oceans, there are big lakes; villages could be built near them once it's safe for people to touch the water. Do you know what swimming is?"

"Well, of course—" She broke off. "I have experienced a dream of swimming," she said slowly and deliberately. "And boats. If there were trees, and wood, we could build some; even Stone Age peoples have boats."

What a strange way to say it, Noren thought: "peoples," plural, and the present tense, too. "You've studied the Six Worlds more than most of us," he observed thoughtfully. "Not only the dreams, but facts stored in the computers. It's not just what you know, but how you think, as if—as if you came from the Six Worlds, like the Founders."

"That's one way to look at it," she confessed. "I—I'm different, I've always told you that . . . and there's the empathy Stefred talks about . . . and I—well, I identify in the dreams, not just the First Scholar's, but the library dreams, too. I mix them too much with reality, perhaps. I suppose that sounds like a retreat, a coward's course."

"No," Noren said. "No, it takes courage—don't you see? Because you're here, in the real world, and you're not deluding yourself, not

121)

even with the Prophecy. You experience those dreams fully, think about them while you're awake, knowing all the time you'll never get out of this prison we're in, not the City but our whole planet—"

"Please don't! You're giving me credit I don't deserve."

"You do deserve it. I know it hurts to talk about this—but Lianne, you *choose* to. Most people don't. They enjoy the library dreams, but in the daytime they can't bear to remember them. I'm like that myself—I push them out of my mind because awareness of our limits here is just too painful. Oh, I can take it; I force myself to think it through sometimes just to make sure I can. But you seem to live with it naturally."

"I—I wish I were what you believe." Lianne's eyes glistened with tears.

"I'll bet I can prove you are." He had led her to a spot in the courtyard shaded by the shadow of a tower; they could look up into the blueness of the sky. "You remember you said once you'd like me to tell you more about the alien sphere I found in the mountains?"

Abruptly Lianne pulled back, withdrawing her arm from his; she stiffened. Noren smiled. "I'm testing you; already you see that. Which is part of the test, because most people aren't even perceptive enough to shrink. They look at the sphere and it fascinates them, and they talk endlessly about what sort of beings the Visitors must have been, and they speculate about what function the thing might have had— and their emotions aren't involved at all."

"But yours are?"

"What do you think about the sphere, Lianne?"

"I'd rather hear what you think," she said levelly.

"I think there's a good chance that the civilization that once came to this world and left the sphere still exists somewhere. That things that used to be real on the Six Worlds are still real, other places. Maybe millions of places. Has that idea ever come into your mind?"

"Yes," she admitted, "it has."

"Do you believe it's true?"

"Certainly. I mean—well, of course they couldn't all have been wiped out by novas, all the civilizations in the universe."

"But you've never heard anybody else in the City mention that."

"I guess I haven't. It's so obvious—"

"No, it isn't, not to the people who don't have what it take to face the thought that we're cut off from them. Lianne, that sphere is physical proof of what used to be only theory. Oh, the Founders knew this planet had been mined, but that could have been a billion years ago. The sphere isn't that old. Right after I found it, I used to try to talk to people about the implications, only they didn't see any implications, they didn't want to see. Somebody told me once that if I'm hoping we'll be rescued—"

(122

"That's impossible!" Lianne broke in sharply. "You mustn't have any such hope."

"I don't. The odds against it are fantastically high; people know that, all right. So they'd rather not think of other civilizations as really existing, existing at this very moment—because once you think of them that way, you know we're in a worse prison here than the First Scholar imagined. We lost more than the Six Worlds; we lost our starships. And since we aren't going to succeed in synthesizing metal, we aren't ever going to get them back. I know *I'm* behind bars; I'm not brave enough to imagine what that means very often, but I do know. I also know what it means for our human race to be maybe the only one in this whole galaxy that's never going to get in touch with the rest. And the look in your eyes right now tells me you know, too."

Lianne didn't answer; the emotion in her seemed beyond words, beyond even what he himself had felt whenever he'd allowed himself to ponder these things. "I'm not trying to be cruel," he said. "I'm trying to show you how much I admire you, how much stronger you are than you think."

She managed a smile. "Stefred's tactics? I'm the one who's supposed to become the expert in encouraging people."

"You have a talent for it. Not only in what you do and say, but in what you don't need to ask—nobody else, not even Stefred, has been able to grasp how I feel about the sphere." He hesitated. "There's another thing. The Council ruled that it can never again be turned on, but the reason wasn't publicized. It's something I learned when I started studying genetics—there's a chance the radiation might be what harmed Talyra's child."

"Oh, no, Noren." Lianne's tone was one not of shock, but of certainty.

"Don't try to spare me. If it was the cause, the fault's mine; Talyra wouldn't have been near it if it weren't for me. Now that I'm sure no other pregnant women came in contact with it, I can't say I'm sorry we found it, because if we hadn't, Brek and I would have died, too, and Talyra would have died sooner—we'd all have died of starvation. But before I learned the radiation may have done harm, I was *glad* we found it; underneath, it almost seemed like compensation for losing the aircar. Even though I know it can't ever help us, even though it makes me feel worse than before about being stuck on this world—just knowing seemed better than not knowing. Talyra believed the Mother Star led us to it. Well, my ideas about its meaning weren't any more realistic." He searched Lianne's face. "Was I a fool, do you think?"

Her hand touched his. "No. Go on being glad; knowing *is* better. And the radiation did not harm the baby, I—well, I can't explain why, call it my crazy intuition, but I'm sure it didn't."

"There's no way you could be sure of a thing like that."

"I suppose not, only what could a portable radiation device be except a communicator of some kind? And they wouldn't have used communicators that could be harmful."

There was a strange intensity in her voice, so strong that he found himself believing her. Her argument was reasonable, yet hardly conclusive; who knew what might or might not be harmful to an alien species? She was not just rationalizing, though—much as she obviously wanted to reassure him, she would not do it dishonestly. Could it really be intuition? Of course not; there was no such thing . . . and still, Lianne's knowledge of things beyond her experience was often truly uncanny.

Twice in the past his reproductive cells had been tested for genetic damage; doctors had handled it. But there was no need to involve a doctor if one knew how to use the computer input equipment and ask the right questions about the data, at least for a man there wasn't. Since to test a woman's reproductive cells demanded surgery, the vaccine, if it worked on men, must be presumed to work on women without this intermediate check. The really crucial trial would be the health of the baby. But before daring to father a baby, he himself must make sure that impure water hadn't affected him as it would have before his vaccination.

He did the test at night, as he'd done the blood tests, when the computer room was deserted. Handling the apparatus, entering preliminary analysis commands, he worked steadily and impassively, without permitting his mind to stray. Only when he keyed the final query did his fingers fumble and his eyes drop from the screen. Cursing himself for his cowardice, he forced himself to look. The report read, FERTILITY UNIMPAIRED. NO INDICATION OF GENETIC DAMAGE. NO KNOWN CAUSE TO EXPECT DEFECTIVE PROGENY.

Noren's clenched hands let go, and he felt weak, reeling with the release of pent-up tension. To his astonishment he found that he was weeping. He had not let himself know how terrified he'd been.

As he emerged from the Hall of Scholars into the brightening dawn, Noren knew elation for the first time since Talyra's death. That was behind him now. The memory would always hurt; he could never feel for anyone what he'd felt for Talyra. But the children he'd have had with Talyra would not have helped humanity to survive. His future children would! They would be the first of a new race, the first born able to live without aid in the only world now accessible to them. *What is needful to life will not be denied us* . . . that was true! There were problems, problems to which he could see no solution, but at this moment they were dim and unreal. If the genetic code of life could be changed, surely other limits could be overcome also. By the Star, Noren vowed, he'd make a *good* world for his children!

His and Lianne's. He was not sure why it had become so important that they be Lianne's—perhaps, he thought, because she, above all women he'd known, would understand the meaning. She saw nothing unnatural in using knowledge to alter life. With eagerness, he turned back into the tower.

He found her in the dream room; she still worked there some nights, and her shift was just ending. "Let's go for a walk," he said. "Now, while it's cool out in the courtyard."

She looked so openly pleased that he was ashamed; his impatience to make plans, more than consideration for her comfort, had prompted this suggestion—and he realized that he did care how she felt about trivial things as well as serious ones. Maybe sunlight really was hard on her. He'd learned Talyra's feelings, all of them—but never anyone else's. Had he tried? Could he become close in that way to Lianne?

"We haven't talked about the secret dream," he said as they crossed the deserted courtyard, their footsteps loud in the hush of daybreak.

"You never seemed to want to." This was true; he'd carefully stayed clear of the topic while unready to pursue it fully. "I understand how it must have been for you, Noren," Lianne went on. "Personal, too personal to speak of. I monitored you, of course—"

"What did that show?" he asked, wondering.

"Only that it affected you deeply . . . in lots of ways. Later, when you asked me what I thought about genetic change, I guessed the dream was involved. And then when I went through it myself and learned how the First Scholar's experience fits in, I knew you must feel—chosen."

"Stefred thinks that makes me dangerous. I'm not quite sure why; I see his point about how hard it'll be to get people to abandon the High Law willingly, but if he's right that it's too late, I couldn't cause any harm by myself. Any implementation is far in the future anyway. So why does he oppose even the research?"

"You don't know?" Lianne asked, surprised. "Noren, of course you couldn't do anything alone that would threaten village culture—and you wouldn't; Stefred's aware of that. But think what it would do to *us,* to the priesthood, if we stopped believing the Prophecy."

"I stopped a long time ago," Noren confessed bitterly. "And it hurts. Stefred isn't a man who'd back away from that."

"Not from the despair," she agreed. "Suppose, though, that you were to win official support for genetic alteration, Council support—and we gave up metal synthesization as hopeless. Gave up the plan to fulfill the Prophecy's promises. No priest, least of all Stefred, could ever again speak those words about knowledge and cities and machines with a clear conscience. Starting now, in our generation, not in our grandchildren's! We'd reinterpret the symbolism among ourselves, but nobody would be able to preside at public ceremonies."

Noren drew breath, horrified by his own blindness. "It would become a real fraud after all, just as I thought when I was a heretic—"

"Yes, that's another thing. Recantation depends on a heretic's being honestly convinced that the whole Prophecy is true, doesn't it? If we revised the official plans, Stefred couldn't recruit any more Scholars; the system would turn into a sham that would no longer work."

Appalled, Noren mumbled, "You don't know how ironic it is, my not seeing it like that in the first place. After the way I took off in that aircar, ready to throw away my life and Brek's proclaiming that the Prophecy is a false hope—" He broke off. "Lianne, I wondered then why all the others didn't feel as Brek and I did. Now . . . they would, wouldn't they, if they accepted the alternative to hoping."

"Of course. And if they did, we couldn't last even till the genetic change could be put into effect. Stefred has to oppose you! He has to keep you from gaining wide support, no matter whether you're right or wrong. That's the only way the priesthood can remain genuine."

"But if I'm right, I've got to have support. It's a paradox."

"Yes. One you'll someday have to resolve. Meanwhile, you and Stefred both have vital parts to play."

"And you, Lianne?"

"I—I can only be an observer," she said sadly.

"More than that, I hope." Noren put his arm around her shoulders, feeling less shy than he'd expected he would. "In the dream— what the First Scholar did, what *she* did—do you believe it was ethical?"

"Not in itself; they knew it wasn't, because the child had no choice and suffered harm. But it was the lesser of the evils they had to choose between."

"Would you make the same decision?"

"In her place, yes, I would."

"I don't mean that—I mean in yours."

"The situation's not going to arise."

"Because of Stefred's opposition? You didn't think I was going to let that hold me up."

"No—no, of course I knew better," Lianne said. "But to prepare a live-virus vaccine—"

"I've already passed that stage. I bent a few policies by using the Technicians' lab, but there just wasn't any other way. And—" He faced her. "—it works. I've tested it."

"Altered your own genotype?" She smiled. "I guess if I'd stopped to think, I'd have realized you had kept on working. I suppose you're going to say you're ready to risk drinking from the waterfall, and I—well, I can't argue. We're walking in that direction. I won't stop you, Noren; I'll stand by and wish you the Star's blessing."

They were indeed approaching the waterfall, though he hadn't planned it. The ring of domes stood dark against a yellow sky; the sun hadn't yet risen above them, but overhead the towers shone with its reflected rays. Noren didn't speak until they reached the garden. Then, barely audible over the splash of the water, he said, "I drank weeks ago. There's been no damage. I thought you might want to do more than stand by."

She drew back, to his surprise suddenly wary. "Noren, I—I don't think I want to hear what you're about to say."

"I won't lie to you. I won't tell you I'm in love with you the way I was with Talyra."

"I know that," she said, hiding her face from him.

"I'll just say I admire you more than any woman I've ever known," Noren went on, realizing this was true. "The research has to go forward; you understand why. But I don't want just that. I want a child, the first child who really belongs to this world—and I care about that child's mother being someone to be proud of. I don't suppose you'd want to marry me, not after turning down a proposal from Stefred; you told me you don't plan to marry at all. If you'd like us to be married, though, we can be. I'll be honored. And if you'd rather we were together for only a while, I'll understand."

Lianne raised her eyes, and they were filled with tears. "You don't understand! Noren, I admire you, too, and I'm flattered that you'd choose me—please don't think I'm not. But you're asking for something I can't give. The first child who really belongs to this world . . . oh, that's ironic, much more ironic than your not seeing why people here oppose genetic change—"

Noren watched helplessly, puzzled by this lapse in Lianne's usual composure. It wasn't like her to give way to emotion; if she did not want him as a lover, she could simply refuse, as she'd refused Stefred and many other suitors. Yet . . . surely he hadn't been mistaken about her feeling toward him; her effort to suppress it had been too plain.

It must be, then, a matter of some past commitment. She might well have been married outside the City, but conviction of heresy meant automatic annulment; under the High Law her wedding vows were no longer binding. Still, she might feel that to break them would be a betrayal of the man from whom she'd been parted.

"Talyra wanted me to have children," he said gently. "If there's someone back in your village you'll never see again, wouldn't he feel the same? He wouldn't want you to remain childless just to be faithful to a memory. We both cherish our memories—and if we're both in the same situation, we won't risk hurting each other."

"Oh, Noren," Lianne whispered, "I never want to hurt you—"

"You won't. You don't have to promise me anything. You'll be better off if you don't; if there was some problem with the vaccine my tests didn't show, I won't be able to have more children after the first, and you've got to be free to have babies with someone else. I accept that."

The words seemed cold. Lianne didn't respond, and Noren moved to take her in his arms, realizing suddenly that she might fear that because he wasn't in love with her, he would offer her no tenderness. "I can't make promises either, I haven't the right," he went on. "But don't you know that while we're together, it'll be real for me? I mean, not like an experiment or anything—"

She wrenched away, almost on the verge of hysteria. "Tell me the truth," Noren pleaded. "Is it the experiment itself? You're not a geneticist like the woman in the dream, you didn't do the lab work personally. I won't be hurt if you believe I'm not competent to have done it safely—"

"No! No, it's not that, I trust your genetic work—you've got to test or there's no hope for this world's future!" Lianne burst out. She struggled to choke back sobs, then resolutely continued, "I can't let you think I don't have confidence in you. Too much depends on this. I'd have your child if I could help that way, only—only I *can't,* Noren. I—I can't bear you a child, I mean . . . that is, I wouldn't get pregnant."

He stared at her, overcome with appalled sympathy. This was the answer to many of her secrets; no wonder she'd declared she would never marry. "Are you sure?" he asked gravely.

Lianne nodded, still weeping.

But she couldn't be, Noren thought. In the villages women always got the blame for childlessness, but genetics had taught him that it could be the man's fault. Lianne wasn't the sort who'd have had enough experience to be sure.

Then too, some types of female infertility were curable. "More's known in the City than in the villages," he reminded her. "It may be that a doctor could help you."

"A doctor—oh, no!" Her eyes widened with genuine dismay. "That's out of the question, Noren."

How odd, he thought—Lianne wasn't easily embarrassed, and besides, she was a medical student. "Haven't you thought of consulting a doctor now that you're a Scholar?" he inquired.

"There's no need—I am already absolutely sure." Her composure restored, she was again speaking with the intensity of total conviction. "Please, let's forget it, shall we? I haven't told anyone else here —I shouldn't have told you, even, only I had to convince you to ask some other girl. You aren't in love with me, after all. It wouldn't have been fair to let you waste time hoping I could have your baby."

That was true, of course. Noren wondered why he was so disappointed.

She had told him to forget it, but he could not. He was distressed for Lianne's sake. *I never wanted a baby,* she had said once long ago—poor Lianne, she had convinced herself she did not even want what she could not have. It wasn't fair that someone so deserving of happiness should be deprived of one of the few joys not prohibited by life in the alien world. And perhaps it was unnecessary! If only she were willing to get a medical opinion . . . strange, how that suggestion had seemed to horrify her even more than the belief that she was infertile.

To be sure, doctors could not always help. There were, he knew, other techniques for conceiving babies mentioned only in the secret genetics file, techniques banned as "obscene" under the Six Worlds' rigid taboo against medically-assisted conception. In theory, it was possible to conceive a baby by laboratory methods and then implant it in its mother's womb; it had shocked Noren to learn this, but by now he had become objective. Yet for him it was not a valid scientific option. Even if people would tolerate the idea, even if he convinced some doctor to support his goal, the surgical and lab procedures were untried; there would be too many variables. If a child conceived by such means wasn't normal, there'd be no knowing whether the genes or the medical techniques were to blame. He was already taking enough risks without departing from the time-proven way of fathering children.

So he must choose someone else. Some woman who wouldn't be hurt—more than ever, after seeing Lianne's emotions, he was resolved upon that. Who, then—Veldry? She was the only one he could think of, and she was unattached at present; her last lover had moved out of her room some weeks back. Inner City rumors being what they were, he'd have heard if anybody else had moved in, as would everyone; and for that reason he could hardly move in himself. People knew him too well not to guess his motive; certainly Stefred did. But Veldry would realize that and would be discreet. She wasn't one to let anyone's secrets reach the Council.

Veldry had experienced the dream; he should at least get in touch with her to find out how she felt about it. Yet somehow he put off doing so. He could not get Lianne out of his mind.

What if Lianne was not infertile, what if it had been her husband's problem all along? Even analysis of her genotype would tell something . . . and he could test that himself! All he'd need would be a blood sample—which, of course, he could not get without upsetting her terribly again. It was tragic for her to be so sensitive, but village-reared women were like that; they felt worthless if they were barren. As if that would matter to a man who truly loved a woman! It mattered in this case only because of the real need for a child. To someone else, to Stefred, for instance. . . .

All of a sudden Noren guessed what kept on troubling him. Lianne evidently hadn't told Stefred; she'd said she had told no one but himself—yet it was probably why she'd refused Stefred's proposal. She had felt unworthy! And that was awful, for though a village man might consider her so, Stefred would not. Stefred did truly love her. Surely he, Noren, would be justified in clearing up the misunderstanding; he had not promised Lianne to keep what she'd said confidential, and in any case, Stefred wouldn't spread it any further.

"Look," he said, confronting Stefred in his study, "I know this is none of my business, but I can't stand by and see two people I care about kept apart when it may be needless. Has Lianne given you any idea why she won't marry you?"

"Not in words," Stefred replied painfully.

"You're not one to give up easily without understanding the reason," Noren observed, probing with the hope that Stefred might already suspect, that it might not be necessary to mention his own discussion with her.

"I know when it's best not to pry," Stefred said. "She has rejected all of her suitors. She—she seems to feel she couldn't make anyone happy, which is of course untrue; but it's something she believes, something from deep in her past, behind the mind barrier I found during her inquisition. I had no warrant to breach that barrier then. I've even less right now."

"Yet you feared she might get involved in a genetic experiment."

"It's natural, in our culture anyway, for a woman to want a baby. If Lianne could have one without facing whatever buried emotions keep her from believing she's desirable for her own sake—"

"Only she can't," declared Noren, aware that Stefred's happiness —and Lianne's—mattered more to him than the risk he was taking by revealing that genetic research still interested him. "Stefred, I—I talked to her about such experiments; I need to know people's views. I asked her how she'd feel personally. She didn't want to discourage me, she favors genetic change—so she was frank. She said she can't have babies at all."

Stefred's eyes lit. "That explains a lot."

"So I thought. She was emotionally upset, extremely so."

"By the Star," Stefred burst out, "I try to make allowances; I know village culture couldn't have been kept from reverting in all ways when it had to regress technologically. I see heretics abused, sometimes murdered, and I resign myself to it. Observing that kind

of intolerance is part of my job. But the other kinds, like sexism—"
With bitterness he continued, "Girls are treated like outcasts if
they're childless; I suppose Lianne's family was fanatic about it. Her
husband may have divorced her for sterility. No wonder she wouldn't
talk about her background."

"And the whole thing could be a mistake," Noren said unhappily.
"I told her she could be tested, but she refused to consider it. Which
is strange, when she's studying medicine herself."

"Not necessarily. She may know enough to realize the odds are
against her. It's a painful topic to stir up—if she weren't emotionally
scarred, it would have come out naturally when I did the initial
psychiatric exam." Sighing, Stefred said, "Now that I know, I can
convince her in time that I think no less of her for it. Yet as you
say, it could be a mistaken idea; it's too bad that she can't be
checked without raising her hopes."

"I could find out from a blood sample if she's genetically sterile,"
Noren told him. "And if she's not, either there's no problem or it's
one that might be surgically correctable."

"She may not consent even to a blood test," Stefred said, frowning.

"Need she? What possible violation of privacy would a simple
blood test be now that she's disclosed the only secret we could uncover by it?"

Thoughtfully, Stefred asked, "You can handle this test alone?"

"The computers do the analysis; it's routine. I've already studied
my own genotype a lot. I'd have gone ahead with hers, but I've no
way to get a blood sample without her knowledge."

"It would be easy enough for me to get it while she's under
hypnotic sedation," admitted Stefred. "Tonight, even."

"Is she still undergoing dreams in deep trance?" Noren asked,
surprised. "I thought only the First Scholar's recordings require
that."

"There are some specialized ones I'm using in her training—a
psychiatrist has to understand the dark side of human nature, and
in our circumstances here, dreams are the only means of learning.
They're rather nightmarish, but she wants to learn, and she can
handle it." Vehemently Stefred added, "Not one Scholar in a hun-
dred could handle the stress at the rate she's accepting it—yet she
feels deficient because she's never gotten pregnant! I can't endure
that, Noren—I can stand losing her to someone else if I must, but
not seeing her underrate herself."

"That bothers me, too," Noren admitted. "I think a lot of Lianne."

Late that night he got the sample of Lianne's blood from Stefred
and took it to the computer room. Carefully he put the test tube into
position and, at the adjacent console, ordered a general genetic
breakdown while framing in his mind the specific queries he would

enter. The entire genotype would be analyzed in short-term memory, but there would be time to get output only on portions directly relevant to his concerns. INPUT ACCEPTED—HUMAN MALE, he was accustomed to seeing as the signal to begin questioning; he expected, this time, to see HUMAN FEMALE.

The delay seemed unusually long. He turned to check the input equipment; it seemed to be functioning. Glancing back at the screen, he saw INPUT UNIDENTIFIED. PLEASE ENTER SPECIES SO THAT GENE MAP CAN BE OBTAINED FROM AUXILIARY FILES.

Noren frowned. There were only three animal species on this planet: humans, fowl and work-beasts—these, plus common plants and microorganisms, could be identified and dealt with by the file already obtained. Auxiliary files stored information only on extinct species of the Six Worlds. In any case the blood was human and should have been recognized as such. The computer system, programmed generations ago by the Founders, was infallible; if it were not, all science would have long since come to a standstill. But could the input device be out of order?

He had divided the blood sample into two tubes, having learned early in his work that tubes were all too easily dropped, especially when brought in concealed under his clothes. He had also learned that it was wise to carry a syringe and extra tubes when working with his own blood; from habit he had brought these with him. He put the contents of short-term memory into temporary storage, drew blood from an often-punctured vein, and proceeded to verify the input operation.

With his blood, it worked perfectly, just as it always had.

He cleared short-term memory again and started over with the second sample of Lianne's blood. INPUT UNIDENTIFIED, the screen announced. PLEASE ENTER SPECIES. . . .

HUMAN, Noren keyed impatiently.

THE INPUT GENOME IS NOT HUMAN, the program responded promptly.

This was ridiculous; he had watched Stefred take the sample from Lianne's arm. HOW MUCH DOES IT DIFFER? he asked, scowling in perplexity.

APPROXIMATE SIZE AND COMPLEXITY OF GENOME IS COMPARABLE, BUT BANDING PATTERN OF CHROMOSOMES IS DISSIMILAR. MORE EXTRA CHROMOSOMES ARE PRESENT THAN CAN BE ACCOUNTED FOR BY ANY KNOWN DISORDER.

HOW MUCH DIFFERENCE AT THE MOLECULAR LEVEL?

THAT CANNOT BE COMPUTED WITHOUT A GENE MAP FOR THE INPUT SPECIES. THERE IS NO INDICATION OF COMMON ANCESTRY; DIRECT MOLECULAR COMPARISON YIELDS NO GREATER SIMILARITY THAN WOULD RESULT FROM CHANCE.

Then somehow the data had been randomly garbled. CAN SEX BE

DETERMINED? Noren inquired, groping.

ON THE BASIS OF MATCHING CHROMOSOME PAIRS, SEX IS FEMALE.

What kind of garbling would leave the pairs intact? It just wasn't reasonable, even if one assumed that the computer program could garble input data, which it never had in any other field of science.

Noren, nonplused, recalled the original data from temporary storage and ran a comparison. The two samples were identical; whatever the problem, it wasn't sporadic. He asked specific questions about physical characteristics, most of which were answered with the comment INSUFFICIENT DATA—and this, had the sample really not been human, would be logical, since lacking a map for the species being analyzed, the program would be unable to locate the particular genes involved. There was just no characteristic he could pinpoint.

Or was there? He had used the blood sample only for genetic data, but short-term memory still contained other data about the blood itself. Personally, he knew little about blood proteins, but he realized that the program could analyze them in much the same way that it could analyze the genes that coded for them. And it could compare them against norms. Slowly he entered appropriate commands.

The blood was *nearly* human. There were, he was told, abnormalities, but none so great as to make the program insist it had come from some nonhuman species. Yet the genetic content of the same blood was undecipherable! It was as if the hundreds of thousands of genes that made up Lianne's genotype had been shuffled; not even those that coded for proteins found in the sample could be located on their chromosomes.

COULD THE INPUT BE FROM A MUTANT HUMAN? Noren asked doubtfully.

NO MUTATION OF SUCH MAGNITUDE COULD PRODUCE A VIABLE ORGANISM. THE EVOLUTION OF THIS GENOME WOULD REQUIRE MILLIONS OF YEARS.

Transfixed, Noren stared at the words while a stunning thought surged into his mind. On impulse he keyed, WHAT WOULD BE THE RESULT OF CROSSBREEDING BETWEEN THIS FEMALE AND A HUMAN MALE?

CROSSBREEDING WOULD BE IMPOSSIBLE, the screen declared. CONCEPTION COULD NOT OCCUR.

She had not said, "I can't bear a child," he remembered suddenly. She'd said, "I can't bear *you* a child."

And she had told him from the beginning that she was different.

This different? A different *species?* But there weren't any other human species, not here, not anywhere the Six Worlds' starships had traveled. The only proof alien civilizations existed was the sphere left on this planet by the Visitors who'd come and gone long before the arrival of his own people's first exploratory team.

The alien sphere . . . a communicator, Lianne had guessed—

she'd been sure it hadn't harmed Talyra's baby. Might she not have been guessing at all? Could Lianne herself be alien, an emissary of some off-world civilization brought here by the sphere's activation?

Incredible as that was, it would explain a lot.

She had been arrested in a village where no one knew her. There'd been a barrier in her mind Stefred could not get through; she'd admitted frankly that she was keeping secrets from him. The City had not awed her, and she had understood the dreams fully from the very first, suffered as if she'd grasped what destruction of populated worlds would be like.

She knew techniques Stefred hadn't taught her. She had incredible insight into things, and into people's feelings. . . .

But she'd been surprised by the crowing of a rooster. She found hot sunlight hard to bear and had spoken wistfully of trees as if she had seen real ones.

Over and over again she'd shown she did not think as village women did. And she knew something about the Unified Field Theory!

Noren's heartbeat quickened as the implications hit him. Lianne —not of his species, born into an alien civilization? But she'd come here on a starship, then! He wouldn't have thought the radiation from the sphere able to cross interstellar space, but there might have been emanations the computer system couldn't detect. There must have been. If the sphere was a communicator, it must be a faster-than-light communicator; he'd turned it on less than a year before her entry to the City, and there were no other solar systems less than a light-year away. The Six Worlds hadn't had such communicators. Only their ships had traveled faster than light; that was why no news of the nova had reached this world except through the Founders. But there might be a civilization with faster-than-light communication capability, a more advanced civilization. It might respond to unexpected signals.

Such a civilization would have metal . . . it could *help!*

Why Lianne alone and not a whole team of aliens? Why the secrecy? Why hadn't the help yet been offered, and why, when Lianne understood how he felt about isolation from the universe, had she not let him know that he would not be cut off forever?

There must be answers. He could not bear to wait till she revealed the truth in her own time. He was, Noren told himself, quite possibly hallucinating in any case; it was too fantastic, too good— literally too good—to be true. Yet everything fit! The more he thought, the more pieces he found that did fit. He would have to confront her with the evidence.

Methodically, suppressing excitement he feared would consume him, he set about transferring the evidence from computer memory onto tape.

(134

* * *

To sleep the rest of the night was impossible, though Noren knew he should get some sleep. Stefred had told him that when Lianne woke from the training dream, they would spend all morning discussing it, might even have their noon meal brought to Stefred's study; he'd been warned not to appear with the results of the blood test until later in the day. Now, he didn't want to take the results to Stefred in any case, not till he'd seen Lianne alone. The delay he must endure before seeing her stretched endlessly ahead.

He sat in his room, going over the taped evidence on his portable study viewer, and watched sand dribble slowly through his time-glass. Surely, he thought, more hours had gone by than it indicated —perhaps it had gotten stuck. Yet as always when tense, he craved solitude, so he could go nowhere to check the time; aside from the courtyard's stone sundials there were only a few clocks in the entire City. Time-glasses must serve to measure passage of hours in personal quarters, for small though the traces of metal in electronic or mechanical timepieces would be, the world did not have even small traces to spare. Or rather, it *had* not . . . now, all at once, there was going to be metal! Each random thought heightened the thrill of it; Noren clenched icy hands and willed the sand to run faster. He could not see people, make casual conversation, with a secret like this on his mind. He could not act as if nothing had happened, as if the world were not about to be transformed. . . .

It was as if the Mother Star itself had indeed sent supernatural aid. There was nothing supernatural about an alien communicator, of course. And yet the fact that he'd crashed at just the right place in the mountains, that Talyra had spotted the sphere and that he'd climbed the cliff to retrieve it simply as a gesture for her sake. . . .

Had she died to summon help for the world?

To be sure, the sphere's radiation evidently hadn't harmed her; and still, the mountain water might have caused teratogenic damage —if not, what had been accomplished by the deaths? He had thought he'd found an answer. Those deaths had led him to study genetics. But genetic change wouldn't be necessary now! Not if an alien civilization, a civilization with metal, had come.

Strange . . . Lianne had encouraged his genetic work. Why, when she'd known all along that it was needless? The acquisition of knowledge was never a waste, he supposed; since for some mysterious reason she must postpone the revelation of her identity, she'd undoubtedly thought genetics a more constructive occupation for him than futile worry about synthesizing metal that could be supplied in its natural form.

But why had she wanted him to risk having a child with altered genes? She'd given herself away over that, admitted a physical abnormality, when she could simply have said she didn't believe human experimentation was justified. Under the circumstances, it *wasn't!* Her urging him to go ahead didn't make sense, unless . . . could it be that there was no real risk involved? A person from an advanced civilization probably knew enough about genetics to gain access to the secret file. She must have studied not only its original content, but what he himself had stored in it; she must know his work was accurate and would be successful.

Was there anything Lianne's people didn't know?

All his life he'd sought knowledge. As a boy he'd been taught that the Scholars knew everything; he'd assumed, on becoming one of them, that he could learn. And he'd indeed learned, Noren thought ruefully—he had learned that too much was unknowable. Though he'd faced this limit when necessary, he had often repressed the thought of it, living day by day without stopping to envy peoples elsewhere in the universe who really did possess the knowledge his own civilization lacked. Could he have gone on that way for a lifetime?

No, he thought as he lay back on the bed, shaking with the release of feelings he'd kept below the surface. He could never have borne it. In time it would have destroyed him, just as living in the village, shut out of the City, would have destroyed him. How could anyone aware of the universe live with closed doors?

The doors of the universe shall once again be thrown open. . . .
Not till now could he fully acknowledge how much he cared. He had said it mattered only for future generations' sake; for one's own sake it was adolescent to care, or so he'd told himself. Growing up was learning not to let oneself long for the unattainable. At least it was called "growing up," but wasn't that merely an excuse for hiding from the pain of longing?

The open universe . . . he'd waited years, hopelessly; now he did not see how he could wait through another half-day.

At noon he went to the refectory on the chance she would appear, but she didn't, though he waited till no more food was being served. She might, he supposed, have eaten in the commons open to Technicians, though that wasn't her habit. Or she might be still with Stefred. What could she discuss with Stefred during all those hours of "training"—Lianne, who knew far more, probably, than Stefred himself? To be sure, her own culture's psychology might be very different from this one's. Perhaps that was why she'd chosen psychiatric training; perhaps her people felt they must understand his thoroughly before any open contact could be made. In any case, she'd been right when she'd remarked that Stefred would give anything to know her secrets. How stunned Stefred was going to be.

Noren looked for her in the computer room, where he now suspected she must spend most of her free time; there was no sign of her. He resisted the temptation to try Stefred's study, for if she was

(136

there he could say nothing, and if she wasn't, Stefred would ask about the blood test. Instead he tried the medical lab; he tried the gym and other recreation centers; finally, in desperation, he went to Lianne's own room, discourteous as it was to visit someone's quarters uninvited. He knocked, but there was no response.

All afternoon, as he combed the Inner City, his tension grew; by suppertime it had become intolerable. He returned to the refectory early, to be sure not to miss her, and ate less from hunger than for a reason to linger inconspicuously. When he was finished with his food, he got back into line and refilled his mug with ale. It took the edge off his nervousness. There was nothing else to do while waiting; more than ever he shrank from the idea of talking to anyone, particularly to Brek and Beris, who, fortunately, were on the far side of the room and had not noticed him. He took pains, after refilling his mug the second time, to sit in a corner where they would not.

When at last he gave up expecting Lianne to come, it was past time for Orison, which she rarely missed. That was the only place left to look. Entering the room late with the service already in progress, Noren stood in the back; he felt giddy, partly with extra ale but partly, too, because Orison still stirred him uncomfortably in a way he could not fathom. He wondered why Lianne, who hadn't been reared by people who believed in its symbols, found it meaningful.

His heart jumped; she was standing only a few rows ahead of him. Her face, raised reverently toward the symbolic sunburst, was more than solemn; he saw to his astonishment that there was worry in it, almost sadness. That made no sense at all. Lianne, above all others present, knew the Prophecy was to be fulfilled. He could understand if she were unmoved by the ritual phrasing. He could also understand joy, the joy believers felt, enlightened ones as well as the unenlightened—yet when he stopped to think about it, he could not recall ever having seen that kind of elation in Lianne. He had supposed she was simply too mature to start out with illusions, that she must sense what the experienced Scholars knew about the odds against survival. How could she not feel joy if survival was certain?

". . . *The Mother Star is our source and our destiny, the well-spring of our heritage; and the spirit of this Star shall abide forever in our hearts. . . . And so long as we believe in it, no force can destroy us, though the heavens themselves be consumed! Through the time of waiting we will follow the Law; but its mysteries will be made plain when the Star appears, and the sons of men will find their own wisdom and choose their own Law.*" No more waiting, Noren thought. No more mysteries. We will not have to find our own wisdom.

The ritual dragged to a close. Noren pushed his way forward to Lianne's side; at the sight of him, the shadow of sorrow in her eyes gave way to brightness. "There's something I want to show you," he said, keeping his voice as level as possible.

On the way to his room they said little, for he could think of no way to express it. How did one tell somebody that one had found out she'd come from another world? He couldn't possibly be mistaken, yet she seemed so—so normal. Her spirits were rising; it occurred to him she might have feared she'd lost his friendship by her refusal to have his child. He couldn't guess how she'd react to his discovery; would she look on it as a betrayal? With the confrontation at hand, Noren became aware that it mattered to him— how *she* felt mattered. He couldn't think of her as alien.

Wordlessly he handed her the study viewer, its tape already rewound and positioned. Lianne sat on the bed and began to read.

Gradually, she whitened; her pale skin turned nearly colorless. Though she was obviously stunned, she didn't seem angry and certainly was not bewildered; the data she was scanning surprised her only by being in his possession. She read through to the end without speaking, her very silence confirming his interpretation of her origin. Suddenly the silence terrified him. He'd hoped, underneath, that she would be glad she need no longer keep up the pretense; but the face she finally turned to him was a mask of pain and despair.

"How did you get the blood sample?" she asked in a low voice.

Noren told her. "We weren't trying to pry," he added. "We meant it for your good, Lianne, we never guessed we'd learn anything except whether you could be cured of barrenness."

"I know. The fault's not yours, it's mine; I said the wrong thing. I got—emotional. If I'd remembered how people in your world feel about sterility, I wouldn't have blundered. I'd have told you I drank too much impure water as a village girl; you'd never have questioned that." To his dismay he saw she was crying again, not hysterically this time but silently, as if she were facing some profound and private grief.

Puzzled, Noren sat down beside her, putting his arm around her trembling shoulders. "I know you must have some reason for not wanting to tell us yet," he said, "but is it really so terrible that we've found out?"

"We?" she inquired anxiously. "You haven't told Stefred, I was with him almost all day—"

"No. I wanted to talk to you first. I guess I felt I needed verification of anything so—tremendous. Lianne, you surely don't believe I think less of you for it, do you? That I think of you as inhuman or something? Why do you mind so much having me know?"

"Because it's you who will suffer for my mistake," she whispered.

"Suffer? Oh, no, Lianne! I suppose you mean you need to keep the secret awhile longer. If that's important I'll go along, and you're right that it'll be hard for me—but I'd still rather know than not know. Even just the knowledge that we're to be saved—" He broke off, perplexed. "Why did you say before that rescue's impossible, that I mustn't hope?"

Lianne met his eyes. "I told you how things are."

"I don't understand."

"There is a great deal you're not going to understand. And you will be hurt by that, as well as in other ways you can't imagine so far. I'd have done anything to prevent it, Noren, because I—I care about you. I wanted your love, I wished I could have your child—that's why I wasn't thinking clearly. I betrayed my responsibilities, and I betrayed you, too, without meaning to. Now it's too late; nothing can undo the damage."

"But Lianne, just because I know a little ahead of time—"

"You weren't ever meant to know."

"That you're alien? But why not?"

"You weren't ever to know aliens came." She drew away from him, pausing as if she needed time to collect herself; when she faced him again she was very calm, composed not just as she usually was, but in a way that made her seem indeed the daughter of a different world.

"We would have to know eventually," he pointed out, "I mean, when it comes to replenishing our world's metal—"

"Noren," Lianne interrupted, "I've got to set you straight, and it's best if I don't put it off. You want the truth, I think, even if it's not pleasant to hear."

"I've always wanted the truth."

"And today—all the hours you couldn't find me—you've been building your hopes on the idea that you're about to receive it, all of it, from my people. That we're here to give you metal, restore the Six Worlds' lost civilization and more." He had the odd feeling that she was drawing this directly from his mind, though she knew him well enough, he supposed, to have guessed that he personally expected more than the Prophecy's fulfillment, that it was her people's knowledge that excited him most.

"Those hopes won't be satisfied," Lianne continued steadily. "We are here to observe—that's all. Nothing in your world will change because of us. It's necessary for you to realize that from the beginning."

Horrified, Noren protested, "You're saying you'd stand by and observe evils you could put an end to? Lianne, I don't believe it!" And yet something in her look frightened him; it was almost as if her words were true.

"You must believe it. I don't expect you to comprehend it yet.

139)

In time, if you have courage enough, you'll begin to perceive what's involved. But meanwhile you must take my word—if you refuse, if you cling to the illusion that we will save your people, you'll lose your own chance to do it. And then nothing can save them."

"Your civilization wouldn't let us die."

"That's a complicated issue. There's more to it than survival—after all, your descendants could survive as subhuman mutants. You want more than life for them, Noren. You want them to regain their rightful heritage. It may be in your power to ensure that. It is not in mine."

"It *is*, it must be if you've got starships," he began; but then a new thought came to him. He had assumed Lianne represented her people—yet it was strange that she was here alone, that she'd been arrested and convicted of heresy, brought into the City without any means of communicating with the others. Could they possibly have abandoned her? Was she herself in fact powerless?

"What are they, your people?" he asked slowly. "Why did they come?"

"We are anthropologists. We have more knowledge than you can envision, Noren, but at the same time less; we visit young civilizations to learn. We aren't the ones who left the sphere on this world, but we did pick up its signals. They were—incongruous. We came to investigate. Not to interfere, only to watch."

"To watch us struggle against hopeless odds?" Noren exclaimed bitterly.

"If you want to put it bluntly, yes."

"You're—inhuman, then, after all, at least your people are."

"From your standpoint, now, perhaps so. There are sides to it you can't see."

"And are you on our side, Lianne," Noren demanded, "or on your cold-blooded observation team's?"

She hesitated. "I'm on both. I wish I could explain more, but I'm bound by a commitment; there's nothing I can do to help you."

Anger rose in Noren; he seized her by the shoulders, pulling her toward him. "Nothing you can do, or nothing you will?" he questioned. "You're not insensitive, Lianne. You've been playing a role all this time, yes, but you do care what happens to us. You couldn't have gotten past Stefred if our people's future didn't matter to you; no Scholar candidate can! And there've been other things you couldn't have faked."

"You're right," she confessed, "I couldn't fake how I felt about you, I couldn't even hide it; you knew when you spoke of the child that it wasn't just that I supported your experiments. Only I couldn't stand in the way of those experiments; they're too important! They're the one chance you have of saving your people, and if they succeed—"

(140

"If? Lianne, you must know the work I'm doing's going to succeed; you wouldn't let me risk harming a baby."

"There's risk in all scientific progress. You're aware of that."

"But you've got advanced knowledge of genetics, surely—"

"I'm an anthropologist, not a geneticist. I know what you're doing is feasible, but I'm in no position to judge the details."

"Not personally, perhaps, but your people . . . I can't keep working by trial and error, knowing there are people around who've already passed this stage!"

"That's one reason you weren't supposed to know," Lianne admitted miserably. "It's going to make what you have to do much harder."

"I can't take risks that are unnecessary; there's got to be another way."

"There is no other way! What can I do to convince you?" She drew a resolute breath, then continued with deliberate coldness, "My civilization's further above the Six Worlds than you can conceive, and we don't share our knowledge with primitives."

Before Noren could reply, she dropped her head; the next thing he knew she was leaning against him. He was dazed—with the ale he'd drunk, with ups and downs of emotion, with the conviction that Lianne could not be as coldhearted as she seemed; instinctively he embraced her. She was warm, not cold at all. . . .

"You're so alone," she murmured. "I can't spare you what you'll suffer from knowing about us. But I might—comfort you sometimes, offer the only thing I'm free to offer—" Though she said no more, abruptly her thought blazed clear in his mind, and outraged, he thrust her away.

"Sex?" he burst out in fury. "Am I on no higher level than that in your view—a primitive who'd be satisfied with sex when you could give me the *stars?*"

Lianne sprawled motionless on the bed where she had fallen, her face set with anguish and resignation. She did not answer.

"I don't need anything from you," Noren said. "Or from your people, either. If they're hoping to observe a so-called primitive civilization's reaction to foreknowledge of certain doom, they'll be disappointed—because we're not going under. I'm going to have children, and I'm going to see to it that others do, too, children who can live on this world without the metal you see fit to deny us."

For a moment a light flared in Lianne's eyes; then, as he went on speaking, their brilliant blue darkened. "That's not all," Noren told her. "We respect each other here, and we respect privacy—but since you don't rank us on your level, you've forfeited all right to be treated as human by our standards. Stefred could have had all your secrets during your inquisition if he'd chosen to take them without consent; he will take them now. Whatever knowledge we can get from your mind, we'll get; and it may be you know the key to metal synthesization after all. You know more about the Unified Field Theory than you admitted—"

"You aren't going to tell Stefred or anyone else who I am, Noren," Lianne declared with clear assurance. "Not ever."

"What's to stop me? I've got proof you can't deny."

"No one will believe the tape; it will only discredit your genetic work."

"They'll believe the computers if the blood test is repeated by experts."

"There will be no opportunity to repeat it. If you tell, I will kill myself, as I would have if Stefred had pursued the inquisition too far in the first place—there's no way he can forestall that. Did you think I came unprepared?"

Noren stared at her in astonishment, sensing beyond doubt that this was no empty threat; she meant it. "Why?" he asked, baffled. "Why is secrecy worth giving your life for?"

"Think about it sometime," she replied quietly. "You won't like the answer, but you're capable of figuring it out, part of it, anyway."

He was too aroused by rage and frustration to think anything out at the moment. He wanted no more of Lianne, not now, not ever except as an information source—yet she remained unmoving, showing no sign that she intended to leave his room. Turning his back on her, Noren strode out the door, realizing only dimly that he'd been left no choice, that he was on his way to find Veldry.

VII

NOREN AWOKE IN A BED NOT HIS OWN, UNSURE OF WHETHER OR not it was morning. In the windowless rooms of the towers one couldn't tell, and his inner time sense seemed hazy. The lamp was on; he could see the tall time-glass in the corner. Its sand had run all the way through—but would Veldry have turned it over as people usually did on retiring? Under the circumstances, that seemed unlikely.

He found to his dismay that he had little recollection of what he and Veldry had said to each other. He'd intended only to ask her . . . somehow it had gone further than that. He ought, he supposed, to be glad. Instead he felt as if something very special had been devalued.

Veldry sat at the foot of the bed, her back to him, brushing her hair. It was long and dark, like Talyra's. He had, he remembered, imagined he was with Talyra, much as he had during the secret dream; Veldry's own identity had been vague, like that of the woman the First Scholar had loved. Only this had not been a dream. He hadn't been wholly himself—he'd been so hot with anger that he'd not thought beyond his vow that he *would* bring about his people's survival—yet he could not say he had not known what he was doing. He'd had too much ale earlier in the evening, perhaps; he'd raged at Lianne's refusal to bring help to the world, and yes, she had roused other feelings too; all those things might explain his impulsiveness. But they did not make what had happened any less real.

He sat up, reaching for his clothes. "Veldry—" he began, wondering what he could possibly say. He had assumed she wouldn't get hurt. He'd supposed making love was something she took lightly. It hadn't been that way; her welcome had been genuine, and her emotions as he'd explained the risk had been deep, though unreadable. That much he did recall.

She turned to him. Her face, of course, was not Talyra's. It was older, and lined with past sadness, though now it was alight with joy. It was also, by ordinary standards, more beautiful; Veldry was considered strikingly lovely. But there was more to her than that, Noren realized, trying to guess her thoughts. He sensed more intellect than rumor credited her with. If only he were better at understanding people. . . .

"Veldry," he said stiffly. "I—used you. I'm sorry."

"Don't worry," she answered, "I've never let anyone use me. One thing I always do is make up my own mind." Then, watching his eyes, she suddenly exclaimed, "Noren, you don't believe me! You really think you came here last night and got me to give something you're sorry you asked for, when it wasn't that way at all. You were the one who gave! You've given me the only chance I've ever had to *be* somebody."

"I don't see what you mean."

"I'm—beautiful," she said slowly, not in a boastful way, but as it it were some sort of burden. "I'm acclaimed for my beauty, and that's as far as anyone's looked. When I was a girl, they called me wild; I guess I was, by their scale of values. I had a lover in the village before I was married; and there, that was a disgrace. But I really loved him. Then I found out that all he saw in me was—physical. That was all my husband saw, too. After a while I left him and started telling people what I thought about the world, only no one listened." With a bitter laugh she added, "They didn't even listen to heresy! If a girl's pretty enough, it's assumed she hasn't any thoughts, let alone heretical ones. Do you know what I was finally arrested for? Blasphemy—the blasphemy of claiming to have made love with a Technician."

"Why did you tell a lie like that?" Noren asked, appalled. It could not possibly have been a true claim; Technicians were forbidden by the High Law to take advantage of village women, who, assuming them to be superior beings, would obey any request without question.

"Didn't you ever want to convince people Technicians were human, and that you were their equal?"

Yes, of course he had. All village heretics defied the caste concept; Veldry's form of rebellion had been imaginative if not prudent.

"Maybe I wanted to see the inside of the City," she went on, "or maybe I just wanted to die trying to be more than the object of men's desire. I knew the Scholars were wise; I thought they'd see what I was, even though they'd kill me for it."

"But Stefred did see, surely. He judged you qualified for Scholar rank."

"Yes. At first I was overwhelmed, it was so inspiring—the dreams, I mean. I wouldn't have accepted rank as payment for recanting; I've never sold myself any way. But the Prophecy . . . well, I was never a heretic about that; I liked the ritual even as a little girl. I liked the thought of a changing future. I was so dedicated in the beginning, Noren. Only . . . there hasn't been anything I could do here, to help change things, I mean. I'm not a scientist, my mind isn't that sort. I know officially the work I do rates just as much respect. But—but men still single me out for my starcursed *beauty!*" She reached out for his hand, clutched it. "You're the first one who's wanted anything more important."

"You've had babies before. That's important."

"Yes, of course, but the men who fathered them weren't thinking about future generations, they just—well, you know. I don't mean they didn't love me, I've never had a lover who didn't claim he was in love . . . only there was never anything lasting."

"Veldry," Noren said painfully, "I'm not sure what I said about us, and that bothers me, because what's between us can't last, either."

"It will! Not you and me, no, of course I know that. Do you think I wouldn't have known even if you'd tried to pretend?" She stood up, began fastening the front of her tunic. "You'd never been with anyone but Talyra before, had you?"

He didn't reply. "I knew that, too," Veldry went on. "You were still with Talyra last night, in your mind, anyway."

"I suppose I was. And it wasn't fair to you," he confessed in misery. "You're *you,* and I didn't respect you enough. It wasn't right."

"How can you say you didn't respect me? You told me future generations will live because of us! That our child will be the first person truly adapted to this world, that from him and others like him will come a race that can survive after the machines break down, and maybe someday, somehow, will get back to the stars. No one ever talks to me about things like that. You did. You asked my opinion of what the woman did in the dream. And when I said I've always wanted to be the kind of person she was, do something really significant and daring, I meant it."

"Even knowing how it turned out for her?"

"Even so—because someone's got to try, somebody's got to take the risks. I admire you for taking them, even going against the Council to take them. You paid me the biggest compliment anyone ever has by guessing I'd be willing to take them, too. That's what matters, not the fact you can't fall in love with me."

"I wish I could, Veldry," Noren told her. "But I'm not ever going to fall in love again."

"Yes, you are," she said gently. "In time, you are. I'm not the right person for you, but in time there'll be someone—not to replace Talyra, no one ever could—but someone different, someone you'll share a whole new life with. And she will be a very fortunate girl."

"I hope you'll find someone to share with, too."

"Maybe it'll happen. I try—every time, I believe it will, only there just aren't many men who look at things the way I do. I—I'll always be happy to know there's one, and that I'm having his child."

"We can't really be sure yet," Noren pointed out, "much as I'd like to promise I'll be back—"

"You won't be back," Veldry acknowledged. "What happened last night couldn't happen twice, not between you and me. But I wouldn't have asked you to stay if the timing had been wrong; I wouldn't have presumed to take Talyra's place without expecting to conceive. You mustn't worry yet—I'm pretty sure there's going to be a baby."

Back in his own room, alone, Noren began facing the fact that there was nothing further he could do until the baby was born. Nothing . . . and he did not see how he could live with his own thoughts, let alone carry on normal relationships with people, considering the magnitude of the secrets he now bore.

He did have to keep Lianne's secret. He was absolutely convinced, as if she'd somehow communicated it directly to his inner mind, that Lianne would in fact kill herself if he told anyone about her. To be sure, he might tell Stefred in confidence—but no, Lianne would sense that Stefred knew. She was too intuitive not to. And if she carried out her threat, Stefred would suffer terribly.

Think about it sometime, Lianne had said when he'd asked why secrecy was worth her life. She'd said it was one mystery he might solve. He'd never approved of secrets. And Scholars weren't supposed to like keeping them; they condoned the guardianship of knowledge only as a necessary evil. How could Lianne have gotten through the tests of candidacy if she accepted an equivalent form of secrecy as right?

For that matter, how had she gotten through them at all?

Stefred had not invaded her privacy. But he must certainly have tested her in all relevant ways, and quite a few issues were relevant. If she did not truly care about the survival of future generations, she would have been disqualified. If she considered herself superior to people, even subconsciously, she'd have been screened out, too; that was one thing for which prospective Scholars were probed very thoroughly. Anyway, it just wasn't possible to believe Lianne's view was as heartless as she'd claimed. He, Noren, had long known how she felt toward him, and the kind of love she'd been hiding could not exist in someone whose inner feelings were inhuman.

The other kind, the outward physical expression . . . Lianne had not offered that before; she'd understood too well about Talyra. How could she have been so inconsistent in the end? It wasn't just that she wanted his love; she'd had her chance, she could have lived with him for weeks without confessing there'd be no child. What

(146

he'd discovered shouldn't have altered anything, for she knew better than to think he'd accept that sort of "comfort" from her. The pieces didn't fit. She'd risked a secret she'd give her life to keep by refusing him, then at the last minute, had insulted him by suggesting. . . .

Oh, Noren thought suddenly, oh, what a fool he'd been! Both times, she had been thinking of the child she couldn't give him. When his discovery had made him balk at the risk of the experiment, she'd insulted him purposely to drive him in anger to Veldry.

She'd taken terrible chances. In his rage he might have gone straight to Stefred if it hadn't been that she was his only link to more information about the aliens. Why must she keep their presence secret? For the same reason the Founders' secrets had been kept—people in general simply could not live with the frustration of knowing themselves to be cut off from the wider universe. Noren was not sure he would be able to live with it, even temporarily. Yet he wasn't sorry for his discovery, not when he'd felt deeply since childhood that it was always preferable to know the truth. Few others felt that way; he and Lianne had agreed on that, the day they'd talked about the alien sphere. *He* had told *her* that most Scholars refused to acknowledge its implications! No wonder she'd realized he could figure out the need for secrecy.

To hide knowledge was evil, yes. But necessary in this case, too, if his genetic work was the only hope. Yet how could it be, when there was an alien starship standing by? Lianne was on his side, but on her own people's, too. She had not said she was in conflict with them; she was their agent, their observer. How could they justify letting the caste system stand another two generations when they could end it by supplying metal? Lianne considered it evil, she couldn't have qualified for Scholar status otherwise, still she wasn't condemning her people's inaction. Besides, after the genetic change was put into effect, the world would lose its metal-based technology, lose the Six Worlds' heritage of knowledge—surely she could not let that happen. And if the aliens must intervene eventually, why not now?

In time, if you have courage enough, you'll begin to perceive what's involved, she'd said. In his anger Noren hadn't stopped to ponder that. He'd indeed been a fool, he now realized; he had expected understanding their ways to be *easy!* He had been picturing a starship like the Six Worlds' ships, "advanced" in the sense of having faster-than-light communicators and knowledge of the Unified Field Theory, but not the vessel of a truly alien culture. He'd imagined no disquieting mysteries—yet at the same time he'd anticipated being immediately given all the answers to the secrets of the universe. Enlightenment didn't work like that, not even for heretics who entered the City as Scholar candidates; one could hardly expect education by aliens to be less difficult than learning about the heritage of the Six Worlds. How blind he'd been not to see the comparison.

Stefred, too, had warned him that he would suffer, that there would be a price for knowledge. No doubt this was also the case with alien knowledge. Noren's spirits lifted. He must face an ordeal, perhaps, but it would be the sort of challenge he'd long ago found he enjoyed.

He must not judge Lianne's people prematurely, he thought as he put on fresh clothes. After all, he'd judged the Scholars throughout boyhood on the basis of false premises and had learned that motives couldn't be guessed from the outside. He would not make that mistake again. Sulking in his room would get him nowhere; he must prove himself worthy to be enlightened. He must proceed with the research they considered essential. Though he couldn't do any more with human genetics till his child's birth, it would be possible to design the genetic changes needed to enable grain to grow in untreated soil. Low priority as that was, it would be constructive. Even if metal became available in time, ability to live off the land would be desirable. Of course! The genetic change would be needed in any case for his human race to be self-sufficient; knowing that, the aliens would see how far he could go without aid. In the meantime, they'd be evaluating his readiness to receive what would ultimately be offered. No harm would come of that. Heartened, Noren went to the refectory for a meal.

Later that day he saw Stefred. "I ran the blood test," he told him impassively. "It showed Lianne's right; genetically there's no chance of her getting pregnant."

"I'm sorry, of course, for her sake," Stefred said, "but someday I'll make her see that she's worth as much as any other woman."

"That shouldn't be too big of a problem," Noren agreed. He did not say, however, that he hoped she and Stefred would become lovers; he discovered to his surprise that this was no longer quite true.

Noren tried, honestly, to work; he sat at a computer console long past suppertime reading technical genetic data about grain. But he could not keep his mind from wandering.

He'd resolved to question Lianne no further till he had proven he could conquer impatience. So that evening after Orison it was she who came seeking him; he glanced up from the console and saw her standing there, looking so stricken that he was overcome by remorse. It hadn't occurred to him that she might need reassurance.

"Lianne, you didn't think I'd stay angry, did you?" he asked.

"I wasn't sure," she replied in a low voice. "I was afraid you'd hate me, but I see you already understand what I was doing—"

(148

How could she? Noren wondered. Intuition couldn't possibly be that specific—and for some reason he guessed she knew about Veldry, too, although he was positive that Veldry would have told no one. Perhaps this was his own wishful thinking; he found he was relieved at the idea of not having to tell Lianne.

"Anyway, that's not why I came," she was saying. "There are things I've got to tell you."

They went upstairs and out into the starlit courtyard. Seeing the sky, Noren felt more awe of it than he'd experienced since his trip into space to retrieve the orbiting starship hull used at the outpost. That memory wasn't pleasant. But now his awe was elevating, not terrifying. Now he need not worry about the meaning of that vast universe; he was with someone who *knew*. Perhaps someday he might be allowed to board her people's ship. . . .

"How many of those stars have you been to?" he whispered, wonder-stricken.

"Orbited? I don't know, I've never kept count. This is the tenth planet I've landed on."

"Counting the one where you were born?"

"I wasn't born on a planet. Only relatively immature human species live that way. We live in orbiting cities, most of us, and keep our home planets as parks."

"Why were the Six Worlds so crowded after the civilization matured, then?" Noren asked. "They had orbiting labs, but not cities in orbit."

"Noren," Lianne said levelly, "the Six Worlds' civilization wasn't mature, that is, your species wasn't—isn't. Inventing space travel's near the *beginning* of the evolutionary timescale." Before he could say anything she went on, "The Six Worlds were unusual in not having orbiting cities at the stage they had reached, though. It was because the solar system had so many planets similar to the mother world. In most systems, colonizing in orbit is more practical than settling neighboring planets."

He turned to her, eager to hear more; but the sight of her eyes cut short his questions. It was as if she'd been crushed by personal tragedy; evidently something far more important than his curiosity was at issue. "Lianne, what's the matter?" he asked. "What's happened?"

"You don't know what it means, my having given myself away," she murmured. "I'm not blaming you for what you did, only—"

"Only what?" Suddenly it occurred to him that her own people might be angered. "They won't punish you, will they?" he demanded, appalled.

"No. All the same, there will be consequences."

"That's what I used to tell Talyra," he recalled sadly, "before I assumed priesthood, when she could see I was unhappy and thought the Scholars must be punishing me for my heresy. Finally she realized the consequences just followed of themselves."

"Yes," Lianne agreed. "But your heresy wasn't a mistake, you had no load on your conscience. The consequences were simply problems you yourself had to face. The position I'm in is more like when you crashed the aircar, except worse. Possibly much worse. I may have upset the future evolution of your species, you see."

"I don't, quite. I guess I see that if I'd refused to keep working on genetics because I don't understand the need, that might be your fault. But I'm not going to refuse. Even without understanding, I'm going to play the game."

"It's more than a game. And it'll be harder for you, knowing about us, than it would have been otherwise. If—if that affects the course of your life, Noren, I'll be responsible."

"Don't worry on my account," Noren told her. "I'll take full responsibility for my own fate, Lianne. And if it does turn out worse than I imagine, I still won't be sorry, any more than I was sorry for becoming a heretic and learning the truth about the nova."

"I realize that," she said soberly. "One part of me grieves because you're going to suffer, yet another part knows you'll think it's worth it. That's not the thing that scares me."

"Then what is?"

"I told you I'm bound by a commitment," Lianne said. "It's— well, formal, like commitment to the priesthood is for you, except it's not just sharing accountability, it's personal. When we're alone or in small teams on primitive worlds, our actions can change those worlds' histories unless we're awfully careful. We swear to put the native people's best interests above everything else, and their best interests normally demand that we not influence them at all. We swear specifically, for instance, to die rather than let them find out about our existence. I'd have killed myself to prevent your knowing, Noren, just as I still would to prevent the secret from going any further—not because you'll suffer from knowing, but because of what it may do to your people's future."

"Our future isn't very bright," Noren observed grimly, "unless you do help us. You could hardly make it worse."

"Yes, I could. I may have already, unwittingly. There are scenarios you don't know about."

"I think it's my right to know, Lianne."

"No, it isn't," she said with sorrow, "but of course you aren't going to take my word for that. Besides . . . in this particular case I think you do have to know. You already know more than you should; you've got to be told enough to give you a basis for the decisions you'll be forced to make. I—I lay awake all last night deciding to be frank with you, even though that means breaking my oath not to disclose anything."

"I don't expect you to give me more knowledge than I've earned," Noren protested. "I've thought a lot, too, and I've figured out a good deal. You'd have refused to support your people's policies if they conflicted with your values, just as a heretic rebels against what's wrong with our system here; you've got the instincts of a heretic in spite of having only pretended to be one during your inquisition. And that means—"

"Wait a minute! What makes you think I was pretending? I was masquerading as a village woman, of course, but everything else was *real*."

"The qualities Stefred judged you on, yes; that's what I'm saying. But the defiance of the High Law, the risks and the enlightenment and the initiation, that couldn't have been real in the same way as for the rest of us; you knew our secrets from the start. That would bother most priests, I guess. It bothered me at first, till I realized that because you weren't gaining anything personally it couldn't have affected Stefred's evaluation of your motives."

"The risk was real enough," Lianne said. "After all, I thought I might have to kill myself. I would have, if he'd probed too deeply."

"Maybe so," Noren conceded. "I—I believe you really would give your life to save us from something you're convinced would harm us. But a convicted heretic expects to die without hope of saving anyone; it's a matter of principle, of standing out against evil. You knew at the beginning the evil was necessary."

"No, I didn't."

"You must have known our life support equipment's irreplaceable."

"I didn't; none of us did when we landed here. We only knew something strange was going on. And what we saw, we didn't like. We thought what you thought when you were a boy, that the Scholars were dictators. There was just one thing that didn't fit: we couldn't understand why the villagers had so much freedom."

"Freedom? Freedom to live in the Stone Age, shut out of the City?"

"Noren," Lianne said gently, "in every similar culture that we've observed, the outsiders would have been slaves of the City—or else equipment wouldn't have been expended on them. We couldn't guess why they were permitted to live, dependent on City aid, yet free to govern themselves, not exploited, not even taxed. It was the strangest setup we'd ever encountered."

"But still a bad one."

"Of course. Not as bad as it could have been, but bad; I was a real heretic in the sense that I believed that. I also believed the

Prophecy was a myth the Scholars had invented to maintain power."

"Didn't the references to the Mother Star make it clear? You knew we were colonists, and you surely knew what a nova is."

"Yes," she agreed. "Only I didn't know the entire Prophecy. Nobody sat down and recited the whole thing; after all, everyone in the village assumed it was common knowledge. We'd heard just scattered passages—and we didn't hear the High Law at all till I got caught breaking it."

Noren stared at her, startled. "You didn't plan your arrest?"

She shook her head. "I filled a drinking jug from a stream right before the eyes of a group of women gathering reeds to weave baskets. It never occurred to me it could be wrong. We're trained to respect local taboos, but drinking the water isn't taboo anywhere, unless it's radioactive or something. We'd only been on the surface a couple of days; we hadn't had a chance to observe the restrictions on food and drink." With a rueful smile she added, "The village women surrounded me, taunted me about what would happen when the Scholars got hold of me. Scared? Noren, the night I spent in the village jail was the worst I'd ever been through, till then, anyway."

"Couldn't your people have helped you escape?"

"Yes, but I chose to see it through. We realized we'd have to get someone into the City sooner or later to learn the facts about this world."

"The villagers must have told you that no one's ever been released from the Inner City," reflected Noren, puzzled. "You couldn't have known then that you'll be free to simply walk out when your job's finished, not if you didn't suspect the truth about the Scholars. So you were risking possible death and almost certain imprisonment—for *information?* Information that not only wouldn't benefit your own people, but that you probably couldn't ever pass on to them?"

"It's a bit more complicated than that," she admitted slowly.

"I'm sure it is," Noren said. "What you've just told me makes me surer of it than ever. We don't rate your help automatically—all right, I won't argue with that. We have to prove ourselves, pass some kind of test. And maybe for me, because I've found out too soon, the testing will be harder than it was meant to be. I'll—cooperate, Lianne. I don't want you to bypass anything for my sake. Whatever I have to go through to earn us a place in your interstellar society, I'm willing to take on."

She sighed. "You have no idea of what you're saying. And I'm tempted to let it pass; you've phrased it so that I could do that without lying."

"If my statement of it is true, we can let it pass for now," Noren declared resolutely. "You came to judge us. I don't fear your judgment."

"Did you fear Stefred's?"

"When I was first brought into the City, you mean? That was different; I had misconceptions about what I'd be judged on."

"So do you now," Lianne said. "That's why I have to warn you."

"What I said *is* true, isn't it?"

"In a sense. It's true as far as it goes, just as the Prophecy's words are true. I'm here to evaluate circumstances, and they're such that you, personally, will have to take on a great deal. Ultimately, if you succeed, your people will attain their rightful place. But it will not happen as you envision, any more than cities will rise out of the ground on the day the Star appears."

"I'm not naive," Noren assured her. "I know I can't imagine exactly what will happen. Later, when I've done whatever's expected of me—"

"That will be the bad time for you, Noren," Lianne said, squeezing his hand. "As if the City had shut you out for your heresy instead of in. It might be kinder of me not to tell you this, but cruel, I think, in the long run; I can't let you build false hopes."

"You've acknowledged we can earn a place among you."

"Yes, in time—your species can—but . . . it's a *long* time . . . long after the Star's light has reached this world."

"Not—in my lifetime?" Noren went cold, beginning to see where she was leading. "Lianne, I can't accept that!"

"Perhaps not. It's asking far too much of you; I never wanted you to bear so great a burden." She was once more close to tears, though her voice was well-controlled. And again, he could sense more than she'd said, as if he had become as intuitive as she. Very, very quietly her words continued. . . .

Noren blinked his eyes, finding himself giddy; his mind was reeling. This wasn't just his own emotion, or even his perception of hers—there were concepts he could not integrate with the words Lianne was saying . . . or was she still speaking at all? Abruptly he became aware of silence. Had she said he must accept the burden for his people's sake, that nothing but his voluntary acquiescence could save them? He did not recall any such words, yet it was not an idea that would have occurred to him; it didn't make sense that acceptance of it could help matters. *Lianne,* he thought despairingly, *you don't know! You can't, no one who's been to ten planets could know what it is to be confined forever to this one.* . . .

Lianne's hand tightened on his. "Let's sit down," she whispered.

The paving stones of the courtyard were still warm from the day's heat. Noren leaned back, gazing up at the stars. *It's not wrong to want the whole universe!* he persisted. *It's not wrong to keep searching for the truth, no more so to demand it of your people than it was to demand it of the Scholars when I was a heretic. I'm willing to earn access to knowledge, but not to renounce it.*

Lianne pressed close to him, not in a sensual way but in a gesture of complete and genuine sympathy. In her eyes was understanding as well as sadness. Somehow she did know. Could this be part of the test? Noren wondered. Was he expected to defy her people's edict, as Scholar candidates were required to defy the teaching that it was wrong to aspire to the High Priests' secrets? *Yes,* he thought dizzily, *she admires strength of will; she no more wants passive acceptance than Stefred wants heretics to recant!*

He faced her. "Look at me," he said, "and tell me that there is no way for me to win your people's aid during my lifetime."

"I won't lie to you—even if I were willing, you'd realize in due course and stop trusting me." *Full trust between us is the only chance we have of getting through what's ahead,* he found himself thinking, though somehow the thought seemed more hers than his own. "There is one way," Lianne continued. "But don't found your hope on that; it's one I don't believe you'll ever use."

"By the Mother Star, I will!" Noren swore.

"Hardly in that name, if you hold it sacred." She tried to smile. "I'm speaking in riddles, as Stefred does to candidates, because I shouldn't be speaking of this at all. And you're not ready; there's a lot you need to know before you can begin to grasp the situation we're in."

Noren was silent. *I won't plead with you,* he was thinking, *but if you're going to tell me some of it, what's wrong with right now?*

"Are you up to that tonight?"

"Yes, of course," he declared, his head spinning so that he scarcely noticed that she had answered his unspoken thought.

"I mean physically—or doesn't the disorientation bother you?"

"Does it show?" Noren burst out, mortified. The odd giddiness did seem to have become physical, and his mind wasn't quite clear; looking back over the conversation he found it hard to recall all Lianne's words. *Am I going crazy?* he thought in sudden panic. *It's not as if I haven't been through plenty of upheaval in the past; I should be able to handle it by this time. . . .*

"This is something you're not equipped to handle," Lianne said. "It doesn't show from the outside, but I get your sensations."

With forced levity he said, "Sometimes I think you're a witch after all and can read people's minds."

"I admitted long ago the villagers would have accused me of witchcraft if they'd known more about me," Lianne replied, not laughing.

Why laugh? an inner voice told him. *Mind-to-mind communication's natural enough*—Horrified, he cut off the thought. He must

(154

indeed be going crazy. Mind reading was only a superstition; he had heard of it in Six Worlds' folklore, but never from any other source. Desperately, his thinking now under firm control, he reflected, *If it were real, Stefred would have mentioned it, surely.*

"Stefred would be even more upset by it than you are," Lianne said dryly, "because he's read everything in the computers about psychology, and he believes the same theories of the human mind the Founders did."

Lianne, what are you doing to me? Noren cried out silently, aware at last that this was not mere imagination, and that it terrified him.

"Nothing I haven't done before with both you and Stefred when I had need," she answered calmly. "I'm simply doing it now on a level at which you're conscious of it. You must know about it to understand my role here, and you wouldn't have believed in it without a demonstration."

"You've been reading our minds all along?" he protested, appalled. "This is what we've been calling intuition?"

"Well, yes, but 'reading minds' isn't an accurate way to describe it. I can't invade anyone's private thoughts—I get only emotions, plus ideas people want to communicate to me. If you want to tell me something, consciously or unconsciously, I know without being told; but nothing you want to conceal is accessible."

"I guess I shouldn't be surprised that you have abilities we don't," Noren said slowly. "You're a different species, after all. But . . . your getting my thoughts wasn't all that happened. I—I think I got some of your thoughts, too."

"Yes. That was the frightening part; I induced you to knowingly accept mental input in a form that's unfamiliar to you and beyond your control. I knew it would scare you, but I had to seize the opportunity that came to do it in a way that wasn't dangerous."

"Opportunity?"

"Strong emotion. That enhances everyone's psychic power; for a person in a culture like yours where the existence of telepathy isn't acknowledged, it's essential, barring some artificial techniques I'd rather not try."

Noren frowned. "Are you saying all human species have this power?"

"This and some rather more spectacular ones I'm not even going to demonstrate. They are latent in all humans; full conscious control of them is possible only to species further evolved than yours, though people with exceptional talent sometimes have spontaneous psychic experiences when the circumstances are just right." She added, after a pause, "A few individuals, like Stefred, use telepathy unconsciously with their close associates."

"Stefred? He does what you do?"

"Not to the same degree, and he's not aware that he's doing it.

You know, though, that he's unusually skilled in understanding people and in winning their trust." She did laugh at Noren's expression. "You needn't be so shocked; there's nothing sinister about it. It's a gift like any other, and you've recognized all along that you don't have the same gifts Stefred has. Yours are different."

"I can't learn to develop such skills, then." The thought pained him.

"No," Lianne said gently. "I could teach you to converse with me silently without feeling dizzy, but there are perils along that road. What comes naturally is harmless. Tonight I forced a level of rapport that was . . . well, let's say a calculated risk. I won't do that again because there's no justification for it; I'll stick to the sort of thing I've done with you in the past—for instance, last night when I convinced you I was serious about killing myself if you didn't keep my secret."

"I wondered why I believed you," Noren reflected.

"It was because I communicated more than words or the idea the words expressed, I also communicated feelings. That level's safe; it's when telepathy is allowed to disrupt your thinking processes that we could run into trouble."

"With your own people . . . you use even higher levels?"

"I have passed on all I've learned of the Six Worlds to the members of my team outside the City," Lianne admitted. "That's one reason you need to know I'm telepathic."

Trying to seem unshaken, he asked, "Have you told them about me?"

"Not that you've learned my identity—they're no longer within range. I've told them other things about you."

"What?" inquired Noren, curious as to why she would have singled him out to be mentioned in what sounded like her official report.

"That the welfare of your species depends solely on you."

He drew back, stunned. Lianne continued, "You've been assuming that only your knowledge of us has put you in a key position. But the position's been yours all along, Noren. The Scholars who've been considering you the best hope for the future are right."

"Lianne, it can't be like that! The fate of a whole human race can't depend on one person—it couldn't even if no alien starship was around."

"Normally it couldn't," she agreed. "We've had occasion before to judge a species' chance of survival, and we've never been able to identify the person on whom it depended, or even say it was dependent on some unknown person. But this is a very abnormal case. There are so few of you, and you have such limited resources, that we know positively that no one else has the potential to do what needs doing—and there isn't time to wait for another such person to be born."

"But I'm not what people think," Noren protested. "I'm not the genius they've been hoping for; if you're telepathic you must know that! I'll try to change things so we can survive here, but I may fail."

"Yes. And your discovering who I am has increased your chance of failure, which is why I'm so worried about my mistakes," Lianne confessed.

"You've no right to be so highhanded with us, to set me up as a gamepiece forced to win or lose this world according to your arbitrary rules," Noren said bitterly. "You can't take it on yourselves—"

"That's just the point," said Lianne. "We can't. We're not wise enough; our intervention could do more harm than good."

"Yet you think *I'm* wise enough?"

"Perhaps not. But you do have the right to act on behalf of your own people." She got to her feet. "There's more to it than this, Noren. First, though, you'd better hear some background—and if we're going to talk all night, let's sit someplace that's private."

She was an agent of what she called the Anthropological Service, the representative not of a single species, but of an organization made up of volunteers from many worlds united in an interstellar federation. The Service was not easy to get into; candidates, it seemed, were tested even more arduously than Scholar candidates and must prove themselves trustworthy during a long and difficult course of training. That was hardly surprising, Noren thought, considering that these people had to be ready to die for their convictions at any time it became necessary on any planet where they happened to land. They also, he gathered, had to undergo hardships other members of their civilization never encountered. Planets were uncomfortable compared to orbiting cities. And the planets visited by observing teams not only had living conditions that were primitive by Federation standards, they were also too apt to be the scenes of disease, violence and wars. The worst of visiting such planets, Lianne said, was not the danger. It was the horror of seeing evils one was powerless to prevent. People who didn't find that painful, who didn't care what happened to other species, were not accepted into the Service. One was required to have empathy.

It sounded like a strange life to volunteer for, yet still, it was the only way to truly explore the universe, see more than the orbiting cities and the planets kept like parks beneath them. Federation citizens outside the Service were not permitted to land on the worlds of species not yet mature; there was too much danger of their doing inadvertent harm. Furthermore, Service life was challenging. Lianne, like Noren himself, was a person who enjoyed that. Other challenges had been open to her—she was rather vague about their nature, and he had the uncomfortable feeling that she considered it over his head—but the Service was the one she had chosen. It was an irrevocable choice; the commitment she'd made was permanently binding, an arrangement that eliminated people who merely wanted a few years of adventure.

She had come to his world as one of three people dispatched to investigate the undecipherable signal of a faster-than-light communicator in a solar system where no such communicator should be. "Only three?" Noren asked, surprised.

"There are a lot of worlds in the galaxy to visit," Lianne said.

"But a starship for three people—"

"It orbited for a few weeks, then went elsewhere."

"And stranded you here? Just the three of you?"

"No. Just me; the others went on. The ship will be back to contact me, don't worry. I've been stranded on alien worlds before." She smiled. "It's not done just for efficiency; it's a good strategy for preventing field agents from getting illusions of power."

Their tangible support varied with circumstances, she told him. On some planets they did keep whole teams for the duration of the mission, and often even offworld equipment. On this one they realized, from having examined the Six Worlds' stripped starship hulls they found in orbit, that they dared not possess any equipment a starfaring people could recognize as alien. Their shuttle abandoned them with nothing but native-style clothes and one concealed signaling device with which they could recall it. They had, of course, observed villages from the air; the team members had been chosen for physical resemblance to the villagers. Being telepathic, they got the meaning of remarks villagers addressed to them, and since one of them was a skilled linguist they quickly learned the language. They knew from the Service's vast experience how to be inconspicuous in the first village they entered and inquisitive in the second. It was a routine mission except for the presence of the mysterious City and the fact that the faster-than-light communicator, which had since been identified as an ancient artifact of a Federation species, was not in the City but in the outpost beyond the mountains—routine, at least, until Lianne's unexpected arrest.

She'd communicated telepathically with the others during her night in the village jail. The team leader had advised her that she wasn't obliged to accept the risk of entering the City—apparently there were situations in which she might have been, but in this case she was free to choose. She'd decided to take the chance. Not just to learn what was going on, though it had become obvious that they were dealing with something that didn't fit known patterns; and not, evidently, to do anything against the Scholars if they turned out to be dictators, since that too would be interference. "There was a reason, Noren," Lianne said, "and what I found here proved the risk was warranted. That's something you'll see later." Having learned he must let her tell it her own way, he nodded and did not interrupt.

She had been thoroughly trained to deal with stress, and at the beginning, even within the City, she had the telepathic support of her teammates. When she was first brought before the Scholars, her only serious fear was that they would probe her mind forcibly under drugs against which she'd be powerless; she had means to commit suicide if that seemed imminent, but the decision would be a hard one, for she could resist most drugs and might not be able to predict what sort they'd use. Fortunately, the inquisition turned out to be quite different from what she'd expected. A few minutes with Stefred and she knew her secret was safe from him, that he would not attempt to make her betray information she wanted to conceal. But at the same time she knew she was facing an experience unlike any that agents had previously encountered in field work. She was being judged by the Service's own criteria of worthiness, by methods familiar to her, even—Stefred approached it as her instructors had, and as an individual he was equally expert. Yet it was not mere instruction. She was aware from his emotions that it was deadly serious, and that by her own code as well as his, it would be unethical as well as impossible to get through such a test by faking.

"According to what you've said about the training you had, you must have known you'd be able to pass it honestly," Noren protested.

"That was the trouble," Lianne said. "I did know, so I wasn't scared—it was fear I'd have had to fake, and I couldn't have, even if I'd wanted to; he's too perceptive to be fooled. You know why he uses stress tactics even with candidates he's sure of. They've got to be genuinely afraid of cracking up before he can proceed with the enlightenment, or else they'll never be certain afterward that they couldn't have been made to recant by terror. I was already certain; I'd been through similar experiences in my training, designed to give me that kind of confidence. But Stefred naturally assumed I simply didn't know what real terror is like. He kept looking for ways to show me, and none of them worked since I'd picked up enough telepathically to realize he wasn't going to subject me to any actual harm."

"How much more did you pick up?" asked Noren, frowning.

"Not anything enlightening," Lianne assured him. "I had no more access to his secrets than he had to mine. But of course, emotionally, he does want candidates to trust him; I knew the pressures he was using were for my benefit. And I knew he wanted me to resist them."

"Is that why you didn't recant in the first place? I've wondered, because from your standpoint, since you were there just to get information and weren't part of our society, pretending to play along with the Scholars wouldn't have been wrong. Especially not if you were offered knowledge in exchange for submission, as I was."

"Stefred didn't use that strategy with me, he never does in cases where he sees the candidate's hoping to learn something that might be passed on to others who oppose the system. Some heretics do hope for that; the bribe was a valid test of motivation for you only because you were convinced that if you accepted it, you'd be the only one to gain." She stopped for a moment; when she continued it was with telepathic overtones of intense feeling. "I didn't know whether or not resisting recantation would be to my advantage, Noren. That wasn't the basis on which I was acting. When we take on this sort of role, we act as we personally would if we'd been born into it. I truly opposed what the Scholars seemed to stand for. If I'd really been a village woman, I'd have refused to endorse the caste system, the Prophecy or the High Law; so that was how I had to play it—otherwise I'd have been lying instead of just concealing things."

"I guess I see," Noren admitted. "There's a difference; *he* conceals without lying, and in fact we all do, as priests. I did with Talyra."

"Yes. The scale of values in the Inner City is much like ours— on most worlds we don't fit in as well, and sometimes we're forced to lie. Here I've lived as if I were one of you. I want you to know that beyond doubt; it's important."

To her, Noren perceived, *important not just because she values honesty or because she needs my trust . . . it's important because of how she feels about me.* "I owe you honesty, too," he said. "I don't doubt you mean all you're saying, but there's one thing you seem to have overlooked. The initial risk, the stress you let Stefred impose on you, your opposition to the caste system—all that may have been real. The ordeals of enlightenment and recantation may have been as rough for you as for any of us. But the sentencing, *that* was sham, Lianne."

She didn't reply. Noren went on painfully, "When we kneel in that ceremony and hear ourselves sentenced to life imprisonment within the City, we believe it. We don't know what's going to happen to us here, either the good or the bad; but we know it's permanent, a real price, not something we can get out of when we're through playing the game—"

(160

"Game? Do you suppose that's all it is to me?"

"I'd like to believe it's not. I guess I do believe, now, that you're sincere about wanting to help us even though you've been taught you ought not to interfere. But you aren't stuck here, as we are. Lianne, the City isn't our real prison—this planet is! All of us who've been through the dreams know that we and our people have been deprived of our rightful heritage. You're pretending to share that sentence when you're really free. That's the deceit I can't ignore, not that your genes are different or that you concealed your origin from Stefred. It doesn't matter that you believe the same things as a real heretic, that you're willing to suffer or even die for them. When you submitted to the sentencing, you were lying, and so you're not a real Scholar—you're acting the part without paying the price."

He could feel her surge of emotion, not anger at his accusation, but a mixture of sorrow and guilt. "I haven't overlooked that," she said quietly. "It's why I haven't assumed the robe."

Noren was speechless; it had not occurred to him that Lianne would see more in religion than a mask for secrets. He'd been assuming she wasn't a priest because she supported the genetic change that would make fulfillment of the Prophecy's promises impossible.

"Stefred doesn't understand, of course," she continued. "He's eager for me to do it because I can't appear at inquisitions unrobed, and he feels that by now I could help new candidates more than the Scholars he's been using as assistants during the open questioning. That's true; and I'd like to take part in ritual, too . . . I'd like to give hope if nothing else. But you are right, Noren—I am not wholly committed. There are roles I can accept here, but not priesthood."

"For you it wouldn't be a religious kind of priesthood anyway, even if your ship never came back," Noren argued, "so why does it matter ethically whether or not you wear the robe?"

"Why wouldn't it be religious? That's what priesthood is."

"Well, you don't believe in the Star—"

"Do you?"

"Not the way some do. I don't believe there are any supernatural powers out there for it to symbolize. But it's come to mean something to me, it stands for truth I can't reach—I need that. You don't."

"Oh, Noren." She did not have to use words; attuned now to the emotional channel of communication, he perceived for the first time what Lianne had been trying all evening to convey. *No one can reach all truth. Even people who've visited many stars can't, people whose resources aren't restricted and who understand the Unified Field Theory. But the more one does know of the universe, the*

*more one longs to reach further . . . and the harder it is to accept
one's limitations.*

"Lianne, I—I take it back," he said awkwardly. "I think it could
all be real for you. Even priesthood could."

"No. When a priest speaks the ritual, he or she acts as spokesman
for the people; that's universally true. I have no right to be your
people's spokesman. I am limited, but not by the same set of
barriers." She smiled and touched his hand. "Don't think I lack
sources of faith. I have my own symbols, after all."

"You do?" Almost before the words were uttered Noren was
thinking, *Sorry—that's a stupid question.*

"It's not stupid. You associate the need for them with your own
world's unique problems; you've never been in a position to
generalize."

He absorbed not only her reply, but the feeling behind it. "Are
the problems of other worlds . . . hard, Lianne? As hard to face
as ours?"

"For individuals, often a great many individuals, they are worse.
You'd know that if you'd ever had to fight in a war."

"I've been more naive that I thought, I guess. I've read what the
computers say about the Six Worlds' wars, yet I can't picture them
as—reality."

"Reading doesn't tell you enough. In the Service we are taught
such things through controlled dreaming," Lianne replied grimly.

"Dreaming? But then when Stefred began it with you—"

"I was afraid," she acknowledged. "You've got to hear the rest
of the story. But since you asked a question, I'll answer it first; I'll
warn you where the story's heading. For individuals, Noren, life can
be worse on many worlds than on this one, and the more immature
the civilization, the more suffering people undergo. For whole
species, though, the problems are soluble. The suffering leads somewhere; it's part of evolution. Your species is experiencing an interruption of evolution—perhaps an end to its progress. That is
far more serious than problems of other kinds. It's terrible in ways
you've not yet conceived. Alone, you would not become aware of
them."

"I want to be aware of them," Noren declared, inwardly dismayed by the cold terror he'd begun to feel. *I've always wanted the
whole truth; why am I afraid now, almost as if I were undergoing
another dream?*

He needed no answer from Lianne. He knew the fear was hers
as well as his, that telepathically he was sharing her emotions, much
as in controlled dreaming one shared the feelings of the person from
whose mind the recording had been made. And it was genuine fear.
Lianne was truly afraid for his people; she was not merely warning

him. She was not even forcing the rapport—he had freedom to reach for it or shut it out, and as always in the dreams, he chose to reach.

Stefred had been unable to scare Lianne; during her inquisition they had reached an impasse, for measures extreme by his standards could not frighten her. When driven to it, Stefred did not shrink from using harmless forms of physical stress; that was preferable to enlightening a candidate who'd not been given the self-assurance to get through recantation, and who might therefore be unjustly but permanently deprived of Scholar status. Lianne, however, had been taught more than he could guess: not only self-assurance, but methods of controlling her physical reactions. Nothing short of real injury could have fazed her. He suffered far more than she did, both from the seemingly harsh tactics he was forced to employ and from his knowledge of the tragedy that might ensue if they failed to challenge her sufficiently.

Ironically, that was the turning point. When Lianne sensed Stefred's growing fear for her, she herself began to feel terror.

She could draw no facts from his mind; she knew only that he was an inwardly compassionate person whose ostensible cruelty was designed to protect her best interests. She'd understood all along that he was testing her rather than attempting to break her, but she had assumed it was to satisfy himself of her sincerity. Now she perceived that he'd been satisfied for quite a while, that the point still at issue was her own awareness of strength; he was preparing her for some mysterious ordeal from which he could not save her. He pitied her even as he strove to ensure that she would meet it with confidence. Lianne could not tell whether Stefred's view was shared by all Scholars or whether he was simply one admirable man playing a dangerous game within a society of tyrants, but she knew he was powerless to spare her the suffering that lay ahead. No hint of its nature came through to her except that in his eyes, the fate in store for her would be permanent, and bravery would be her sole defense.

Till this point, she'd expected she could learn the City's secret and then be rescued in some way; Stefred's feelings made her realize it would be more complicated. There might be no chance of rescue; she might face ceaseless, futile punishment; worst of all, she might learn nothing to justify her sacrifice. But she did not falter. The unanticipated terror hit swiftly, and it took only an instant for her to pass from fearlessness to courage.

Though she showed no outward sign, Stefred was sensitive enough to her emotions to be immediately aware of the difference and to see that she could now be safely enlightened. Thus her fear was compounded, for his inner relief was mixed with worry. He could not guess why she'd slipped suddenly to the verge of panic; could the foregoing stress she'd withstood too well have brought on a delayed reaction? Always before he had calculated accurately; for the first time he found himself dealing with someone he could not understand—someone he must subject to the dream sequence without anticipating what unusual problems she might face in it.

If he had foreseen how great those problems would be, or if he'd been aware that had he shown her the Dream Machine in the first place there'd have been no need to bother with any other stresses, he might never have dared to begin the dreams at all.

The dream sequence was not the first step in enlightenment; since non-Scholars were ignorant of their people's true origin, some basic facts of astronomy had to be presented at the outset. This was done in Stefred's study, but he and Lianne were not in the study at the moment he judged her ready. As they walked through the corridor, they passed the dream room, the door of which stood open with complex equipment, sinister in appearance to the inexperienced, plainly visible. "Take a good look," Stefred said casually. "If you persist in your refusal to recant, you will spend a great deal of time strapped into that chair." The remark wasn't meant to be cruel; it was a routine instance of the tactics he used with everyone: a true statement that was unnerving when heard as an implied threat, but heartening when remembered later as one successfully withstood. In the light of Lianne's proven fortitude, he expected her to gain an immediate sense of triumph. To his astonishment and dismay she nearly stumbled against him, her face ashen, and in that moment their fear fed each other's.

"I'm glad he'll never have any suspicion of how rough he made my last hours of ignorance," she told Noren, "because he'd be horror-stricken by what was in my mind. I'm not sure I ought to describe it to you, even."

"You recognized the function of the equipment, I suppose," Noren reasoned, "and if they train you to understand things like wars that way, no wonder you were nervous. That's nothing to be ashamed of."

"We're conditioned to fear controlled dreaming, yes," she agreed, "and not just because it's the only means of showing us evils that don't exist in our own civilization. It's through dreams that we're taught to meet fear itself; after all, we couldn't be seriously afraid of our own instructors. I'm used to training dreams, I don't mind them however scary they are. But there were worse possibilities." She turned to him, her eyes large with remembered terror. "Some cultures use controlled dreaming in ways Stefred is too innocent to imagine."

"I'd be surprised if there's much that Stefred is naive about," observed Noren. "He's read a lot of things he doesn't speak of, evils that sometimes occurred on the Six Worlds. If you mean controlled dreaming could be used for torture, well, even I've imagined that, and I'm aware that it wouldn't be harmless. But you knew he wouldn't do it."

"I wasn't sure how much power he held; I thought I might be taken over by some higher authority—he was afraid of something bad happening to me, certainly, and I realized that what he'd said was less a threat than a true warning. I could deal with torture, though, if it were temporary—"

"It couldn't very well be permanent."

"Yes, it could. A body can be maintained indefinitely with life support equipment and dream input. Only that's not the worst, because if the mental input is pure nightmare, the brain dies relatively soon, and I did know that wasn't going to happen to me; he was thinking in terms of wasted life, not lingering death. The other thing sometimes done isn't called torture; there are worlds where people actually choose it. A person can be kept alive year after year on a machine like that with *pleasant* dreams."

Noren struggled with sudden nausea. "Lianne—that's *horrible*."

"Of course. To you and to Stefred and to me, to anyone who values consciousness. But it matched the pattern of what I knew at that point. There are societies where it would be considered fitting punishment for heretics, and others where it would be viewed as a merciful alternative to imprisonment in close quarters. I had visions of a compartment somewhere in the City with row after row of encapsuled dreamers, like frozen sleep quarters on a slow, primitive starship except with no oblivion and no promised awakening."

"I'm—not sure I would have held out, faced with that."

"I'm not sure I would, either. Unless a person was sure that public recantation would really aid dictatorship, the other form of submission would be worse; it would be wrong to hold out just for the sake of stubborn pride. But the next thing Stefred told me was the part about having already passed the point of no return."

"Oh, Lianne." Noren put his arm around her, found she was trembling. "I've been blind to so much."

"I'm not looking for sympathy, you know that," she said quietly. "But understanding how I'm vulnerable is related to the rest of what you're going to need to understand. The next part's even more so, only you won't like what you hear."

"I have to hear it. I want to. But—but Lianne, it's hard because I've always thought of the universe as, well, *good,* somehow. In spite of freak disasters like the nova, I've believed there are more than enough wonderful things out there to balance."

She was radiant for a moment; he sensed an emotion new to him. "There are!" she burst out. Then, slowly, "There are wonders past your imagination. But if I were to show them to you at this stage, you would only feel more bitter. Right now you believe that I am heir to all the glories while you are doomed by fate to a dark prison world. You must see that darkness, too, is universal; then later you'll find that you do have access to some of the light."

Of course, Noren thought as the surge of elation ebbed. *You've got to have seen more good than I have, or else you couldn't possibly bear to confront all you're telling me about.* Aloud he said, "If I've shown any courage in my life, it's been only because I've had no choice. But you, you *chose*—not only here, but at the start, when you chose to be exposed to evils you would never have had to know exist. I admire your strength more than ever; don't think my finding out who you are has changed that."

"You chose, too, by becoming a heretic," she answered.

"I couldn't have been anything else on this world."

"No, because you wouldn't have been content not to look at all sides of things; but it was a choice all the same. Elsewhere you'd have had more options, and you'd have picked the one that let you see farthest. Which on any world would have meant looking at darkness, just as my choice did." With a wry smile she added, "That's why you share my horror at the idea of perpetual sweet dreams."

He shuddered. "Lianne—when you were hooked up to the Dream Machine for your first session, did you really think that was what would happen?"

"No, I knew better by then. I'd been shown the films of the Six Worlds and the Mother Star before that point, and I recognized a nova when I saw one. I'd begun to piece things together—and it was more of a shock than you've guessed, worse than the other, much worse."

The hardest act she'd put on had been concealing the fact that she understood the film of the nova. There was no actual revelation of the Six Worlds' destruction in that film, but for Lianne, of course, its mere identification as the Mother Star was the key to the colony's situation; it would have been even if she hadn't received Stefred's powerful emotions. The Service had known from the beginning that the people of the planet were not only colonists but lost colonists, out of touch with their world of origin. That had been evident from the converted starships used as living quarters in the City, which like the orbiting hulls were made of an alloy that couldn't be melted and used for other purposes with the facilities available. Lost colonies, however, were not particularly uncommon; in the early phases of every civilization's interstellar expansion, some starships failed to get home. Descendants of their passengers weren't necessarily in danger—they often survived successfully enough, and in due course, were contacted by later explorers of their own species. In any case they were not the sole representatives of their species. The Service did not worry about the welfare of lost colonies.

Novas were another matter entirely. And when Lianne perceived that she would be forced to dream of the nova, she wasn't at all sure she would be able to endure it.

Her experience in controlled dreaming, in voluntary acceptance of nightmare, made it harder rather than easier. She knew in advance that this would be so. She realized that the dreams were ordinarily used with people who did not have any foreknowledge about novas, or even about worlds unlike their own; for them there would be terror and emotional pain—but there would not be complete grasp of significance. They would not absorb anywhere near all the feelings of the person who'd made the recording, while she would share those feelings fully. And she would suffer other feelings beyond that. One experienced a dream according to one's own background, and her background was such that to her, destruction of an entire human species was an ultimate, intolerable evil. Lesser evils she'd been taught to bear on the basis of evidence that they occurred in all species and were thus apparently part of the evolutionary process. But what answer was there for an evil that robbed all the rest of meaning?

The Service was, of course, aware that novas sometimes destroyed populated solar systems. But never before had such a case been observed; once a nova was detected, there was no way to determine whether the planets of the star had been populated or not. If the star of a Federation solar system novaed, the event was predictable and the population was evacuated. The same was true when a known immature species was similarly endangered—

"Wait a minute!" Noren broke in. "You're saying that if your Service had been observing the Six Worlds before the nova, it would have saved the people?"

"Not all of them; that would have been impossible. But enough to make sure your species was safe."

"But then you're admitting you do intervene sometimes."

"If nothing else can prevent extinction, yes. There is no evil worse than extinction of a whole human species; the Founders were right about that. Every Scholar who recants is right about it. I know what you're going to ask next, Noren—but don't ask it, not yet. Hear me out."

Deeply though she feared the dreams, having grasped what they would contain, Lianne had been obliged to undergo them willingly —not only by the role she was playing with Stefred, but by her own oath to the Service. Her awareness of the nova changed everything. She now knew that the colonists might be the sole survivors of their home system; it was her responsibility to find out for sure. And if they were indeed the only survivors, it was her responsibility to determine whether or not they had the resources to go on surviving.

The dream sequence proved even more taxing than she'd anticipated, for she identified in a close personal way with the First Scholar; she hadn't expected recordings made by anyone with insight so far ahead of most of the people of his civilization. The agony was somewhat tempered by his courage, yet on the other hand, she knew his specific hope for survival to be groundless. It was evident to Lianne that the nuclear research goal was unattainable with the City's facilities—she drew more detail from his thoughts about these than less knowledgeable dreamers could—and she knew from the start what Noren had learned gradually, what most other Scholars, even Stefred, still could not bring themselves to believe. If they relied on synthesization of metal, the colony was doomed.

Furthermore, there was the edited state of the recordings to cope with. "It was bad in the way Stefred explained it to you," she told Noren, "more of a torment than he realized, in fact, to have my mind held within unrealistic limits, because I was so accustomed to full recordings. If you hadn't done what you did to spare me that, there's no telling what would have happened. I wouldn't have refused to recant; even knowing the editing was drastic, I trusted Stefred enough to believe it hadn't been done for deception. But I might have cracked up during the later part of the dream sequence."

She had not been in touch with her teammates at that point; when she'd first grasped the nature of her inquisition, she had broken off with them so as to have no unfair advantage. She had asked them not to resume telepathic communication until she initiated contact herself, and she'd resolutely refrained from doing so not only during the intervals between dreams, but throughout the ceremony of recantation. They had witnessed that ordeal without understanding it, as friends of other heretics did. Afterward, however, she had passed on the whole story, and she'd told them what they already saw from the discoveries she reported: there was no question of her leaving the City until she had learned whether anyone had found the route to permanent survival of the colony.

"Genetic engineering, you mean!" Noren exclaimed. "But I didn't find out about it till weeks after you recanted. Why did you stay so long?"

"You'd begun to be interested in genetics—I'd learned that much."

"Telepathically?" he inquired uncomfortably.

"No, at least not till you came to me with the secret recording. I sensed your goal then because I already knew you'd studied the field, and also because I'd been looking for the same thing you had

(168

in the full version of the First Scholar's memories."

Did it give you nightmares, too? he wondered. He'd never told her of his own.

"I have skills for gaining access to my subconscious mind," Lianne said, "so I perceived the clues he left without being disturbed by them. I didn't follow them through; I waited to see what you'd come up with."

"What would you have done if I hadn't found the secret file? The timing was quite a coincidence, after all—generations passing, and then its being discovered the year you got here."

"Not really a coincidence; your finding the sphere in the mountains triggered both my arrival and the events that led you to pursue genetics. As to what I'd have done if you hadn't pursued it, well, after a while I'd have used telepathy to steer you in that direction."

Noren frowned. "You mean you can control people that way?"

"Definitely not. They must choose to respond, but I sensed you would; I had you identified as the potential leader even before I knew you were on the right path."

Keeping himself under rigid control, Noren ventured, "What if there'd been no potential leader?" He would not ask the more fundamental question directly; Lianne was aware that the inconsistencies in what she'd revealed were obvious to him. *You were trained by the same principles Stefred follows,* he thought, *and like Stefred, you expect people to work out the answers on their own. . . .*

"I could have told you the answers hours ago," she agreed, "but you'd simply have rejected them. I had to give you the emotions, the conflicts, make you feel the paradox for yourself. I've tried to state enough of the facts for you to resolve it."

Slowly, Noren said, "You're sure in your mind that if there'd been no potential leader, the outlook wouldn't be bright. In that case your people would save us, as they would have from the nova, because nothing else could prevent our extinction."

"Save you from extinction, yes, since there's no greater evil."

"But some other evil would follow that they couldn't save us from," he went on painfully, "something I don't know about." *That's got to be how it is—I've had proof that you feel as strongly as I do about what happens to us: Stefred's judgment, and now direct communication from your mind to mine. What's more, your feeling is tied in with how you feel about the Service; the conflict's not between two loyalties, and you're not so timid as to stand back just for fear your action might miscarry.*

"The results of intervention are well known from the Federation's past history," said Lianne, her voice remote and sad. "In the early days some species were brought in too soon; it was thought mature

169)

civilizations could help young ones, that if an effort was made to respect their cultures, it would work like the merging of ethnic groups on a single mother world. But that's not comparable."

"Why isn't it?"

"Different cultures on a mother world are made up of people of the *same* species. There's no difference in length of evolutionary history involved. But with separate species that have evolved on separate worlds, a certain level has to be reached before contact is fruitful, before it's safe, even. If a species isn't old enough biologically, all the struggle of its past evolution goes for nothing."

"You mean because the struggle turns out to have been unnecessary? But that's saying still earlier contact would have been better."

"No! The struggle is necessary; no species can evolve without it —the struggle to solve its own problems, I mean. Its people can't hold their own among biologically older peoples without that background. And their potential contribution to galactic civilization can't develop, either. If a species turns to absorbing knowledge from others before gaining enough on its own, its unique outlook is lost. It has nothing to give, and the spirit of its people dies, Noren. No more progress is possible for them, and since it's genetically impossible for them to interbreed with other species, their descendants are doomed to be like retarded children in the eyes of the Federation. The Service is dedicated to making sure that never happens where there's an alternative."

Noren pondered it. Finally he said, "Lianne, I can't argue with the goal, but . . . it's not as clear-cut as it sounds. There are more factors to weigh—"

"Of course there are. That's why I'm still here."

"To judge not our worthiness, but the odds against us?"

"To obtain data so that judgment can be made." She reached out to him, fear surfacing once more. "Don't you see, I'm just one person, quite a young person, we're talking about a decision that demands the collective wisdom of all the mature species in the galaxy! The Service will make it—but they will not tell me while I'm here, Noren. As long as I'm among you, I'll be given no more power than you have; they won't tell me the odds, or what's best for your world, any more than they will tell you."

VIII

IT WAS ASTONISHING, NOREN THOUGHT, WHAT ONE COULD ADJUST
to when one had no other option. He wouldn't have believed he
could behave just as he always had since his entrance to the City
—rise, dress, eat, work hour after hour at a computer console,
even mingle naturally with people—knowing that the world was
being observed by an alien civilization. Yet he did it. Weeks passed,
and it became habit to push thoughts of that civilization from his
mind and get on with the demands of routine living. He learned
to treat Lianne almost exactly as he had before, and incredible
though it seemed that the existence of secrets between them could
go unnoticed, she assured him those secrets were safe.

"The most anyone might wonder," she declared matter-of-factly,
"is whether we are lovers. And since they wouldn't mind if we
were, it makes no difference if they guess wrong."

"What about Stefred?" Noren inquired miserably. Despite the
value he'd always placed on honesty, he was now hiding the genetic
experimentation, hiding the existence of the aliens, hiding the true
nature of his relationship with Lianne. For Stefred to have a false
impression about that relationship would be one thing more than he
could endure.

"Stefred can see you don't love me," Lianne said with pain. "Do
you think I'd let him believe you do, when I'm forced to deceive
him so many other ways?"

The deception was a deep grief to her; though Stefred would
never know the full extent of it, it wasn't failure to win her love
that was going to hurt him most. He was counting on her as the
heir to his work, yet in time, when she disappeared from the City
—something no Scholar had ever done—he'd assume that she was
a deserter. Nor was that the only misapprehension she was foster-
ing. "It's not just that you won't carry on after him," Noren observed sadly, "but you already know more about the job than he
does—"

"Not more about the techniques he uses, but I'm trained in some
he's never dreamed of. And I'm not qualified to teach him such

171)

skills even if it were permissible; I can tell myself it's a kindness not to let him suspect what he's missing."

"But Stefred wouldn't look at it that way," Noren protested, "any more than I do."

Lianne sighed. "I know. But Noren, he would choose to reject access to knowledge for the sake of the principles he believes in. As you would. As you both did, in fact, when you were candidates."

"Then, I thought the Scholars were going to kill me," Noren reflected grimly. "The prospect of having to live with the choice wasn't something I considered."

Day by day, he learned to live with it—though in this case, he'd really been offered no choice. He told himself that if he were, he would of course choose to act in the long-term best interests of his species. He took pride in schooling himself to seem impassive, and that skill came back, for throughout boyhood he'd been obliged to conceal his feelings from his family. He'd been a heretic for years when they'd supposed him simply a muddle-headed dreamer. Now he was again a rebel: against the Scholars' opposition to genetic research, and on another level, in the privacy of his deepest mind, against the relentless hands-off policy of Lianne's people. By day, he turned from this second rebellion to devote his attention to the first. He proceeded with preliminary computer work so that if a chance ever came to test genetically altered crops, he would be ready.

At night it was harder. Nights had been hard in any case since Talyra's death; now, lying sleepless too long in the dark of his lonely quarters, he could not help imagining the wide universe that was Lianne's heritage—that, if things were different, might well have been his. It *should* be his! He could not accept the fate that barred him from it any more gracefully than in boyhood he'd accepted the idea of being forever barred from the City. Inwardly he raged just as he had then. And despite himself, despite his sureness that Lianne was truthful, he began to hope for a similar outcome. She'd admitted she did not know what her people would decide about his chances, that in fact there was much involved that was beyond the grasp of younger field agents. So was it sure that he would be offered no aid? There could be no open contact between cultures if that had proven invariably harmful, but in secret . . . what harm could be done if they enlightened a few individuals in secret, accepted a few, perhaps, into their own ranks?

This vision built up gradually, so that he was scarcely conscious of its formation. The Service to which Lianne belonged was mysterious in a way that excited him, drew him, as in his adolescence he'd been drawn to the mysteries of the City. The senior members took on qualities he'd once attributed to Scholars, untarnished by the assumptions he'd then had about the Scholars' motives. Knowing that Lianne trusted these elders implicitly, he let reverence displace the resentment he found intolerable. They were immensely powerful and wise, surely, beyond his furthest conceptions; their minds, their culture, their technology were infinitely advanced— and they could give him answers if they chose.

He did not expect them to make it easy for him; he did not even want them to. His growing dream-scenario included unimaginable trials, which surpassed the stress of Stefred's challenges as those had surpassed his boyhood guesses about what Scholars might do to a steadfast heretic. The attempt to picture them was rather pleasantly terrifying. Inside, he longed to feel as he had during his earliest days as a Scholar, confident of his ability to handle himself in any situation that might arise. The ordeals of his candidacy had built that confidence, and he would be happy to endure further ones to get it back. The awesome Service grew in his mind as the one agency that might do for him what Stefred no longer could.

That he must first prove himself was only fair. Yet since Lianne's people would not let his species die, they would not ask him to achieve the impossible—therefore what he was striving for must be possible. They might not come right out and say so, even to her; but neither she nor he himself, much less this planet's inhabitants, would be allowed to come to harm. Had not her fellow agents taken a solemn oath to put the best interests of the worlds they visited above all other considerations?

The elation he'd first felt about the success of the genetic experiments began to return. Seen as a test of his abilities, the work no longer seemed futile, and he realized the Service was indeed wise; he would not want aliens to take over a task he himself could accomplish. With rising spirits he looked forward to the birth of Veldry's child.

She had not told him in words that she was pregnant, for they could not talk privately without fear of gossip; but one evening, after the appropriate interval of weeks, she had paused by the table where he was sharing a meal with Brek and, imperceptibly, nodded. Her face had shone with something deeper than its beauty; and in that moment he became aware that he too had crossed the line from bitterness to acceptance—even, at times, to joy. A child, *his* child, first of the new race that would someday regain its place in the universe. . . .

There was, to be sure, the fact that without metal the City's technology couldn't be maintained; and once it was gone, people couldn't rise back out of the Stone Age. Without metal they'd have no chance of reaching the stripped starship hulls that orbited the world to which they'd be forever confined. So logic told him.

But now there was another logic. It couldn't happen that way! The permanent loss of technology would mean the end of his civilization's evolution just as surely as extinction would, and far more surely than would premature contact with the Federation. Thus there had to be a way out of the trap, though neither he nor anyone else in the City could yet perceive it; there *had* to be, or else Lianne's people would consider intervention justified. There could be no point in withholding aid for the sake of not interfering with evolution if evolution was going to stop anyway.

He did not question Lianne directly about this; he guessed that one of the trials he, and no doubt she herself, must meet was despair over the Prophecy's eventual failure. If he were given the answer to that despair, there'd indeed be outside influence on the course of the world's history, for armed with an answer, he could easily win Stefred's support—even majority support. Besides, he was sure Lianne would not be told anything specific she would be obliged to keep from him.

Yet she evidently had faith in the Prophecy. She'd affirmed it at her own recantation, after all, knowing the attempt to synthesize metal was doomed to fail, and she insisted her only pretense concerned her background. Lianne never laughed at faith. "You have to believe in something," she told him once, "and the more worlds you visit, the truer that is. Terrible things do happen. I've seen them everywhere—and here, the nova, I couldn't bear that if I didn't trust the universe further than I can see."

"How did you learn to trust it?" he asked, genuinely puzzled.

"Well . . . at the Service Academy, I suppose I started there; I never saw any of the bad things when I was little. At the Academy we have rituals, like Orison only far more complex, with telepathy in them, deep levels you can't imagine; the old, experienced people, who've seen hundreds of worlds, participate. They show you the dark side, they make you feel horrible at some points, but then they show the good . . . and it seems you'll never be afraid of *anything* after that. You are, of course. In the real world, you are. But you can't ever forget that there are forces stronger than fear."

Noren caught a hint of her emotion, though it was communicated on a level he didn't know how to receive. For an instant he grasped the key concept: evil that couldn't be banished could be transcended. . . . *It all fits,* he thought; but the perception quickly faded, and he could hold no more than memory of a state in which he'd have given a great deal to remain.

Dazedly, as his surroundings became solid and familiar once more, he said, "I've—felt something like that before, I think."

"Yes, in the last dream, when the First Scholar was dying."

"*He* knew? But how? And why don't I remember better?"

"Such knowledge can be attained by all humans," Lianne told him, "but without expert teaching it usually comes only at times

(174

of crisis, and then only to those ready to open their minds. It's not based on logic, it's truly intuitive, a matter of sensing how the universe *is*." Compassionately she added, "You don't understand me. I could force rapport but you'd fight it, as you did even while you shared the First Scholar's dying thoughts. He was an old man who'd reconciled the two sides of his nature, while in you there's still conflict. That's why you remember mostly terrifying feelings from the deathbed dream."

"I remember his faith for the future."

"His future, or the world's?"

"The world's, of course—the Prophecy. The ideas that became the Prophecy, anyway, that we now know were deluded hopes. He never had delusions about himself; despite what's been put into the liturgy, he knew perfectly well there wasn't any future for *him*."

Shaking her head, Lianne said, "What one draws from a controlled dream is limited by one's preconceptions, I know that in principle—all the same, it's hard to believe you missed so much."

"What? Lianne, did I miss something significant?"

"Only to you. And perhaps," she amended thoughtfully, "to your effectiveness in the role you'll have to fill. Don't expect to handle all the problems ahead with logic."

Noren frowned. "I know the value of faith; I admit we can't keep going without it. But on the other hand, we can't solve our problems with it, and the trouble is that most Scholars are trying to! I thought it was because I do follow logic instead of clinging to the Founders' illusions that you believe I'm the one destined to make survival possible."

"Yes, but logic alone won't be enough." For a moment she seemed on the verge of adding something illuminating, then hastily she declared, "I mustn't speak of this; it's too soon."

Did she know the details of what the Service would demand of him? Noren wondered. That he must trust its elders was clear, and perhaps . . . perhaps she was saying he must go further, place faith in them of the sort his fellow-priests vested in the admittedly-symbolic Star. That was reasonable . . . that was the logical answer to a lot of questions for which he could see no other. It explained how Lianne could find meaning in religious ritual, for instance. He had never fully understood religion; its symbols were uplifting only when he managed to view them as an affirmation that the unanswerables would be answered, by his descendants if not by himself. But the Service already had answers. If one were to say the words with that in mind, not some vague future acquisition of knowledge, but contact with beings who possessed it. . . .

He tried it the next time he attended Orison. *What is needful to life will not be denied us* . . . not if the Service is watching out for our welfare. *The sons of men shall find their own wisdom . . .* of course, if the Service knows all human species ultimately do so and that when they do, they become ready to join the Federation. *There is no hope but in that which lies beyond our sphere . . .* yes, and it existed! Now that he'd met proof that it existed, things made sense, more than they ever had while he'd thought such assurances must be accepted blindly. The Founders, to be sure, had been blind; if they'd been right about those promises it had been for the wrong reasons. Possibly that was what Lianne meant by true intuition. Or perhaps it was fortunate chance—but in any case, she herself was in a position to know, and so, now, was he. He need only trust her people.

For the first time, Noren began not only attending Orison regularly but assuming the rotating role of presiding priest. He'd presided at Vespers occasionally for Talyra's sake, but never at the services open to Scholars alone. The mere fact of his priesthood did not require it of him; the placing of one's name on the roster was strictly voluntary. Somewhat to his own surprise he found it exhilarating. Was this merely because he knew secrets others didn't? he asked himself in dismay. No—he still hated the secrecy. He longed to tell what he knew. And the only words in which he was free to tell it were those of the poetic liturgy. It was the knowledge itself that buoyed him, convinced him at last that those words were justified.

No one commented at first on his new assurance; the extent to which one took on priestly functions was something never mentioned except by one's closest friends. Noren noticed, however, that people seemed pleased—perhaps they thought his active endorsement of religion signified a return to the specific goals of the Founders. Almost certainly this was Stefred's assumption. Lianne, who knew better, was strangely silent.

Veldry also knew he hadn't returned to orthodoxy, yet she came to every service at which he presided and was clearly elated by his public commitment. Her face, watching him, was at times as rapt as Talyra's had been. It was probably a matter of traditional faith, Noren realized; not being a scientist. Veldry hadn't quite grasped that his abandonment of metal synthesization meant that without outside aid, the Prophecy could not come true. She knew only that he rejoiced in the child she carried, that his hope for the future was genuine. She seemed not to need to know why.

Brek, however, had known Noren too well not to wonder. They were no longer as close as they once had been. Their companionship had been strained by the dark seasons after Talyra's death when Noren had found it hard to watch the bliss with which Brek and Beris awaited the birth of their own baby; then after that baby was born, the disagreement about genetic experimentation had become a barrier to much conversation. He knew Brek would be shocked by what he had done, and he couldn't have confided in him anyway, for Brek had not sought to experience the secret dream—by which, Noren felt, he would very likely be even more shocked. The love between Brek and Beris was too bound up with conventional values to permit any thought of risking its fruitfulness. Beris was by now again pregnant and they were both ecstatic; Noren found it hard to meet their eyes.

But having shared his past crises of conscience, Brek was well aware of what full honesty had always meant to him. So it was Brek who cornered him one evening and demanded, "What's going on, Noren? I've seen people change, but not this much! You swore to me that it's impossible to synthesize metal, yet if you believed that, you wouldn't be still affirming the Prophecy at all, let alone going out of your way to do it formally in priest's robes. What do you know that the rest of us don't?"

"Stefred doesn't feel a need to ask me that," Noren temporized.

"Stefred hasn't been hearing you argue that we should hedge our bets by creating biological freaks," replied Brek grimly. "He has no grounds for suspecting you've given up on the Prophecy's promises."

This was partially true; since the Council had rejected the idea of genetic change, Noren had stopped expressing his opinions on the subject in front of members. He stood helpless, inwardly debating how to answer Brek. He did not think he could get away with a direct lie even if that tactic weren't repugnant to him; and besides, there was no lie that would serve to explain away Brek's bewilderment. Best, then, to use half-truths to forestall further questioning, even at the cost of deliberately breaking their remaining ties of friendship.

"I do know things the rest of you don't," Noren admitted flatly. "I know we have just one chance to survive and only as an active priest will I have any chance of winning leadership away from narrow-minded diehards. I'm sorry if what I'm doing violates your principles."

Brek paled. "It violates yours," he said incredulously. "It's a betrayal of everything you've always stood for."

Miserably, Noren turned away in silence. Not until afterward did he reflect that the First Scholar himself had been obliged both to betray many of his principles and to purposely let his motives be misunderstood. Of course, things wouldn't be as bad for him as for the First Scholar. Though he might be very much alone against opposition from even the few men formerly close to him, he would not face the loneliness of total responsibility. He had the support of Lianne and her people. Strange, he thought; for years he'd felt alien in the world, and now aliens were the only friends he had.

177)

                                    *   *   *

Lianne was not quite his only friend; there was also Veldry. But it wasn't safe to let that friendship become known to anyone. That he was the father of her unborn child was perhaps the only such secret in the City about which no rumors existed, and a secret it must remain till he was ready to confront the Council with the proven success of genetic engineering; people wouldn't need much insight to see that if he'd chosen to have a child by Veldry there must be more involved than an ordinary love affair. So, aside from customary courtesy to her when they met publicly, he was forced to be content with seeing her during the services where he acted as presiding priest. She always stood in the front row on such occasions. Time passed, and he watched the child grow. Women, being proud of pregnancy, did not wear clothes of a style that masked it, as Lianne had told him they did in some cultures; he didn't have to count weeks to be aware of the baby's approaching birth.

The prospect both thrilled and terrified him. He dreaded the hours he must wait while Veldry was in the birthing room and half-hoped he wouldn't know when her labor began; but one evening when he went to the dais to begin Orison, she was not in her usual place. Under the blue robe Noren's flesh turned to ice. She never failed to appear when he presided; there could be only one cause for her absence. She had given birth without trouble in the past, he thought —surely there was no danger, and yet with this special child for whose genes he was dually responsible. . . .

Somehow he got through the ritual, his voice unfaltering, his hands steady as he raised them. *"May the spirit of the Star abide with us, and with our children. . . ."* No one would send him word—they would ask Veldry if anyone was to be informed, and she would say no. He might hear no news until long after the child was safely delivered, perhaps not till the formal announcement was posted. There would be a festive meal, for all births were celebrated, but probably no private party; Veldry's beauty had won her few friends among the women. He wished he could have been with her when she entered the birthing room, could have said something encouraging; maybe she too was now frightened by the risk they'd taken. Maybe she was afraid to see the baby. Would they even let her see it? No, under the stern tradition of sacrifice that permitted Scholars no contact with their children, she would see it only if no wet-nurse was available. But if it was not healthy, she would be told. She could handle that, Noren realized. Veldry had plenty of strength; she did not need to draw on his . . . unless, perhaps, that was what she'd been doing all this time during the services. Was that why she'd been eager to hear the words of faith proclaimed in his voice?

After Orison, Lianne spoke to him. He'd never told her who had conceived his child, but no doubt she'd sensed it telepathically, and

(178

in any case she knew by the time elapsed. "Go to the computer room," she said quietly. "I'll bring you news as soon as there is any."

"You? But what excuse—"

"I'm a medical student, and since fortunately I'm a female one, the midwives won't think it strange if I ask to attend a birth. Who did you think was going to get a sample of the baby's blood for genetic analysis?"

He hadn't thought. What went on in the nursery was not for men to ponder. "While you wait, you'd better start examining this world's customs," Lianne advised, only halfway amused. "I really don't know how you'd get that blood sample without me, though no doubt you'd come up with some scheme as you did in the case of my blood. And I don't know how you're going to check on the child's health after it's adopted by villagers, either."

Nor did he, Noren thought ruefully; he'd been aware that he must test the genetic health of his grandchildren, but how was he to know who they were? No Scholar knew! No records of parentage were kept when babies were adopted; the Technician women who placed Wards of the City—presumed by the adoptive parents to be village-born orphans—made sure only that they went to good homes. Originally he had supposed that once genetic experimentation started, record-keeping would become possible. Particular children could be placed under surveillance, for Technicians who visited the villages routinely reported to Stefred on those identified as potential heretics; Noren himself had been watched from early childhood. But without Stefred's cooperation, this would be impossible to arrange. And after the child had been given out for adoption, it would be too late to trace where it had gone. That wouldn't happen till it was old enough to be weaned, of course—perhaps by then, the need for secrecy would be past.

Check on its health, Lianne had said. He'd somehow assumed that either it would be born healthy or it would not, and that if it was all right, the only further step would be verifying passage of the altered genes to the next generation. Now, waiting for word, Noren began to consider factors he'd thrust from his mind during Veldry's pregnancy. The child's health must be continuously monitored. In the population as a whole, genetic disease was virtually nonexistent, for all who'd come from the Six Worlds had passed genetic tests. However, it was theoretically possible that the genetic alteration he'd done could have affected genes besides the ones he'd changed purposely, affected them in some way not detectable at birth or by computer analysis. And of course one test wasn't enough; he must monitor many children. How was he to find enough volunteers? Noren wondered despairingly. For a long time he'd pictured himself displaying with triumph a normal son or daughter whose very existence would make the objections melt away; now with the time at hand, he realized that no matter how healthy the baby was, there was nobody he yet dared confide in.

Hours crept by. He was too agitated to think clearly. *Tomorrow,* he thought, *if the child's all right . . . and of course it* is *all right, the Service wouldn't have let me go through with this otherwise. . . .*

He looked up, suddenly sensing Lianne's presence. Simultaneously, with sickening fear, he sensed that in her mind was shock, horror—more than she'd displayed since the night he'd confronted her with his discovery of her identity. Her face was dead white. Noren found himself paralyzed; he could not even speak. *The baby?* he pleaded mutely, knowing that she was reading his thoughts although her own were shielded from him.

A trace of color came back to her, and she smiled. "You have a strong son." Hastily she added, "He's fine, Noren—no problems I can see."

"What's the trouble, then? Is Veldry—"

"She's fine, too. It was an easy birth. I—well, they were using hypnosis to ease her pains and that made her receptive, so I couldn't resist helping a bit." At his evident bewilderment Lianne explained, "The way I helped you deal with the effects of purple fever. By communicating wordlessly, giving her skills that can't be taught with words."

Weak not with fear now but with relief, Noren was unable to piece things together. "Do you feel guilty about using telepathy that way?" he asked slowly.

"No, certainly not. There's no harm in my helping people as individuals. Veldry doesn't know why the birth was easier than usual any more than you knew why your convalescence wasn't as bad as you expected, and in both cases I prevented needless suffering."

"But when you came just now, your face—"

Lianne's smile faded. "Noren," she said cryptically, "you've a long way to go. The road's rougher than you've let yourself think, rougher in some ways than you've any grounds for anticipating. And when I'm startled into remembering that, I can't always control my feelings. Let's not talk about it now! Let's just be happy because the baby's so healthy."

"You're certain he's perfectly normal?" Noren persisted, striving to attain the state of elation he'd assumed would come naturally.

"As certain as anyone can be by looking at him. But I'm not omniscient, Noren, and I'm not as competent to judge his genetic makeup as you are."

She hadn't brought the blood sample with her; she declared he was too tired to handle it effectively and insisted that he get some sleep. It being impossible to visit the birthing room, Noren followed this advice. He woke exultant, so exultant that as he ran the tests he was not even nervous.

The standard programmed analysis of the baby's genotype, completed rapidly by the computer system, revealed no genetic defects of types known to the Founders. Noren's own painstaking work, the many hours at a console during which he examined the coded data in detail, proved that the change he'd made to his own genotype had indeed been inherited by his son. The genes involved were, of course, dominant; it had been designed that way so only one parent's genes need be altered in the first experiment. This meant the boy could metabolize the normally-damaging substance in native vegetation and water without ill effects, though verification would be needed after he was mature. Not all his descendants would inherit the same capability, however; the changed genes were unavoidably paired with the unaltered recessives that had come from Veldry, and chance alone would determine which would be passed to particular offspring of the next generation. From now on, since the vaccine was no longer untried, it must be used on both parents.

And yet, Noren thought, that would not be an adequate test unless the experimental children intermarried, or at least agreed to relationships of the kind he'd had with Veldry. How was he to arrange that? To deprive them of free choice would be unthinkable; Scholars saw to it that heretics were subtly encouraged, but no other interference in villagers' lives was permitted. Even if he managed to keep track of the babies, there would have to be a lot of them before enough data could be obtained to prove it was safe to inoculate the whole population.

So what next? "What's your next step?" Lianne challenged when they met late that evening; and Noren became uncomfortably aware that underneath, he'd hoped she would tell him. Had he not gone as far as it was possible to go without Service guidance? What constructive end would be served by letting him waste time in further groping, considering they must have analyzed what he ought to do?

"I don't know what to do now," he said, thinking that perhaps this direct admission was required of him. "But you, Lianne—" He stopped; he still could not speak openly of his conviction that he'd be ultimately enlightened. "You know the people in the City better than I do," Noren went on slowly. "I'm not good with people; you are, and you've some degree of access to their minds. Who can you name that might be open to the idea of volunteering?"

"I can't name anyone," she replied soberly. "Oh, I would, Noren —I am permitted to help you in any way I could if I were truly of your people, even by using psychic powers abnormal among you. But if you have any potential supporters, they're keeping their thoughts to themselves."

"How can everyone be so shortsighted?" Noren exclaimed angrily.

"They aren't in a position to judge metal synthesization," Lianne pointed out, "and they'd rather believe you are wrong about it than that the Founders were."

And they have no grounds for believing the Prophecy can come true without it, Noren remembered. If he had not learned Lianne's identity, neither would he; to go on affirming religion's promises under those conditions would have been impossible.

"There's more involved," Lianne said. "Not all of them feel that losing technology would be intolerable; they don't all see, as you do, that it would mean the end of your civilization's evolution. But as long as they believe there's hope of synthesizing metal, they can't endorse an alternate plan; they're afraid the caste system might be maintained longer than is necessary for mere survival."

"But we wouldn't maintain it if the alternate could be implemented!"

"No? For a while you suspected even the Founders had done so."

"It would be a—a hard decision," he conceded. "There'd be a fight over it; some would say that as long as there was any chance of bringing the Prophecy to fulfillment, we should keep the capability even though it would mean keeping the castes. I haven't faced that because I knew, even before you told me, that the Founders' plan offers no chance."

Lianne's eyes weren't visible in the darkness of the courtyard. "You must face what you're asking your followers to face," she said levelly.

Yes. I can't be spared anything merely because I know the point's a moot one, he perceived. Knowing nothing of the Service, what would he say? After a long time he ventured, "There might be a compromise. The research outpost's set up for the nuclear work; we could move the essentials there so they wouldn't be lost when the City's opened to everyone and its resources are quickly exhausted. Each Scholar could choose personally, whether or not to go there. But oh, Lianne, the aircar traffic would stop, and the people who went would be exiled futilely—"

"*You* know that."

"And knowing, I should try to talk them into it?"

"It may be the only arguing point you have. But it won't be enough; to win out, you'll have to—to act, Noren."

He pondered the implications. "In the end, when the genetic change is accomplished and I'm old, I'd have to go there myself and continue nuclear research. Die there as leader of that lost cause."

Her calm tone gave way to hesitancy. "Perhaps."

He would have to promise that, certainly, and he would have to mean it. He couldn't go to the outpost until his work was finished, since the computer complex was indispensable to analysis of genotypes, but afterward . . . wasn't it what he'd have wanted, if he hadn't known the truth about Lianne? To preserve technology, some remnant of knowledge at least, simply as a monument to what the Six Worlds had once accomplished, after sharing of metal with the Villagers made maintenance of the City impossible? The gesture would be empty now; this must be why Lianne had told him he'd suffer for his discovery. Whatever the Service offered him, he must return to play out the charade, unless the real route to restoring technology appeared during his lifetime.

"I'll do whatever's necessary," he declared, wondering if he was as sincere as he wished to be, and if she could assure her seniors that he was.

"I believe you will," Lianne agreed, not happily. "But even action won't be enough; people need—inspiration. You'll have to give them that."

As a priest gives hope. In the past he'd given little of anything, though he'd tried; he'd often offered the truth, which was what he most valued, only to have it rejected.

"Noren," Lianne said suddenly. "You're willing to give, I know that, yet I—I think you also must learn to receive. You're—you're more isolated here than I am, even. You don't know how to interact."

His heart ached for her; she, warm and loving by nature, had made her feeling toward him plain, and in this he'd been the one to reject the offering. "You do understand, don't you—" he began, knowing that with her, there was no need to complete the thought in words.

"About Talyra? Yes, very well—more than you do, maybe."

He didn't probe her meaning; he knew only that although it had been nearly two years since Talyra's death, he could not love Lianne in the same way. There were times when he wanted to. He certainly wasn't held back by the fact that she was alien, and although that made marriage impossible, since it precluded an honest commitment to permanence, there was no rational reason for not turning what City gossip now held to be fact into the truth. Even Stefred, long ago, had said any man Lianne loved would have his blessing. Perhaps he hesitated only because Talyra had said simply that he must have children, not that he should love for love's own sake. Yet he sensed that there was more to it than loyalty.

Besides, he must indeed have more children. With Veldry? She was as dedicated to the future as the rest of the Scholars, and less narrow-minded. Maybe he should marry her. She would accept him; he could make her happy; on his side, it would be no worse than any other marriage of convenience. Veldry had taken no lover since the night their child was conceived, and if for his second genetically-changed baby he turned to someone else, she would be hurt as he'd never expected her to be. He did not want to seek another bride. Why, then, did he not want to marry Veldry, either?

183)

It did not matter what he wanted. If he married her, he could acknowledge their son publicly without implying anything extraordinary; most Scholars would be surprised but not suspicious—yet on the other hand, if any did support his proposal, they would recognize that he had acted upon it. Lianne would let it be known that she was barren; that was no shame among her own people and would not bother her. With rumor as it stood, he would appear to be giving her up on that account, which would show potential allies that his talk of genetic change was more than talk, more even than cold science. It would be seen as a human commitment. A gesture, a symbol, yes—but in such things lay power. Only so could he inspire anybody to follow him.

But he did not look forward to the end of Veldry's confinement, knowing what he must say to her when he told her of his joy about the child.

Women stayed in the birthing room three days, then rejoined friends and loved ones at the noon meal in the commons. Everyone came forward to congratulate new mothers; Noren had no chance to speak to Veldry privately. No one saw anything odd in the warmth of his felicitations, or even in the fact that he took the chair next to hers—Lianne was on his other side, and it was assumed they were simply being friendly. Veldry was radiant. "You've given a great gift to the world," said Noren, and his intensity was noticed only by her; the people present thought it merely a conventional phrase. All children were gifts to the world, and especially all Inner City children, whose parents must give them up for adoption. But Veldry took his true meaning without need of further words.

"I am fortunate," she replied; and that too had double meaning. It struck him that when they married, many would be less surprised by his choice than by hers; desiring her for her beauty, they would be envious. There was envy in their looks as they waited for the unnamed father to appear. It embarrassed him; he should not acknowledge the child, perhaps, until the interest had died down. So he told himself.

To see her alone, he would have to go to her room; that he felt himself obligated to do. But that evening when he joined the group gathering for Orison, she stood in the front row; and it dawned on him that he—never attentive to religious observances—had overlooked a more obvious duty: she'd assumed he would arrange the roster so as to preside at the ritual Thanksgiving for Birth. Hastily he found the priest scheduled to officiate and with the excuse that he wouldn't be free for his regular turn, asked to switch, donning a borrowed robe in lieu of his own. There was no time to review the service. He had heard it, naturally, but had never read it through, and almost stumbled over the substitution of "this mother" for "these parents" which he should have been prepared to manage smoothly; otherwise he found the experience strangely moving. Veldry came forward—without kneeling, of course, since it was not fitting for one Scholar to kneel to another—and met his gaze with high spirits as he placed his hands on her head in the formal gesture. *"The blessing of the Star's spirit has been bestowed upon her, for she has given herself freely in love and in concern for the generations on which its light will fall; now in their name we acknowledge their debt to her, and wish her joy in the knowledge that her child will live among those whose heritage we guard as stewards."* Her child, and his! Ever after, he'd know that somewhere a part of him lived on. . . .

She expected no private talk, Noren perceived as she stepped back. It was too soon for her to start another pregnancy; without conscious decision, he put off making any move. Days passed. And then early one morning, awakened by a knock at his own door, he opened it in dismay to Veldry.

He hardly knew her; there were lines in her face he'd never noticed before, and she was red-eyed from weeping. "What's wrong?" he demanded, his voice rough with anger not at her, but at whoever had found out and now scorned her. It was the only explanation he could think of, and marriage would not mend matters, not if she with her pride had been reduced to this by someone's branding of the experimentation as "obscene."

"I—I don't know how to tell you," she faltered. "You don't deserve so much tragedy in your life—it's not fair, when you meant to do good."

"Look, Veldry," Noren said, gripping her shoulders, "I'm ready to face up to anything that happens—don't worry about *me*. But I won't stand for it if people are blaming you for trying to do good yourself. I'll take full responsibility, I'll lie if I have to, say I didn't tell you till afterward—"

"Noren," she broke in, "no one's found out. No one ever will. But the baby's—dead."

"What?" His legs buckled; he reached out for support, and Veldry clung to him, led him to the bunk where they sat side by side. "How—*how?*" Noren whispered.

"The nursery attendants don't know. He was just—weak, as if he hadn't had enough to eat, though he'd been nursing well. He . . . he was never strong after the first, Noren, only I didn't want to see it, I kept thinking he'd gain weight soon . . . I didn't nurse my others personally, you know, I didn't have anything to compare with. The women who took care of him between feedings didn't tell me because there wasn't anything to do except hope. But when I went in yesterday morning, I knew something was wrong. I held him all day, but finally in the night he stopped breathing."

"Didn't they call a doctor?"

"Yes, near the end, but he wasn't sick in any of the ways doctors can help with."

"The doctor must have said something," Noren protested.

Veldry was silent. "You can't hide it from me," he urged. "He was my son; I have to know what the doctor thought he died from."

"Well, at first she said malnutrition, but we knew he'd had plenty of milk." She didn't meet his eyes.

"Would you rather I talked to the doctor myself?" he asked gently.

"No! If you're going to crack up, it had better be here instead of in front of people." She turned to him fearfully; he wondered if she thought that like a traditional village father, he might blame her for failure to produce a perfect infant. "She said," Veldry continued, "that apparently this baby's body couldn't get the right nourishment from milk, couldn't—metabolize it properly."

"That's crazy! All babies live on milk."

"Of course, but she said there could be something wrong, some congenital problem—"

Congenital. The room spun around Noren. "A genetic defect, you mean."

"The doctor didn't know if there could be a defect just like this, she said she'd have to ask the computers."

"It doesn't matter what the computers say." Noren's voice was cold, remote; in his own ears it didn't sound like his own. "Don't you see, Veldry, whether such a disease has occurred before or not —and the blood test I did shows it hasn't—in this case I *created* it. I altered the genetic pattern of metabolism. I brought a baby to life who was foredoomed to starve."

"You couldn't have known ahead of time," she said in a carefully rehearsed tone, "and you tried the metabolic change on yourself, you told me—the baby's metabolism was like yours."

"Yes, I tested it on myself first. But I don't drink milk, after all; there isn't any milk on this planet except human milk. Probably I can't metabolize it any more, either." He wondered how he could have been so stupidly, tragically blind as to believe he'd checked everything.

After a long pause Veldry said steadily, "We knew there was risk. We wouldn't have done what we did if it hadn't been a choice between that and letting all our descendants die. We'll grieve, we can't ask not to suffer—but you musn't blame yourself."

"I can't not blame myself," Noren declared.

"I—I suppose that's true. I guess that's part of the burden you've taken on. And I still admire you for taking it, Noren."

Hazily, he was aware that he should comfort her, should turn from his own guilt and despair long enough to give her the support that was her due. He did not know how. He couldn't marry her, of course; he would never be able to remarry, since to attempt a second alteration of his genes would not test the change to be used on other people. To father a child for his own sole benefit would not be a justifiable form of human experimentation. So there was nothing he could offer Veldry.

Not till she was gone did he reflect that he might have offered the solace of ritual words. With Talyra he'd used such words to mask secrets; Veldry, who knew those secrets, also viewed them as a source of strength. Though she had long ago accepted accountability for the Scholars' stewardship by assuming the robe, she never functioned as a priest, perhaps less from scorn of convention than from lack of self-respect. She honored his active priesthood and must have wished him to exercise it in sorrow as in joy. But he couldn't have done so even for her sake—not when his newfound grounds for faith had proven hollow.

How could they, Lianne's people, have let it happen?

Strangely, he felt no resentment against Lianne herself, nor did he shrink from companionship as he normally did in times of anguish. It was to her quarters that he went, following an urge he did not stop to question.

He was not sure how much he told her verbally. Lianne held him, and wept. Noren too shed hot tears, not only of grief and remorse, but of outrage. "How could they?" he demanded. "I expected trials, defeats—but how could they let an innocent baby—"

"It wasn't a question of letting; they had no way to know. We aren't gods, Noren."

"Gods?" He did not know the term.

"I forget," Lianne said, "that concept's not in your world's religion, and I don't suppose you've read much about the cultural history of the Six Worlds. In many cultures the power symbolized here by the Star is personified, attributed to supernatural beings. Primitive cultures worship whole groups of gods, but civilizations advanced enough to know there's only one Power often conceive of it as a Being, too. The Founders didn't happen to have that tradition. Some Federation worlds do."

"They believe there's a *being* off in the sky like the Star, controlling things?"

"Well, not in a physical sense. It's simply a different symbol." She sighed. "It's hard to explain when you don't understand the Star either; you're so literal-minded, Noren. The point is that we acknowledge a power beyond our own power. We're not gods in the Service, and we don't play at being gods! To see ourselves that way would be blasphemy."

Forcing himself to speak levelly, Noren reflected, "It would be . . . making light of the truth, you mean. In the village people called me blasphemous; they cared less about truth than I did, or so I thought. I knew the power's not in a magic star. You're saying it's not in the Service, either."

"No more than in the Scholars," Lianne said gently, "who would be gods to the villagers had not the Founders very wisely used an impersonal star as the symbol of something higher. You don't want to be worshiped; do you suppose my people do, or that we merit it?"

"Oh, Lianne." As understanding flooded his mind, he was overcome by a sense of sin unlike any he'd experienced before. "I—created my own false symbol; I've been imagining them as gods, all right. You don't know—" He broke off, unable to confess that he had done so consciously even when performing the offices of priesthood.

"I know," she admitted miserably. "When I came to tell you about the baby and found you thinking such thoughts, I was horrified. I saw then why acting as a priest had been getting easier for you, and I knew that sooner or later I'd have to set you straight."

"Don't worry about it," Noren said grimly. "I can see for myself. I knew in the beginning there was risk, only I didn't want the responsibility—after I found somebody to pass it on to, I refused to believe it was real. But it has to be real if it's to accomplish anything. If your people were gods, what I'm doing would be futile after all."

"You'd be merely a puppet—your whole race would become puppets—if we could protect you from error," she agreed, "or even if we could ensure your ultimate success."

He sat hunched over on Lianne's bed, his head buried in his hands, unable to think of the future. Going out to face people, bearing the secret not only of the baby's existence but of his accountability for its death, was past contemplation. He could not endure that even privately. Starvation . . . the baby had *suffered*. Even the subhuman mutants like the First Scholar's son didn't suffer. He had accepted the risk before learning about Lianne, but somehow he hadn't pictured it in these terms.

Lianne's arm was warm across his shoulders. "I prayed you wouldn't have to learn through disillusionment," she was saying, "and I evaded my job. I should have been prepared. Though I couldn't have saved the baby, I should have kept going to see him —but I was a coward. I knew if he wasn't thriving I wouldn't be strong enough to tell you. Yet now in the space of a few hours you've got to make a very difficult adjustment, when I could have bought you more time."

"A few hours—I don't understand." He was not sure he'd be able to accept the consequences of his failure in weeks, let alone hours.

"You've got to preside at the service for the baby," Lianne said.

"Lianne, I can't!" he burst out, appalled. "I couldn't do that even for Talyra, and now, after my—my blasphemy, I can't ever preside as a priest again. I couldn't anyway in this case; I couldn't stand up and declare it'll turn out for the best, knowing the death was my fault."

"It's going to be hard. But you are obligated."

"You're right, of course," he conceded. "Veldry will expect it, and I owe it to her."

"Noren," Lianne questioned after a short silence. "Do you intend to go forward with the work?"

He didn't answer; she, being telepathic, ought to know he wasn't ready to talk about that. "If you do," she continued, "you're obligated not just for Veldry's sake but for everyone's. When you tell future volunteers about this baby, they'll know whether or not you were the one who spoke at his death rite."

Yes, and if he was not, they'd feel he was either too weak to accept the responsibility or not convinced that the experiment had been justifiable. There would then be no volunteers. Furthermore, there might not even be opportunity to seek any, for the secret would be out. It was a father's place to arrange the service for a dead child. If he himself presided, it would be assumed that the father was unwilling to reveal his identity and that Veldry had simply gone to the priest who'd officiated at the earlier Thanksgiving for Birth; but if he sought a substitute, there could be no hiding the reason for his involvement.

"There's something more," Lianne went on. "Now's a bad time to stir up an issue I've held off raising, yet it's only fair to warn you." Her arm tightened around him, and he sensed, beneath her sorrow, the ache of a deeper one—pain not merely for the present tragedy, but for some other that lay ahead of him. "You've no conception yet of where you're going," she said. "You're thinking that if you can get through this one service it will be the last act of your priesthood. Don't look at it that way. Make it a beginning, not an end; it's as a priest that you must lead your people later on."

Noren raised his face, startled into anger. "I told Brek that," he recalled bitterly. "To protect your secret I led him to believe I'd turned hypocrite. But I'm not a hypocrite, and I won't use priesthood as a route to power."

"Do you think I'd want you to do it hypocritically?"

"No more than you want me to create congenitally defective babies," he replied, his voice harsh, "but I suppose hypocrisy too can be justified in the name of survival. Reason tells me it can. Well, you've sometimes said I rely too much on reason. About this, I'll follow my feelings."

"And your feelings don't include faith right now. But they used to, before you found out who I am."

"In survival of my race, yes. Not in the Prophecy's promises, not after I became sure that genetic engineering is our only chance to survive. If the Service isn't backing those promises, I can't affirm them any more than the rest of the Scholars can give them up."

Hesitantly, Lianne said, "I affirmed them, knowing the Service hasn't the power to make them come true."

"On what grounds?" Noren challenged, thinking with regret of how logical his speculations about her motive had seemed.

"Your reasoning wasn't all wrong," Lianne told him. "I was sure when I went through the recantation ceremony that some way does exist for your descendants to regain the technology that will be lost here, so that the Prophecy can ultimately be fulfilled. If that weren't true, open intervention by the Service would be judged essential, because without it the evolution of your species would reach an end worse than the consequences of artificial interruption. And you are right that we wouldn't let you engage in human experimentation to no purpose if such intervention were considered inevitable. We'd intervene now, not as gods but simply as human beings abiding by ethics, balancing lesser evils against greater, just as you do."

"But then your people know the way!"

"Yes, they must—but that doesn't mean they can make sure it'll be implemented. They're dealing in probabilities, not certainties. They too need faith; but we have evidence that they do have grounds for it."

Noren's head swam. "If you hadn't come, I wouldn't know that. I couldn't act as a priest, yet you say it's in that role I must lead—"

"So by speaking like this, I've altered the odds," she admitted. "I haven't an answer. We are . . . agents, Noren, not only as representatives of the Service, but in the sense that once we interact at all, we influence histories to an extent we're not able to compute. It goes back to what I said about trusting the universe. Things we can't explain do happen, things like your finding the sphere that saved your life and that brought us here, for instance—they are not mere coincidences; they follow statistical laws other than laws of random chance. But we can't predict which problems will be solved by such events."

"Lianne, don't hold out on me," he pressed. "Will I receive help in finding the solution once I've gone as far as I can alone?"

"As much as I'm able to give you," she replied, her voice low.

"I mean the part you don't know. Does the Service tell individuals facts that can't be announced openly to their cultures?"

"Occasionally, if there's urgent need. It must be done very subtly. In this case, to prevent the harm that would result from disclosure of our existence, it would have to be managed in some way that would make your possession of advanced knowledge seem natural both to your fellow Scholars and to this world's future historians. That may not be feasible. And the time may not be ripe for it in your era; it may be that the genetic change must be thoroughly established before the next step is taken."

Resentment flared in him again. "They'd let me live my whole life in ignorance of what they foresee? It's not fair."

"Life's never fair to people who set out to change things. In the normal course of progress, strength to strive can hinge on not knowing the future; they won't tamper with that course unnecessarily."

"What if I'm not strong enough to keep striving?" Noren began, but then, in a stunning flash of insight, he knew. All Lianne had told him in the past meshed as with a kind of awe he stated slowly, "The decision is mine. It has been, all along. If I quit, they'll step in and give us aid."

"Of course." Lianne's eyes glistened. "I never denied that it's in your power to make them do it."

"I—got things backwards. I believed if I proved deserving enough, I could gain help; I thought they were testing me."

"You mean you wished they were." She tried to smile, adding, "Not being tested is harder. I know; I've lived both ways, just as you have."

He'd been living, since his discovery, for the day when he would pass their test and feel triumphant. Now, uncertain not only of his strength but of his talents, would he be right to go on gambling with infants? It wasn't as if he had no option. . . . He savored a bright vision: open contact with the alien culture; ships landing, unloading more metal than anyone had seen since the Founders' time; the Prophecy fulfilled in his generation, cities rising almost literally overnight in accord with the villagers' naive expectations. The caste system abolished forever. Knowledge freely available to him and to everyone, not merely the Six Worlds' stored heritage, but greater wisdom than the Scholars dreamed could exist. If open contact was deemed unavoidable, there'd be no point in further delay. One word from him, and he could have all he'd ever longed for; his contemporaries could have it too . . . and there would be no more defective babies.

But it would mean the loss of his people's potential; overshadowed by older species, they would never evolve to Federation level. Future generations would pay the price.

"You have the power to decide," Lianne repeated. "At the start, I had it. I could have lied in my initial reports, said there was no one here fit to carry your people forward. But I judged that you and Stefred and others I'd met would want to be the ones to pay."

There was nothing else to be said. After a while, when he felt able to talk without weeping, Noren went to arrange the rite for his dead son.

IX

IN THE DAYS THAT FOLLOWED, NOREN IMMERSED HIMSELF TOTALLY in analyzing what had gone wrong with the genetic change. His error could not have been avoided, he found; it had not been a stupid mistake or even a careless one. And it had been made initially by the geneticist of the First Scholar's time whose design he had followed. She, like himself, had been forced into human experimentation long before it would have been tried if test animals had been available. Success at so early a stage would have been almost miraculous.

With painstaking care, he redesigned the change and went back to the Outer City's labs to prepare a new vaccine. He injected himself with it to make sure it wasn't virulent, but that, of course, proved nothing about its genetic adequacy; it must be tested on someone whose genes hadn't been previously altered. His agonized doubt over whether he'd have the courage to perform such a test was mitigated, somewhat, by the fact that he saw no immediate chance of finding a volunteer to perform it on. As long as he was busy, he pushed that problem from his mind.

He continued to preside at religious services whenever his turn came. Lianne insisted that a sincere commitment to the priesthood was indispensable to his task, rather than simply a means of gaining power among the Scholars; but she would not explain further. She seemed deeply troubled by the issue. "The knowledge of your course must grow from within you," she told him. "It's not beyond your reach, not something you need outside help to discover. To give you specific advice wouldn't do you any good; while you're unready to face it, I'd only cause you more pain."

"Lianne," he protested, "I'm ready to face *anything;* I've never backed off from the truth, not knowingly, and I won't start now." Which she ought to realize, he thought indignantly.

"It's because I do realize it that I believe you have a chance of achieving the goal," she replied, grasping more than he'd said, as always.

"I can tell you're not happy about what you're concealing," he said forthrightly, "and I wish you wouldn't try to spare me. I'd feel better knowing the worst." Actually, he was sure nothing could be worse than the things to which he'd already resigned himself. The prospect of more pain did not seem to matter.

"There'll be time enough to worry about it later," Lianne declared. "I'll say only that winning the villagers over will demand greater sacrifices than you've considered."

Greater than the sacrifice of contact with her civilization? She did not know his mind as well as she seemed to, Noren thought in misery. Even so, he'd lost peace of conscience, the ability to have children, all hope that the Six Worlds' technology could be preserved. He'd accepted the likelihood that he would end his days in exile at the now valueless research outpost beyond the mountains. "I've considered becoming a martyr like the First Scholar," he said dryly, "but giving up my life wouldn't do any good—and barring that, I don't think there's anything left for me to give up."

"That's because you don't see how much you have to lose," she observed sadly.

Contemplating this night after night, Noren confessed inwardly that it did dismay him, not so much because he minded being hurt— he felt past minding, numb—but because of his evident blindness. Why could he not perceive what Lianne foresaw? He tried, yet it eluded him. The fact that the means of gaining village support for a change in the High Law eluded Stefred also, and that she apparently expected no insight into it on Stefred's part, didn't cure him of self-doubt.

He saw little of Stefred these days, but Lianne was, of course, a go-between. There was no hostility on either side, nor even open opposition. Stefred allowed Noren to go his way without interference, presumably because he did not guess how far he had gone. Not guessing, he must feel that he, Noren, had turned his back on constructive science, that his youthful promise had gone sour; the thought of this was hard to bear. Some said such things openly of him. He now argued for genetic research and was viewed less as a threat to the established order than as the City eccentric. It had happened before, he'd heard: Scholars disillusioned in youth had become fanatic champions of impractical schemes, and while their right of free speech had been respected, the quality of their judgment had not. He must list the admiration of his peers among his losses, Noren knew, although never having cared much what others thought of him, he did not count it a great sacrifice. The loss of his closeness to Stefred was something else again; he missed that, and like Lianne he hated the deceit he was forced to practice upon the one man in the City most worthy of confidence.

He was free to study genetics; any Scholar was free to study anything—but to devote years to it, abandoning all pretense of research into metal synthesization, was out of the question. Genetic research fell in the avocation class, like art and music. Inner City people were expected to perform essential work, if not out of sheer dedication, then merely because they received food and lodging. Noren, as a trained nuclear physicist, volunteered for a shift in the power plant; and thereafter, since he spent even longer hours on the genetic work, he had a bare minimum of time left to eat and sleep. Fatigue added to his numbness, and for that he was grateful. Only work could insulate him from despair.

Veldry continued to attend Orison whenever he presided; seeing her there in the front row tore at him emotionally. One evening she approached him after the service and asked to talk in private. Too much time had passed for that to start gossip, he decided, and in any case he could refuse no request of Veldry's. He went with her to her room, suppressing with effort the memories it stirred in him.

"Noren," Veldry said, "the risk has to be taken again, doesn't it?"

"Yes," he agreed in a low voice. "I've—reconciled myself to that. Only there's no one I can ask."

"You could use a volunteer who doesn't need to be asked."

"I don't expect to be let off that easily. Who'd offer, when there's no support for genetic change even in principle?"

"I'm offering," she told him simply.

"You—what?"

"I'm willing to try again whenever you're ready."

"Veldry," Noren protested, reddening, "I thought you understood. You and I can't try again; my genes are damaged, and if I tried to repair them it wouldn't be a valid test—the risk to the child wouldn't be warranted. The new vaccine has to be used before the man drinks unpurified water."

"I do understand. The man doesn't have to drink it, the woman can. Genetically it doesn't make any difference which parent gets the vaccine, so I'm volunteering to be inoculated."

"Oh, Veldry," he burst out, deeply moved. "It's brave of you, but you mustn't have a baby who might die, not twice—"

"I lost my special baby," she said softly. "I want another to take his place—and anyway, why should more people than necessary get involved before we know it's safe? I'm already committed. It's better this way, really."

Perhaps it would be, Noren thought. It had meant a lot to her; perhaps the chance of a happy ending was worth the danger. He paused, embarrassed, wondering if she'd really grasped the extent of the risk she was taking. "What if I fail again?" he asked.

"You won't."

"I may. I refused to accept that, the first time; I told you the change I'd made might not work right, but I never actually believed it. Now I do, and it has to be considered."

"I wouldn't be the only woman in the world to have lost two children."

"You'd lose a good deal more," he reminded her. "You'd lose your ability to have normal ones."

"I've had my share in the past."

"That's not the only thing," Noren said bluntly. "There are only a couple of doctors in the City qualified to sterilize a woman, both of them senior people we don't dare to confide in—"

"I've had my share of lovers in the past, too," Veldry broke in. "I thought I'd made clear that I want to do something more with my life."

"But—if you should ever find the man you've been looking for, the one who'll see beneath your beauty and whose love for you will last—"

"Then it will last till I'm past the age to have babies, and if he sees beneath my beauty, Noren, he'll know that's not such a lifetime away as you think." She smiled ruefully. "You'd be surprised, I suppose, if you knew just how old I am—but didn't you ever wonder how it happened that I'd experienced the full version of the First Scholar's dream recordings long before the secret one was found?"

He drew breath; he had indeed wondered, for he'd assumed she'd arrived in the City only a few years ahead of him, and young people rarely sought the full version. It hadn't occurred to him that being beautiful might mask the usual effects of age.

"I ask just two things," Veldry went on levelly. "First, I've got to have your permission to tell someone the truth about the first baby."

"Well, of course; I wouldn't do this unless the father of the second one was informed. May I—ask who it's to be, Veldry?"

"No, you can't," she replied. "That's the second thing; I may never be able to name him to you, though I'll get you a blood sample." After a short pause she added slowly, "I may have to tell more than one person, and I can't consult you about who. Do you trust me to choose?"

"You mean you're just going to . . . persuade somebody?"

"I'm in a better position to do that than you are, after all." Bitterly she continued, "I've got one asset, which has never done either me or the world any good; is it wrong for me to take advantage of it the one time I might accomplish something worthwhile that way?"

"No," he said. "No, maybe this will make up for all the grief it's caused you. I trust you, Veldry. Tell whoever you need to, just so the facts don't reach anyone who'd put a stop to the birth of genetically altered children."

"If I have a healthy one," Veldry declared, "nobody can stop it. Under the High Law I have a right to get pregnant as often as I want, and my genes will be changed for good."

* * *

With grim determination, Noren injected Veldry with the corrected vaccine; when the alteration of her genes had been confirmed, he and Lianne stood by her while she drank from the courtyard waterfall. Veldry, having been told that Lianne was barren, not only shared the widespread assumption that she and Noren were lovers but rejoiced that they could remain lovers despite the necessity that he father no more children; in her eyes, Lianne's apparent curse had become a blessing. He could not yet be sterilized; there was no doctor at all in whom he could confide, and the High Law prohibited sterilization except in cases of proven genetic damage. Unlike the First Scholar, who had been in the same position, he was young, and he was realistic enough to know that a time might come when this aspect of his personal sacrifice would become more burdensome than it was in his present state of depression. He might someday want love, and Lianne would not be in the City forever . . . but at that thought he turned, wounded, from all such reflection.

He drew back from a deep relationship with Lianne, even from the friendship that had grown strong between them. She knew him better than any human being ever had; she understood his dreams, his longings—his whole outlook on the world—in a way that hadn't been possible for Talyra. It was due not only to her telepathic gift, but to the compatibility of their minds. With Lianne he knew, for the first time in his life, what it was not to be lonely. Yet this kinship of spirit had become a searing agony. He wanted desperately to glimpse the universe as she had seen it, to share the ideas she was now willing to discuss, but at the same time he could not bear to talk of them. What he could not have, he must forget, or lose his grip on the routine of everyday living. To his dismay he found himself avoiding his sole chance to exchange thoughts about the things that mattered most to him, shunning all reminders of the realms he had renounced.

There was little time to talk to Lianne anyway, considering his double work load; when he saw her, he fell into casual comments on daily happenings or technical points of the work. He was not fully aware of the extent to which this was deliberate. Looking back, however, he knew his one opportunity for real communication was slipping away. Lianne obviously knew, too, and was saddened. It occurred to him that she, left alone in his world for an indefinite number of years, was desperately in need of his companionship though she was resigned to not having his love. If she was the only person in the City he'd found who *cared* about the universe, the reverse was even more true. He was nevertheless powerless to help himself. Inwardly aching, he let their moments of contact run out in empty conversation.

Some weeks after Veldry had begun drinking unpurified water, she told him, radiantly, that she was pregnant. She seemed even more elated than she'd been the first time; Noren thought with chagrin that her courage outmatched his own. He was pleased by the news, but he could scarcely feel good about it—he knew that as time went on his terror would grow in pace with the growing child. How could Veldry be aware of the life so intimately close to hers without terror? And did the man she'd induced to experiment look forward calmly to the coming of a possibly defective son or daughter? "I don't suppose . . ." he began awkwardly.

"That I can say who the father is? No, he made me swear not to tell even you."

With discouragement, Noren reflected that he would never be able to sway people, as a priest or otherwise; he just wasn't the kind of person they confided in. Did someone think, after all the risks he'd taken privately, that he'd betray a supporter who desired secrecy, much less spread rumors about one brief and probably extramarital relationship?

"I'll say, though, that you'd approve of him," Veldry added, her eyes alight with fierce pride.

"He's made you happy, then. I'm glad."

"In the way you did, yes, he made me happy. He offered me respect, and he'll share my feeling about the child whatever happens. But I meant you'd approve of him as—well, since you can't be the biological father of the new race yourself—"

So the man was admirable, not a casual lover but someone who truly cared about future generations. For that he was thankful. Yet he was not sure he'd wholly approve of someone unwilling to declare his convictions openly. To conceal the experimentation was one thing, and necessary; but experimentation would serve no purpose unless the idea of genetic change eventually gained defenders.

Since he seemed unable to progress toward finding any, he finally broached the topic with Lianne. "No amount of sacrifice on my part will help matters if the majority can't be won over," he complained.

Lianne was silent, thoughtful, for a long moment. "What was the hardest part of what the First Scholar achieved?" she asked slowly.

Noren pondered it. Not martyrdom; that had been only the climax. Not the secret genetic experiment, which had achieved nothing in his time. "The worst was having to endorse a system he knew was evil," he said. "We all know that, and we all relive it."

"Yes, you reconcile yourselves to it, to the pattern of hardship his plan demands. But he himself had to do more. He had to break away from his society's pattern. The truly difficult step was to accept the fact that a social structure like the one the Six Worlds had—the one he was used to and believed worked best—would not work in this colony. You experienced his turmoil over it in the dreams, but you probably got so wrapped up in the ethical issues that you haven't grasped what a tremendous innovation it was for him to think of making any change at all."

"I guess I haven't."

"I have," Lianne told him, "because I've studied lots of societies I can compare. People normally want to hang onto what they're used to; the villagers' feeling about the High Law is simply an exaggerated form of a tendency that exists in every culture. What's more, so is the rigidity of the Scholars' view. It affects even your own thinking. You're resigned to the necessary evils, therefore you haven't separated the customs that are still necessary from those that aren't."

"Are you saying I've condoned evils that needn't exist?" he protested, shocked.

"No, but you've taken everything as a package, without examining what's essential as opposed to what's merely traditional. For the Founders, changing their old system was hard not just because it meant condoning wrongs, but because it involved abandoning traditions. The First Scholar was the only one among them who question those traditions enough to see that some could be altered."

"And if I were his equal, I could do that here?"

"Because you *are* his equal, you *will* do it."

"That doesn't sound—sacrificial," Noren said. "If I'm not expected to lose my life in the process, where can I go but up?"

"There are more basic things than life in the life-or-death sense."

"What?" he pressed, sensing she was on the verge of giving away more than she felt she ought to reveal.

"Your culture's framework—the pattern of living that makes your life tolerable here under the harsh conditions this world imposes. So far you've pictured only how you might pursue your goal within that framework, and you see no other way. Neither do I, I'm afraid."

"Now you're really scaring me," murmured Noren.

Lianne's smile seemed forced. "That's a good sign. It shows you're starting to think along the right lines." Soberly she added, "To someone who's known only one culture, merely defining the framework is scary. I remember! When we join the Service, we renounce allegiance to our native worlds, and we're required to analyze thoroughly what it is we're putting behind us."

"That's different," he reflected. "You do it because you want the new framework the Service offers; you don't have to strike out on your own without one."

"I never claimed *I'm* the equal of the First Scholar," said Lianne.

Startled, Noren shielded his thoughts from her, unwilling to let her sense the dismay in them. "I . . . think I just got the point," he said.

It was disconcerting to realize he had not questioned all his premises; as a heretic, had he not always been a questioner? Had he not, since, challenged the Founders' plan itself? He'd never hesitated to break rules when he saw purpose in it; now, during the next weeks, Noren began looking for rules to break. None seemed relevant to his cause.

He could, to be sure, devise plans that went against custom. For instance, it would help tremendously if the outpost were turned into a center for genetic research instead of nuclear research. Genetically altered crops could then be grown there by Scholars, who, beyond the mountains, did their own farming in any case. He'd by now nearly completed his computer work on the design of the changes necessary for growing food without soil treatment, weather control or irradiation of seed; at the outpost he could test them personally. By an even more radical breach of tradition, parents of genetically altered children might rear their own families at the outpost, which would eliminate the large problem of keeping watch on those children and arranging intermarriages between them. But there was no way he could take over the outpost in the face of majority opposition. Besides, such a course would be useless for bringing about eventual genetic change in the villages, and that, rather than the research, was his main problem.

The seasons passed. Veldry once more became great with child, and it was Noren who felt the sickness by which she herself seemed untouched. "What did you do to her during that last birthing?" he asked Lianne. He had read that posthypnotic suggestion could be employed in powerful ways, though neither she nor Stefred had ever insulted him by offering it as alleviation of anxiety.

"Nothing lasting," Lianne assured him, following his thought. "I only helped with the delivery; now, I think, she's got a real sense of destiny. But you are right that hypnosis can do more than anyone here uses it for. I was appalled when I first saw how commonplace it is in the City; many societies misuse it before they understand the powers of the mind."

Noren waited, hoping to hear more; he still knew little of those powers, and it was a subject she usually steered away from. "I needn't have worried," she went on. "Stefred is competent; he knows what not to try, and the others trained in induction don't go beyond hypnotic sedation and anesthesia for physical pain. I stay within comparable limits, though I'm tempted sometimes to use my own training."

"I wouldn't want—anesthesia, not for mental things," he told her.

"Of course not. But hynosis can increase awareness, too. I could open whole areas of your mind that you've shut off—" She stopped, sorry, evidently, to have said something that might tantalize him.

"I suppose that isn't permitted," he said, unable to keep bitterness from his voice.

"Technically it isn't, but that's not what holds me back. It would be . . . disorienting, Noren. You'd be badly scared at first."

"Well, I wouldn't let that matter," he declared with sudden hope.

"All the same it would interfere with your functioning as a scientist. You'd have to adjust to new states of consciousness; you wouldn't be able to work till you'd regained confidence in your own sanity."

"Like—like after my space flight," he reflected. *Like what?* Lianne's thought echoed, and he recalled that she could not know; he'd never told anyone but Stefred what had underlain his panic in space, where he'd been literally paralyzed not by physical fear but by what was happening in his mind. He rarely thought of it himself any more, having learned to put such things aside and get on with life. Now, at Lianne's silent insistence, he let it well into memory: the detachment from ordinary reality, the horror of feeling that nothing had meaning in a universe too immense for rational comprehension. . . .

Lianne was speaking, urgently and aloud. "Those are feelings you connect with religion?"

He shook himself back. "I felt them first at Orison," he admitted, "though not as strongly as later on. I know they don't make sense; I doubt if they did even to Stefred, despite what he said about its being normal to get upset by unanswerable questions."

"They make sense," Lianne stated positively, surprisingly undisturbed by this most painful recollection of his past. "The fact that you've experienced them is—significant."

"Stefred called it a sign of strength." Noren had never fully understood that, though he'd tried to take Stefred's word for it.

"He was right, as he usually is within the limits of his knowledge. What's puzzled me is how anyone as strong as you could have shied away from them entirely, both the dark side and the bright. Now I see. You went part way on your own, young, in circumstances of great stress; and you got burned."

"Part way to what?" Noren whispered. *What bright side?*

"To another state of consciousness where perception is not tied to reasoning. If you want a physical explanation, such a state involves separate areas of the brain; but it's more than that, and more complicated. People react differently. Some find it pleasant—euphoric, even—but it can be terrifying, too, especially to anyone who values reason as much as you do."

But it's a way to see more of the truth, he thought, sensing from her emotion that the abyss that had haunted him was merely a stage on the road to the sort of mental power her own people possessed.

"I've been concerned," Lianne said, "because your culture has no real mystic tradition. The Founders were scientists and preserved little of what they could not analyze. The computer record glosses over what other values were cherished on the Six Worlds. Normally, you see, a planetary civilization at your level has both science and mysticism; and both are needed to reach the levels ahead. Your

(200

people's religion does inspire nonrational consciousness to some degree; evidently it did even in you. Yet City society doesn't encourage that, and Stefred isn't aware of what it signifies. The apparent meaninglessness of the universe is only one face of the coin. There is a state of—of *knowing* the meaning, knowing in a way beyond faith that everything fits together." Sighing, she added, "I can't describe it any more than you can describe the bad part. There are no words."

"You could show me . . . telepathically, couldn't you?" *Please, Lianne, please don't withhold this from me!* he pleaded silently.

"I have tried," she said gently. "At Orison I've tried to reach you, but you shut me out. I know why, now. You were burned once; underneath you're afraid to enter those regions again."

"Never mind that. Use deep trance if you need to; I'm willing."

She pressed his hand between hers, meeting his eyes. "Noren, to get there artificially, through hypnosis or drugs, is extremely dangerous. I'm trained to some extent, I could keep you from permanent harm, yet even if there weren't that past panic to be overcome, it would interrupt your working life. With that trauma, it would mean a much longer interruption than average. I'm not a psychiatrist in my own culture, you know; I can do more than Stefred only because a standard Service education covers far more information about the mind than Six Worlds psychiatrists possessed. I am no better qualified to heal you quickly than he was."

And in the future when his work was completed, Noren thought in anguish, she would be gone. If it ever was completed, ever could be. What would it be like, having saved his people, to know that Lianne was out among the stars somewhere, seeing worlds he could never see, probing spheres of consciousness he could not attain?

She shivered, as if the sorrow were more hers than his own; he found himself wanting to hold her. But on the point of embrace, they both stood back. There was nowhere that could lead except to tragedy.

"At least it helps to know a bright side exists," he said resolutely.

"It exists, and someday, if you hold your mind open to whatever inner experiences may come, you can reach it spontaneously. You have the proven capacity. To pursue that way actively simply isn't your role."

No, and to turn back from it was merely another sacrifice his role demanded. He wondered how many more there were going to be.

Somehow he got through the suspense of Veldry's pregnancy; through her confinement; through the Thanksgiving for Birth that followed the delivery of a healthy baby boy. He'd privately hoped he might learn the father's identity from that service, but Veldry forestalled him. "It would give away his secret, to you at least, if he arranged to preside," she said. So the regular roster was evidently followed; as it happened, ironically, it was Stefred who officiated. Noren wondered how Lianne hid her feelings from him, and what he would say if he knew what he'd inadvertently blessed.

Veldry wasn't permitted to nurse her own child this time, since there was no lack of wet nurses; but Lianne visited the nursery often enough to provide assurance that nothing was amiss. Gradually Noren's dread gave way to elation. The ensuing relief, however, was shadowed by the realization that his grace period was over—he must delay no longer in finding volunteers to produce other children.

The solution dawned on him unexpectedly. One evening in the refectory a new Scholar, a man named Denrul, joined the table where he was sitting with several friends; Noren, rather amused at first, watched him rest his eyes on Veldry with something akin to adoration. Denrul, though older than most novices, was too recently admitted to have lost his awe of City women, and he'd as yet heard none of the long-standing gossip. Her beauty, for him, overwhelmed all else. Or did it? There was more in Denrul's gaze than desire; Veldry's own eyes lit with response, and Noren perceived that hope had wakened in her once more. Telepathy? he thought wryly. Maybe it was; maybe that was what love at first sight always was. In any case the two seemed well on the way to becoming love-stricken.

A new Scholar, Noren thought with sudden excitement—one whose ties with City tradition weren't yet formed. As a recruit barely a week past recantation, Denrul's idealism would be at its peak; that did not seem quite fair, and yet why not, except because he was just the sort of person who might be swayed? If to try to sway such people was wrong, then so was everything else he, Noren, had done; his instinct to avoid taking advantage of immature consciences was, perhaps, merely a sign of conflict in his own.

"Yes," Lianne told him, "Denrul would be receptive—so would most candidates I've worked with, if approached early. I wondered when you would think of it."

She now worked with them—he hadn't stopped to consider that, for her discussions with candidates were as confidential as Stefred's own. Unrobed assistants had always monitored some phases of the enlightenment dreams; Lianne was by this time fully trained to do so routinely. Thus the novice Scholars, their first few days after recanting, knew her better than anyone in the City aside from Stefred, and they trusted her equally. Most of them were adolescent; all were elated by their triumph as heretics; all expected to adapt to new ways. Even more crucially, fresh from initial exposure to the dream sequence, they were loyal to the First Scholar alone. The secret dream, by Council decision, had thus far been made available only to people who'd experienced the full version of the First Scholar's other dream recordings: a policy Noren now saw was aimed toward restricting it to those with long-standing commitments to the Scholars' traditional goals. He had been charged by the First Scholar's words with full authority to decide who should be given access; he recalled that at first, Stefred had feared the power this gave him. Power, yes! Novices would emerge from that dream ready to support what they'd see as an underground movement within the still-mysterious Inner City society. There were not enough of them to affect policy decisions, but as volunteer parents they would suffice.

During the days he pondered this, Veldry and Denrul spent much time openly in each other's company. It reached the point where Noren wondered if she'd already told him; she'd have to explain about her genes, of course, if they became lovers, and in inoculating her he'd authorized her to reveal his own role as she saw fit. But when he brought up the subject, she seemed surprisingly embarrassed. "No," she said. "He'd agree, but it shouldn't come from me; that would be—seduction. You tell him, Noren. Tell him the truth about me, the whole truth. And then—" she blinked back tears "—then whatever he wants to do is up to him."

Noren sought out Denrul, and they had a long talk. "You understand," he said at the end of it, "that I'm asking you to perjure yourself as far as the Prophecy's concerned. That's what the others won't do, and you've recanted on that basis of believing they won't. To become a Scholar, at the same time realizing that according to our present knowledge, what you affirmed in the ceremony's false after all, won't be easy. Especially when you'll, well, gain personally—"

"Veldry? Noren, that's not how I feel about her," Denrul protested, shocked. "I'd never involve her in anything I had doubts over."

"I've told you frankly that you'll be far from her first lover."

"I will not," Denrul declared. "I'll be her husband if she'll have me at all."

"That's the village way," agreed Noren, wondering uneasily whether Denrul's fervent words reflected true devotion to Veldry or merely his inexperience with the Inner City's less-strict conventions.

"It's the only way right for her," insisted Denrul. "Look, here's a woman you say has had her choice of men—yet she thinks more about what's best for her descendants than who she chooses? I say she wants more than love. I say she deserves a partner committed to more."

"So do I," Noren admitted with relief. "But you see, people not in on this secret have no way of knowing what she really cares about."

Although Denrul had been won to the cause of genetic change without the secret dream, Noren was unwilling to alter the genes of anyone who hadn't experienced it. To be sure, it was too harrowing in some respects for anyone unready for the full version of the others; but it could be edited—Lianne was as skilled in that process as Stefred. During one long, agonizing night he went through it again, serving as monitored dreamer while she prepared a version suitable for those who'd recently completed the enlightenment dreams. This she kept in her personal possession. Denrul was told to sign up for library dream time; and on his scheduled night, she arranged to be on duty. Shortly thereafter, pale but resolute, he returned to Noren for inoculation.

A few weeks later, Denrul and Veldry stood up at Orison and to everyone's amazement exchanged marriage vows. Veldry wore everyday beige trousers instead of a traditional red bridal skirt, and there were no officially designated attendants; Noren, who couldn't publicly have assumed that role without arousing comment, found himself in the less welcome one of presiding priest. It was his regular turn, Veldry having carefully checked the roster, so when the newlywed couple stood before him to receive formal benediction, it was assumed they had no special friend to perform the office. The blessing was taken for a routine one. To Noren, however, it was a turning point: his own confirmation of total responsibility for other people's risks.

He joined them afterward for a private feast in Veldry's room, at which Lianne was the only other person present. She poured from a large jug she had brought, and Noren proposed the conventional toast: "To this union—may it be fruitful and bring lasting joy."

They drank. At the first taste Veldry seemed ebullient and Denrul perplexed; Noren, in bewilderment, burst out, "By the Star, Lianne, this stuff's like water! Couldn't you find any better ale?"

"Under the circumstances I thought watered ale might be more appropriate," she said pointedly, "considering where the water came from."

Denrul's puzzled frown gave way to bravado; with shaking hands he drained his cup without pausing. Indignantly Noren protested, "Lianne, that was cruel. At a marriage feast, a time for celebration—"

"No, Lianne's right," Veldry interrupted. "It's melodramatic, maybe, but not cruel. It's got to be like this. I mean, if we believe in what we're doing, believe strongly enough to overthrow the old traditions, we've got to establish new ones. We need to dramatize! Life's not all abstract science and ethics."

Lianne was brimming with exhilaration; it was as if the ale had been more potent than usual instead of less so. "I propose a second toast," she said, "to the day when stream water will be drunk sacramentally at village weddings."

In high spirits they finished the contents of the jug. Denrul—who like many heretics had sampled impure water before his arrest— passed the safe limit in a single evening; only for him was it a crucial step, since the others had consumed plenty of such water before. The symbolic significance in the act was nevertheless strong; for Noren in particular it was a poignant reminder of what he had lost, what he had yet to hazard before the gamble could pay off.

Later, walking back to his own lodging tower with Lianne, he mused, "I couldn't see for myself what Veldry saw; is that why I'm not getting anywhere, why I'm blind to the path ahead?"

"Partly." Lianne seemed troubled; the elation she'd shown earlier had faded. "I—I gave you a clue, Noren, in my toast; I don't think I overstepped my role because both Veldry and Denrul got what I was driving at. You . . . several things could cause you to find that harder."

"I've never liked ceremony, that's one, I suppose—though what happened in there was good. Were you doing something to us with your mind?"

"Nothing more than people usually do with their minds under such circumstances. That's one of the things you don't grasp about ceremony."

"Well, nobody here knows about psychic things."

"Not consciously. But they sense what's going on, as Veldry did —and as Stefred would. He'd deny the existence of telepathy, but he could predict exactly what the effects of the symbolic action would be."

"Why doesn't he, then? You say the clue's in your suggestion about watering the ale at village weddings, but he maintains villagers wouldn't be willing to drink unpurified water at all. And I should think a wedding would be the last occasion they'd pick to do it."

"There's a gap between existing tradition and what must replace it," she agreed. "Stefred can't bridge that gap; he's too bound to the conventions the Founders established. You are freer—precisely because you've stood off from religious symbolism, you are free to reinterpret it as the Founders reinterpreted their own. You've already tried that once, mistakenly, in trying to make gods of us—"

"And I'll not repeat that mistake."

"Have you analyzed it, though?"

Not as well as he should have, Noren thought with chagrin. His mistake, as with his earlier errors concerning religion, had been in trying to name the ultimate. He was willing now to call it the Star and let that go. But Lianne was talking not about ultimates but about concrete things: the provisions of the High Law, for instance. The things that not only could change, but must. The Law forbade drinking impure water; she foresaw not merely the breaking of that Law but its reversal, for people would never ignore religion on a formal occasion like a wedding. He'd imagined their hoarding what little purified water was left simply to serve wedding guests. . . .

"Oh, Lianne," he murmured. "I'm beginning to guess where you're leading—but if symbols can be manipulated like that, turned around and given whatever significance someone wants them to have—"

"It is dangerous," she admitted. "Like everything else, it's a principle that can be put to ill use, and on most worlds both unscrupulous men and sincerely deluded ones have misused it. Here there are exceptional safeguards, which you will have to override."

It was true, he reflected, that the Founders had deliberately created the symbols and ritual of a new religion in the first place; what they had done could in principle be redone. Yet conditions had not been the same. "I don't think Scholars would ever revise the basic symbols," he declared. "That's not as simple as creating a little ceremony to express our own feelings about defying a taboo we've already decided to ignore at our own risk. There'd be—well, no *authority* for it. People don't just make up their minds to change what things mean. The Scholars won't take my word for scientific facts; how can we expect that I can alter their religious views?"

"We can't," Lianne acknowledged. "The kind of thing we did tonight will help form a small group of dedicated volunteers to produce genetically altered children. What I proposed in the toast was something altogether apart; it concerned not the Scholars' religion but the villagers'."

"But one's got to lead to the other."

"Really? Who believed in the symbols first when the Founders established them?"

The villagers did, Noren realized, confused. The Founders gave them the Prophecy and High Law believing in the ideas behind the symbols, but it was the villagers who took them at literal face value; only later, when village-born heretics were brought into the City, did those symbols acquire true religious significance within the walls. "But we can't alter people's views by a proclamation from the Gates," he protested. "How can the interpretation in the villages change before it's changed here?"

Lianne stopped and faced him, reaching for his hand. "You're beginning to ask the right questions," she said, almost with sadness. "Noren, we are coming perilously close to things I must not say to you. If that last question is answered, it must be by you and you alone—not so much because I shouldn't intervene as for your own

(206

sake. I—I couldn't bear to have you change the shape of your life on my word."

She gave his cheek a light kiss, then turned quickly and hurried across the courtyard toward the tower where she lodged. Noren was left listening to the echo of her footsteps.

It was not long before Veldry was pregnant again; by that time, the group of volunteers had grown by another couple and several young men—novices still in adolescence—who were willing to be genetically altered as soon as they could find brides. That, of course, was the major problem, since relatively few girls became Scholar candidates; once a man's genes were altered, he would never be free to love Technician women, who could not participate in human experimentation. For this reason Noren decided to accept couples only, and their number was necessarily limited by the number of female novices who entered the City. It seemed a bit unfeeling to tell these women that if they wished to serve the cause of human survival, they must choose husbands immediately from among the eligible men on the waiting list; yet after all, in the villages most marriages were arranged by families. Few girls grew up expecting to marry for love. Though men and women alike were free to refuse the dream Lianne offered them, none did so, and none, having experienced the dream, refused to support the First Scholar's secret goal. They were not yet priests and had been told by Stefred that they need never assume the robe; the conflict between endorsement of the Prophecy and advocacy of genetic change was not severe with them. More significant, Noren suspected, was the fact that in working for the latter they were continuing to oppose authority. A new Scholar's biggest problem was generally turning from heresy to support of the established order.

The risk to the children was no longer a great worry, with Veldry's baby thriving well. The worst part of the whole business, for Noren and Lianne, was the extent to which they were deceiving Stefred. He had always been close to each Scholar he'd brought through candidacy; now all the new ones, within days of recantation, were being sworn to stop confiding in him. Noren feared some might break this oath, but Lianne seemed to see no danger. "It's not as if he's going to suffer any harm," she pointed out. "Oh, he'll feel hurt if he finds out about the conspiracy, but they don't realize that. He's still Chief Inquisitor to them; though they trust his integrity, they don't know he's vulnerable to personal feelings."

"You and I know." Noren bit his tongue; he was sorry that had slipped out, for Lianne was in a far worse situation than he was. She worked with Stefred, saw him daily and discussed the progress of these same novices with him. Furthermore, Stefred was still in love with her, though he'd long ago given up hope of her returning that love, and there was now small chance of his finding happiness with anyone else. Were he to be attracted to some newcomer, that woman would be committed to genetic experimentation before he was free to speak.

Denrul had chosen medical and surgical training, realizing that a physician who knew of the experimentation was desperately needed. On the side, he completed the computer training program in genetics, and Noren began tutoring him privately in the details of his own more advanced work. He himself must have a successor, in case . . . in case of emergency, he told himself firmly. The Service was not going to take him away aboard the starship, not ever. But the work was too vital to depend on a single person's presence; and besides, Denrul, who was to specialize in medical research, had more access to lab facilities than Lianne. There was even the possibility that after he was no longer being supervised, they could produce the genetic vaccine in the Inner City instead of having to make clandestine excursions to the officially off-limits domes.

Noren rarely saw Brek any more except at large gatherings, but when he did, Brek's troubled look was haunting. It was not only that Brek now thought the worst of him. Nuclear physics, for Brek, was finally producing the disillusionment Noren's greater talent had found there earlier. Even his happiness with Beris seemed affected. One evening, when she wasn't present, he approached Noren and said miserably, "You were . . . right. It's hopeless. I want you to know that I—I understand, better, why you gave it up. I can even forgive hypocrisy now; it's not like when we were younger, I can't seem to give up priesthood myself, and you—you never felt as I did about the Star in the first place. You at least believe we have *some* way of surviving."

"Are you sure my way's wrong?" Noren asked slowly.

"Maybe not. Maybe I'm simply a coward—only Beris . . . I couldn't let Beris—"

"Even if there were healthy babies before hers?" Telling Brek would do no harm now. He would never betray anyone, and though he might be shocked, sickened, by the now-available dream of the First Scholar's involvement, it would lend weight to what he'd viewed as an indefensible position. Things were not the same as before the birth of Veldry's son.

"That's a hypothetical question," Brek declared, "to which there's no honorable answer. I couldn't ask others to do the dirty part."

"Nor could I," agreed Noren; "but the issue's not hypothetical any more." He went ahead with the whole story.

"There's no excuse for me, for the way I doubted you," Brek said when he'd heard it all. "I've known you too long and too well.

(208

I'm not saying I could have done what you did—I've never been as strong as you—but I should have known things weren't as they seemed. I'll talk to Beris. I'll go through this dream; I owe you that much. Only . . . about the Prophecy . . . I'm not sure. Even if we keep working at the outpost, we'll know that cause is lost—"

"We know now," said Noren sadly.

Hypocrisy about it wasn't a solution—not for him, not for Brek, not for anyone. Yet neither was abandonment of the symbols. They must be reinterpreted, not abandoned; he'd known that since the night of Veldry's wedding . . . but how? How?

"I've been going at it backwards," he said to Lianne. "Destruction of symbols doesn't work, I know that! I tried it in the village when I was condemned for heresy, and then later I crashed the aircar on the way to trying it again; Stefred permitted it both times because he knew there was no danger of my succeeding. Yet I've still been thinking in those terms, and so has he. We can't ever get people to break the High Law by destroying their belief in it—"

"No more than the First Scholar could have overcome people's attachment to the Six Worlds by revealing those worlds were gone," she agreed.

"He gave them something *constructive*," reflected Noren, "turned a symbol of tragedy into one of hope."

"That wasn't a unique concept," Lianne said. "Successful religions of many worlds have been centered on symbols with transformed significance."

"Then what we do with watered ale at wedding feasts is more than dramatization of our defiance?"

"Well, it represents defiance, but not just of the Law. We defy our fear of destruction, Noren, and our confinement within the limits this world's environment imposes. It's a small thing, of course, not the equivalent of the Star and not nearly so powerful. Yet many religions do incorporate rites that involve food or drink with symbolic meaning; that's a missing element in what you've got here, where there are only negative taboos, and it would fit naturally."

"But nobody not already willing to drink impure water would accept it, or get any lift out of it if they did."

"No. By itself it's not the answer."

"What is?"

"Read up on the Six Worlds' religions, how they originated, how they changed," Lianne suggested, evading a direct answer.

He'd come to the end of the genetic design work and had found no way to experiment with plants past the sprouting stage, so he followed this advice—and was soon absorbed in a field of inquiry wholly new to him. In the past, he'd questioned the computers about beliefs; now he sought detail about the histories of those beliefs. It fascinated him and at the same time disturbed him . . . so many of the beliefs were manifestly untrue. And yet, it was not true that a miraculous star controlled the destiny of this world, either. Had the symbols of the ancients, even those taken literally, been less valid?

To be sure, evil as well as good had been done in the name of religion. Evil men had exploited religious feelings to attain their own ends; things done to certain heretics surpassed the worst of Noren's boyhood fears about his own fate. There had been hideous episodes in which whole opposing populations had slaughtered each other in the belief that their causes were holy. Manipulation of symbols could indeed, as Lianne had acknowledged, be dangerous. But the danger lay in the character of the manipulators. *Anything* could be twisted, perverted, used to destroy people's freedom, their minds, even their lives; still a man of integrity could lead without destroying. The First Scholar had done it. Before him, there had been others. There had been not only prophecies, but prophets, doing their best to combat whatever evil they were faced with. An appalling number of them had, like the First Scholar, died as martyrs. Unlike him, some had been openly worshiped after their deaths, yet, Noren realized, the worthy ones never sought this, would never have wanted it personally; it was a price to be paid for the victory of the truths they'd lived for.

Time went on; Noren resigned himself to an interval of inaction. Although he discovered no answers relevant to his own world, he felt he was gaining insight. The pain of past losses had dulled, and while he could not call himself happy, his appreciation of the Inner City—of his access to the computer complex and the Six Worlds' accumulated wisdom—began to return. It was anguish to know that Lianne's people had far more knowledge than the computers, knowledge he could not attain; still he had by no means exhausted the resources available to him. *More than you can absorb in a lifetime,* Stefred had promised him long ago; and that was true. Lianne herself knew only a fraction of what the Service knew.

Lianne too was unhappy, but not on that account; she grieved for him more than for her own deprivations. Increasingly, she shielded even her emotions. He wondered if she missed her people despite her insistence that she did not. "It's normal in the Service to spend long periods alone," she declared, "that is, apart from our own kind. I'm not really alone. Here, I'm among people equal to my own; with individuals, the evolutionary distance doesn't count. That's significant only for cultures."

Another child was born to Veldry, a girl, Denrul's daughter. Soon afterward, a son was born to the second genetically altered couple, premature but otherwise healthy. That made three healthy children, two of whom had the altered genes from both parents, and since several other couples had been recruited—including Brek and Beris —more were already on the way. It was almost time for the first child's weaning. He would be sent out for adoption soon; a plan for keeping track of his whereabouts must be made.

"Is this the tradition I must somehow overthrow?" Noren asked. "We can't rear families in the City, both because there isn't room and because the castes mustn't become hereditary; but I suppose the custom of losing track of our children isn't essential. It was set up merely because the Founders felt Scholars should sacrifice normal kinship ties."

To his surprise, Lianne shook her head. "It's far more important than that; the system couldn't work without it. If Scholars' children weren't reared as villagers, indistinguishable from the others, a question would arise that no one here's ever raised: the question of how much more survival time could be bought if some villages' life support were cut off. There'd be a kind of division even the castes don't create."

Horrified, Noren protested, "We're stewards! We couldn't possibly prolong life on this planet by not spreading the resources equally."

"That's what a starship captain does in an emergency," Lianne pointed out. "Where it's a choice between death for some and ultimate death for all. And that's what it would come to when the time ran out here with no metal synthesization in sight. The Founders foresaw it. They barred specific records of adoptions because they knew Scholars wouldn't cut off their own offspring as long as there was any alternative."

"It's a tradition I can't tamper with, then."

"You can't abolish it," she agreed, "but you'd be justified in modifying it because with genetic changes, the villages will be self-sufficient. It won't matter if the advocates know where their children are. . . ."

She went on talking, but Noren was deep in thought. As always, it came back to the problem of how to withdraw City aid without bloodshed. Religious sanction . . . but he was no closer to knowing how to provide that than he'd been seasons ago. "You told me to study how the Six Worlds' religious traditions changed," he said reflectively, "but things were different there. The leaders with new ideas, the prophets, weren't shut away in a City, and usually they weren't the official priests. They were often considered heretics, as far as that goes. They lived among common people and interacted with them."

There was an abrupt silence; Lianne cut off what she'd been saying in midsentence. "Priests here begin as heretics," she said, her blue eyes focused on his. "And they do grow up among the people."

"But as heretics they can't persuade anybody to change. I know; I tried it! And after they get in a position to speak with authority, they're isolated."

Lianne kept on looking at him. "Must they be?" she asked quietly.

"Well, of course; the most basic tradition we have is our confinement to the City—" He broke off, struck suddenly, horribly, by the implications of what he had said. *Tradition*. By tradition, Scholars did not mingle with villagers. When he and Brek had planned to defy that tradition, they'd gone as relapsed heretics, not as priests, and would not have been recognized as Scholars. But if a robed Scholar were to walk into a village square, people would listen to what he told them, listen in a way different from the way they listened at formal ceremonies. On the platform before the Gates, Scholars were anonymous figures; in a village they'd be seen as individually human. . . .

Or superhuman.

Faintness came on him as the blood drained from his face. "Set out to become a prophet, you mean? Lianne, I couldn't!"

She remained silent, waiting; he sensed her sympathy, but not whether the thing he was now thinking was what she'd foreseen all along. "I couldn't," he repeated. "You didn't grow up here yourself; maybe you don't know how villagers feel about us. They'd worship me! It would be everything the First Scholar wanted to avoid when he set up our anonymity—why, they'd follow me around, treat every word I uttered as holy."

"Well, yes, that would be the idea," she agreed. "They would accept what you said in personal contact with them when they'd never tolerate it as a sudden ceremonial proclamation. They'd get used to the idea of a coming change, over the years—"

"Years!"

"Oh . . . I assumed, that is, I was thinking in terms of the preparation years being the main point. The genetic testing of crops will take a long time, too, and you could handle it yourself—" She bit her lip, hesitant, unsure how far he had gone in the perception of something obviously well-developed in her own mind.

"We won't be able to delay more years after we prove the change is safe to implement," Noren protested. "It's bad enough having to wait for the first generation of babies to grow up."

"You don't have to wait shut inside the City."

"Start talking to villagers *now,* not knowing for certain that implementation's going to become possible?"

"You're confident of the vaccine now."

"Three normal babies, yes, I'm confident enough to use it on as many Scholars as will accept it. But I'm not ready to risk the entire species. And—and if I promised such a change, people would want a demonstration; that would mean human experimentation on villagers, which is unthinkable."

"If it's unthinkable, Noren," Lianne said bluntly, "you had best say so before Veldry's baby is adopted. When that boy matures, you will have human experimentation among villagers whether you like it or not, with the first child he begets. The gene pool of the species will be permanently affected. Surely you weren't counting on his being convicted of heresy before ever touching a girl."

He had been. Without thinking it through, he'd pictured the children becoming heretical enough to reach the City while remaining conventional enough to marry young—and getting arrested in that short interval, as he himself had been, mere days before his planned marriage to Talyra. It was true that with their adoption he'd be committed to tests involving non-Scholars. Perhaps a small-scale experiment with village volunteers would be no worse.

That paled, however, beside the other issue. To personally visit the villages . . . but of course, it would be impossible. "Stefred wouldn't let me go outside the City," he said, ashamed of the inward relief that swept through him at remembrance of the obstacle.

"Stefred can't keep you from going," Lianne argued, "any more than he can stop me when I go."

"Not from walking out the Gates, no—but if I spoke to villagers he'd have me brought back and lock me up from then on." The Technicians who reported to Stefred kept in touch by radiophone and aircar; village affairs were quickly known in the City, and Stefred would not hesitate to use force if he believed the people's welfare was at stake.

"I think you're mistaken," said Lianne slowly. "Noren—Stefred knows human experimentation has gone on."

"Knows? You told him?"

"Of course not, but do you think anyone as perceptive as he could remain blind so long, when we recruit all the novices?"

"But if he knew, he'd have put a stop to it."

"No. Interference would be an even worse threat to the Inner City than supporting you would be; social interaction here is founded on the right of each Scholar to make his or her own decisions. Stefred can't override that when the experimentation does no harm to people not involved in it. If he felt that there was danger of children with defective genes being sent to the villages, he'd act, but he trusts your scientific competence."

"Have you—discussed it with him?" Noren asked, appalled.

"No! Never—and I haven't picked up much from his mind, either; he shields more than when I first knew him, as if he has secrets of his own. But he's an excellent psychologist, after all, and on that basis I can predict his reactions, even his reaction to the idea of your speaking out publicly."

"He left me free to do that before because he judged me bound to fail," Noren said. "If he kept his hands off again—well, I wouldn't be willing to do such a thing as a mere gesture. I'd have to believe I could succeed; yet if in principle I could, he'd be duty-bound to prevent it. The Council would force him to."

"You underestimate Stefred. He has more independence than you give him credit for—and more courage." Lianne's eyes filled with tears. "More courage than I have, Noren."

"I don't understand—"

"Because there's so much you don't yet see, and I—I'm not brave enough to tell you. Stefred will be. Since he can stop you anyway if he wants, you have nothing to lose by talking it over with him. As a favor to me, will you do that?"

"Yes," Noren promised, putting his arm around her, realizing from her trembling that she was even more upset than he himself. "If a time comes when I feel I should talk to villagers, I'll talk to Stefred first."

He tried to drive the idea from his mind, but it would not let him be. The more he thought of it, the more he knew it could work. It would demand unprecedented personal sacrifice, as Lianne had foreseen; the idea of receiving homage was repugnant to him. The prospect of doing so in official ceremonies when he got older was bad enough; this other would be infinitely worse. He had never liked villages in any case and would despise whatever time he spent there, all the more so because his role would encompass all the most difficult aspects of priesthood. Yet several ends would be served by it: not only alteration of the villagers' attitude, but the crop testing—which he could accomplish with the aid of Technicians under his orders—and continuous observation of the children through successive visits.

The one thing he did not see was how Stefred could let it happen. But he had never known Lianne to be wrong. And he'd promised her to discuss it with Stefred, rash though that seemed. She avoided him during his days of deliberation; she seemed afraid to confront him, afraid even to meet his eyes. Noren knew he must get the decision over with.

"Yes," Stefred admitted when Noren asked, "I've known for some time you are experimenting. I don't know exactly who's involved, and I don't want to. It's a matter for individual consciences."

They were alone in the study, in the old way, the old atmosphere of trust strong between them; it was as if there had never been any rift. Never again, Noren thought, would he stay away from the one person with whom he felt free to express his deepest thoughts. Even with Lianne he was not as free as he was with Stefred; between Lianne and himself, on both sides, was the tension of holding back feelings. And he feared hurting Lianne, whereas Stefred, as she'd perceived, had unlimited strength to face whatever needing facing.

"I've hated deceiving you," Noren said, knowing the words

(214

weren't necessary, knowing too that one deceit must continue. He could never reveal Lianne's identity or the fact of her people's existence; but with the reasons for that restriction, Stefred would concur.

"You've had to deceive me," Stefred acknowledged. "As I've deceived you, pretending not to know."

"I'll spare us both and tell you the next step outright." He did so, finding the words came easily. Stefred's face, listening, was unreadable.

For a long time after Noren finished he was silent. Then, wonderingly, he said, "It . . . might work. It's bolder than anything that's occurred to me, further from the principles I've spent my life upholding. Strict isolation from the villagers is indispensable to their freedom under our system, yet while we hold to it, the High Law can't be altered. In contact with villagers . . . there would be a chance. We'd have a chance, while otherwise there is none."

"You're saying you'd *support* me?" Noren asked, incredulous. To his chagrin, he felt more dread at the thought than elation.

"No," Stefred told him. "If we should commit ourselves to your plan and fail, the morale of the Inner City would be destroyed just as surely as if I had supported you all along—and without the Inner City's stability, the villages would be doomed. I can't risk that, even knowing this change may be the only means of saving our remote descendants. I have a responsibility to the intervening generations."

Noren found himself tongue-tied, unable, somehow, to argue. Had he come to Stefred hoping that he'd be overruled and would thus escape the burden of carrying out a plan he hated?

There was another pause. Then in a low voice Stefred said, "It's impossible for me to support you. But if you take it upon yourself to act, I will look the other way, Noren."

"I—thought you might. The idea depends on your treating it as you have the experimentation. Yet in this case, how can you get away with that?"

"The Gates are unlocked; we are held here only by our freely accepted obligation to follow the First Scholar's rules. If you decide your conscience leads you elsewhere, no one will hear that the issue was discussed between us."

"But wouldn't tolerance on your part be the same as support as far as most Scholars are concerned? If I'm allowed to come and go, they'll see you're letting me do it."

Stefred's eyes widened with surprise that faded into evident pain. "By the Star," he murmured, "I've been wondering how you of all people could propose this scheme so calmly. I assumed you understood what you'd be taking on." He rose and came to Noren, laying a steady hand on his shoulder. "I didn't say I could permit you to

215)

come and go," he said quietly. "Only to go once, with the assurance that as long as you incite no violence you won't be brought back by force."

Stunned, Noren formed words with difficulty; his mouth was so dry he wondered if they were audible. "Leave the City—permanently?"

"You'd best think in those terms. Many years from now, after the genetic change has been accomplished, you might be able to return; but our society will be so altered that neither you nor I can make sure predictions."

It hardly mattered. Years . . . enough years for the babies to grow up and have babies of their own, then for inoculation of the whole population . . . and then the cutoff of the purified water supply; if he made people accept that through their trust in him, he would have to stay with them while it was happening. Yes, to be exiled that long would be the same as permanence.

He had never imagined that kind of exile. From the morning he'd first seen the City, its bright towers dazzling with reflected sunrise, he had believed he would live and die within its walls. That thought had uplifted him even while he'd assumed he would die soon. He'd invited capture for the sake of one brief glimpse of such existence. There had been disillusionment; the City was not the Citadel of All Truth he'd envisioned, shouting his heresy before the Gates in defiance of the Law that barred them. It did not hold all he'd expected to find; not, he now knew, all he might find elsewhere in the universe. It was nevertheless the sole repository of knowledge in his world, and its contents had been ample compensation for what was formally termed "perpetual confinement." How could he give up that sustenance? Access to knowledge was his life's core. He'd contemplated eventual exile at the research outpost, but only with the supposition that stored knowledge would be transferred there, that it would become the last bastion of knowledge when the City's technology wore out. To leave the City now, to live in a Stone Age culture among people with whom he could never speak of matters not taught in the village schools, without the computer complex, without tapes or even books apart from village tales and the Book of the Prophecy. . . .

This was the step to which he'd been blind, blind because he could not face the thought of it; the thing of which Lianne had warned, seeing it far in advance—yet lacking the courage to open his eyes. This was the thing she'd known only Stefred could tell him.

"I can't make it easy for you," Stefred said, "and harsh though it may sound, I wouldn't at this moment even if I could."

"Because you want me to fail," Noren said, not bitterly but in simple acknowledgment that Stefred's compassion and his duty were at odds. "You've always opposed genetic change, apart from believing it couldn't be brought about safely; you don't think it's the lesser of evils."

"I do think it is. I must be ruthless with you because I want you to succeed."

Noren turned in his chair, looking up at Stefred in utter astonishment. He could not speak.

"I look far ahead, as you do, Noren," Stefred went on. "I can't say it's wrong to put survival of our species ahead of all other goals, important though they are. I oppose you only because it would be self-defeating to put short-term survival at risk for the sake of long-term survival. Now for the first time you've come to me with a plan that entails no such risk. Of course I want you to succeed in it. But it's more demanding than you realize, and you must face that from the start—only by doing so can you become strong enough to deal with the problems you'll meet."

No doubt, Noren thought numbly. If he could find courage to accept exile from the City, he'd have courage to do anything; as usual, Stefred understood him perfectly. "I'm . . . not sure I can," he confessed. "I've borne everything else so far without cursing fate, without asking why it has to be me who gets hurt. Yet this is so ironic—I'm just about the only person in here who doesn't look at City confinement as a sacrifice—"

"It is not ironic," Stefred said, drawing his own chair close to Noren's and sitting down again. "The fact that for you the sacrifice works the other way is providential. Noren, priesthood itself is founded on voluntary sacrifice. The Scholars who are homesick for the villages would have buried guilt feelings if they returned; and you will be in a position where you can't afford not to feel wholly sure of your worthiness to fill the role in which you'll be cast."

"I don't feel sure," Noren protested. "Oh, I know that I haven't got selfish motives for letting people worship me. But I'm not really qualified to inspire them. I haven't any gift for it; I'm a good scientist, but in dealing with people I'm—inept."

"I would not let you go if it were otherwise," Stefred told him. "That handicap, too, will work for rather than against you."

"How, when I need to win their confidence?"

"You will win it through your symbolic role and your integrity alone; you'll be in no danger of receiving personal adulation. For a natural leader, even one who didn't want homage, there would be that danger; by his very charisma he would, against his will, become a god. That's a concept you may not be familiar with—"

"I've read," said Noren shortly, not mentioning that it was from Lianne that his knowledge of gods had first come. "The idea's blasphemous."

"To you, yes, as it should be. To villagers it would seem a natural extension of the supposed superhuman stature of Scholars.

And that fact creates peril, Noren. Our system keeps power-seekers from the priesthood, it even eliminates those who might be corrupted by the collective power we do have; but it cannot completely protect against the possibility that a natural leader in close contact with villagers might be tempted to use his power to serve unselfish ends beyond survival of the species. He might impose his own concept of what's good for people upon them; that's one reason such contact has been prohibited. What's more, the people would welcome a godlike leader. They would demand that he take responsibilities they can better exercise for themselves. Someone gifted enough in leadership to assume them would not be the right person to enter the villages as prophet; but you, I trust."

Lianne had known these things, too, Noren perceived. They must have entered into her initial judgment of him as the only Scholar qualified to bring about genetic change. "What would happen," he ventured, "if I couldn't keep my promises to the people—if the genetic alteration I've designed fails in the next generation, or if the Council refuses to implement it after it's proven?"

Stefred hesitated, frowning. "There would be no harm done," he said, "at least not by your actions. That's why I can safely let you go."

"But the people would lose faith; they'd feel betrayed—they might not trust Scholars at all any more."

"You won't be speaking for the Scholars, though they'll assume you are." He leaned forward and met Noren's eyes unflinchingly. "If the experimental change fails, I will denounce you as no true priest but a renegade, and they'll believe not what you've said, but what's said of you in the formal ceremonies—because the latter will be what they'll then want to believe. Does that risk frighten you?"

"No," said Noren resolutely. With quiet despair he became aware that Stefred had been speaking for some time in simple future tense, assuming that his choice was already firm, and inwardly he knew he was indeed committed. He was not sure he could endure exile or fulfill the role he must assume; beside those things, public humiliation seemed a minor ordeal. Apart from failure itself it did not scare him.

"It should," Stefred informed him. "I'm not sure you see all the consequences of failure."

"I'm satisfied enough with the vaccine to stake my chances on it."

"You realize that if you are publicly banished from the priesthood, the villagers may kill you?"

He hadn't, but as Stefred said it he knew it for truth, and nodded. How he'd changed, he thought—long ago, when he and Brek had resolved to become real renegades and repudiate the Prophecy, they'd expected death at the hands of the villagers; but now he felt none of the resignation he had then. He no longer had any hidden desire to become a martyr.

"There is something more," Stefred continued. "As you say, if the vaccine proves safe, majority opinion among Scholars may still hold fast against implementation of genetic change. I will have the power to override the Council decision, secretly if necessary, and I won't hesitate to use it if I am sure the villagers will give up City aid willingly. My highest loyalty is, and always has been, to them and their descendants. But if at the time you've set for the change they're against it, or so divided that interruption of the pure water supply would lead to widespread violence, it will be no better than if the vaccine itself had failed. I'll still have to denounce you and even your own followers may turn on you; if they do, I'll lift no hand to save you. Do you understand why?"

In a low voice Noren said, "It would be the same kind of situation as it was with the First Scholar; people were justifiably angry, and he led them to take it out on him instead of killing others. I have to—to plan it that way from the beginning, don't I . . . make sure that if I fail, I'll be the only one to bear the blame."

"Yes," Stefred said gently. "I'm trusting you for that, too. I couldn't very well refuse to after all these years of saying you're more like the First Scholar than any other man I've known."

Noren looked around the familiar study, realizing with a shock that after this day he might never enter it again. More than any other place in the City it had been home to him; more than anyone else in his life, excepting only Talyra, Stefred had been family. Now if they ever did meet again, Stefred would be *old.* . . .

He stood up. "We can't communicate, can we," he stated, knowing the answer.

"No. I'll have reports on your actions from Technicians, but you must not send direct word, and you won't know what's happening here."

"It's better if I don't; it won't be good news."

"You'll be despised by all but your secret supporters," Stefred agreed, "and I can't openly defend you. If the Council wants you stopped, I will have only one weapon to ensure your freedom—the argument that you've made promises for which you must take personal responsibility."

Promises. A new age; a new kind of City built by common men, of stone; new seed that would flourish in untreated land. Machines, yes—to villagers any unknown object was a Machine. Knowledge, too, for who was to decide the bounds of knowledge? He could make it all fit the Prophecy, and the people would never know what they must lose.

Stefred's face was drawn with pain. "This is true priesthood," he said, "to take the universe as it is and affirm what we cannot alter. What's humanly possible to change, we will. We must change even our own biological design when survival demands it. But we have no power to reorder the world to match our hopes. If there is no way to preserve our ancestors' knowledge—if despite all our striving, its loss is inherent in the nature of things—then we must affirm that fact without despair. The Prophecy is a metaphor, not a blueprint. It proclaims a future better than the present. That's the only absolute we can have faith in."

His throat aching, Noren stood mute while Stefred embraced him. Then he turned quickly, knowing he must go before tears surfaced.

Stefred called him back. "Noren," he said. "Noren . . . make a good future for my son."

What a strange way to put it, Noren thought; the children of Stefred's wife must now be full-grown, and he had never mentioned any particular one, nor had he acknowledged other offspring. "The future belongs to the new race," he said firmly. "Perhaps to some of your son's children, Stefred, if he accepts genetic alteration himself in his later life."

"He won't need to. He was born with genes adapted to this world."

"Born—" Noren's breath caught; in shock, he whispered, "Veldry's son . . . *yours?* But she wouldn't have—"

"Wouldn't have revealed your secret to me, no. But watching you preside at the service for her dead baby, Noren, I guessed; I knew you too well not to realize there was just one reason you could have been suffering as you were. I also knew Veldry well enough to anticipate what she'd do next, and when I saw her begin to smile at men she had previously discouraged, I confronted her with it. She'd had no hope of finding anyone who approved of the experiments; she was ready to sacrifice her pride by offering herself to one of those unlikely to care one way or the other. I spared her that, at least."

"You were willing to take the risk, knowing how my son died, knowing yours might die too or else live with some horrible handicap, and that if he didn't, if things turned out well, you could never tell anyone?"

"Not even you—I couldn't have told you if you were remaining here; the others would read it in your eyes. My stand against genetic change is all that's prevented the idea from tearing the Inner City apart. But did you suppose I could favor your goal and let the burden rest on you alone?" Himself close to tears, Stefred went on, "You must bear the heaviest load; I can't spare you any part of it —but I can't spare myself, either."

"Oh, Stefred." He could neither spare himself nor be spared, Noren thought; the worst, for Stefred, was yet to come. Lianne would disappear, and in that grief he'd be unable to see any purpose.

Abruptly, inspired by unconscious telepathy, Stefred said, "Noren, you mustn't tell Lianne; it would ruin her recruiting system. Unless . . . it just occurs to me . . . she may go with you. If she offers, you must accept for the sake of her happiness as well as yours."

"The rumors aren't true," Noren said. "We aren't lovers; I thought you knew that."

"I know that so far your love is unconsummated—but I also know, perhaps better than you do, that it exists. It would be harmless for the two of you to share the village work. I would . . . miss Lianne, miss her a great deal, but I could train another assistant who'd win novices to your cause."

"No," said Noren steadily. "Lianne has her mission, as I have mine. After tonight we won't see each other again."

In the computer room, after he'd generated the tapes of essential data, checked and rechecked, realizing that this was his last opportunity ever to question the computers personally, Noren recalled the secret file once more, for courage. He reread the First Scholar's last words to him: MAY THE INFINITE SPIRIT GUIDE AND PROTECT YOU; AS I DIE, YOU WILL BE IN MY THOUGHTS.

When he'd experienced those dying thoughts in dream form— that most intense transfer of knowledge which, like all other kinds, would now be unavailable to him—they had concerned not genetic change, but the Prophecy. Were the promises indeed one and the same? As Stefred had said, the Prophecy was metaphor. The First Scholar had not composed its words. *It's there in my mind, but I've never been able to frame it as it should be,* he'd thought through his pain. *I'm a scientist, not a poet.* . . . He, Noren, was also a scientist. Would he be able to find adequate words for new promises, or would his sacrifice be futile?

He should wait, perhaps, and compose the words before going. But if he waited, he would wait forever; he would lose courage, not gain it. He might already have lost what had carried him through the day. . . . Motionless, clinging to the console he might never touch again, he found he could not choose a question to be his last.

His head dropped, and he wept.

Lianne found him there long after midnight. Noren turned slowly, reaching out to her. "Lianne," he said in agony. "I *can't.*"

She touched his face with cool, gentle fingers. "You have no choice."

"Yes, I have choice! No one's path is predestined; no one's required to take on the job of saving the world."

"I didn't mean that. I meant you've already chosen. You may feel you can't go—but can you stay?"

No. It was as simple as that. He could not stay in the City, aware of what he might achieve outside it; if he tried, he would only come to despise himself.

Lianne held him close as they left the computer complex, giving him no chance to look back. They sat on a stone bench in the courtyard, under fading stars. "All this time," she murmured, "all this time, nearly four years, I've known you would go before I did. That you'd give up not just the things you longed for, but those you already had."

She too was an exile, Noren thought, though her renunciation of her heritage was temporary, and he'd done little to ease her loneliness. His arms tightened around her; now that it was too late, all the pent-up passion he'd denied was rising in him: passion not only of his body but of his yearning to reach Lianne's world. Just when had he stopped measuring Lianne against Talyra? He would always love Talyra, but she had been dead four years; she wouldn't have wanted him to mourn indefinitely. He hadn't waited solely for her sake. He had held back, unwittingly guarding himself against this moment, the moment of the inevitable parting. And now that it had come, it was no easier for his long self-restraint.

"I don't know why I wasted the years," he said with remorse. "I wanted to love you, but I felt—frozen. Sometimes I think I'm the one who's alien."

"I understood how it was with you, Noren. As a child you lost your mother; as a man you lost your bride—you couldn't love only to lose again. You were afraid to give your heart, and I wouldn't have wanted less."

"Yet you knew we'd lose each other, too, and you weren't afraid."

"I'd have taken the time we could have rather than none," she acknowledged. "But people are different, born different, and not only because of their genes. You were born to stand apart, as you were born with a questioning mind."

"Maybe it's a good thing, since I'll always have to," he declared. His position would be solitary past the endurance of a warmer person. Furthermore, a Scholar in the villages could love no woman; in the eyes of the people, any such relationship between castes would be shockingly unnatural. It was no longer important that his genes were damaged; no situation where it mattered could arise. And anyway, he would not want anyone but Lianne. He'd given his heart despite himself, long ago; he would not give it a third time even after she was gone from the world.

Would he know when she was gone? Someday the starship would return; would he look up some night and see a light move and know that was the moment when she was lost to him? When the doors of the universe were for him irrevocably closed?

Her face was wet against his, and sobs shook her body. *Oh,*

Lianne, he thought, *how could I have deceived myself so? If I'd been as honest about my feelings as about my beliefs, we'd have had what people think we've had. . . .*

"We have the rest of tonight," Lianne said. "We still can have memories."

He took her into the lodging tower, and for a few brief hours of his last night in the City, Noren's spirits were lifted.

X

IN THE MORNING, NOREN TOOK THE BLUE ROBE FROM BENEATH
his bed, opening the storage compartment quietly so as not to wake
Lianne—though he knew she was only pretending to be asleep. She
was right; there must be no farewell. Neither of them could get
through it without breaking. He would need his strength for this
day, and for the days ahead.

He had no real plan. "Take things as they come," Stefred had
advised him. "You've always been quick-witted and resourceful;
rely on those assets instead of trying to deal with what you can't
foresee. You have the right instincts. You'll find them more effective
than you expect."

Lianne had put it somewhat differently. "You will receive—
inspiration, Noren," she'd said seriously. "I don't know how to explain this to you, but I am sure, from many worlds' experience,
that it is true. Unconscious functions of the mind play a part in it,
but one draws, too, on something outside oneself."

"If that were true universally, Stefred would know," Noren had
objected; but he'd recalled as he did so that Stefred wasn't aware
even of telepathy.

"He knows," Lianne had replied. "He said, 'May the spirit of
the Star go with you,' didn't he?"

Naturally he had, and he'd said it with more feeling than people
did on less momentous occasions. Now, suddenly, it occurred to
Noren that the common, conventional phrase might—like the equally
improbable-sounding prediction of the Star's physical appearance—
reflect an actual concrete fact. Was the difference only in the extent
of the Founders' understanding?

He took his blue robe and the clothes he wore, nothing else. As a
condemned heretic he had arrived in the City with nothing and
he'd acquired nothing during the interval, for as stewards, Scholars
were not permitted personal belongings. The data tapes he'd generated he took to the Outer City lab, placing them in the custody
of the Technician in charge, with specific orders about their storage.
From there, he proceeded to the City's exit dome. His hand trem-

(224

bling, he pushed the button to slide back the heavy Gates. They began to open, revealing blinding white pavement beyond; Noren touched the button again to reverse them as he stepped through.

From the outside they were, of course, unopenable.

He was prepared for the panic that hit him; having been conditioned to it both by dreaming the First Scholar's death and by his own initiation ordeal, he knew what he would feel. There was no ugly mob now, still he found himself flinching as he approached the platform's edge. Here the First Scholar had been struck down; here he himself had been pelted with dirt during the reenactment to which he'd been subjected, without warning, at his recantation. He had not been outside the Gates since that day. His trips to and from the outpost had been made by air; Scholars never stood on this platform except during public ceremonies. The first such ceremony of one's priesthood, he'd heard, was a grueling test of nerve: one was sent out alone so that remembered terror would counter one's aversion to mass obeisance. One was not expected to endure either for more than a few minutes; prolonged exposure to kneeling multitudes was unheard of.

Noren started down the long flight of steps, wide steps up which crowds swarmed at recantations and on feast days. The steps, too, held memories. Talyra had stood on them, watching in anguish as he'd faced abuse, humiliation and finally the sentencing; he had believed then that he would never see her again. Would she be living now if there'd been no reunion? She might have died anyway with her first child, no matter who she'd married. That was something he would never know.

Before recantation, he had been on the steps himself; it was there he'd been recaptured after his escape from the village had proved useless. He had been injured and penniless; he'd known it was only a matter of hours till Technicians would apprehend him—but he had reached the walls of the City. And the sight of the City had so stirred him that nothing else seemed to matter. The sound, also . . . there had been music, his first experience with the awesome electronic music he'd since come to take for granted. It had heartened him. Was it not better, he'd thought, to die defiant than to be dragged to his fate like a work-beast marked for slaughter? And might he not shake the crowd's blind faith if he could induce the Scholars to act openly against him? A blue-robed priest had emerged from the Gates to preside at Benison, the daily ritual for opening the markets; when that priest had read from the Book of the Prophecy, Noren had cried out against the apparent falsity of the words. He'd kept shouting his protests till Technicians stunned him; the crowd assumed the Star itself had struck him down for his blasphemy. He had known better, and he had believed himself doomed to torture and execution, yet inside he had hardly minded;

225)

for they had carried him through the Gates into the City. The City . . . the one place on the earth he had ever wanted to be.

Now, years later, he looked back up those steps toward the again-impenetrable walls and the glimmering towers beyond. They shone in the hot sun of midmorning. He could not gaze at them any more; it hurt too much, hurt more deeply than the sting of his watering eyes. . . .

And besides, at the foot of the steps, a small, eager cluster of people was gathering.

This was, in their view, a blessed day. It was something to tell their grandchildren: the day a Scholar descended the steps, the day they knelt within reach of his hands! There were a few Technicians in the group; these might have seen Scholars at close range before. But the villagers certainly hadn't. They had not been sure whether a Scholar's hands were made of ordinary flesh or were, perhaps, translucent. Noren steeled himself and extended his arms in blessing. He had no right to deprive them of that. This first congregation was composed of reverent people, those who cared about the Prophecy, the future; the ones who did not care had remained in the market stalls. His appearance being unprecedented, no custom compelled anyone to come forward; he had not beckoned; these had approached him as seekers of hope. They looked to him for what he himself had once thought to find within the City. *A priest gives.* . . . If they wanted a tale to pass down to their descendants, well, he was here to make sure they could have descendants to pass it to.

"May the spirit of the Mother Star abide with you, and with your children, and your children's children," Noren said with solemnity. "I have brought you good news of the coming age."

It was both easier and harder than he'd expected it to be: easier because words did come to him, sincere words that left him feeling no taint of dishonesty; yet harder because he had not foreseen the practical problems that would arise.

He had known he would attract attention, but that was an understatement. People flocked to him. They knelt silently, not cheering— for that would not be seemly—but simply waiting, eyes devoutly raised toward the sky; and after he'd passed, they got to their feet for a better view. Whether they heard what he said was questionable; they were too absorbed by the thrill of his mere presence. But at this stage, that did not matter. He was a long way from asking them to break the High Law; what he must accomplish at first was simply to win their trust—and that he could do only by being worthy of trust. More and more clearly, as the first day passed, Noren understood why Stefred and Lianne had believed he might succeed where equally worthy Scholars would fail. Only his mood of self-sacrifice was making this possible. If he had come to the people in any state other than total despair about his own future, he could never have borne their veneration; as it was, he didn't have to remind himself that he had no ulterior aims.

It was not, of course, necessary for the people to venerate Scholars as they did; that was no part of the Founders' design. No Scholar had ever encouraged the belief that priests were superhuman. It had arisen spontaneously over the generations, and there was no way to stamp it out, for the sole alternative to being seen as transcendent would have been to become all-too-human tyrants. But now, Noren saw, there was some chance he could counter that belief; he could demonstrate his own humanity. He must move very carefully, however. He must retain authority to speak, and given a choice, he preferred mystical authority to individual authority. Better that he should be classed among impersonal beings than that he be considered an idol in his own right.

The fact that he'd be assumed to be superhuman was his chief protection against being recognized as a former heretic; no one in the first weeks would be likely to look at his face, and he'd soon have grown a beard. People saw what they expected to see. As long as he kept away from his home village, where he might run into his father or brothers, there was small danger. His family would be unlikely to speak out in any case, lest they be accused of blasphemy; the provision that only older Scholars could appear publicly was meant to prevent multiple recognitions rather than particular ones. He had been away for a number of years, and was not the same person he once had been. The years had aged him more than they'd have aged a carefree farmer.

He had no plan as to where to go; but it soon became apparent that without declaration of a destination, he would never get away from the market area outside the walls. People would block the roads; as word spread, they would travel from far and wide, leaving farms and village shops untended. Furthermore, it would soon take on the atmosphere of a carnival. His first listeners might be devout, but they would soon be joined by the merely curious; before long everyone, even the nonchalant, would want to see the show. Huge crowds always came to the markets for festivals, such as Founding Day and the Blessing of the Seed, and the ceremonial appearance of Scholars was not the sole attraction. A trip to the City outskirts was a welcome break in humdrum lives; but that was not the kind of foundation he should build on.

Escape, to be sure, would be simple. He had only to command, and Technicians would put an aircar at his disposal; they would take him unquestioningly wherever he ordered. And indeed, if he was to visit outlying villages, that would be the most practical way of getting there, as well as the way everyone would expect a Scholar to arrive.

But it didn't seem the best way. *You have the right instincts,* Stefred had said; and instinct told him that though he had full power to command Technicians—a power that couldn't be taken from him unless he was ceremonially banished from the priesthood —he must use it only for the essential indirect access to lab facilities needed to continue the genetic research. He did not want to ask Technicians, even those eager for the honor, to fill his personal needs. Nor did he want to do what everyone would expect. The whole point was to get people used to changes. . . .

Inspiration, when it came, was a flash of light. He found himself speaking almost as one did in the controlled dreams, not knowing what was to come, afraid, yet at the same time confident. "I will build a new City," he said, "beyond the end of the longest road: a City without walls, without towers; and the unquickened land there will bear fruit. And in this, no Technicians will aid me. . . ."

It was tantamount to a declaration that the sun would stop in its tracks and rain would fall up instead of down; everyone knew that unquickened land—land not treated by the Technicians' machines —did not, and could not, become fruitful. Such words from anyone but a Scholar would have merited not mere derision, but the charge of presumptuous blasphemy. And, Noren thought grimly, even he had sown seeds of potential retribution. If he did not make good his words, if the genetically altered plants would not grow in untreated soil . . . well, this was the sort of commitment Stefred had warned he must make. Carefully, he did not specify exactly when the miracle would come to pass; but there would be a limit to people's patience. Omniscient as they thought him to be, he had placed himself at their mercy.

That idea, strangely, was heartening. It made their present adulation much easier to face.

"Beyond the end of the longest road" was a long way, a journey of many days on foot even without stops in intermediate villages. He had made such a journey before; the village of his birth was far out on one of the spokes that radiated from the City, and after escaping, he'd traveled inbound by night, sleeping in farmers' fields during daylight hours. Only at the end, after his injury, had he dared accept a ride in a trader's sledge. Now he would not ride at all. People would be glad to build a sledge for him, to harness a team of their best work-beasts, to spread sand before it as it traveled so that its runners would glide more smoothly than on a routinely sanded road. To them, that would seem fitting. Yet even had he possessed miraculous power to produce wheels, which without wood or metal couldn't exist, he would not have ridden, though he knew his stamina would be taxed.

City dwellers were not hardened as villagers were; in years of confinement, one lost one's physical prowess. Even his labor at the outpost was now far behind him. The oppressive heat, hour after hour, began to drain him, and he appreciated, for the first time, how Lianne felt about it. As a boy he'd been inured to heat, had never known the cool relief of a tower's interior. He could become inured again; in his renunciation of the City, he had not counted physical comforts among his sacrifices. All the same, he found to his surprise that his body's demands were the cause of his first role crisis.

If villagers thought Scholars ageless and sexless, they gave even less thought to such mundane matters as these awesome beings' bodily needs. Noren didn't recall this until he realized that he was thirsty. He had been on his feet half a day in the hot sun, speaking to groups most of that time, repeating the same blessing over and over. No one had offered him a drink of water; it would never occur to anyone that he might want one. He could, of course, ask for it—but that was awkward. No one had pure water in hand, and in any case, how could he pronounce the blessing in one breath and ask for a drink in the next? It would be undignified. He himself wouldn't mind that, but his audience would; he must uphold the ideal image they expected. His mouth got drier and drier. He began to wonder, half-seriously, whether the sacrament of drinking impure water should be established far sooner than he'd planned; but no, he could not yet break the High Law in their presence. There was not even any impure water, since streams close to the City were all diverted to the purification plant. Longingly, as he left the market area, he eyed roadside taverns.

By the time sunset approached he was, by supreme irony, suffering more seriously from thirst than from any emotional burdens.

The blue robe was a hot garment, never designed for long wear; under it, sweat drenched Noren's clothes. How, he thought in dismay, was he going to wash? How would he manage other bodily functions that might be assumed unnecessary for Scholars? He could not remove the robe except in privacy, and at a farmyard cistern there'd be none; as for excusing himself to use a privy, the very thought was ludicrous.

These concerns overrode that of food; but he'd eaten nothing all day and eventually must do so. This was the one such problem he'd considered before leaving the City. Technicians, when in the villages, bought food; they never took from the villagers without paying. But he could have carried no large amount of money, and in any case, people might be insulted if he tried to pay. No one had ever dreamed of such an honor as seating a Scholar at table; yet an honor it would be, and in that one respect he must let people serve him. He must also, he now saw, request a private sleeping room— though it would mean turning its occupants out—as well as the unheard-of luxury of an individual wash-water jug and slop jar. His hosts would hardly begrudge this, but he disliked the thought of demanding privileges. Furthermore, it wasn't quite the fashion in which he'd choose to prove himself human . . . or was it? On second thought, Noren decided, the vulgar gossip that would spread would be a healthy thing.

He had not traveled far the first day, for he had spent most of it with the market crowds. By nightfall they had thinned out; after once being blessed, people didn't presume to follow him without invitation. He must eventually, he supposed, choose followers. It wouldn't be fitting to go alone, and he'd rejected the idea of a Technician escort such as would appear with a Scholar before the Gates. Besides, to build a new "city" he would need help, and it must come from people willing to abandon their past lives, willing to take the frightening steps he would ultimately ask them to. But that was in the future. For now, he could think no further than water and rest.

At the crest of a long hill overlooking the City was a farmhouse. Leaving the last cluster of suppliants, Noren, dizzy with fatigue, climbed the path to its door. To his immense relief the family saw him coming and met him outside. "May the spirit of the Star be with you," whispered Noren hoarsely; the formal greeting was now, and must remain, automatic, for it would be a terrible breach of courtesy to inadvertently omit it. "I should like to share your table if I may."

The farmer, a graying man, was so stunned he couldn't reply; but his wife was a woman of presence. "Reverend Sir, you will be welcome," she said simply. She met his eyes squarely, even from her knees; Noren liked that.

"If I enter your house, you must not kneel to me," he said. "That is fitting only in public places, and I wish to be your guest." He wondered if he would be able to stand on his own feet long enough for the others to rise to theirs.

They gave him a room, obviously their own, and after he'd bathed, a hearty meal. Like all farm and village families, they had ample food and no need to apologize for its quality, since only one type of food existed; he was served bread and stewed fowl, just as he would have been in the Inner City's refectory. They waited silently before eating; he realized they expected him to recite the customary words. It had been many years since he'd done that, though he'd used those words in other rituals. *"Let us rejoice in the bounty of the land, for the land is good, and from the Mother Star came the heritage that has blessed it. . . . And it shall remain fruitful, and the people shall multiply across the face of the earth. . . ."* That took him back to his childhood, even to the time when his mother was alive, and to the later time when he'd burned with resentment at the idea that she'd been led to believe in the Scholars' blessings. What would his mother think if she could see him now?

"I must rise at dawn and be on my way," he told the family, "for

I go to build a new City. . . ." They listened solemnly to the new prophecy that had in a single day become more real to Noren than that of the Founders. No one, not even the old man, seemed surprised. It fit; it was right; it was *natural*. It was the business of Scholars to build Cities, to make the land fruitful, to enable the people to multiply. The change was not going to be hard to effect after all; it required only his wit—and his willingness to pay the price.

At daybreak he stood on the hilltop and watched the sun rise; as he'd seen the City first, coming by another road down this same hill, he looked his last upon it. The lighted beacons atop the towers faded as the sky brightened. Sunlight struck the silvered surface of the domes, which from this distance appeared as a single scalloped wall encircling the tall spires within. Inside one of those towers, Lianne would be waking. . . . Resolutely, Noren turned his back on the scene and started down the other side of the hill.

Gradually his life assumed a new pattern, a pattern composed not only of what he must cope with on the journey, but of his blossoming plans for its end. So the First Scholar had felt, embarking upon another "impossible" scheme, hating his own role, expecting no happy ending for himself, yet believing more and more that it would work. That future generations would be saved by it. It was so simple . . . one committed oneself *first,* and *then* faith came! Noren had never understood that; even after experiencing the dreams repeatedly, he had not. But both Stefred and Lianne had seen.

Stefred, though unable to see the specific way to success till it was pointed out to him, had committed himself by fathering Veldry's child. He would not have done that without believing underneath that a way would be found. There was the child to consider; he would not have risked that child's welfare merely out of kindness to Veldry or desire to support Noren's cause.

Noren, too, had believed strongly enough to take risks. In the end, he had committed himself not to mere risk but to outright sacrifice. Yet in his conscious mind, he'd been uncertain that it would achieve anything; he had left the City less out of faith than out of the knowledge that to stay would be to concede defeat. He had imagined a long period of vagueness—of grayness, like the moss-covered land into which he'd come—during which he must live in utter despair. He'd thought it would be like the time at the outpost, only more permanent. It wasn't. Once his commitment was complete, he felt hope, even excitement. The pieces began to mesh. The plan was really going to enable his people to survive!

The experimental children, all of them, must live in the new "city"; Stefred would be able to arrange that. It had already been agreed that they'd be named by their parents according to a code both he and Noren could recognize. Having them sent where he ordered wouldn't be hard, for village-bound Technicians were accustomed to obeying Stefred's instructions without informing other Scholars; and if his interference with normal procedures ever came out, he'd have only to say his aim was to make Noren answerable for those children's welfare. Already, word of the new prophecy would have reached him; he would contrive to delay the adoption of his son till he heard that the settlement was established. He would understand that the children must eat food from unquickened land.

Their adoptive parents also would have to eat it, which meant they must have their own genes altered. This, the human experimentation among villagers, was the part Noren liked least, yet it wasn't as if it were an untried change, and he'd already resigned himself to the fact that a comparable situation would arise as soon as the children came of age. Better to have them together than scattered throughout the population, and better, too, to place them with families composed of volunteers. The couples would give informed consent; he could tell them the essential truth in terms they'd understand. People would come to his settlement as Technicians sought admission to the Inner City, knowing the hardships involved, but nothing of the real reason these must exist.

Noren's own task, apart from bringing to pass the miracle on which he'd now staked his life, was to choose the residents of—of what? He spoke of it as a new city, but he could not think of it that way in his own mind. The research outpost had been conceived as "a new City beyond the Tomorrow Mountains," but everybody called it simply the outpost. Villages had names: Abundance, Prosperity, and so forth. He named the planned settlement Futurity. He began to talk about it by name. Rumor spread ahead of him; it was not long before people in the villages he entered were already believers in the place, starting to wonder who would be fortunate enough to live there.

They turned out to meet him now in holiday garb, green instead of everyday brown, adorned with the blue glass beads that symbolized religious devotion. They filled the village squares as they normally would on feast days. Their bearing toward him was not so much worshipful as jubilant; his coming was cause for celebration. The farther he got from the City, the truer this was, for not everyone had opportunities to travel—some had lived to old age without a pilgrimage to the Gates, and had not seen Scholars even from a distance.

It was impossible, of course, for him to individually bless every man, woman and child in each and every village along the road; he spoke to those on outlying farms, but in the centers he held services. Once, he thought ruefully, he had shrunk from the role of presiding priest at small City gatherings; now he was assuming it before hundreds—and on those occasions, he could not stop them from kneeling.

He was also asked to bless wedding parties. Weddings were solemnized by village councils and blessed, when possible, by Technicians as the Scholars' representatives; but naturally people were eager for the unprecedented distinction of a benediction from a real priest. At first Noren wondered how there could be so many weddings; were these boys and girls marrying hastily simply because of his appearance? No doubt a few dates were advanced, but he soon learned that some couples were traveling long distances on connecting roads from villages on other radials, bringing their families and friends along. His days were long, hot and thirsty, but at night there was invariably a wedding feast—and he saw that when the time came to introduce innovations, there'd be no lack of enthusiasm.

He did not mind weddings or the rites of Thanksgiving for Birth; services for the dead were another matter. The first time he was called upon he was, unreasonably, stunned. It was the job of Technicians to conduct such services! But no one sent for the Technicians when a priest was present; instead, they thanked providence for their good fortune, and in fact it was whispered in his hearing that the aged woman who'd died, after outliving her grandchildren, had declared that now—having seen a Scholar with her own eyes— she could depart in peace. Horrified, shivering despite the heat, Noren went through with the service, though of course the Technicians had to be summoned first to bring the aircar, which he was incapable of calling down from the sky as he'd been expected to. Watching it lift away afterward, he nearly lost his self-control; his face was wet with tears. What would happen when there were no more aircars? Ultimately, when genetic change was complete, recycling of bodies would not be necessary; his new crops would have genes to recover trace elements efficiently from organically fertized soil. But the people, who knew nothing of the disposal of bodies in any case, would wish to continue sending them to the City as long as the City stood. It was a symbol not to be lightly cast aside. And indeed, thought Noren, did he not want his own body to go there; did he not wish to think that in death if not in life, he would someday return?

He got through that service by rote, as he had the one for his son, without letting himself think of the words. But it wasn't the only such rite he performed, and the words did bother him. *Not in memory alone does he survive, for the universe is vast.* Was it right to tell the people something he wasn't sure of? They trusted him! He owed them comfort, and yet. . . . *Were the doors now closed to us reopened, as in time they shall be, still there would remain*

233)

that wall through which there is no door save that through which he has passed. Lianne didn't think such words were foolish, although she had no more real knowledge of the matter than he did. And he had none, after all; he certainly did not know they expressed a false idea—he could not say it was false any more than he could say the Prophecy was. Like the Prophecy, those words were more metaphor than blueprint.

As he perceived this, much fell into place for Noren. Most villagers had a naive view of the Prophecy: they thought Cities would rise overnight on the date of the Star's appearance. The Scholars considered themselves enlightened; yet he'd wondered, lately, whether their view might not be equally naive. Not false, as he'd feared in his despair over the impossibility of metal synthesization, but—well, oversimplified. Too literally tied to the Founders' specific plans. The First Scholar himself had known better than that! He'd made provision for genetic change, knowing that would mean loss of technology; yet the ideas of the Prophecy had all been in his deathbed recording. It was on those ideas he, Noren, was now drawing in his own words to the people, rather than on the interpretation priests were taught, the narrow interpretation that kept them from facing the real world. Stefred knew. It had been he who'd declared it wasn't a blueprint. But he knew, too, that most Scholars would hold to their interpretation as fiercely as the villagers to theirs. They would not pursue truth to a third level.

Was that why he now felt no hypocrisy? Noren asked himself. Because, paradoxically, he still cared more about searching for truth than did others?

One evening as he entered a village, people took him to the house of a sick man; he stood appalled by the bedside, his mouth dry with more than the thirst of the weary day behind him. They expected him to cure the man! They believed Scholars could do anything. If he failed, as he inevitably would, they might think him no true Scholar; yet if by chance the man survived, he could not accept the credit that would be accorded him. There were limits beyond which he would not go.

"I can do nothing," he said, inwardly groping for inspiration. "You must call the Technicians; illness can be cured only with Machines."

"The Technicians came yesterday, and said they could not help. But surely, Reverend Sir, if you merely speak the words—"

It was possible. Noren knew from things Lianne had said that faith could often heal; if the man was a believer, and heard, he might recover—even from an illness beyond the skill of City physicians, he might. But he also might not. Some things mind could not do. If only he knew the diagnosis . . . but no, it was better this way. It was better if he himself did not know the probable outcome.

(234

"May the spirit of the Star abide with you," he said gravely, placing his hand on the sick man's hot forehead, "and if it be fitting, may you be healed; but rest assured that the light of the Star falls on realms beyond this earth." He turned, and to the family went on, "Do you think we Scholars would permit any deaths if we could prevent them? We are but stewards, guardians of the Star's mysteries. The power to give life or take it is not ours. I do not know how long this man will live."

And because this was true, they nodded in acceptance and let him go his way. If he'd been certain the man was dying, Noren perceived, what he had said would not have satisfied them: they'd have sensed a presumption of power at least to foresee. Only by keeping an open mind could he function as a prophet; he must make no predictions, good or ill, unless sure beyond logic that they were genuine.

He had as yet no permanent followers, though people walked with him from village to village. Usually, now, he lodged with the heads of village councils, these being the most prominent citizens, deferred to by others desirous of the honor. It was ironic, considering the scorn he'd once received from the council of his own village, which had tried and convicted him; when he asked himself whether his hosts would do the same, he knew that most would. He didn't like to think of what might happen to youths of these villages who dared to express doubts about his status, yet wasn't he serving his original aim? The more heresy he inspired, the better. It was good if boys and girls looked upon him and were set to thinking, good for the world, and good for them, too, in terms of their real fate if they were condemned on that account. But it was not good on the part of those who did the condemning. They were not the sort he wanted in Futurity, and because he couldn't take heretics either, since to protect them would deprive them of their birthright, he must find some way to make contact with the folk who stayed in the background. Those like Talyra. . . .

Thoughts of Talyra came often to him, for with her he had shared the open land. He had sat with her on the gray moss; walked with her down roads like this, lined with dull-hued fodder and purple shrubs, past the green of quickened fields; taken her in his arms under the wide sky alight with silver crescents and the red bead of Little Moon. The memories, all too poignant, came back—still he could not wish for those days. That part of his life was gone. His heart would always be in the City . . . or, when Lianne went, would it go with Lianne? Noren honestly did not know. It hardly mattered; that life was gone, too. Only his goal remained.

Dwellings grew fewer as he traveled outward from the City, and villages were farther apart. There came a night when he stopped at a lone farmhouse once more. The man and wife were respectful but less diffident than most; were it not for the now-tattered blue robe, he thought sadly, he might have talked with them as friends. Yet he sensed that they were troubled. No family was present, and the woman, beneath her courteous welcome, eyed him with the desperate plea for aid he'd now seen, and helplessly sorrowed over, in too many people to count.

After supper she approached him privately. "Reverend Sir, I wish no favor," she said, "yet for my husband's sake I will speak, since you have paid us honor such as we could not have hoped for. As you see, we have no children. We are undeserving of anyone's esteem. Yet he has not divorced me, shame though my barrenness is on us. If I merit punishment so heavy, can it not take form that falls on me alone?"

"Barrenness is not a punishment," Noren began; but then, having learned much from Stefred's ways, he added, "Do you feel you are justly punished, and if so, why? I warn you that you mustn't lie to me."

The woman drew breath, then met his eyes steadily. "I am aware of no weighty sin. I thought you, Reverend Sir, might enlighten me; for it's hard not knowing what I've done wrong."

If she had been guilt-ridden or had shown false humility, he would not have pursued the matter, but he saw that this woman and her husband were fit parents; if they could have no children of their own, why not some of his wards? Traditionally Wards of the City were placed only with large families, for barren wives were considered unworthy; but that was senseless. Besides, he must take only childless couples, since he disliked the thought of inoculating young children who'd been born with unaltered genes, and he did not want to limit the settlement to newlyweds. He alone would have authority to place the experimental babies—that was necessary, since only he would know which were in fact siblings who must grow up as foster-kin lest they later, unknowingly, intermarry—and no one would challenge his decisions.

"You have heard me speak of Futurity," he said slowly, "where barren land will become fruitful. Unfruitful marriages will also be blessed there. I cannot promise that you will conceive a child if you come, but whether or not you do, you will be mother to Wards of the City."

She dropped to her knees despite his earlier prohibition, joy and gratitude illuminating her plain features. Noren took her hands. "It will not be an easy life," he warned. "Get up and call your husband, and I will tell you what the people of Futurity must venture."

Before he left the next morning, they had pledged to sell their farm and come after him. They were mature, reliable people, a good balance to the adolescent couples who would of necessity make up the majority of the Chosen Families; to them, he decided, he would give Veldry's children.

The alteration of people's genes must be done dramatically, for it must be made clear from the start who was free to drink impure water and who was not. Furthermore, people would want the assurance of a rite. They would even want the rite to be frightening; though ordinarily the injection involved was painless, they'd feel better afterward if it were made an ordeal. Again following what Stefred had taught him of initiations, Noren realized that it would be necessary to give the volunteers proof of their own worthiness. Also, almost too late, he remembered that in the case of those to be married the injections must take effect before the weddings, and in fact brides must be required to swear by the Mother Star that they were not already with child. He dared not inoculate a woman who might be pregnant; the effect on the unborn baby's genes would be too uncertain.

In the last village, therefore, he waited. He spoke of how Chosen Families must qualify, and word spread, by the traders and by radiophone; before long barren and betrothed couples began arriving from other regions. Most were years younger than himself, youngsters fresh from school eager to embark on a glorious adventure. They made him feel ancient—as, now full-bearded, he indeed must look to them, if they looked beyond his priest's robe at all.

He'd expected to call on the village for help in building, but he soon saw that that would be a mistake. There were far too many volunteer couples; he had to make the conditions hard. They must be willing to raise the new "city" unaided, stone by stone. It was well, and necessary, for them to come anticipating miracles; but all that could be done without miracles they must do for themselves. This wasn't only a screening strategy, he realized. Later, they would take pride in what they'd accomplished.

Gradually, through many interviews, he chose those with the soundest motives. He explained the goal with half-truths, nonetheless valid for being partial. "Families grow, the villages grow, there are more and more people every year; and this is as it should be under the Law. Yet the City does not grow at all. A time will come when the world needs more farmland than can be quickened, more water than can be made pure; the Technicians will have too few Machines to serve everyone. The Law does not say this, for the Law does not speak of the future. The Prophecy does not say it, for the Prophecy tells of the time when the Star will become visible. But the Scholars know it. They know someday the Law must change, and my work is to teach you to live with tomorrow's Law. To this, if you are willing, you will be sealed; but if you choose it, you cannot go back, nor can your children. You will belong to Futurity as Technicians belong to the City. . . ."

237)

They were, Noren feared, spellbound. One by one he listed the hardships: no preexisting village comforts, no buildings except those they raised themselves, no City goods such as traders sold elsewhere. Limited social contacts outside the community. Poverty unprecedented in their world, since they'd have no harvests or craftwork to sell and no time free to work for wages. Mysterious changes in the High Law that would not be spelled out in advance; still more mysterious risks that might extend to their descendants. Most sobering of all, a rule that their children must marry as he decreed or face charges of heresy. Noren had read enough to know that while many of these provisions would, under other circumstances, be wholly unjustifiable, in most societies it would nevertheless be easy for a self-proclaimed prophet to find people who'd voluntarily comply with them. The magnitude of Stefred's trust in him impressed him anew. What he was doing was dangerous, though it was a lesser evil than extinction, lesser even than the caste system his work would ultimately abolish.

Yet Futurity would indeed produce heretics, or so he hoped. His people, like all other citizens, would be free to choose dissent; and it wasn't as if the dissenters would suffer harm.

He gave orders by radiophone; Technicians from the lab came out by aircar, bringing the genetic vaccine. They did not know what it was, of course, and since they were used to inoculating villagers against disease, they wondered only that he took personal charge of the equipment. They knew nothing of the rite held that evening for the chosen couples alone. The volunteers themselves did not know the true significance of the needle to which they submitted, though since it was a metal object they looked upon it as holy. "It will mark you as pledged to Futurity," he told them, "and ever after, until the fruit of Futurity is spread throughout this world, you and your children will be set apart. I believe the spirit of the Star will favor you, but I have no sure foreknowledge. You are the vanguard, for good or for ill; if your children should sicken, it would be a sign that peril threatens the coming age. Against such peril the world must have warning. What is new must flourish in one place before it can flourish everywhere. Do you accept the role of forerunners, knowing these things to be true?"

Individually they gave assent, elated not only by the honor of being chosen, but by their own excitement. Noren wasn't gentle with the needle; he knew how Stefred, or even Lianne, would handle it, and overcame his reluctance to offer a symbol more memorable than words. The triumph in the initiates' faces told him he'd judged accurately.

But this rite was not the real test, either of them or of him; so far he had not asked them to do anything against their inclinations. Nor had he presented them with any conflict between their image

(238

of a Scholar and his demands on them. To induce them to break the High Law's taboos would be far harder. With growing apprehension, he faced the thought that the time for that step was at hand.

The weddings were to take place in the new community, and the feast, Noren declared, was to be attended by its members alone. Farewells to friends and relatives must be made before departure. "You will set forth to no household," he warned, "and the moss of the wilderness will be your marriage bed. But from your children and foster-children will come new strength for the world, and the light of the Star will shine upon the City you establish."

So at last, beyond the end of the road, Noren came to Futurity; high on a knoll, looking out toward the Tomorrow Mountains, he chose its site. At sunset the people climbed to it in wedding garb: red skirts for brides, red-trimmed white for those already married, with white tunics for everyone but him. He himself wore, as always, the blue robe; and it occurred to him that he would be the only person there that night who would sleep alone.

They stood in a circle around a blazing moss fire as one by one, the couples exchanged vows and received his blessing. When the solemnities were over someone started a song, and the others joined in while two went to the campsite to fetch ale for the toast. Returning, they said to him in puzzlement, "Sir, most of the jugs are empty; there's not even any water—"

Though he'd been waiting for this discovery, Noren felt a sick chill of fear. If their trust in him was not strong enough, the whole scheme would fall in ruins—and he found himself worrying less over his own fate, or even the world's, than about the feelings of these young people whose wedding night would be spoiled. How had he had the audacity to think he could make the occasion joyous for them?

He kept his voice calm. "This is the mystery for which I've prepared you, for which the rite set you apart from your generation. We drink water fresh from the land, here; fill the jugs from the stream and you will not be condemned. A day will come when the High Law is changed, but you and your children need not wait for that day. Here grain will grow in unquickened fields; did you think you were not to harvest it, though that too is now contrary to the Law?"

Their eyes widened in shock; they had been reared to believe that eating or drinking anything impure was not only sinful, but likely to have dire results. Even those who suspected that prevalent nursery tales were exaggerations knew that to consume impurities, or merely to use pots made of unpurified clay, was an offense equivalent to heresy for which one would be sent to the City in bonds.

239)

After a long pause one woman spoke out, saying, "Reverend Sir, you are testing us, lest having been honored, we might think ourselves above the Law; perhaps also you test again our willingess to endure hardship. There is no need. We will go thirsty, and hungry, too, if you ask it of us. Rest assured that we won't defile what is sacred."

Aghast, Noren realized they'd naturally take it that way; having picked the hardiest and most dedicated, he could well imagine their abstaining even through heavy labor within sight of the stream. They might persist till they collapsed, trusting him, ironically, to eventually provide them with sustenance. And though he could pronounce water pure by decree, that would do nothing toward freeing them from dependence.

"This is indeed a test of courage," he said soberly, "but not the sort you suppose. I know what it is to deny thirst, for I have done so; once I came near death thus, seeing that to use impure water would be a wrong. Yet I have also done something else. I have drunk such water deliberately, in dread of the outcome, for the sake of those who may face an age when the City cannot supply the world. The Star did not strike me down for it."

They all stared at him, amazed less by his impunity—for could not a Scholar do as he pleased?—than by the implicit admission that he was neither immortal nor exempt from fear. Noren stood up, opening the fastenings of the blue robe to show the commonplace clothes underneath. "Look at me," he said. "I am human, a man like other men, although it has been given to me to know mysteries. I will not tell you impure water did not harm me. It did, for someone among the Scholars had to pay the price of new knowledge. But it harms me no longer and has not harmed anyone to whom I have done what I did to you in the rite of pledging; the spirit of the Star revealed to me what I must do. From that same source I have knowledge of how to make grain sprout in this wasteland. Someday all will have such knowledge, for does not the Prophecy tell us that a time will come when the Scholars no longer are guardians?"

The young couples remained very still, clinging tightly to each others' hands; but he knew they were responding to him. "I forbade your families and friends to attend your marriage feast," Noren went on, "because it must not yet become known what we do here. Village people would bring you to trial; they would send you to the City for the Scholars' discipline, and from that I cannot, and will not, shield you if you are charged. But once Futurity's land bears fruit, people's feelings will change. They will acknowledge you subject to a new Law and will look forward to the age of that Law: the time when all land will be fruitful and all wedding feasts will be as this one."

(240

Slowly, the faces circling him took on confidence. "We will fill the jugs as you command," said someone at last; and as several went to do so, Noren, striving to keep the mood to which he'd roused them, started a familiar wedding hymn:

May the Star of our hope be with us,
As the joy of this night we celebrate.
May the heirs of our love be many,
As the world of its light we await.

He took the water they brought him and mixed in a scant portion of ale. "This is a night of celebration," he said, smiling, "and who would not wish ale on such a night? Yet it is also something more. That is what the water means: henceforth, when in love we give life to children, we are pledged not to the world that must pass but to the one that must come." Raising his cup, he added, "I will drink first, and on my head be it. I have performed rites and made prophecies, and have not been struck down; yet should they prove false, in the end I will be stricken. The Star's spirit will be withdrawn from me; my priesthood will be nullified; I will be accursed in the sight of the Scholars, and indeed of all people, if I lead you unwittingly to harm."

The cups were passed around, in readiness for the toast; people handled them not fearfully, but with awe. Plainly they believed in him. The only thing they did not believe, thought Noren in anguish, was his last statement. They did not guess there was real danger of its becoming the truest prophecy of all.

"To these unions: may they be fruitful and bring lasting joy." Hiding the shaking of his hands, Noren drank; and all the others followed.

The ensuing seasons were hard beyond measure; looking back on them afterward, Noren wondered how anyone had endured. Backbreaking labor was, of course, taken for granted by farm and village people; the clearing of fields with stone tools and the erection of stone buildings did not dismay them. Hunger was a newer concept —since the time of the Founders, the full burden of any food shortage had been taken by the Inner City, and a Scholar, by instinct and by training, shrank from the thought of villagers having to subsist on short rations. Yet though native plants could now be safely eaten, their taste was unpleasant; and alone, they were not nutritious enough to sustain anyone whose time was spent doing heavy work—they were no substitute for grain crops. Trusting Noren wholly, the people of Futurity would have expected their land to bring forth a harvest in the first cycle after clearing had he not warned that they must stretch the meager supply of grain their dowries and savings would buy. "I cannot know when the land will bear fruit," he was obliged to tell them. Privately, he was afraid it might not happen before he himself, who took no more than one scant serving of bread a day, was close to starvation. He could have requisitioned supplies from the Technicians, but the power of his scheme lay in forgoing City aid. He must prove it was possible to survive without that; his people must put their faith in the new way.

Delaying work on their own homesteads, they built a dwelling for him, built it tall, at the summit of the knoll, although the stones couldn't be brought by sledge when there was no road. It was not his idea; they did it out of love. Noren could not demur, for he saw that such a building was vital. Futurity was to be a new city, and the mark of a city in their eyes, evidently, was less the presence of actual towers than the presence of a resident Scholar. The Scholar must, to satisfy them, be fittingly housed. As he mounted his steps for the first time—steps unlike any ever built in a village—he found himself aware, with a stab of pain, that this might be where he would live out his years. Many years . . . even worldwide implementation of genetic change would not free him to leave these people. He owed them more than bountiful harvests.

The steps became the center of the community; he held Vespers there. Each evening after the service, the others gathered around informal bonfires, but he soon found that accompanying them put a damper on the fun. They revered him; they loved him—but they would not tell jokes or sing bawdy songs until he had retired into his house and shut the door. They'd have been shocked to know Scholars enjoyed such activities; for him to say so would not be seemly. It would deprive people of something they valued. It was his good fortune to have been born a loner, Noren realized, because he could never again be anything but alone.

Once a small plot of land was cleared, his genetic work progressed. He ordered a radiophone sent out, and Technicians in the Outer City labs read to him from his data tapes as instructed; when necessary they carried scientific materials to and fro by aircar. If computer analysis of genotypes was needed, they were told to leave the samples in a place where he knew they'd be found by Denrul— who was to have been informed of the situation by Lianne—but Noren communicated no more with Denrul than with Stefred or Lianne herself. His supporters in the City would keep track of his progress, for those who'd assumed the robe were as free to command Technicians secretly as he was. Direct contact, however, was out of the question. The safety of what he was doing depended on his complete repudiation by the City in case of failure; no Technician must be given grounds to testify that Scholars had done more than watch. He was honestly glad they resisted the temptation to send messages.

(242

All the same, indirect contact with the City was harder to bear than the dreamlike detachment that had dominated the first weeks of his exile. Now again functioning as a scientist, he could not forget that his work would lead to the end of science—that his success would mean exile for others as well as for him. To his people, he spoke with hope of "the day when all the world will live as Futurity lives," the day when no land would be quickened, no water piped from within the City's walls. But on that day the City would begin to die. Was it true that in time a means of regaining technology would appear, or was Lianne's faith in this only illusion? *Cities shall rise beyond the Tomorrow Mountains, and shall have Power, and Machines.* . . . He used those words in ritual and now considered himself honest; he had, in Futurity, dropped the capital letter from his conception of "cities" and no one had been dissatisfied, so no doubt the same would be true when it came to power and machines. He could accept that. He was willing to search for a truth beyond truth. And yet . . . Lianne had said that without technology evolution would stop. That particular truth was more than metaphorical, at least it was unless the Service, too, was naive.

He did not often think of the Service. He did not even think of Lianne as alien. He'd be satisfied, Noren thought grimly, with the City and with the Lianne he knew; but they were as inaccessible now as the rest of the universe was.

His plants, after a few terrifying setbacks, grew vigorously. On hands and knees with a stone cultivating tool, his robe cast aside in the hot sun, Noren laughed at the irony: this was the way he'd started, in his father's fields, and he'd despised every moment of it. His brothers had derided him for lack of persistence. If they could see the effort he now expended on nurturing each slender stalk, they would think it a greater marvel than the vivification of unquickened land.

The people of Futurity were surprised less by the plants' growth than by the fact that there were so few. "Did you think I could raise my hand and bring all the fields to life at once?" Noren chided, realizing as he spoke that they had indeed thought so. "It takes work! It is with plants as with people, as you well know: the seed of a few in time engenders many. I will give you seed for planting, but I cannot produce it any faster than these grain stalks can."

So in the first cycle, "harvest" meant only seed for the test garden, though he held the traditional ceremonies; but on that day a greater event occurred. Stefred knew, of course, the date of the harvest festival, for this was fixed according to season zone, staggered region by region for efficient use of land treatment machines in the villages; the invariant climate had nothing to do with it. Thus it was that as Futurity's citizens gathered for the Blessing of the

Seed, Noren looked up to see an aircar appear unsummoned, bringing Technician women who gave three Wards of the City into his care. And the oldest of these children had Veldry's features, but his eyes were like Stefred's own.

The arrival of the children, which Noren placed with the couples to whom they had been promised, marked a change in the settlement; while there was still hard work and hunger, living became less camplike and more family-oriented. Many of the brides were pregnant, and though Noren could not banish all worry over that large group of genetically altered babies, sustained by unpurified water from the time of conception, he managed to conceal his mixed feelings. He kept up his dual work as priest and scientist, but was no longer required to lead in practical matters; Futurity elected its own council and began to make civil laws.

The new crop sprouted, a patch large enough to be seen from aircars. Word of green shoots in unquickened earth soon spread, for the Technicians, by whom it was also viewed as a miracle, had occasion to talk in village taverns. Despite lack of a road, people began arriving to see the wonder. Having expected this, the community had built ordinary rain-catchment cisterns so that visitors could quench their thirst, and the absence of pipes to the City was not noticed. The council also built a wall around the test garden; sightseers were charged a fee, not only to obtain much-needed funds for grain but to keep the precious young plants from being trampled. This Noren approved with considerable relief. His religious services, however, were open to all comers, and he now spoke of a time when the miracle would extend elsewhere. He mentioned, without emphasis, that this would bring changes in the High Law. The idea did not bother anyone. His status as a prophet was firm as long as both the plants and the adopted children were thriving.

The veneration he received still bothered him, and yet, he reminded himself, the quickening of land with Machines had been considered supernatural in the first place. Who was to say what "supernatural" was? He'd made no claims that were not true, and none he was not backing with his life. Was it worse, really, for people to assume what they did than for Stefred to believe that psychic powers were against nature? If Lianne were to display her gifts openly—not only the gifts he, Noren, had been shown, but others at which she'd merely hinted—the villagers and Technicians wouldn't be the only ones to believe they were seeing miracles.

He was once again besieged with pleas for blessings; people approached him whenever he emerged from his door. During his journey, he'd been so dazed by his new role that, except during rites, he'd pronounced the words of the benediction mechanically. Now he searched the faces of the suppliants and tried to convey personal warmth each time he said them. Once he wouldn't have

(244

been able to do this; he perceived that he had grown. He knew more about giving than he had in the City. And he knew the pattern of his years was formed: to give, and receive nothing; to live, as had the First Scholar, without hope of attaining more than the world's future good.

And then one morning as he raised his hands for the hundredth time in the formal gesture of benison, Noren froze, seeing an upturned face so like Lianne's that he must be dreaming. . . .

It was not Lianne, of course; it was not even a woman. The man who knelt before him had . . . what? Not piercing blue eyes—though the eyes were what drew him, they were green, not blue. Not white hair or near-white skin. The impression of resemblance had been an instant, instinctive thing that didn't bear up under analysis. Or . . . could it have been a purely mental resemblance? Yes—not likeness, but the touch of a mind similarly trained. A powerful telepathic touch. He knew, in less time than it took to say the blessing, that the skill behind it was greater than Lianne's and would be used at a far deeper level. *Don't panic,* he told himself. *Reach as you would in controlled dreaming, open your mind to whatever experience may come; nothing will happen to which you have not consented.* And in the next moment he realized he'd not told himself this at all, but had been wordlessly informed.

They paused only a brief time; no one nearby noticed anything strange. But to Noren it seemed that hours were passing. There were no words, it was not silent conversation. He sensed none of the man's thoughts as he had sensed Lianne's, and though he reached out for knowledge, he was given none. Instead, all he felt— all the pain and uncertainty and longing, the anguish of exile, the hunger to search out truth, all the fears and regrets of his past, the grief for those he had lost . . . and, too, all his hopes for the future, all his faith born of commitment to them—rose to the surface at once. He was engulfed, overwhelmed. His head roared, and light blazed behind his eyelids; he was reeling. . . .

He opened his eyes and met calm green ones that held not reverence, but something quite like it: a mixture of sympathy and awed, startled admiration. "Reverend Sir, I am honored by your blessing," the stranger said with sincerity.

Struggling to maintain his balance, Noren repeated it. "May the spirit of the Star go with you—wherever you may travel."

"May it abide with you also," replied the man softly, rising from his knees, "and with all people of this earth, until the Star's light falls upon them and the Prophecy comes to fulfillment."

It was a farewell. This could be no one but an alien from the starship, which meant the starship had returned for Lianne. They would be leaving: in mere days, or even hours, they would leave this world forever. Noren knew he had been examined and found

245)

equal to his task; he knew, as he had long known, that he would receive no help with it. He had not expected them to relent, had not even wanted them to, in view of the cost—the decision had been his, and he did not wish to alter it. He should now rejoice, for he had just been told specifically that his sacrifices were not vain, that not only survival, but fulfillment of the Prophecy, was judged assured.

But he did not feel like rejoicing. When the stranger had gone, Noren retired into his house and threw himself down on his moss pallet; and for the first time since leaving the City, he wept.

Several days passed. Noren got through them with set face and level voice, but his hard-won, precarious peace had been shattered. No fire of hope warmed his words of blessing. He felt no joy at the sight of the flourishing green seedlings that meant salvation of the world. For him the light had gone out, as in due course, the lights of the City would flicker and then fail. He had saved his people—but he was no longer able to care.

He was not sure why this was so. He had learned nothing from the alien's visit that he'd not been expecting, and the only words said to him had been a confirmation of faith in his world's future. Furthermore, he'd received clear assurance that he need not doubt his fitness to fill the role in which fate had cast him. Why then did he doubt more than ever? Why did he not just fear, but *know,* that his strength would not last a lifetime?

Lianne's departure? But he had known for years that she must leave his world. His last night in the City, he had faced how much that mattered to him; still he had risen from their bed and walked out through the Gates alone. He should be buoyed by that memory, not crushed, for if he had done that, he'd have courage for all lesser things—only he did not think he'd be able to do it twice. It was a foolish point to be unnerved by, Noren thought miserably. That was one test to which he would not be brought again. Lianne was gone. . . .

No. He was not certain she had gone yet; the starship had arrived, but had not necessarily departed . . . and before it left, Lianne might come to say goodbye.

That was the source of his despair, Noren perceived suddenly. She might come, thinking him strong, and he would not be strong enough. He had the power to make her people stay. He had only to say he was quitting; that he was not a prophet, not a savior, but human; that it was their job to save worlds, not his. They were not gods, but neither was he—and he was alone while they were many. He'd done all that could be asked of him. He could return to the City with Lianne and let them finish what he had started.

As he thought this, lying sleepless on his pallet while dawn bright-

(246

ened the stone casing of his window, he looked up and Lianne was there.

It was telepathy, he realized, not coincidence; he'd never have guessed she might come had he not sensed that she was close. She had left the City by darkness, and under cover of darkness the alien shuttlecraft had brought her here. It must be waiting nearby to return to the starship. They'd hardly deny her a brief visit; Lianne too was human, and in love.

As she stood in the doorway, her hand white against the matting she'd drawn back, he felt her love sweep over him: a far more powerful mental radiance than she'd loosed within the City's walls. He understood that this was the telepathic mode natural to her, and that love heightened it, that physical love would heighten it still more. She had suppressed it to spare him, even during their one night together; she hadn't wanted him to glimpse what he was giving up. She had not wanted to show him what true intimacy was among her kind, what powers his own mind could attain, through love, that no less intense experience could awaken.

But now it seemed she herself was weakening; her thought was more for him than for his world's welfare, or even for the bright realm to which she'd soon return. Their loss of each other was a grief that would be with her always. And Noren found that what hurt most was not anything he had sacrificed, but the heartbreak he had caused her.

He lay motionless, not daring to go to her. "Lianne," he said, his voice flat and remote. "Don't come in. Don't even speak to me. Leave quickly, while there's still a chance."

She moved close, ignoring the words. A blue blur brushed his cheek as she bent down, the sleeve of her robe . . . how odd that was; he'd never seen Lianne robed before. All these years, despite Stefred's puzzled disappointment, she'd been adamant about refusing priesthood. She had remained unwilling to make a sham commitment lacking permanence. Now, he supposed, she'd had to wear a robe in case people saw her enter his house, and after all, no Scholars would ever know. Yet if she did encounter people, they'd kneel to her! That would be still worse than it was for him; she would feel she had no right to pronounce the blessing.

"Please go," he repeated, not looking at her face.

"Don't you want me here?" It wasn't really a question, and her voice was light; in the emotion he sensed, love overpowered all pain.

Noren sat up, resisting the urge to take her in his arms, knowing that even to kiss her would mean defeat of the cause to which he'd given himself. "You know how much I want you, how much I'll always love you," he said tonelessly. "But you don't know, I guess, that I have limits; maybe you think I'm as superhuman as the villagers do. By the Star, Lianne—" He broke off, aware that the phrase, in this case, was not profanity; he meant it seriously. "In the name of the Star, I ask you to leave this world before all that's behind us loses its point. I'm on the verge of cracking up right now. Maybe, just maybe, I'll get my nerve back after you're gone; but if you tempt me to keep you here, I'll do it—at the cost of everything we both believe."

She dropped to the pallet beside him and took his face between her hands. "You won't have to," she said. "I'm staying."

Stunned, afraid of the thoughts that idea roused in him, Noren drew away from her touch. "Staying? You'd let the ship go and come back for you another time?"

Very quietly Lianne said, "It won't be coming back, Noren."

He stared at her, appalled. "That's not possible. Your people wouldn't abandon you." He wanted her to stay, yes, but not at that price. Not if she'd be exiled from her heritage as he was from his.

"They haven't abandoned me," she told him. "I chose."

"Chose *this* world, when you could have the whole universe?"

"Not quite the whole universe. There's a lot more to it than this galaxy, after all; everybody's got boundaries, and life is life, on one world or a thousand."

"I—I can't look at it that way," confessed Noren dazedly.

"I know you can't. That's one reason I'm here."

"To enlarge my prison by sharing it? Lianne, what good would it do me to know you were suffering, too?"

"Oh, Noren. I'm not going to suffer, not as long as we have love."

Abruptly, he grasped the whole of what she was offering. She would not stay in the City; she was no more free to return there now than he was, for she'd have told Stefred she was joining him so as to spare Stefred's feelings by not disappearing unaccountably. She meant to live here, in Futurity. She would share not only the exile, but the commitment—that was why she had assumed the robe.

But how could she? "Your oath to the Service—" Noren protested.

"I won't violate it. The Oath demands that I put the best interests of your people above all else, but my being with you isn't contrary to them. I won't be intervening. I'll be living just as you do."

As he did. Years without respite from the oppressive heat she found so taxing outside the towers; hard physical labor in the fields, using Stone Age tools she'd never before handled; isolation not merely from her heritage but from such sources of knowledge as she'd had in the City, poor as they were by her own civilization's standards . . . and the burden of priesthood among people not even her biological kin—people who, once they discovered the healing powers she wouldn't deny them, would venerate her in a way not merely symbolic. Whatever she said now, she would suffer. And she might not always have his love, for there was still danger that the genetic change would prove unsafe, still a possibility that he might fail and die for it. If the people turned against him, Lianne might die too or she might not; she might outlive him in any case, for the lifespan of their species wasn't the same: she'd already lived more years than he had, perhaps many more, and yet she didn't age as fast. For her to stay with him awhile was one thing, a thing she evidently wanted to do. But she must not send her people away forever.

"Surely someday they'll come back for you," he said.

"No. Besides, I don't want them to. I couldn't bear to have you come to hate me."

"I could never hate you."

"You could, and would, in time, Noren—if the starship were going to return for me, yet not for you."

He was silent. She was right, of course; he wouldn't be able to suppress envy—but he wouldn't have let her know. . . .

"I'd know. I'm telepathic, remember? But even if I weren't, I'd have known, whatever worlds I went to, all the rest of my life."

Noren drew Lianne to him, embracing her, no longer doubting his own self-control. He had feared he'd not be strong; now he knew better. He loved her too much to be anything else. His destiny demanded sacrifice, but hers did not, and he would not let her suffer for his sake. If she must go with the ship or remain permanently, then he must make her go.

"Lianne," he said slowly, "you once said I was born to be apart. That's true. I am what I am, and you can't soften it. Maybe it all has meaning, I don't know—I guess neither of us knows the why of things. Maybe my losing everything, *everything,* is in some way necessary to the future of this world; anyway so far it's seemed to be, and I don't mind paying that price. I'm not paying it for nothing. The man who came from the starship affirmed the Prophecy—"

"From the ship? When?" Lianne broke in, obviously startled.

He told her, perplexed by her surprise. "That was before I told them I want to stay," she said, frowning. "There was no need for such a mind probe, certainly not then. And that man, he's senior to most of us, he deals with basic policy; he rarely leaves the ship personally. I didn't know probes of that kind were ever tried with people of immature species. Was it . . . painful, Noren?"

"In a way. He warned me not to panic; I assumed it was something telepaths do routinely."

"Not like that. Deep wordless communication is used privately between people close to each other, but a full one-way scrutiny of motives done by a stranger, fast, and in public—very few untrained people could stand up under that. It's a technique we reserve for special occasions. It has been done to me in Service rituals, was done yesterday by the same man, in fact, during my formal leave-taking aboard the starship." She shook her head, puzzled. "I wondered why he didn't argue more against my choice; now I see. But why didn't he tell me he'd met you, or even that he'd been down to the surface?"

"What did he tell you about the Prophecy, about how our civilization is to regain technology?" Noren asked. "He knows our evolution won't stop, I could sense that; and anyway, they couldn't have made a decision to withdraw unless they knew the answer."

"He knew," she agreed. "But he didn't inform me; he said that by staying here, I'd forfeit my right to hear what they expect."

"Not even whether the key will appear in your lifetime?" Noren protested indignantly. "Why would they be so merciless?"

"Because they realized that I love you," Lianne told him, "and that I'd pass all my knowledge on to you."

"They didn't trust me not to tell anyone about them, then."

"Oh, yes. If they hadn't trusted you, they wouldn't have allowed me to stay as living evidence. They withheld what they did for my sake—to make sure I really wanted to spend my life with you and wasn't doing it merely to buy knowledge for you that your task doesn't require."

"I couldn't endure having you give up the stars for my benefit," he declared, trying to steady his voice.

"They realized that, too," she said. "They aren't merciless; they simply take a long view of mercy."

Then they were waiting for her; they had trusted him not only with future generations' welfare here, but with hers, and had known he would say what must be said to send her back to them. Unless. . . .

"Lianne," he asked, trying to contain the sudden hope, "you told me subtle intervention's permitted, sometimes. If there were a way we could keep our technology without synthesizing metal, some way we can't ever discover, and they could give me a clue to it—would they?"

"Yes. Yes, and knowing you were probed before I left the City makes me wonder . . . only it doesn't fit. They don't lie, and they did tell me specifically that my decision was final, that no ship will return here for any reason in our era."

A cold thrill, excitement mixed with dread, came over Noren, and he smiled. "It does fit! There's still a chance, in the time before they leave orbit—they knew you'd want to be with me when the clue is offered. They'll surprise you too, or perhaps you'll even be needed to interpret, I know they won't make it simple for either of us—"

She pulled away from him, staring. "Noren, I thought you understood. They've already left orbit. They're light-years away by now."

Shock drained him. "Are you sure?" he whispered, disbelieving.

"Of course I'm sure. If an agent decides to stay on a planet, there are—formalities. They aren't painless because there's got to be a guarantee that it's an informed choice, and not a hasty one; I knew in advance what I'd have to do. I watched the ship go last night. The point of light was there and then it was gone; and the special links with me were just—cut off. Instantly, when the ship went into hyperdrive."

He couldn't speak, but his horror reached her silently. "Noren," she pleaded, stroking his hand, "Noren, don't lose heart now. They didn't tell me the answer; but when they said farewell, they weren't grieving, not even for me. Telepathically, I could tell they weren't; and if they'd believed us doomed to live out our lives in tragic futility, they would have been. What we do will lead somewhere, even if we never know where."

"It's not that," he said, "not the thing I'd already come to terms with. It's you, Lianne. Don't you see, I wouldn't have let you stay behind."

"Why do you think I didn't come here till they were gone?" She settled back against his shoulder, her white hair soft against his skin. "I wouldn't have let you decide, and I wasn't sure how to make you believe it'll be all right for me; only now that's easy. You've been probed by one of the most skilled elders of my people, and you *know* he grasped all your feelings. Remember that he probed me, too."

Slowly, Noren absorbed it. *Life is life, on one world or a thousand.* She did not need to see more worlds; her life was here. The rest of the universe existed; it was full of wonders—and just knowing that was enough. Enough even for him, now that he did know. This world was not a prison, but a base; one might choose one's base freely, but one could not escape the necessity of choosing. Was it possible, perhaps, that on the level veiled in mystery one chose the worlds into which one was born?

He held Lianne close. They sat quietly, not even fondling each other. There was time ahead for that, and Noren knew it would be good, that there would be a union of spirit as well as of body that would illumine all the dark years confronting them. Though the doors of the universe were shut, Lianne could open a window; and he no longer feared to look through.

Suddenly, rays of sunlight flooded the room. "It's morning," said Noren, as if waking from sleep. "It's a bright morning."

He stood up, putting on his tunic and then his blue robe over it, and turned to Lianne. "We've got obligations, you know. You aren't going to enjoy being a prophet."

"A culture," she told him, "can have only one great prophet at a time. I serve as a priest, but you are more. That, I think, must be what the mind probe was meant to confirm."

Side by side, they stood in the doorway as people came up the hill toward his dwelling; it was time for Benison. Lianne looked and whispered in astonishment, "Noren, practically all those girls are nearly ready to give birth."

"Well, their weddings were all held on the same day." He smiled. "This is what we've worked toward, isn't it—new life, a new generation that's born adapted to this world? It's a good thing you've had some medical training, seeing as I forgot to include a midwife among the settlers; you got here just in time to deliver a lot of babies."

He took her hand and led her out before the assembled people. "Tonight is to be a feast night," he announced with rising happiness, "for I will ask you to witness my marriage to the Scholar Lianne."

Epilogue

AS IS WELL KNOWN, THE SCHOLAR NOREN BECAME A LEGEND AMONG his people. The usual image of him is as a white-bearded patriarch, revered Archpriest to the world of the Interregnum Era; that he was still a young man when he came out of the City is rarely remembered. That his exile outside the walls involved self-sacrifice is never so much as imagined, although those who knew him best did note that in his eyes, even at the moments of his greatest triumphs, was an inexplicable sadness. This seemed something of a paradox, for beneath the wisdom all acknowledged were intuitions of deeper things—things concerning the vast universe of which the Prophecy spoke—and there, he evidently found more light than dark. There is thus little doubt that his consort Lianne showed him visions of realms she had explored, and that she opened his questing mind to more than she herself had seen in them.

In the closing years of the Dark Era, the settlement at Futurity flourished. The first harvests were small; most of the grain was kept for seed and the rest ceremonially consumed by the few Chosen Families then in residence. But word of the miracle spread. As each new crop sprouted, crowds came to see it, and to be blessed by the Scholar who was already accorded a status different from that of other Priests, different even from that of the Scholar Lianne who stood at his side. He could have taken power over all the land in those years. People would have believed anything from him—except that his prophecies might yet fail. That knowledge, like the knowledge that such failure would turn men to vengeance, he kept to himself; yet he claimed none of the authority that could have been his. By his word, the City remained the world's center. His task was not to abolish the High Law, but to herald the age of its transformation.

Within the City, where this goal soon became openly known, the Scholar Noren was held in contempt. He was viewed as a defector, and a dangerous one; only the belief that he must stand answerable for his prophecies saved him from seizure. Few of his opponents felt—or wanted to feel—that the Law could be changed with safety, or that the promises of the Prophecy as traditionally interpreted might not be essential to survival. Alteration of human genes, in the second generation if not in the first, would surely prove as ruinous as it was indecent. For this, in the villages, Noren alone must be blamed; only so could the City's life-support role be preserved. And meanwhile, grain was growing in untreated soil, grain that might be consumed by the unfit were it not for Noren's presence. He was therefore left alone; but among the Scholars he was already a scapegoat, not merely for anticipated disaster, but for the lack of progress toward metal synthesization.

This injustice even his secret supporters encouraged, telling themselves that the First Scholar's pose as a mad tyrant had been comparable. Aware that a means of retreat must indeed be left open until genetic change was fully proven, they were obliged to become more secretive than ever, lest their cause be won too soon. For slowly, their number grew. There were more heretics than there used to be, youngsters stirred by Noren's subtle discouragement of the caste concept. With such as these, he was merciless; he stimulated their rebellion and then contrived for them to be condemned, knowing they'd hate him for the betrayal, yet knowing, too, that they must be led to claim their birthright. Once enlightened in the City, their bitterness turned to loyalty; Lianne had seen to it that recruitment of novices would be continued by her successor. By this means, over the years, Noren won a large following among the Scholars: a following inspired by him personally. The Scholar Stefred, foreseeing this, bided his time. He continued to champion tradition, forestalling the showdown until the outcome was assured.

Genetic work continued, led by Noren outside the City and Denrul within, through the unquestioning Technician intermediaries. The genes of the newborn were tested. More Wards of the City were adopted, and more Chosen Families admitted to Futurity. Changes were made to the vaccine so as to impart heritable immunity to the planet's lethal diseases against which vaccination in each generation had till now been needed; these were tested on Scholars by Denrul before being used in Noren's rites. Offspring of the first families were inoculated against disease like all villagers, but for those of couples chosen later, that was no longer required; it would become impossible, after all, once the City's technology failed. This was the last of the genetic alterations indispensable to human survival. When it was complete, Noren went on working: he designed vegetables to supplement the monotonous diet of grain. It was now also possible for the flesh of work-beasts to be eaten; but this he kept from the citizens of Futurity in fear that it would be called an abomination.

Futurity's children came of age. They married within the community as arranged; the few who refused were tried by the council for their defiance and delivered to the City for discipline—to Noren's private satisfaction. He did not send word to Stefred that one of these was his son; it would not help the boy to be the only known child of Scholars to attain Scholar rank in turn. That much of tradition must stand. But he confessed in his own heart that he'd fostered that child's nonconformity.

The children had children of their own, and all were born genetically healthy. *There will be a time when all the world shall live as Futurity lives,* the Scholar Noren had prophesied, *and this will be in our era, before the Mother Star appears to posterity. Scholars will come forth to bless unquickened fields, and to mark all people, that they may turn from the old Law to the new.* To the day of this event, all villages looked forward with gladness. No date had been given, but within the City, supporters and opponents alike knew the time for the change was ripe.

They awaited Noren's word. For he would choose his day, and they must respond: either in full agreement, or—as many feared— through a split no longer dangerous. The supporters were numerous enough now to take control; they would destroy the water purification plant if need be; but they would not see the castes maintained in the name of the original Prophecy's lost cause.

On Founding Day, the Scholar Noren spoke out, spoke to vast crowds at Futurity rivaling those before the City's Gates. As always, Technicians recorded his words, and those words were soon heard in the Inner City.

But they were not the words anyone expected to hear.

I will build another new City, Noren had said, *on the shores of a great lake two weeks' journey hence; and it will be called Providence. And those in Providence will live as do those in Futurity; but there will be Technicians among them, and all villagers who work there will become Technicians.*

Among the Scholars there was both bewilderment and outrage. Had Noren, at the last moment, succumbed to the temptation to save the City at the price of keeping the castes? Or had he found evidence that genetic change was unsafe after all and so retreated to save his own life? Comparatively few would follow him two weeks' journey into the wilderness, for not enough pure water could be carried to supply anyone whose genes had not been altered; those few would not rise against him for the failure of his promises to the rest of the world. And if they were offered Technician status, they would become his sure defenders. Thus the Scholars were of a mind to forbid this new scheme. Some believed genetic change should be implemented without delay, while others felt he should be publicly repudiated—and nearly all agreed that he should be brought back, by force if necessary, to give an accounting. But the Scholar Stefred trusted Noren, and because he had not aided him in the past, his word prevailed. The City waited, uncertain and afraid, while Providence was established.

After the new community's first harvest, on the day of the Blessing of the Seed, there was yet another prophecy. *When all harvests are as this and no fields of the world need be quickened,* Noren declared, *the Scholars will go back into the sky from which they once came. By the time of the Star's appearance, they will return; and there will be a new Founding. And from that day forward, our world will be as the Prophecy promises.*

This was clearly impossible. There was not enough metal in the world to restore space travel; all Scholars knew that. The shuttle still existed, and was operable; it had been used in the establishment of the outpost beyond the Tomorrow Mountains. But the starships in orbit were stripped hulls. Though in theory, the process of decommissioning them carried out by the Founders could be reversed, there were not enough resources to restore even one; there would not be enough even if the life-support equipment unneeded after full implementation of genetic change were diverted to it. Moreover, were a space journey to become possible, there could be no chance of fulfilling the Prophecy by it. The Founders had searched thoroughly but futilely for a solar system from which metal might be obtained; without the coordinates of such a system, the chances of stumbling on one were negligible. So it was said that Noren had been too long away from the computers, that his judgment was warped—or worse, that his longings and his power had driven him to madness.

Yet the Scholar Stefred, now the oldest and most respected member of the Council, still refused to countenance any interference; in his thought was that the First Scholar had feigned madness for worthy ends. "Let Noren come to us in his own time," he insisted. "For better or for worse, this world's future is in his hands. If he is mad, which I do not believe, he nevertheless has the people behind him; they will not break the High Law without his sanction. And if he fails in the end to give it, full blame must rest on him for the promises unfulfilled."

Thus the building of Providence went forward without purpose the Scholars could discern. They reconnoitered from aircars going to and from the outpost; the lake seemed more than a symbol of water now safely used for bathing. Much activity went on there, structures were built at the edge, and people approached these almost as they would holy things like Machines. It was recalled that the Founders' plan for the transition period preceding fulfillment of the Prophecy included a phase during which villagers would earn Technician status by machine-aided work—but without metal, what semblance of machines could Noren have placed on the lakeshore?

Several seasons passed. And then one morning, fair like all mornings, the plaza before the Gates began to fill with people, though no ceremony was scheduled; and word came through Technicians that the Scholar Noren would soon arrive. Without precedent in his years away from the City, he had commanded that an aircar be sent out to him. He had broadcast a message by radiophone, heard in all villages as well as by his contacts in the Outer City: he would appear at the Gates, and many Scholars would come forth to greet him.

The aircar did not drop into its accustomed dome, but instead came to earth in the plaza outside the walls. Before a crowd surpassing any ever assembled there, the Scholars Noren and Lianne alighted; and with them were two citizens of Providence. Technicians cleared a path for them as they ascended the steps, while Scholars indeed came out to meet them, as many as could stand upon the wide platform—and for the first time in history, the Gates stood open after all had emerged. They invited Noren to pass through; but he shook his head and remained on the topmost step, facing the Scholar Stefred.

"I will not enter the City," he said, "until all people of the land are free to do so. I have come today for a different purpose." As he spoke, the man and woman of Providence came forward; they did not kneel, but stood beside him, holding between them a large clay bowl, which they handled as a sacred thing, raising it in the manner of a seed jar presented for blessing.

"These are the firstborn of Futurity," Noren said, "who now show you the gift of Providence; grant them in my presence their rightful status as Technicians, according to the Law."

Leaning forward, Stefred looked into the bowl, and saw with amazement the unmistakable glint of metal.

"I have at last learned how it can be obtained," said Noren, smiling.

To the people, this was a lesser miracle than the blossoming of unquickened land; having been taught that all metal had been brought into the world by Scholars at the time of the Founding, they viewed a repetition of the event as not especially surprising. But to the Scholars on the platform, it seemed a truly supernatural feat. They wondered, in that moment, if Noren might not possess in truth the powers village tales had long attributed to him.

"This is not my own doing," he told them solemnly. "I must not be credited with it, now or ever, for it is a blessing of the Star."

"And . . . the Prophecy?" Stefred, his voice hushed with awe, spoke for everyone: all the Scholars who had kept that faith and all those who had in sorrow relinquished it for the sake of their people's assured survival.

257)

"Our faith is vindicated," Noren declared, "if we are now willing to give up our guardianship and turn to other tasks. I did not wish to raise your hopes before I was sure; but to my people last Seed Blessing Day, I told the literal truth. Though there is not enough metal on this earth to fulfill the Prophecy, what is accessible is sufficient to restore one starship. In time, we can mine other worlds as the Visitors once mined here. What we lost to them has been amply repaid."

Then to the Scholars, in a voice too low to be heard by the multitude over the music that swelled forth, Noren explained his discovery. The metal could be extracted from lake water and wet soil, not by any method the Founders had known, but by genetically altered bacteria—which was, no doubt, a routine process on worlds less rich in ore than the Six. For it had been suggested to him not by sheer genius, but by a new alien artifact found the previous year near Futurity.

"The *Visitors* used this—this genetic process?" Stefred asked.

"So it appears." Noren's face was impassive. "The artifact contains coded symbols; Lianne and I were able to decipher them. Once I had the fundamental idea, genetic engineering of native bacteria wasn't difficult."

The incredibility of this explanation was apparent. In the first place, it was an almost fantastic coincidence for Noren to have found one alien artifact, the radiating sphere, just at the place where he had crashed in the mountains. That another such coincidence could have occurred was past rational belief; the odds against it were incalculable. And even supposing that it had happened, how could any artifact of those long-vanished miners reveal that they'd used bacteria in such a way? Furthermore, if they'd indeed done so, why had they not completed the job, taken the last traces of metal? Why had the bacteria not gone on extracting it during the interim if there'd been any left—or if they had, why had the Founders not seen?

These questions and more went through Stefred's mind as he listened—but he knew they were, and would remain, unanswerable. He did not suppose that even Noren had answers to them. Yet one could not deny evidence before one's eyes merely because logic said it couldn't exist. Noren was extracting metal from low-grade unminable deposits, and he would not lie about how he'd learned to do so; there was in fact no other way he could have learned. Moreover, his next words confirmed what he had claimed.

"There is also a star chart," Noren went on calmly. "Its symbols, too, are decipherable and can be fed into the computers. Whether or not we find aliens by following where it leads, we need not worry about failing to find planets."

(258

A chart of solar systems unknown to the Founders could not have been derived from any source other than the Visitors.

So the Scholars Stefred and Noren embraced, and many prophecies were affirmed to the people; then all priests withdrew into the City save Noren and Lianne. In the days that followed, the Scholars embarked on new work: some to effect genetic change in the Outer City and villages; some to mine distant lakes; some to prepare for the immense task of refitting a starship. And Noren, from his base at Providence, watched with mixed feelings—for he knew that to equip the ship, the City must die.

Yet in his heart was a great thankfulness. For that death must precede a rebirth, and the rebirth would be to a greater destiny than the other Scholars imagined. Only he and Lianne knew the truth about the scope of such a destiny.

He had indeed found an alien artifact. He had shown it, by now, to the City's scientists; the star chart was in their hands. They would believe the only thing they could believe: that it had been left by the aliens they knew about, the Visitors. History would never record that other aliens had come and gone, much less that discovery of the artifact near Futurity had not been coincidence at all. But Noren knew, knew surely enough to stake everything on faith that its chart would lead the ship to planets that could be mined. For among the symbols decipherable by science, there had been one that seemed meaningless; and this Lianne had known for the Service emblem.

It must be done very subtly, she'd told him long before. So subtly that had he not left the City, it could not have been done at all, not, in any case, in his era. Yet the data contained in that small capsule would make the difference between descent into a permanent Stone Age and ultimate rise to Federation level. It was for this the alien elder had come on that long-ago morning, not merely to probe his mind. The decision had been made then; and the Service had gone away in the certainty that he, Noren, would search out all the knowledge accessible to him.

The Dark Era drew to its close. The people of all villages were inoculated; their unquickened land was sown; they knelt with joy beside the streams of their land while Scholars blessed the water in Noren's name. The people dipped in their hands and drank gladly, knowing themselves one with the earth, with the fruits it could bring forth; and though they still revered the City, they looked to it no more for sustenance.

The Technicians moved from the Outer City to new villages beyond its walls, for the Outer City was not liveable any longer. Its power and air conditioning were gone, no water was piped in, all metal that had been used there was sent back into the sky. Every day the shuttle rose and returned. Gradually, the towers too were abandoned, except for the Hall of Scholars where the computer complex was preserved; the Scholars still in the City slept in the open courtyard. The water purification plant was shut down, and no one noted the day on which no more water came through the conduits to village cisterns.

No City goods were now sold in the markets, for there was no longer any way of manufacturing anything beyond what could be made of stone, clay, fiber, wicker and hide. To these crafts the former Technicians turned, taught by village masters, and village craftsman thus earned Technician rank; furthermore, all people in the world could earn it by a few weeks' labor at lakeside mines. It extended to their children, so that in the next generation no one of lesser status would be left. Only the Scholars remained apart, as priests; but it was made known that their offspring did not succeed them. Henceforth priesthood would be an honor to be sought freely, though still attained through mysterious ordeals to which one must submit of one's own will.

Through the years of the starship's refitting, Noren continued to live in Providence, supervising the work there and the training of those who went to other lakes. He had sworn not to enter the Gates until they could remain open, which till the ship was equipped, could not happen. And perhaps he no longer minded exile; he can hardly have wanted to see the City's lifeblood drained. Bit by bit, all he valued within was taken—finally even the computer complex, which had provided the instructions for restoring interstellar travel, was split into components. All that would be left, once the ship had gone, was memory preserved with minimum power. The City would stand as an empty shell.

Most Scholars did not grieve over this; they were afire with enthusiasm for the space expedition. A large majority were going; among those with scientific training, few but the aged would stay behind. It was a perilous venture, to be sure, and there could be no hope of quick return, for unless they found an alien civilization —which Noren privately knew they would not—power and supplies were not sufficient for a two-way trip. They would have to build an outpost on a new planet, and stay there many years while they utilized its metal to establish mining and manufacturing facilities. *Not on this world only, but on myriad worlds of innumerable suns shall the spirit of the Star abide. . . .* Metal would, of course, be returned to their people once large-scale mining capability had been developed and more starships recommissioned; but perhaps, too, new worlds would prove more habitable than the old. Many might choose to emigrate to planets with richer resources. The Star might already be visible there, if those planets were within a smaller radius from the nova—priests who were now alive might set eyes upon it! And so might the children of the new race already born. Meanwhile, the world was safe; the stars beckoned; and the Scholars were content. Only the Scholar Noren stood apart.

The Scholars will go back into the sky from which they once came, he had prophesied, *and by the time of the Star's appearance, they will return; and there will be a new Founding. And from that day forward, our world will be as the Prophecy promises.*

But Noren would not live to see that day. In his time, the world would be far poorer than before, since all but remnants of its technology must go with the ship—and only he could lead the people through that hard age. Only from him would they continue to believe the promise.

He could not go with the ship himself.

It is not certain when this knowledge came to him. Perhaps he knew from the start, from the hour he first held the star chart in his hands and perceived the unlooked-for outcome of his endeavors: the doors of the universe would be opened for his people within his own lifetime. Yet it was his dream, his most cherished wish, and through him it had come to pass . . . must he not have felt, at least for a little while, that the universe might be opened for him also?

He never confessed this, except perhaps to Lianne. He kept working. There was time for one last genetic project before the computer's power was lowered; young geneticists now openly helped him; and as his final act as a scientist, he gave the world trees. Knowing from Lianne what a lakeshore settlement should look like, he planted them thick beside the water, hiding the ugly traces of the completed mining. They were, naturally, mere seedlings, and in a world where wood was unknown, his prophecies about what they'd become were soon mixed with legend.

The time of embarkation came. Having endured the departure of her own people's starship, Lianne was well prepared to uphold him through the farewell rites, which were formal and were held before the Gates. It was a day of rejoicing. Noren filled the role expected of him, and no one noticed that she kept closer than usual to his side. When in the end the Scholar Stefred came to them, with sorrow in his eyes unlike any before seen there, Noren perceived that he was not glad to go; for him, too, the hour of parting was bitter. "Why?" Noren asked. "Why leave this place against your wish when you cannot live to return to it? We will need priests here; who will judge their worthiness and teach them to dream?"

"Lianne can do that," Stefred replied. "This is my world, and for its people I've lived; I would not choose to die in exile. But my presence here would tear it asunder. The Scholars staying are loyal to me, while the people are loyal to you; and it is you who are most fit to be Archpriest."

So at last, when the shuttle had ascended on its final trip, the

Gates of the City were thrown open, never again to be sealed; and the Scholar Noren went in to his tabernacle. It was a symbol still, a holy place, a place not to be defiled by the people now free to enter. He would see that they entered with reverence. He stood with Lianne between the silent towers that could not, in their time, be relighted; crescent moons illumined the courtyard. And Noren knew he had now come into his own.